The
Fairies
Return

ODDLY MODERN FAIRY TALES

Jack Zipes, *Series Editor*

Oddly Modern Fairy Tales is a series dedicated to publishing unusual literary
fairy tales produced mainly during the first half of the twentieth century.
International in scope, the series includes new translations, surprising and
unexpected tales by well-known writers and artists, and uncanny stories
by gifted yet neglected authors. Postmodern before their time, the tales in
Oddly Modern Fairy Tales transformed the genre and still strike a chord.

Kurt Schwitters | *Lucky Hans and Other Merz Fairy Tales*

Béla Balázs | *The Cloak of Dreams: Chinese Fairy Tales*

Peter Davies, editor | *The Fairies Return: Or, New Tales for Old*

The Fairies Return

Or, New Tales for Old

COMPILED BY PETER DAVIES

Edited and with an introduction by
Maria Tatar

PRINCETON UNIVERSITY PRESS

Princeton and Oxford

First published by Peter Davies Ltd., © 1934

Introduction copyright © 2012 by Princeton University Press

"Jack the Giant Killer" by A. E. Coppard is reproduced by permission of David Higham Associates Ltd.

"Godfather Death" by Clemence Dane is reproduced by permission of Pollinger Limited and the Estate of Clemence Dane

"The Fisherman and His Wife" by E. M. Delafield (© E. M. Delafield, 1934) is reproduced by permission of PFD (www.pfd.co.uk) on behalf of the Estate of E. M. Delafield

"Little Snow-White" by Lord Dunsany (© The Estate of Lord Dunsany) is reproduced by permission of Curtis Brown Group Ltd., London, on behalf of the Estate of Lord Dunsany

"Sindbad the Sailor" by Eric Linklater (© Eric Linklater, 1934) is reproduced by permission of PFD (www.pfd.co.uk) on behalf of the Estate of Eric Linklater

"Ali Baba and the Forty Thieves" by A. G. Macdonell (© A. G. Macdonell, 1934) is reproduced by permission of PFD (www.pfd.co.uk) on behalf of the Estate of A. G. Macdonell

"The Little Mermaid" by Lady Eleanor Smith is reproduced by permission of Lady Juliet Townsend on behalf of the Estate of Lady Eleanor Smith

"Little Red Riding-Hood" by E. Œ. Somerville (© The Estate of E. Œ. Somerville) is reproduced by permission of Curtis Brown Group Ltd., London, on behalf of the Estate of Edith Somerville

"O, If I Could but Shiver!" by Christina Stead is reproduced by permission of Writers House LLC as agent for Christina Stead

"The Sleeping Beauty" by G. B. Stern is reproduced by permission of the Society of Authors as the Literary Representative on the behalf of the Estate of G. B. Stern

Requests for permission to reproduce material from this work should be sent to Permissions, Princeton University Press

Published by Princeton University Press, 41 William Street, Princeton, New Jersey 08540

In the United Kingdom: Princeton University Press, 6 Oxford Street, Woodstock, Oxfordshire OX20 1TW

press.princeton.edu

Library of Congress Cataloging-in-Publication Data

Llewelyn Davies, Peter, 1897–1960.
    The fairies return : or, new tales for old / compiled by Peter Davies ; edited and with an introduction by Maria Tatar.
        p.   cm. — (Oddly modern fairy tales)
    Includes bibliographical references and index.
    ISBN 978-0-691-15230-1 (hardcover : alk. paper)   1. Fairy tales—History and criticism.
I. Tatar, Maria, 1945– II. Title.
    GR552.L54 2012
    398.2—dc23

                                        2011053129

British Library Cataloging-in-Publication Data is available

This book has been composed in Garamond Premier Pro and ITC Fenice

Printed on acid-free paper. ∞

Printed in the United States of America

10 9 8 7 6 5 4 3 2 1

Contents

[vii

CONTENTS

The
Fairies
Return

Introduction

Old wine is often all the better for being
re-bottled; perhaps old wives' tales
are like that, too.

—*Big Claus and Little Claus*

How do you breathe new life into forms considered archaic,
dated, passé, old-fashioned, or, worse yet, obsolete? Peter
Davies set himself that challenge when he published *The
Fairies Return*, an anthology described on its dust jacket as
a "Christmas book written by a number of distinguished
authors. It is a collection of well-known fairy stories retold
for grownups in a modern setting." Moving the tales from
times past, from the nursery to the parlor, and transforming
the wondrous into the quotidian (and vice versa) was a challenge he issued to "several hands"—fifteen contemporaries,
most of them on familiar terrain when it came to fairies and
folklore. Together, they created a rich mosaic, with each vibrant tile telling us as much about Great Britain in the era

following World War I as about the culture from which it was drawn.

The Fairies Return offers sophisticated fare for adults rather than primal entertainment for children. Moving in a satirical mode, it delivers on the promise of what "satire" originally meant: *satura*, or a mixture of different things blended to suit discerning tastes.[1] Not only do we have a variety of tales drawn from Denmark, Germany, France, and the Orient (in addition to England), but we also have authors who choose targets that include evils ranging from predatory behavior and political corruption to drug addiction and social ambition.

The fairies invoked in the title of this volume made their first official print appearance in 1890. "Who says that English folk have no fairy tales of their own?" Joseph Jacobs asked in his preface to *English Fairy Tales* published in that year.[2] For over half a century, Edgar Taylor's 1823 translation of tales by the Brothers Grimm had dominated the fairy-tale marketplace. *German Popular Stories*, illustrated by George Cruikshank, consisted of tales selected from the Grimms' *Children's Stories and Household Tales* (published in two volumes in 1812 and 1815), and it was an instant bestseller. Nearly every decade after 1823 witnessed a new translation of selected German tales into English, culminating in Margaret Hunt's 1882 rendition of the complete corpus of tales, along with a critical apparatus. Jacobs was not wrong to be defensive when he assembled eighty-seven British tales from oral traditions and put them between the covers of a book.

Why did it take so long for the British to publish their answer to the Brothers Grimm? Jacobs attributes the lag to "the lamentable gap between the governing and recording classes and the dumb working classes of this country—dumb to others but eloquent among themselves" (1). He concedes that many of the stories in *English Fairy Tales* are imports: "I have acted on Molière's principle, and have taken what was good wherever I could find it" (2). There are some imports from America, Scotland, and Australia, but the collection as a whole is English, and Jacobs is careful to concede that other national collections contained some of the same *classes* of tales but that he sought out the uniquely English version of international tale types. In sum, the British tales are not derivative of the German, the French, or the Italian but constitute an indigenous body of lore.

Jacobs's introductory remarks go far toward understanding the Anglicizing of tales from Europe and the Orient in *The Fairies Return*. The settings are Devonshire, Scotland, Ireland, and London—anything but the native soil from which some of the tales sprang. As importantly, the untroubled appropriation of stories from the world over suggests that the tales have truly become British, that they have migrated with ease into a new culture and medium, making themselves available for literary adaptation and refashioning, once they established themselves as part of a native storytelling tradition.

The half-century between Jacobs's *English Fairy Tales* and Peter Davies's *The Fairies Return* witnessed what Virginia Woolf famously described as a change in "human character," a change that took place "on or about December, 1910."[3] Her observations about the novel complement Walter Benjamin's pronouncements about a sea change in traditional storytelling after World War I. The eloquence so prized by Joseph Jacobs had vanished: "Less and less frequently do we encounter people with the ability to tell a tale properly. More and more often there is embarrassment all around when the wish to hear a story is expressed."

4]

For Benjamin, the key year in the great shift from an era that narrated lived experience to the age of information is 1918: "Was it not noticeable at the end of the war that men returned from the battlefield grown silent—not richer, but poorer in communicable experience?... For never has experience been contradicted more thoroughly than strategic experience by tactical warfare, economic experience by inflation, bodily experience by mechanical warfare, moral experience by those in power."[4] The storytellers who once passed experience "from mouth to mouth" and whose lives were intimately bound up with the stories they told are no longer with us.

The Fairies Return reminds us that stories endure nonetheless, particularly once what Jacobs called the "recording and governing classes" saw the tales as bonding agents for national identity. The British writers who took up tales by "Perrault, the Brothers Grimm, Hans Andersen, the authors of *The Thousand and One Nights* &c." made them their own. In the international thicket of characters and plots, they found plenty of material for fashioning stories that they could make their own—and in many cases had already been made their own—with the local colors of social and political satire. The tales themselves migrated into the *terra firma* of literary invention, with authors who, for the most part, had been writing novels and plays for adult audiences. Peter Davies, head of the publishing house that issued *The Fairies Return*, must have decided it was time for a comeback for fairy tales, on this occasion with stories that would be British, literary, and, for the most part, playfully satiric rather than experientially communicative and unmediated.

Pairing satire with fairy tale seems, at first glance, to be a marriage of two supremely incompatible partners. Satire, in the traditional sense of the term, has a historical specificity and strong social mission generally absent from traditional tales, which take place in a vague and remote "once upon a time" with characters hungry for wealth and power. It engages in what one critic calls "demolition work," with a view toward reform in its indictment of vice and praise of virtue. But precisely in its juxtaposition of extreme vice and extreme virtue, satire comes to resemble the fairy tale, which often stages something of a morality play by punishing vice and rewarding virtue.[5] The tellers of tales, like literary satirists, see the world as "a battlefield between a definite, clearly understood good . . . and an equally clear-cut evil."[6]

The moral crusades enacted in fairy tales can easily degenerate into grotesque excess and a playful carnivalesque spirit, erasing or discrediting all attempts to impose a moral or message. Satire too can operate in a more open-ended mode, engaging in inquiry and exploration rather than in a predetermined plan of attack. Mikael Bakhtin tells us that the Menippean satirist creates extraordinary situations to provoke and test philosophical ideas rather than to convey definitive answers.[7] In *The Fairies Return*, satire occasionally takes a back seat to playful provocation. When E. M. Delafield, for example, takes up the Grimms' "Fisherman and His Wife," she imagines how modern-day desires would change the course of the wife's requests and of the husband's relationship to those wishes for wealth and power. Instead of flattening out the tale and turning it into a straightforward condemnation of female ambition, Delafield poses questions about the nature of wealth and power and provokes speculation about how the vibrant "What if?" of fairy tales can evolve, later in life, into the disenchantments of "If only!"

Both satire and fairy tale are driven by lack, by a sense that something vital is missing and that social circumstances have made life short, nasty, and brutish. They may begin in a dystopic setting, with dire need, messy fixes, and cruel injustices, but they also offer or point the way to a better world, where wrongs are made right and injuries repaired. If satire is missing the rainbow promise of the "happily ever after" found in fairy tales, it contains the Enlightenment promise that reason and wit will lead to steady improvements. Both satire and fairy tale, by aiming to expose social injustice, contain within them the principle of hope so carefully theorized and elaborated by Ernst Bloch.

Bloch's essays on fairy tales emphasize their utopian spirit. "Once upon a time" refers not just to the past but points forward to a "more colorful or easier elsewhere," a place where courage and cunning can help you change your station in life, to win "the herd of elegant cattle and ninety bucks in cash" that enables Little Claus to live happily ever after in the version of the tale told by R. J. Yeatman and W. C. Sellar in *The Fairies Return*. For Bloch, the element of hope—the anticipatory illumination that allows us to imagine a better world—also endows fairy tales with "a piece of the Enlightenment that emerged long before there was such a thing as the Enlightenment."[8]

If *The Fairies Return* reveals just how comfortably satire can settle into the fairy tale, modernizing it and equipping it with a critical edge sometimes lacking in its traditional forms, the volume also reveals what is lost when satire's rhetoric of exposure invades fairy-tale discourse. Satire, with its historical specificity and commitment to topical issues, does not inhabit a "once upon a time" but the "here and now." Gone are the wonders of Cinderella's magnetic beauty and the horrific snarls of a talking wolf in Grandma's bed. What we have instead are stockbrokers and socialites, rubber stamp makers and shopkeepers, ordinary folk beleaguered by villains and monsters that haunt the real lives of adults rather than the imaginations of children.

In an anthology of fairy tales and fantasies by Victorian women writers, Nina Auerbach and Ulrich Knoepflmacher comment on how quickly fairy tales can undergo a sea change: "The wild magic of fairy tales, so guardedly approached even by the finest of didacticists who dominated earlier juvenile literature, now seemed to license a new generation of writers as well as readers to be deviant, angry, even violent or satirical."[9] The writers for *The Fairies Return* felt almost duty-bound to tap into the transgressive energy of folk narratives and to provoke, unsettle, and inflame in ways that the Victorians had never even imagined.

Satirists, as Matthew Hodgart has shrewdly observed, have "always accepted the risk of failure." Committed to exposing public abuses, they can become ensnared by the "ephemeral and transitory events of [the] day."[10] In *The Fairies Return*, we may occasionally feel lost in the woods. Why are the giants in Coppard's "Jack the Giant Killer," named Demos, Kudos, and Osmos, and why are they persecuting the inhabitants of London? But some things never change, and A. G. Macdonell's "Ali Baba and the Forty Thieves" remains as topical and on the mark today, in its indictment of fraud and corruption, as it was in its own day. Peter Davies' volume may not always be completely transparent, but it gives us all the abundance, variety, excitement, and revelation we might expect to find in the hybrid form of satire and fairy tale.[11]

The Fairies Make Mischief

"Jack the Giant Killer" introduces *The Fairies Return*, and it is one of two British tales included in the volume. A. E. Coppard's Jack is a trickster, outwitting and slaying three oafish ogres terrorizing England, "husky, fascinating, agile leviathans" who seem friendly and well disposed to the British but in reality feed off them. Their cannibalistic activities are ignored for a time, but soon London is covered with "stays and stockings, kimonos, pants, wraps, hats, and shirts." How do the people react? First there is denial (the kindly giants must have been distributing clothes to the poor), then the government orders an "enquiry," and finally there is retreat into isolation: "But a dark terror invaded every private mind; all ran from the presence of the giants and hid as best they could." It takes a fisherman from Cornwall—a likeable fellow who is willing to slay the giants for love as much as for money—to deliver the country from evil.

The breeziness of Coppard's pastiche of one of Britain's most celebrated folktales (only "Jack and the Beanstalk" is perhaps better known) ought not to blind us to the political message embedded in it. The date of publication is 1934, and only a year earlier, Hitler had already begun to violate the terms of the Treaty of Versailles. Just a year later came the occupation of the Saar, followed in early 1937 by the move into the demilitarized Rhineland to occupy what had been intended as a buffer zone between Germany and France. It is hard to imagine that Coppard did not have German military might in mind when he made creative mischief with his trio of predatory giants. The slaying of the final giant at sea hints at the importance of naval preeminence at a time when England was moving into an era of political and economic decline.

Clemence Dane's "Godfather Death" reminds us of how Britain had not yet recovered from the casualties of the First

World War. She begins her version of the folktale by quoting from the Grimms' story of that title, and she hews closely to its plot. Drawing attention through citation to the moment at which Death gives his godson the gift of a career as physician, she moves in an elegiac mode, revealing that mortality throws its shadow over everyone. The Grimms' tale too emphasizes Death as the great leveler, and, for the two German tale collectors, it represented a democratic principle in a world otherwise ruled by strict hierarchies dividing rich and poor and creating social injustices. Both the Grimms and Dane show Death making its one great exception. Seeking some connection to life, Death agrees to serve as godfather to a boy who grows up to be a celebrated physician. A superb diagnostician, the young man has divined Death's secret of standing at the head of a bed when hope is lost and at the foot of the bed when recovery is possible.

Clemence Dane, also known as Winifred Ashton, creates an *alter ego* named Clement, a boy who grows up in an era permeated by disease and warfare. Death has "harvested" the field of war, and it does equally well in the "swamp mists" of the Devon village in which Death's godson is born. In those precincts, Death flourishes and befriends the local doctor, the one man willing to invite him in and shake his hand. When he becomes godfather to the doctor's son, he also becomes ensnared in a situation in which he must, one day, betray the person he has promised to protect. Not to be outwitted, Death, by making his godson a physician and imparting a secret to him, creates a loophole for himself. The Grimms'

Death wants his revenge once the secret is betrayed, and he engineers an accident that leads to the physician's death. Godfather Death has a similarly "malicious look" on his face when he acts "clumsily" and fails to position the physician's candle stub on the taller candle that is his son's. There may be occasional reprieves, but Death cannot be cheated.

"The Fisherman and His Wife" moves readers from war zones to the battle of the sexes. E. M. Delafield, prolific as diarist and novelist, modeled her tale on a story borrowed by the Brothers Grimm from the painter Philipp Otto Runge. Written in a Low German dialect, the tale seemed to possess, in its colloquial qualities and pungent ingredients, a folkloric authenticity lacking in some of the items collected by the brothers. The Grimms seemed unaware of the tale's kinship with "The Fisherman and the Genie," a narrative gem from *The Thousand and One Nights* in which a poor man casts his net into the sea three times, each time retrieving worthless objects. On the fourth try, he pulls out of the sea a copper jar, opens it, and finds himself at the mercy of a genie's wrath. The fisherman manages to trick the genie and put him back in the jar.

The German tale is inflected quite differently, with a husband and wife, the one content to live in a pigsty, the other with unbridled ambition that reveals not only the monstrosity of greed but also of feminine power. Delafield gives us a new twist, with a young author named Alured as husband, and a wife named Barbara, who is described as "an unreasonable and overbearing young modern if ever there was one."

The knowing narrator is on to the fictional author/fisherman, who has a bad case of writer's block and not much talent in the first place. Alured knows that "poetry does not come forth from palaces," and he longs for quarters more modest than the estates and castles conjured by the magical flounder he catches. In a climax that parodies the wife's desire to become omnipotent and usurp God's role, Barbara's last wish backfires, and the Papal palace is turned back into the tiny cottage of the story's beginning. Alured, unlike his folkloric kinsmen, does not discover contentment. Instead, he longs to have had Barbara's opportunities and to have taken advantage of the offices she occupied. Ambition does not know gender in Delafield's moral calculus.

Edward Plunkett, who published under the name Lord Dunsany, was an expert in chess, a cricket player, a supporter of scouting, and an avid hunter who advocated for animal rights (he was known for opposing the "docking" of dogs' tails). This diversity in interests is mirrored in the expansive repertoire of genres he commanded: fiction, drama, screenplays, poems, and essays. Lord Dunsany's "Little Snow-White" is set in modern times and continues in the vein of social critique with an aristocratic cast of characters that includes Lord and Lady Clink, along with Blanche, Lord Clink's daughter from a first marriage.

Instead of an optical device, Lady Clink consults an acoustic wonder to determine who is the fairest of them all: "Oh gramo, gramo, gramophone, / Which of us is the fairest one?" The huntsman of the Grimms' "Snow White" is replaced by a chauffeur named Clutch, who secures the requisite "tongue and heart" by running over a random pedestrian. The trees in the forest are supplanted by lampposts in the tale's new urban setting. And Blanche is taken in by a group of hardworking miners in exchange for managing their household.

Tragically incapable of exorcising the demon of envy, Blanche's stepmother, like Snow White's wicked stepmother, compulsively consults the beauty oracle in order to assure herself that her sexual rival is out of the way. Lord Dunsany's evil stepmother does not dance to death in red-hot iron shoes. Instead, she confronts social calamity after her daughter marries, losing her standing and the opportunity to be presented at Court. Dunsany takes the traditional pairing of murderously jealous and cold-blooded stepmother with innocently sweet girl trained in the art of good housekeeping, retaining its drama, but draining triumph from the victory of girl over mother by turning both into frivolous creatures devoted, above all, to appearances. This is no infatuated reworking of the Grimms' tale but a cynical commentary on a culture that has funneled passion into purchasing power and false status symbols.

Anna Gordon Keown disenchants the exotic entertainments of *The Thousand and One Nights* when she turns Aladdin into a retired undertaker living in a Scottish township. A cheerless fellow who once had "a thousand and one subtle devices" for advertising his services, this Aladdin might have devoted his last days to growing cucumbers for the local show but for an "itch." The desire to "polish" his Gaelic leads

[13

to incantations that mysteriously coalesce into a spell that conjures a naked demon.

The uncivilized creature, grotesque and deformed, quickly becomes a society favorite, winning prestige for the undertaker even as he becomes a source of intense anxiety for him. The demon not only has horns and a tail—which are challenging to keep hidden from view—but also a habit of making shocking statements that reflect his true nature. But the passion stirred by the alien and exotic works such magic that the good folk of Drumlochrie applaud when the demon incites them to crime and engage in floor-thumping when he insults them. A shameless entertainer, the demon feels quite at home in bourgeois surroundings, and Mr. Aladdin must strain his resources to find a way to disencumber himself of the otherworldly pest. Anna Gordon Keown, like many of the authors anthologized in Davies' volume, seems fascinated by the ability to resist registering surprise in the face of the outlandish. In any other setting, the demon would not have to show his tail to create shock effects. But in Great Britain, as long as the tail of the demon remains tucked in, out of sight, he can be offensive and abusive, intrusive and unkempt. And rather than being recognized as the scoundrel that he is, he becomes, in a move that reminds us of the modern-day search for re-enchantment, a source of wonder and fascination.

A. G. Macdonell's "Ali Baba and the Forty Thieves" resituates the celebrated tale from *The Thousand and One Nights* to contemporary London. With the wry wit and gentle satire that became his trademark style after the publication of *England, Their England* in 1933, Macdonell makes light of the craving for wealth and power at the heart of fairy-tale passions. His two brothers are descended from a shopkeeper named "Barber," whose deeply divided loyalties to Ireland and Scotland manifest themselves in the birth of sons who incarnate the stereotypical traits of the two nationalities. Cassim Barber, with all the tough-minded business instincts and "relentless realism of the Irish race," prospers after investing the wealth inherited from his father. Alastair, by contrast, is a "dreamy, unpractical Scotsman" who writes novels for a living.

[15

The treasures in caves and the wonders of magical commands are transformed in Macdonell's tale into the wonders of margins and mergers, with a Sesame Finance Syndicate that is "little better than robbers." Through "one of those electrical mysteries which are beyond ordinary comprehension," Alastair makes a fortune in finance, and, with his newfound wealth, basks in the glow of prizes and awards for novels that once languished in bookstores. Like his rich and greedy counterpart in the Arabic tale, Cassim learns of the scheme and attempts unsuccessfully to replicate his brother's success. In a denouement that replaces the slave-girl Morgiana, the tailor Baba Mustafa, and the jars of oil with J. P. Morgan, Doctor Baba Mustapha, and shares of Samarcand Oil, the Sesame Syndicate collapses and only one of the thieves survives to set himself up in a new firm. Macdonell's tale of financial intrigue, corporate treachery, and passionate greed reads like an allegory of modern times and reminds us that fairy tales, with their focus on primal fears and desires, are easy to tailor to modern socioeconomic conditions. Skillfully demystifying a tale from long ago and far away, Macdonell reveals how deeply the quest for instant wealth in fairy tales is tainted by deception, treachery, and greed. But the hero who wins a fortune, a kingdom, and the hand of a princess manages to succeed without ever becoming implicated in the tale's nexus of greed and guilt. Dumb luck is always on his side. Alastair Barber is Jack, Lucky Hans, Fair Ivan, Tom Thumb, and all the other dreamers and numbskulls who are by nature deserving of good fortune and thereby escape the fate of their rapacious, evil fairy-tale brethren.

Helen Simpson's "Puss in Boots" turns to the Gallic tradition to make a much more subtle point. She too relies on contrasts by pairing the hero, not with a brother who embodies everything the hero is not, but with a feline sidekick who is as shrewd, worldly, and duplicitous as the miller's son of the tale is naïve, artless, and innocent. Puss in Boots, blessed with a master so kind that he spends his last shilling on boots for the cat that is his sole inheritance, shields his master from the predatory forces surrounding him. Jack Millerson may believe that "honesty is the best policy," but Puss knows that engineering satisfaction requires wits, ferocity, patience, and, above all, the ability to bluff.

When Charles Perrault wrote down the tale "Puss in Boots," he appended a lesson for "young people," a message that, once registered, is more like a mugging than a moral.

By asserting that diligence is worth more than acquired wealth, it contradicts sharply the logic of the plot. When another, equally irrelevant moral about clothes, appearance, and youth is added, there is a sudden shifting in the tectonic plates that support the story. Perrault's story does not, as the first moral insists, celebrate the superiority of "industry, knowledge, and a clever mind" over "mere gifts from others." One could challenge that wisdom in any number of ways, most obviously by arguing that the inherited cat was in fact far more valuable to the miller's son than anything else. Helen Simpson understood clearly that the mysteries of the partnership between miller's son and cat are entertaining rather than enlightening. To be sure, Puss is an expert in survival, and he steers his master toward wealth, power, and a title. But in the end he is little more than a comic *alter ego* to the earnestly honest Jack Millerson, a feline figure who makes possible the idea that luck will always be on the side of the hapless, naïve simpleton of fairy tales.

Eleanor Smith pays homage to Hans Christian Andersen in her modernized version of "The Little Mermaid." Inspired by the Danish author's "gift for pathos and romance," the well-traveled British writer set her story in the new fairy-tale realm of Hollywood. Mary Domville grows up in Canada, but there is something exotic about her family. Her six elder sisters have the "dark exuberant beauty of gipsy girls" (Smith believed that her paternal great-grandmother belonged to the Romani people), and Mary herself, though "fair-haired," has skin as brown "as an Indian's."

Andersen's Little Mermaid was an upwardly mobile creature of the sea, striving to acquire, above all else, a soul. Drawn to the sights and sounds of an urban setting, she makes a pact with a Sea Witch, exchanging her voice for legs and the ability to live on land. When she fails to capture the heart of the human whose love could have endowed her with the treasure she sought, she has the chance to kill her rival but instead plunges into the sea. Hers is not a return to nature. Instead she has the opportunity to become a Daughter of the Air, acquiring a soul after three hundred years of good deeds. Andersen, despite the Disney interpretation of the tale, uses romance and courtship as little more than an alibi for writing about salvation.

Retaining Andersen's feverish pathos and just as exactingly avoiding real romance, Smith gives us a human longing to return to nature. Never at home in the world of parties, rituals, and ceremony, Mary Domville is "shy as a squirrel" and happiest when roaming the countryside, paddling a canoe, or building a wigwam, a skill she learns from an Indian servant named "Little Moose." When we read that Mary can "swim and dive like a fish," it becomes evident that the profusion of animal metaphors and nicknames reveals not only an alliance between Mary and Little Moose, but also a mutual bond with nature: "They belonged to it."

Mary's encounter with a fortune-teller on the occasion of her social debut translates her from nature into culture. Hollywood beckons, and, despite the risk of pain and suffering prophesied by the fortune-teller, Mary cannot resist its allure and travels to the very place where her beloved David Darrell makes his home. Hollywood, as the site of illusion, artifice, and counterfeit fantasies, is the opposite of everything to which Mary had been drawn before the liminal experience of a social debut. And yet her infatuation with Hollywood is prefigured in her devotion to a marble figure of a boy— its art proving more seductive than Little Moose's lessons in building wigwams. Smith's Mary, like Andersen's Little Mermaid, suffers from the tyranny of art over her imagination, and there is not the slightest whiff of the tragic in her return to nature, where human life and marine life merge in a soft tidal flow.

In her "Little Red Riding-Hood," the Irish novelist E. Œ. Somerville puts nature at war with culture, and her Moira Cloca-dearg (another Mary, but this one of the Red Cloak) struggles valiantly to resist the beautiful blandishments of a fairyland. At age ten, Moira is promised a pair of shoes by a Cluricaune, an Irish fairy resembling a leprechaun. Wisely refusing, she understands that she will be bound to follow the Cluricaune wherever he goes, even into a lake. At thirteen, exquisite music draws her into a fairy realm, and she incurs the wrath of the wee folk by kidnapping a pony she names Lusmore.

The cultural distance separating Somerville's narrative about the dangers of fairies lurking everywhere in nature and the story of Little Red Riding Hood told by Charles Perrault several centuries earlier is not as great as it might first seem. Both Moira and Little Red Riding Hood find it a challenge to resist the temptations of beauty and nature, both failing to see peril where there is beauty. Seduced by the "divilment of the fairies," Moira nearly falls into dark waters so deep that she would never have emerged from them. But it is in the portrayal of the Wolf that the two narratives diverge.

Cornelius Wolfe, or Curley Brech, is a "wild lad," and he is widely known as a mischief-maker, the "divil's own play-boy." But he is also a convert to love, and he carries out Moira's errand to grandmother while the girl is captivated by the challenges of the hunt. Masquerading as grandmother, he throws himself on the girl and holds her tight. This encounter, embrace rather than threat, marks the end of Moira's romance with fairy foxes, those elusive creatures that led her to the magical realm. As a grown-up Red Riding Hood, Moira moves from nature to culture, and the little shoe thrown after Moira and Cornelius Wolfe as they emerge from the Chapel—a shoe that you would not get "the like of in the whole world, no, nor in the globe of Ireland neither"—is a sign of exactly what Moira has lost in abandoning the world of the fairies.

That special shoe returns to haunt Robert Speaight's story, "Cinderella," a high-minded attack on the excesses of fairy-tale romance and royalty. Cinderella, in this retrospective narrative of a middle-aged woman's life story, has grown up, and she is neither widow nor divorcée but what Anglo-American cultures once referred to as a spinster or old maid. The slipper in this Cinderella story was fashioned in silver thread by a holy woman: "For the feet that stumble and the heart that does not fail." And although its history is written upon Cinderella's brow, her story is put on paper by a narrator who discovers "Cinderella's secret" in a dream and is compelled to "inscribe her story."

"Cinderella" is our quintessential rags-to-riches story, an international tale about a modest girl of humble origins whose magnetic beauty and dazzling clothes win her the heart of a prince. Magic traditionally made things happen in her story, whether in the form of a fairy godmother or a tree that showers down a dress of gold and silver. Cinderella has never been aligned with philosophers, but in this story she comes to be compared to Christ, Socrates, and Shakespeare. Her road to sainthood—she becomes a counselor, confidante, and guardian to those in need—begins at sunset, with a journey that culminates in an encounter with the splendors of "dissolution." There is almost "too much beauty" in the silent mysteries of the night, as she descends into a valley fraught with symbolic meaning.

This Cinderella becomes a martyr, a young woman who seems to make a mad dash from the beautiful mysteries of the physical world to the brutal mysteries of the metaphysical. The awful secret she discovers right near the altar of love has to do with betrayal, suffering, and "eternal crucifixion": "love's mystery laid bare." Her sacrificial atonement for the sins of the King whom she once idealized and idolized takes the form of custodial devotion to the scores of lost souls seeking her advice and care. Although politics are treated with more than a touch of cheerful cynicism, Cinderella is declared to have become "the consolation of all her world." Her role as a mender of souls (she specializes in the resolution of marital disputes), it is solemnly declared, will create for her a happily ever after. Here, the fairies have returned to make real mischief for those who aspire to fairy-tale romance. Compassion and good deeds have replaced passionate melodrama.

Christina Stead's "'O, If I Could but Shiver'" is anything but an exercise in sublimation and instead takes us on an X-rated odyssey with a hero driven by raw desire. Stead's source is "A Fairy Tale about One Who Left Home to Learn about Fear" from the *Children's Stories and Household Tales*. Although the term "fairy tale" appears in the Grimms' title, the story recorded by the two brothers is more or less an extended anecdote, with a series of self-contained episodes, each taking a burlesque turn. It is the stuff of campfire tales, designed to send chills up the spine of listeners and to inspire the very affect the hero lacks. The Grimms' hero possesses the loopy innocence associated with fairy-tale numbskulls and simpletons. They can perform heroic feats in large part because fearlessness shades so effortlessly into courage.

If cheerful naïveté and generous goodwill characterize the Grimms' hero, cynicism, greed, and a voracious sexual appetite distinguish Stead's protagonist. His first feat leaves no human wreckage behind, but, in the second phase of his odyssey, he becomes the accomplice to a counterfeiter, whom he outrages by seducing his three daughters and sister. Tossed into prison, he tunnels his way out and lives miserably for a time, "assisting" in murders and druggings and living in a "maze of rotten tenements" described with baroque excess. There is a "foul, green, rotting staircase, covered with rags, cobwebs and filthy emanations of households," pans filled with "the mingled excreta and spittle of all the families in the house," and children making "immature love round an open cesspool." Even this horrific dystopia is incapable of producing shivers in the hero.

Lludd, Stead's hero, marries, fathers children, divorces, remarries, fathers twins, and is thrown in jail for failure to pay alimony, all the while carrying on with various young women. The organizing principle for his adventures is reduced to egotistic sexuality, and the inability to shiver becomes secondary in the mind of everyone but Lludd. Yet, shiver he does, and Lludd receives his comeuppance in a forced return to his first wife, who is "much older" now, "wrinkled and wasted," yet with the "fires of passion" still burning bright. One libidinous fiend meets another. Lludd's wife has become "a man-eating ogre," so "savage" in her lovemaking that Lludd finally learns to shiver, and shivers thereafter day and night. The Grimms' tale of an adventurous innocent who settles down to love and marriage (the cold bucket of minnows that finally gives him the shivers is a metaphor for sexual pleasure) is transformed into an anti-fairy tale about the enduring tortures of love and marriage, a horror story guaranteed to give readers, if not the shivers, then the creeps.

Charles Perrault's "Sleeping Beauty in the Wood" is brought up to date in Gladys Bronwyn Stern's "The Sleeping Beauty," a story that proclaims the defeat of fairy-tale romance even as it brings magic back to a disenchanted world. Beginning with an incantatory "once upon a time" and ending with a "long joyful flight," it also takes the couple "deep into the dying day." The old-fashioned mingles with the new when Roy and Queenie (Stern relishes word play, giving us a British "Roi"), who reside in Briar Park, settle down and have a child named Rose. At her christening party, Rose is toasted and endowed by the guests with every virtue: beauty, chastity, courage, good horsemanship, charm, a marvelous figure, a brain for higher mathematics, and so on.

Roy and Queenie have abandoned a life of carousing for the sake of their daughter, whom they raise in the rural delights of Briar Park. They cordon their estate off from the world, and, as "converted rakes," they ensure that their daughter will grow up in a "crystal vacuum" that is wholesome, unblemished, and "ineffably dull." Yet Queenie preserves one addiction, and the uninvited guest who startles everyone by appearing at Rose's christening predicts that the mother's frailty will be the daughter's undoing. "If you ask *me*," he declares, "Queenie's child won't be long in her teens before she picks up the use of Queenie's pretty little needle; the same pretty little needle whose prick has sent so many of our débutantes to cold ruin and a colder death."

What is strictly forbidden becomes the source of irresistible temptation, and, on her fifteenth birthday, Queenie's daughter pricks herself with a needle and falls into a deep sleep. It is then that magic happens. A plane crashes near the outskirts of Briar Park, and from its wreckage emerges Chalmers Prince. Making his way through the hedges, he finds the drugged Rose, also known as Beauty, and presses a kiss on her lips. The curse of drugs and alcohol is lifted, and a sleeping Beauty is borne aloft into a life of adventure. Pleasure may reside in the ruins of fairy-tale romance—in vintage wines and grains of morphine sulphate—but Chalmers and Beauty lift themselves above and beyond it to soar off "across the hills and far away."

"Grimm's Not the Word" captures perfectly the spirit of Hans Christian Andersen's "Big Claus and Little Claus," and R. J. Yeatman and W. C. Sellar use that phrase as the subtitle for their refashioning of the Danish tale. The two authors, who pulled the tale out of the editor's hat, discover—much to their astonishment—that murder, adultery, brutal beatings, blackmail, and treachery constitute the core of fairy-tale magic in Andersen's story. Blending the telling of the tale with responses to questions posed by the "kiddies" listening to the story, the authors create a raucously energetic narrative that leaves a trail of corpses, as Little Claus plays trickster to Big Claus and others, outwitting them and turning the tables at a dizzying speed. The hectic pace is ramped up by a sassy and sarcastic conversational style of such expressive intensity that the authors' proposal to collaborate with MGM to make a horror film does not seem in the least implausible.

Andersen's unrepentant hero reminds us that folktales were once a way of fighting back against vulnerability and powerlessness. It was precisely the tough struggle for survival, with its accompanying sense of defenselessness when it came to poverty and disease, that bred a folklore authorizing its heroes to acquire power at any cost. The passionate attachment to power through violence remains a fact of life in many of the once most popular tales, where the body becomes both object and target of power through ceremonies of torture. The hero is cheerfully in control, and it is he who is charged with disciplining bodies and administering justice.

When tales like "Big Claus and Little Claus" crossed over into the nursery, along with other canonical tales, they produced a form of astonishment that can be divined in nearly every sentence of Yeatman and Sellar's retelling of the story. Cultural amnesia has made us forget that these stories were once told by adults to multi-generational audiences. The true wonder of the fairy tale, as this collection so potently reveals, is its ability to migrate into new spaces and to transform itself as it moves across cultures, eras, and generations. Stories that were once told around the fireside and read to children from books are refashioned in this volume in ways that require us to develop a form of bifocal vision that keeps our sights trained on the story told but also puts us back in touch with how the story was told in times past. When the fairies return, we see them in double vision.

In this volume, a generation that had lived through World War I and spent over a decade in its shadow revealed its loss of faith in happily ever after. Drawing on traditional tales in print collections, the authors represented take on a range of topics that embrace the timeless and universal as well as the topical and local. Creating narratives that reveal the capacity of fairy tales to frame utopian fantasies as well as to expose social realities, their real legacy is encapsulated in the title of one of Ernst Bloch's essays: "The Fairy Tale Moves on in Its Own Time."

Peter Davies Brings Back the Fairies

On the title page of *The Fairies Return* appears an apology to the memory of Charles Perrault, the Brothers Grimm, Hans Christian Andersen, and to the anonymous authors of *The Thousand and One Nights*. We find there also the name of the collection's godfather, a man schooled in fairy lore. Peter Davies was no ordinary publisher and editor, and to understand exactly why a grown man might find it fascinating to bring the fairies back to England requires a look at his personal, as well as professional, life. For this is the man whose name will be forever associated with J. M. Barrie's play *Peter Pan, or the Boy Who Would Not Grow Up*. This is the man who, with his brothers, served as the model for a character who has become part of our cultural imagination and whose name is nearly synonymous with youth, pleasure, play, and enchantment. However elliptically related the life of Peter Davies may seem to the content of *The Fairies Return*, the stories in that volume were, in the final analysis, commissioned and made possible by a childhood in which fairies mingle with pirates, dogs and their masters dance in public parks, and birds transform themselves into babies.

Peter Davies may have been a sober businessman, but he also understood just how impoverished the world could become once it was disenchanted, whether by the mere fact of growing up, or by the steady rationalization sped up by the Weberian forces of capitalism and modernity. His imagination may have been intense, but he himself was not unhinged. He was not so naïve as to think that the world could be re-enchanted with *The Fairies Return*. But he did understand that the tales once told to us in childhood had magical qualities that could be revived and rescripted in ways that could reanimate us as reminders of the gap between fairytale fantasy and social reality. It was a matter of harnessing their natural energy to the oddities and eccentricities of modern life, and it is no accident that the writers recruited for *The Fairies Return* were all expert observers of modern British manners and mores.

Peter Davies, born in 1897 in London, was one of five sons of barrister Arthur Llewelyn Davies and Sylvia Llewelyn Davies, herself the daughter of the celebrated novelist George du Maurier. He, along with his brothers, was adopted by J. M. Barrie after both parents died within a few years of each other, Arthur in 1906, Sylvia in 1910. Peter Davies was still an infant when J. M. Barrie famously entertained the two older Llewelyn Davies boys, four-year-old George and three-year-old Jack, with antics that included twitching his ears, elevating one eyebrow and lowering the other, performing magic tricks, and boxing with his St. Bernard dog Porthos. At the time, Barrie, who hailed from Scotland, was a renowned London journalist, novelist, and playwright, married to the talented actress Mary Ansell, with whom he resided at 133 Gloucester Road, on the south side of Kensington Gardens.

An animated storyteller, Barrie worked magic with children, drawing them into a world of make-believe as he told stories about fairies lurking in Kensington Gardens and setting up household in the roots of trees. All the social awkwardness that Barrie felt around adults mysteriously vanished when he was around children, who were not at all unnerved by the way he alternated between playful expressiveness and concentrated silence. A child who participated in the gatherings recalled Barrie as a "tiny man" with a "pale face and large eyes and shadows round them." She described the matter and the manner of his interactions with children: "He looked fragile, but he was strong when he wrestled with Porthos, his St. Bernard dog. Mr. Barrie talked a great deal about cricket, but the next moment he was telling us about fairies, as though he knew all about them. He was made of silences, but we did not find these strange, they were so much a part of him . . . his silences spoke loudly."[12]

In Kensington Gardens, Peter Llewelyn Davies was introduced to a new mythology rooted in the geography of the London park, which Barrie had populated with birds and babies, fairies and flowers that walk on their own, along with an old crow named Solomon Caw and a boy named Peter

Pan, who rode around the Gardens at night on his goat, "playing sublimely on his pipes." It is in those stories that Peter Pan, a creature Betwixt-and-Between, had his origins. Within a matter of years, he migrated from Kensington Gardens into the pages of a novel named *The Little White Bird* and finally, in 1904, onto the stage as the boy who would not grow up. By then Barrie had befriended the parents, and the two families became close over the years.

Peter Pan bears the Christian name of the Llewelyn Davies' third son, but he is in many ways a composite character, created over the years through stories told in Kensington Gardens and adventures played out at Black Lake Cottage, where Barrie and his wife spent three summers with Arthur, Sylvia, and, eventually, all five boys. The woods were transformed into a tropical forest in the South Seas; the boys became heroic figures doing battle with redskins and pirates; and Barrie himself played the pirate Captain Swarthy. Barrie took dozens of pictures, added text, and had everything bound together in a book entitled *The Boy Castaways of Black Lake Island, Being a record of the terrible adventures of the brothers Davies in the summer of 1901*. Its author was designated as Peter Llewelyn Davies, and its publisher was J. M. Barrie.

Three years later, *Peter Pan, or the Boy Who Would Not Grow Up* captured the imagination of London when it was performed at the Duke of York's Theatre. Many of the adventures staged at Black Lake Island entered the script, and, in the dedication to the first printed edition—the play was written in honor of "the five"—Barrie described his work as being "streaky with you still, though none may see this save ourselves." Peter Pan may have been named after #3, as Barrie charmingly put it, but he reveals: "I always knew that I made Peter by rubbing the five of you violently together, as savages with two sticks produce a flame."[13]

Peter Davies, in later years, referred to the play as that "terrible masterpiece." In the late 1940s, he wrote: "What's in a name! My God what isn't? If that perennially juvenile lead, if that boy so fatally committed to an arrestation of his development, had only been dubbed George, or Jack, or Michael, or Nicholas, what miseries would have been spared me!"[14] Although many believe that Michael was the true inspiration for Peter Pan, it was Peter Davies who was burdened with the emotional baggage attached to being the model for a character who incarnated eternal childhood and performed miracles every year in London theaters. "Peter Pan in Bridal Party," the *New York Times* trumpeted when he served as best man at his brother Nico's wedding. "'Peter Pan' Is Named," that same newspaper proclaimed when he was included in Barrie's will. The reporter captured just why Peter Davies agonized over the identification with Peter Pan. After describing Davies' marriage to Margaret Hore-Ruthven in 1932, the article goes on to explain exactly who he was: "Mr. Davies, who, as Peter Pan, was known as a Boy Who Would Never Grow Old, has led almost a double life. Although he is an adult, married man in charge of a business enterprise, the apparently immortal fantasy of Peter Pan has always been associated with him."[15]

Some might have taken pleasure in the association with the playfully irresponsible Peter Pan, but not Peter Llewelyn Davies. The "miseries" of Peter Pan were dwarfed by the real-life tragedies visited on the Davies family year after year. The last and perhaps the most melodramatic of these events came when the sixty-three-year old Peter Davies hurled himself in the path of an underground train at the Sloan Square Station in London.

Peter Davies was a boy of just nine when his father had surgery for cancer of the jaw. Arthur Llewelyn Davies died a few months after the painful surgery, which left him unable to speak. He was a mere thirteen-year-old when he lost his mother to what was probably stomach cancer. J. M. Barrie adopted the five boys, sending them to the best possible schools and supporting them well into their adult lives. But one calamity followed another. Two of the five boys died young. A stray bullet killed George when he was stationed in Belgium on the Western Front in the early years of World War I. And Michael was drowned, most likely in a suicide pact with another student named Rupert Buxton, while at Oxford.

Peter Davies, like his brother George, volunteered for military service when war broke out, and he shipped to France, where he worked as a signal officer. There he experienced physical hardships and emotional trauma so powerful that his brother Nico wrote, on the day after he committed suicide: "The 1914 War ditched Peter, really." His brother's health, both physical and mental, had deteriorated so badly by the time of his death that "he would have lived with hardly a smile."

The exact motives for Peter Davies' suicide are far too complex to fathom and will forever elude us. The potent mix of personal tragedies, alcoholism, and general existential despair are impossible to sort out. We do know that Peter Davies returned from war and lived with an artist named Vera Willoughby and that that relationship led to a temporary break with Barrie—Uncle Jim did not approve when they moved in together. When the affair was over, Peter [33 reconciled with Barrie, who arranged for an apprenticeship in publishing with Walter Blaikie in Edinburgh and with Hodder & Stoughton in London. Peter Davies Limited was funded by Barrie and enabled Peter to work with his brother Nico to establish a respected publishing house that flourished for many decades.

Peter's eldest son Rivvy long ago made the claim—from a nursing home—that Barrie's failure to leave the bulk of his fortune to his adopted boys led to his father's suicide. While it is true that Barrie left most of his fortune to his secretary Cynthia Asquith, who had developed a close personal, nearly familial relationship to her employer, sums were given to the boys as well, both during Barrie's lifetime and at his death. Nonetheless, Rivvy made the following claim: "My childhood was unhappy because of what was happening to my father. I could see that he [Barrie] was ruining everything. From the moment I was old enough I was aware that my father had been exploited by Barrie and was very bitter. . . . My father didn't really like Barrie. He resented the fact that he wasn't well off and that Barrie had to support him. But when he was cut out of the will, he was livid and tremendously disappointed. . . . He started drinking heavily."[16]

Rivvy's words are no doubt an exaggeration, a protective mantle against the actual facts of his father's illness (he was suffering from emphysema) and depression (his wife had Huntington's Disease and his three sons were possibly carrying the genes for it). After World War II, Peter had become obsessive about delving into his family's history, reading thousands of letters and documents inherited from Barrie and consulting family friends about Barrie and his relationship to Arthur and Sylvia. The history came to be known as *The Morgue*, and the documents in it provide not just a family record but also a pathological desire on the part of the family historian to linger obsessively over details—even going so far as to interrogate his nanny—and sift evidence in order to understand unfathomable mysteries of the heart. Peter's need to get to the bottom of what he saw as a love triangle was doomed, and in 1949 he wrote: "Alas, the more one learns of those sad days, the sadder the tale becomes."

Peter Davies' childhood reads in many ways like a fairy tale, not the "happily ever after" variety, but one more like the many chain tales recorded by the Brothers Grimm in which misfortune breeds hard luck which in turn begets misery and finally leads to tragedy. The attraction to fairy tales may have stemmed not only from a childhood filled with stories about fairies, but also from a deep hankering for the gold with which fairy-tale heroes are showered once they emerge from loss, hostility, and conflict. We do not know exactly who chose the titles of the tales that were to be transformed, but, in the absence of a named editor, we can assume that Peter Davies himself took on that task. He ranged widely, from *The Thousand and One Nights* and the Brothers Grimm to Charles Perrault and Hans Christian Andersen.

E. Arnot Robertson's "Dick Whittington" could not be included for copyright reasons, but everything else is there, as a testimony to the inventiveness of the British imagination when it comes to making the most of fairy tale wisdom and providing challenges to it. Fairy tales have always had the capacity to puncture bourgeois propriety and speak truth to power even as they fuel our fantasies and fears. In this volume too, they are to double duty bound.

Notes

1. The connection of satire to "satyr" has long been refuted. I have profited from Gay Sibley's arguments about *satura* in *"Satura* from Quintilian to Joe Bob Briggs: A New Look at an Old Word," in *Theorizing Satire: Essays in Literary Criticism*, ed. Brian A. Connery and Kirk Combe (New York: St. Martin's Press, 1995), pp. 57–72.

2. Joseph Jacobs, *English Fairy Tales* (London: The Bodley Head, 1968), p. 1.

3. Virginia Woolf made the observation in an essay entitled "Mr. Bennett and Mrs. Brown," published in 1924, and the phrase serves as the title for Peter Stansky's book on Bloomsbury: *On or About December 1910: Bloomsbury's Intimate World* (Cambridge, MA: Harvard University Press, 1996).

4. Walter Benjamin, "The Storyteller: Reflections on the Works of Nikolai Leskov," in *Illuminations* (New York: Harcourt, Brace & World, 1968), p. 84.

5. Claude Bremond, "Les bons récompensés et les méchants punis: Morphologie du conte merveilleux français," in Claude Chabrol, *Sémiotique narrative et textuelle* (Paris: Librarie Larousse, 1973), pp. 96–121.

6. Alvin Kernan. *The Cankered Muse: Satire of the English Renaissance* (New Haven, CT: Yale University Press, 1959), pp. 21–22.

7. Mikhail Bakhtin, *The Problems of Dostoevski's Poetics*, trans. R. W. Rotsel (Ann Arbor: University of Michigan Press, 1973).

8. See the two essays "The Fairy Tale Moves on Its Own in Time" and "Better Castles in the Sky at the Country Fair and Circus, in Fairy Tales and Colportage," in Ernst Bloch, *The Utopian Function of Art and Literature: Selected Essays*, trans. Jack Zipes and Frank Mecklenburg (Cambridge, MA: MIT Press, 1996): pp. 163–85.

9. Nina Auerbach and U. C. Knoepflmacher, *Forbidden Journeys: Fairy Tales and Fantasies by Victorian Women Writers* (Chicago: University of Chicago Press, 1993), p. 3.

10. Matthew Hodgart, *Satire: Origins and Principles* (New York: McGraw-Hill, 1969).

11. The volume was reviewed shortly after publication: "The Fairies Fly," *Times Literary Supplement*, November 22, 1934: 818.

12. Pamela Maude, *Worlds Away* (London: John Baker, 1964).

13. J.M. Barrie, *Peter Pan and Other Plays*, ed. Peter Hollindale (London: Oxford, 1995), p. 75.

14. Llewelyn Davies Family Papers. General Collection, Beinecke Rare Book and Manuscript Library, Yale University.

15. September 18, 1937, p. 21.

16. Andrew Malone, "The Curse of Peter Pan," *Sunday Times* (January 1, 1995).

[The Fairies Return]
Or, New Tales for Old

BY SEVERAL HANDS

With reverent apologies

to the memory

of Perrault,

the Brothers Grimm,

Hans Andersen,

the Authors of

The Thousand and One Nights

&c.

Jack
the
Giant
Killer

A. E. COPPARD

In the days of the Cheerless Charter, when the whole land was filled with people who had nothing to do and kept on doing it, three giants came, and the deuce knows *where* they came from or *how* they came, but come they did and there they were, Demos, Kudos, and Osmos. Everyone knows what a giant is supposed to be like, but for centuries no one had believed in monsters; Gog and Magog, Blunderbore, Cyclops, King Kong, and the Long Man of Wilmington, were creatures we had read about but could give no credence to, and so, despite those wonderful photographs in *The Morning Post*, the verifications from the cinema Gazettes, and a special supplement issued by *The Radio Times*, sceptical parsons living in the country, who would not take advantage of the special excursions run by the L.M.S., continued to shower letters on the press explaining that these images were nothing more than a mirage induced by occult mediums, or else were a walking advertisement for somebody's breakfast cereal. They could not, and you—my dear reader—could not, suppose anything like the reality of these three colossuses stalking one behind the other on silent crushing feet that filled a roadway, their faces resembling Big Ben, and hands that could lift a motorbus in Cornhill and toss it like a box of matches into St. Paul's Churchyard. Whenever one of them took a pinch of snuff and sneezed, the metropolis for a moment was in a shower of rain. And there was no getting rid of them; they out-topped St. Paul's and in three strides could traverse Whitehall. We were like gnats—we *were*—wrestling with elephants.

What the devil did they mean by it? What did they want here?

They had come to save the country—they said.

From what?

You will see in good time—was their answer.

Whence had they come?

They came—they said—from Who-knows-where.

And where is that—may we ask?

Who knows—was the reply.

And who's Who?

They answered—Who.

Well, in a world where wisdom was snatched from your mouth before it could be uttered, you couldn't get away from talk like that.

'Welcome!' cried the populace, crowding to the tops of all the high buildings and using binoculars to spy the ropes of hair in the giant ears and the teeth like tombstones.

'Behold!' the giants pleasantly bellowed. 'Behold, and trust us.' And there were the three of them, husky, fascinating, agile leviathans, going for a short stroll as it might be, barging like three balloons from St. Mary Axe to the pond at Fulham till the half of London was in a traffic block—well, [41 you couldn't believe it till it was seen and then, holy, holy, holy, there was no doing anything with them, they were that big and they were so benignant.

Where did they live now? What did they eat? Wait awhile, I am coming to that. At first there was such a furore caused by their visit that nobody cared for anything else. It was a circus, though it was at once seen that no known building could accommodate such monsters. They did not seem to eat or drink, they were friendly and well-disposed, their only offence was their size, but the uproar their proximity created could not be allowed to continue. Sport languished, religion was postponed again, parliament was counted out day after day. Something had to be done. The L.C.C. were particularly anxious about their new bridge—and we know what happened to that! The three great affable huskies were forbidden to go here, go there, or do this, that, and the other, but still they went and still they did. Traffic stopped, work stopped. The police were ordered to do something about it, but what could policemen do?—with handcuffs the size they are? Even if they could have arrested them they could not try them anywhere or imprison them anywhere; you could not get them into a police court, you could not have got them into Crystal Palace even; the Old Bailey was not large enough to fit the half of *one* giant in, let alone three!

One fine day the Chancellor himself went out to make an inspection of them. They were down by the Monument. He saw them and took note of them. He did not like them much. They were dressed like ordinary men, at least Demos and Osmos were; they were in lounge suits, while Kudos wore a frock coat, a top hat, and carried an umbrella, and when he raised his hat to air his head the shadow of it swept over Billingsgate and several acres of the city. If he had opened the umbrella no doubt the Chancellor would have gone home to bed. And there was this Demos bending down a bit. You could see he had a large red patch on the seat of his trousers. People on the top of the Monument were poking their hands through the railings and marking crosses on the red patch with pieces of white chalk. Osmos was being attended to in the same popular way, but his patch was a black one. Kudos, standing upright with his umbrella hung over his wrist, was tossing bits of chalk to everybody. The giants seemed to enjoy this performance, but the people enjoyed it still more. The Monument took close on a thousand pounds that day. There were queues stretching across London Bridge and along the streets as far as Blackfriars and Aldgate. The uproar was terrific so the Chancellor took his megaphone and called up to the giants:

'Hoi! Which is the head man of your bunch?'

'I am,' said Demos.

'No. It's me,' Kudos said.

'Bah!' cried Osmos, 'I could bite the two of you in half.'

Now the Chancellor was one of the country's wise wise men; he had read everything in the newspapers and knew quite a lot.

'I'll make a test of you,' he said, thinking of a little bit of a puzzle he had heard in his childhood. 'What is truth?' he shouted up.

And Kudos said: 'Nothing but what becomes you.'

Demos said: 'Nothing but what the world wishes you.'

But Osmos' answer was: 'Nothing that I can't improve upon.'

Then they all three suddenly yelled: 'How's that?' as though they were appealing for l.b.w.

Everyone was paralysed into silence by the sound of that vast yell which must have echoed far over the Weald of Kent. The people stopped marking their crosses on the seats of the mighty. The Chancellor continued his conversation. Big Ben was striking a quarter to four.

'O ho!' laughed the Chancellor through his megaphone; 'so you can improve upon truth, eh?'

'No!' thundered Demos. 'Never!'

Kudos glanced at his brother and smiled. Osmos, on the other hand, nodded his head in affirmation.

'How?' asked the Chancellor.

'By ignoring it,' Osmos said.

Kudos beamed upon him.

The Chancellor shrugged his shoulders and in doing so dropped his megaphone. A constable picked it up, but before he could restore it Osmos stooped from his great height and whisked up the Chancellor between his colossal finger and thumb—as you might lift a hairpin. Away, aloft, the Chancellor was reft, helplessly squeezed, the breath torn out of him by the speed of the giant's movement, while his admiral's hat flew off him and fluttered down on to the roof of Cannon Street Hotel. When the poor Chancellor came to himself he found he was standing on what might seem to be a large platform, only it was soft and warm, was queerly uneven and had a peculiar smell. He realised he was very high up in the air. The six eyes of the giants were glaring close above him. He saw what he stood upon was Osmos' bare hand, palm upwards. It was a gigantic palm, it swayed and quivered, and the Chancellor grew sick with horror, for the city lay below him, too far for him to take a peep at it. He staggered and screamed for mercy. The giants, it seemed, were puzzled by him.

'What is he saying?' Kudos asked.

'I cannot make him out,' said Demos.

'Must be on the wrong wave-length,' explained Osmos. 'Where's his loud speaker?' And peering down into the upturned faces of the crowd Osmos at length espied the policeman who was still holding the Chancellor's megaphone. Adroitly he stooped, and snatching up the policeman handed him to Kudos. Very carefully Kudos picked the megaphone away from the policeman—much as one plucks a thorn from the finger—and handed it to the Chancellor.

Then he laid the policeman on the palm of his huge hand and with a jolly twinkle in his eyes he blew at him as you might blow a feather. The unfortunate peeler was puffed into the air in a vast arc over London Bridge, describing antic letters in his flight—the letters X and C and Y—until he shot with a quiet squirt into the Thames just beyond the Old Swan Pier, so quiet indeed that nobody would have noticed him had they been there—which, of course, they were not, every collier, schooner, coble, and barque of the sea being utterly deserted in the excitement of the hour.

Meanwhile the Chancellor, perceiving his precarious state, was harrowed by deathly fears. The three faces were breathing on him hard enough to blow him after the policeman if he had not had the wit to drop his megaphone and fling both arms around a gold ring on Osmos' middle finger. What with the heat of the sun and his burning dread he thought of crawling into a long dark tunnel facing him, until he realised that this was actually the sleeve of Osmos' jacket. The finger of the giant began to roll him over and over, quite playfully, but it was so sickening and dangerous that the Chancellor grabbed his megaphone again.

'What do you want?' a vast voice roared, like a train in the Underground.

'Nothing, nothing whatever,' quavered the Chancellor. 'Only put me down again, please!'

The giant laughed; his tongue resembled the slimy body of a hippopotamus. A commotion in the street below drew his attention. A crowd of little men each arrayed in glittering helmets were wheeling a red fire-escape between Osmos' feet. They hauled on a rope and an extending ladder crawled slowly upwards beyond the giant's knees. Osmos made a gesture to blow the Chancellor away just as he had served the policeman, but Kudos snatched him up in time, saying, with a reproving smile: 'No, no. Allow me.' He bent down and placed the fainting Chancellor in the outstretched arms of the fireman on the ladder. Osmos called after them: 'If anybody wants anything, give 'em beans. Beans is good for you.' The giants smilingly watched the man descend the ladder with his sacred burden amid tumultuous cheering. The ladder was then folded up and wheeled away. The giants strolled nonchalantly off.

They always walked on and on until it was night, when they disappeared in the darkness, though where they slept was a mystery, unless it might be, as was confidently surmised, somewhere in Epping Forest. No one had noticed the loss of the policeman, and the giants, though visible from day to day, did not work any serious harm beyond dislocating the entire life of the community. They were so harmless that the pigeons often settled on them in flocks. As for eating anything, it was never seen of them. Indeed, you could not begin to imagine the bulk of substance they might require to devour, or where they could obtain it; a rick of hay would have been no more than a quid of tobacco in such jaws. As time went by people thought they must be archangels, or the three wise men from the east, or something from a different planet entirely.

And yet, something had to be done about them. You could not permit them to go on stravaiging about the city of London just like that . . . you . . . could . . . not . . . because, well, because it was not allowed, not in the city of London. Occasionally it happened that they were not seen for days, and then the House of Lords with the whole bench of bishops combined would declare that they must not be allowed to return. They returned. *The Daily Express* advocated their immediate banishment and entire removal. How? Well, you had the whole resources of modern civilisation at your disposal, hadn't you? Ah, but those resources were demonstrably inadequate, for just as you could not with all the means at your disposal even arrest the monsters, neither could you with the whole canon of English law to select from frame an indictment; and if you had discovered anything of the kind you may be sure the writ wouldn't have run. Staunch upholders of law and order at any price suggested the use of aeroplanes and tanks; a gentleman in the Isle of Wight who had not so far set eyes on the giants said they ought to be run over by motor-buses, while some went so far as to hint darkly at poison gas or bigger and brighter bombs. But the insurance magnates pointed out that you could not adopt such measures without great damage to property, as well as possible danger to innocent human life.

And then, one summer morning, as a night-watchman named Drake was trailing home from his duties at a sponge factory in Ealing he discovered a pair of grey flannel trousers lying in the middle of a side street off Gunnersbury. It was a curious thing to find in a public roadway, even at that early hour—between six and seven it was. An ordinary pair of trousers. The watchman picked them up. They were a little torn. There was three and sevenpence in one pocket and the half of a green cinema ticket in the other. The watchman smoothed the garments, folded them, laid them carefully in his work-basket, and passed on. He had not gone more than fifty yards further before he espied a lady's shoe in the gutter. He picked it up. He turned it over and over. 'Well, I be damned,' he said. It was a good fashionable shoe, glacé kid, fairly new, with high heels, and of a medium size. 'Where there's one,' said the watchman, 'there's sure to be a mate to follow it.' So he dumps his basket on the kerb, looks down, and creeps along. Can't see anything more. Looks round and about and sideways. Nothing. Not anything. Not a thing. Looks up. Sees something.

'Well, I be double damned!' says he.

It was the companion shoe, hanging up in the twigs of a sycamore tree just outside 'The Plume of Feathers.'

'Might a bin *made* for the missus!' said the night-watchman, and he popped the pair of shoes into his basket underneath the trousers.

Away he goes again, and believe it or not, he was passing a congregational church in the extraordinary solitary purlieus of Chiswick, and happening to glance over the railings at a printed bill about fleeing from something, what did he see— what else? He saw a bowler hat. Belonging to nobody. It was propped sideways on the steps of the sacred edifice. Opens gate and picks up hat. It was a good black hat. It fitted him.

'If we're going on at this rate,' says he, 'I'd like it to snow bandboxes afore I gets any further.'

Looks around. Nobody about. But it was uncommon quiet just there; the sunlight seemed queer, the roofs were too clean, the pavement too tidy. Begins to feel uneasy. Fancies some eyes are watching him behind some window blind.

'Might be only a plant,' he mutters. 'Or else—it might be a crime!'

So, quickly propping the hat down on the steps again exactly as he had found it, he rushes off to the nearest police station, mumbling: 'I believe it's a murder!' Arrived at the nearest police station he sees a crowd of people all carrying articles of clothing—the obvious as well as the unmentionable—in their arms. Found in the streets, all of it! Everybody had some, stays and stockings, kimonos, pants, wraps, hats, and shirts, and they had all come to report their finds. Everywhere, over half London, they were finding chunks of raiment, some costly, some poor, most of it badly torn, and soon the police stations were stuffed to their ceilings with masses of discarded attire.

What was the meaning of it? It couldn't be murder after all—there were too many clothes. For the same reason it couldn't be a crime either. Was it a university lark, or a new dodge for a flag day? Had some almighty old clothes man gone mad? There was a heat wave on at the time, but you could hardly believe so many people had gone nudist all of a heap like that—unless perhaps they had been smitten with sunstroke. The midday press contained no news at all about the discoveries, and consequently, right on until noon, there was no public stir, but by lunch time the evening editions had got wind of the matter. At question time in the House of Commons on the following day there were some facetious exchanges, one wag of an M.P. from Glasgow suggesting that the clothing had been thus secretly broadcast by the kindly giants for the use of the destitute poor in the heart of the empire. The minister complimented the speaker on his humour and its patriotic tone, but assured him that far graver possibilities were involved; much of the clothing had already been identified as belonging to numbers of people who were reported to be missing. He had ordered the fullest enquiry into the matter.

This announcement at once sent the wildest rumours into circulation. Certainly hundreds of persons had disappeared. They had left their clothing behind. Their clothes were here, but they had gone. And something else was gone—the giants! They had not been heard of for some days. What did that portend, if you had any logic in your wits and could put two and two together? It was of course the giants, the giants! And what had they done with the vanished persons? To what folly had they persuaded them? Were they in captivity, or merely modestly hiding because of their lack of attire?

Not a vestige of them, beyond their clothing, ever came to light again, and when the giants once more strolled unconcernedly into town there arose a wild clamour for their immediate extermination. But a dark terror invaded every private mind; all ran from the presence of the giants and hid as best they could. There arose no bold defiers of a menace that could not be defined, the metropolis was in a state of panic and public duty was ignored. Streets were lined with empty buses and abandoned cars, shops were closed, houses bolted and barred; except for the striking of town clocks the place might have been a silent desert.

About this time a young fisherman from Cornwall was visiting his aunt who kept a ham-and-pie shop in Camber- well. He was a likeable young fellow and his name was Jack. One afternoon Jack and his aunt were at tea, eating prawns and talking earnestly about the giants. She told him of the great reward that had been offered for their extermination.

'I shouldn't want all that for it,' said Jack.

'Not ten thousand pounds!' shrieked the good lady.

'I wouldn't mind it,' the youth replied. 'I wouldn't refuse it, in a manner of speaking, but of course I'd do it just the same for love.'

'Then,' cried his aunt, 'for goodness sake get a move on!'

'I will,' Jack said, and putting on his best hat he bolted for the Underground. The giants were not on view that day, but it was the only safe mode of travel in those troublous times. In twenty minutes he arrived at the Boss's house and asked to see the Boss. He saw the Boss. The Boss had his daughter with him. She was a fine piece, as plump as a leveret, and her name was Primrose. She sat down beside their grandfather's clock and looked at Jack. The more she looked the more she liked. She grew quite fond of him. His hair was red and his figure was good. He liked her and the look of her.

He told the Boss he would undertake the extermination of the giants. 'Pray do,' said the Boss. 'I myself will privately double the reward, for I don't mind telling you that nobody does a solitary thing although I worry myself to a wafer all day long.'

'Never mind the reward,' Jack answered.

'What!' cried this Primrose. 'It is twenty thousand pounds now, and you are but a poor fisher lad!'

'I know,' said he; 'and of course I wouldn't mind it, in a manner of speaking, and I wouldn't refuse it, but I'd do it just the same for love—if you understand me rightly.'

The beauteous Primrose went up to him and put her two milk-white hands on his shoulders. 'I do,' she murmured. 'You are the dream of my life.'

'Pass the word,' said Jack, 'and it's O.K. with me.'

'About these people,' interrupted the Boss, 'these people who are missing? Nobody seems to *know* anything, nobody seems to *do* anything; I worry myself into a wafer all day long. We must find out where those persons are before we . . . we . . . attend to the giants.'

'Sorry, sir. There's nothing to be done about them now,' Jack sadly replied.

'What do you mean? "Nothing to be done?"'

'Prawns,' Jack said.

'Prawns?'

'That's it, I'm afraid, sir. These giants hang around London because there's millions of people here, shoals of them.

They only eat about once a month, but when they do get hungry they make a tidy clearance. They catch 'em coming out of the theatres at night, pick 'em up just where they fancy and tear the skin off 'em—that's their clothes, you see, they couldn't stomach that—and there you are. Just the same as prawns. That's why you find their clothes scattered all over the place.'

The Boss took off his spectacles and stared at a rectangular rose in the hearthrug.

'Do you ... um ... do you mean they ... um ... they ... er ... ?'

'That's it, sir.'

The Boss took a handkerchief from his breast pocket and pressed it anxiously to his chin.

'Tut! tut!' he said. 'That kind of thing ought to be stopped. Instantly. I can bear with a little judicious robbery, but violence of this kind I will not permit. Shall I give you an order on the artillery?'

'Not a chance!' Jack declared, and explained. 'You could bomb 'em, you could blow 'em in half, easily you could, but you couldn't get rid of the remains. They're too big. They'd block the streets for months and rot and stink and give all London a pestilence.'

'Well, do something, will you, my honest lad?' the Boss pleaded. 'Will you do something about them?'

'I will and all,' replied the bold young fisherman. 'Shall I see you again?' he asked Primrose.

A. E. COPPARD

'Any time you like,' answered the princess—for such she undoubtedly was. And then as he faded out she shrieked: 'Ring me up! Excalibur 2760!'

'Skoal!' came the faint reply.

The horrible secret was out, and citizens hid themselves more tightly than ever from the dastardly cannibals, who, though seldom seen, were known to be at large, for one night they wrenched off the roof of Knightsbridge Barracks, helped themselves ruthlessly, and on the following morn Hyde Park was found to be strewn with military pyjamas. It was the immensity of the giants that paralysed all effort; the heart trembled, the mind shrivelled, before the problem of their appalling bulk. You might shell them, but you would certainly destroy half London in the process and kill ten thousand honest citizens. And when you had killed the three accursed ones—what then? It meant something very contagious indeed.

Even so, opinion was divided upon this question of whether you ought or ought not, much as it had been over the earlier dispute between the Mr. Cans and the Mr. Cants in which, as is well known now, there were thousands of Cans who could, but very often forgot and therefore didn't. Occasionally there was a lull in the ghastly depredations and the populace breathed hopefully again. At one such interval public attention was happily diverted by the astounding discovery of Cupid's skull. This well-authenticated relic was found in one of those ruined corridors of Poland by a friar named Levinsky, who at once presented it to the British Government in return for a bag of remuneration.

Jack the Giant Killer

But time flies, and honest Jack was leaving no stone unturned in his pursuit of the giants. Daily he strove and nightly he schemed, with the image of the princess ever in his soul, to come at those vast villains. He went on his bicycle to the borders of Epping Forest. He took a good look round. There were a lot of trees. He did not go into the forest but sat down close by. A voice was wailing in the sylvan groves:

Fee

   Fye

      Fo

         Fum.

Then a crash came through the forest as though a tornado was blasting it. Now, Jack, my boy! Up he jumps and flees for his life, pell-mell but nimble-footed as a roe, away from the trees and across the open fields. One look behind him he gave: a giant in a tall silk hat was bounding after him! Over hedge and hurdle and ditch Jack sped in the fastest speed ever recorded by mortal man, racing towards some electric pylons at thirty miles an hour at least, maybe forty—I should not be surprised to hear it was fifty miles an hour—but it was all too much like a tadpole trying to defeat a seal. As Jack passed a pylon the giant gave one whoop and a leap for the final jump on him. The giant's foot caught in the wires of the Grid, there was a sort of fluffy hoot, like a flash of magnesium, and down cracked Kudos as dead as a cooked cod. The current had struck him and he was cooked too.

After tearing on for another mile or so—just to make sure—Jack pulled up, fresh as a daisy. The Giant, far away be-

A. E. COPPARD

hind him, lay stone dead. He made quite a blot on the landscape. Jack gave it another ten minutes but it did not stir. The other giants did not seem to be about, so Jack decided to go back and have a look at Kudos. And, do you know, he had some difficulty in finding him! As he got nearer and nearer the corpse seemed to be sagging and dwindling like a pricked balloon, waning and compacting, and by the time Jack reached the pylon all he could see was the clothes of the giant stretched out quite flat and empty across a couple of fields. There did not seem to be any sort of body inside the clothes. One of its great boots was stuck like a barn at the end of the trouser legs, the other boot was all twisted and burnt, still smoking. Over in the next field, where the coat lay and the head ought to have been, the starched collar and the tie were still in place but there was no head and no neck. Jack took a walk all over the coat. He reckoned it was a hundred yards long. About half-way across he felt a lump under his foot. He cut open the coat and drew out a tiny brown body. It was Kudos, shrunk to the image of a child's doll.

'There's a bit of a moral in this,' said Jack, 'if I could only think of it.'

However, he put the doll under his arm and was soon mounted on his bicycle again. When he came to the post office he sent off the doll in a parcel to the Boss's daughter. With his mind scheming and still scheming he lodged for the night at an inn called 'The Rouse Me and Suffer,' but after a pleasant sleep he rose betimes, took up the telephone and called for Excalibur 2760.

'That you?'

'Yes,' she said.

'Get my parcel?'

'Yes,' she said.

'What d'ye think of it?'

'The little doll? Too delicious! Frantically sweet, dear John! But didn't you know—I gave up dolls years and years ago? Yes, don't ask me how long, I forbid you. I don't collect them now.'

'Ah, but it's not a doll,' he explained; 'it's Kudos! I got him yesterday. That's his remains. Please show your father.'

It took him no end of a time to convince Primrose of the reality of this giant's demise. It did not seem credible to her that what had seemed so much could be so little after all.

'There's a bit of a moral in that,' said Jack.

'Perhaps there is, dear, but I am so afraid papa will not believe it is really one of the giants. I know he won't want to pay you any of the reward for this little thing.'

'It's O.K., kid, take it from me,' said Jack. 'And never mind the reward; of course I wouldn't refuse it, not in a manner of speaking; I'd do it just the same for . . .'

'Another three minutes?' the operator interrupted.

'No!' said the princess hastily. 'Time's up, John. Au revoir. And thank you so much.'

'Skoal!' came the faint reply.

Well, the Boss made out he couldn't believe it. And he *wouldn't* believe it—you would have thought he did not *want* to—until the clothes of Kudos were found lying just as

A. E. COPPARD

described by Jack and the whole populace proclaimed him their national hero. By that time Jack was away on his lonely mission, bent on ridding his country of the two remaining incubuses.

The corpse having so conveniently shrivelled, the Boss thought this must be due to some peculiar law of the giants' nature and he forthwith removed the ban on their slaughter. Speedily the defensive resources of civilisation were mobilised to contrive an end of Demos and Osmos, but giants are stubborn things; they are subtle, and they are swift; the death of Kudos and the vast preparations for war caused them to shift their ground; in short, they bolted. Darkness covered their retreat. None knew where they had gone or where the terror would break out next. The country held its breath. But Jack was inspired, he knew it was his destiny to rid the fatherland of its foul curse and he trailed the brutes as far as the black country. It was their first sally into the heart of Merry England, though they can have seen but little of its tender beauty for their flight was more rapid and silent than a meteor flowing through the starry sky. Harried by hunger they made a nocturnal foray into the more illustrious parts of Wolverhampton. The mind shudders to recall that dreadful calamity . . . suffice it to say that Demos and Osmos separated there. Whether they quarrelled, or parted merely for tactical reasons, will never be known; one thing is clear— Osmos turned back that night and sped towards the sea.

On the following afternoon Primrose was knitting in her boudoir when the telephone bell gave a slight ping. Thinking it to be only a false call she did not trouble to answer it, but she was soon roused by a long, confident peal. Wearily she picked up the receiver and said 'Hallo?'

'That you?' asked a well-known voice.

'Johannes!' she breathed in emotional surprise.

'Speaking from Wolverhampton. Got another giant this morning, kid!'

'I beg your pardon?'

'I put paid to Demos all right, girlie.'

'Do you mean . . . he is dead?'

'That's it. Between here and Shifnal. I pushed him down a coalmine.'

'Pushed him! You *pushed* him!'

'Well, in a manner of speaking. I mean to say that's how I fixed him. It was a cute bit of work and he fell for it. He's at the bottom now, along with the rats and the sewage, so I shan't be able to send you a doll this time!'

'No, please do not think of it!' cried she. 'I gave them up years and years ago, dear; do not ask how many, I forbid you!'

'He hung on the edge of the pit with his hands, but I pick-axed him for twenty minutes and down he went at last with a pretty mouldy plump. Tell your dad, won't you? And I say, Primrose. I'm feeling pretty good, Primrose. I want to say . . . Are you there, Primrose? Primrose, are you there?'

There was no answer. He guessed she had run to inform the Boss. He rang off.

Time ticked by, water flowed under all the bridges as hard as ever, but young Jack did not allow any grass to propa-

A. E. COPPARD

gate under his extremities. Osmos, the last of the accursed ones, was in flight and our hero traced him across The Wash and along the desolate coast of East Anglia. The mammoth would not leave the coast, he kept ever by the shore, and at the rumour of his approach every ship had left its port and scurried out to sea. Time and again Jack was sure that Osmos was meditating some desperate attempt to reach the Baltic.

He meant to baffle him, and to master him.

One night, when the wind was still and the sea as placid as a bowl of wine, with a long stream of honey-coloured moonlight sluicing from shore to sky, Jack watched the giant steal from the shades of Benacre Wood and approach the quiet lapping waves. As though in weariness the monster drooped and sank down with his head between his hands; his shadow stretched across the marshy plains behind him like the mask of a hill. After a while he stirred. He began to take off his clothes and at last stood up, naked from head to heel, and paddled into the sea until the water reached his knees. There he raised his hands aloft as though invoking the aid of an agency in some realm unknown and very far away, and across the motionless air the words of a beseeching appeal droned from his lips:

'Maresull eetotes anassull eetotes akiddle eetivy.' Beyond all doubt the monster's grief was keen. Those sad, mysterious words floated down to Jack hidden in a bush of furze. The huge head swayed from side to side as though its eyes were searching heaven from the north to the south. For long they sought, but in vain. Tears as big as oranges plopped into the water between the giant's knees. Dropping his arms disconsolately Osmos returned to the shore, donned his clothes, and slunk back to the wood. Jack crept and crawled to a safer place, then rose and cantered away until he came to the port of Lowestoft in the pale light of dawn. The harbour was empty save for one gallant ship that had steamed in during the night. The skipper sat smoking at ease in the bows of the ship. Jack hailed him:

'What ship, old tar?'

The captain's answer came like music that is trumpeted, and Jack knew him for a friend and jumped aboard.

Now this ship was bound to the northern seas on a whaling campaign and had put into Lowestoft for bait.

'I'll show you some bait,' said Jack.

'You will! What bait can you show?'

'Nothing to pay for,' Jack answered, 'and it'll bring you a thousand pounds.'

'Is that so?'

'It is and all,' Jack declared.

'Tell me more,' said the skipper.

So they conferred and they agreed. A plan was made.

When night fell again and the sea grew gloomy there was bustle aboard the ship. It was time to up-anchor and steal away. They did so as the moon began to rise. The sad waters glistened cheerfully when the vessel rippled out to the ocean roads. In a while she was standing off Benacre Wood where the giant was lurking. All her lights were doused as she floated slowly in; no tiresome tide betrayed her, no ominous wave; the sea itself was sleeping. Jack and his companions waited and peered and waited. They had not long to wait; far off on shore the very wood seemed to rise up and the shipmen quivered in astonishment as the Thing emerged. They saw him cast off his clothes and come wading into the shallows, his arms held aloft and his voice intoning: 'Maresull eetotes.' The ship, so small, was hidden in the darkness beneath his gaze, but the moonlight shone full on one side of his accursed body. On came Osmos, swinging his head from side to side, until he was no more than a gunshot off.

'There she blows!' roared young Jack, and bang went the harpoon gun with a roar that rattled the windows of the lighthouses. The harpoon flew to its mark and buried itself in the giant's midriff. Osmos stopped, looked down and put his hand to his stomach, but already his knees were crooking and he sprawled headlong into the sea like a crashing tower. The ship's bell rang out for full steam ahead and away went the gallant whaler far into the North Sea, trailing the horrid leviathan in its wake until they were fifty miles from shore. Then Jack stopped the ship and put off with the captain in his gig to make sure that Osmos was dead. He was. Quite. So they fixed the boat anchor in one of his ears and the skipper clambered up through the giant's hair on to the top of his belly and removed the harpoon. He wanted to carve off the giant's head but he didn't know how, and anyway the ship hadn't a derrick strong enough to hoist it on board, so Jack just hacked off the giant's thumb and heaved it over his shoulder into the boat. They left the carcase for the crabs and sharks of the sea to devour, and set a course for home.

'We will make,' Jack said, 'for London Town.'

So to London Town they went. Good heavens! the metropolis was raging to do honour to its young deliverer. But Jack had only one thought in his heart, and the skipper went with him to help carry the giant's thumb to the Boss's house.

'Welcome,' said the Boss to young Jack (and to the skipper he said: 'I am pleased to meet you'). 'Welcome, I have been wearing myself to a . . .'

'Papa!' interposed the princess, 'the skipper is anxious to return to his ship; time and tide wait for no man, and money talks.'

'That is so, indeed,' the Boss sighed, and he gave Jack the twenty thousand pounds.

'Now go away, papa, do!' the princess said. The Boss went upstairs.

Jack gave the skipper the thousand pounds he promised him, and another thousand for good luck.

'I shouldn't do that!' cried the princess. She snatched the extra thousand away from the skipper and said: 'Be off with you!' The skipper went downstairs.

'Now you must help me count the reward,' said Jack to Primrose.

'O bother the money!' she replied, with a coy air.

He said: 'Ah, well; I can count it myself I suppose. It doesn't matter, of course, and I'd have done it for love, but you know the way it is with me, honey?'

A. E. COPPARD

The princess put her two milk-white hands upon Jack's shoulders.

'I do,' she murmured. 'You are the dream of my life.'

And almost before he knew where he was she had married him.

Godfather Death
A Tale

CLEMENCE DANE

Then came Death striding up to him with
withered legs, and said, 'Take me as godfather.
I will make thy child rich and famous, for he
who has me for a friend can lack nothing.'
The man said, 'Next Sunday is the christening;
be there at the right time.' Death appeared
as he had promised, and stood godfather
in the usual way.

When the boy had grown up, his godfather one
day appeared and said, 'Now shalt thou receive
thy godfather's present. I make thee
a celebrated physician.'
—'Godfather Death,' *Grimms' Household Tales*

Death's godson was born some thirty years ago in the smallest and oldest of Devon villages, a village remote from society, high roads, and a drainage system. The few cottages were bowed under hundred-year layers of thatch, and the floors of those cottages were flagged with paving stones from the castle on the hill. The castle on the hill had been burnt down in the Wars of the Roses, and a wood had grown up above the forgotten foundations. For some centuries now the returning gipsies camped in it, cooked their poached rabbits in the fireplace of the great hall, backed their caravans into the raspberry-canes and nettles, and sheltered from the eternal rain under the beeches which grew on the edge of the ditch that was once the castle moat.

The gipsies could escape from the rain. They enjoyed the summer, poached the woods, exploited the near-by fairs, and, as autumn came, moved on. But the villagers never escaped from the rain. Moistures, half-cloud, half-dream, hung about their encircling hills for nine months of the year, for ever condensing into fine, relentless rain, which soaked the woods, slid across the meadows, drained into the lanes, and rolled on down the ditches to the village pond.

The pond lay in the centre of the village and at night the jack-o'-lanterns danced upon its bright green coverlet. It drained away into a stream which ran through a rushy swamp. This was full of kingcups in the spring. Later in June the tall yellow flags of the iris encamped upon it. The village children called the iris 'candlesticks,' and, reaching after the brightest, messed themselves to the knees in the rich evil-smelling ooze.

Godfather Death

All day long the dragon-flies darted and wheeled above the camping-ground of the flags like so many aeroplanes. Indeed, if you imagined yourself two inches high, the place at once became a battle-field, glorious with the bright uniforms of flowers and insects, terrible with the battle-calls of frogs, the ping of midges and the heavy artillery of the bumble-bees. But though it was a battle-ground, it was not till autumn that death came with the poison gas of the swamp mists. Then there would be a burial or two of the old and feeble in the Norman churchyard, while the gentlefolk would hurry off to winter sports in Switzerland to escape 'the influenza.' But the villagers saw it out, year after year, and when the young and vigorous also died like flies, their thousand-year memories awakened and they called it 'plague.'

The rector and the doctor did their best, that death-stricken winter thirty years ago; and the squire sent a handsome cheque, and was there anything he could do? But the rector did not answer, because he had died two days before the letter arrived, and his elderly wife followed him before she could answer all the letters of condolence, let alone business communications. Then the retired linen-draper from Exeter was struck down with his household of daughters. Three died, and the fourth, in deep mourning, took her father to Torquay and the house was shut up. These absences and deaths emptied the village of its gentlefolk. Then the retired post-mistress succumbed; but her niece, who took the infection, survived to nurse and bury the one servant and the sexton's wife.

CLEMENCE DANE

So there was no one left to help the villagers but the village doctor, whose wife was expecting a first child. The doctor, dosing himself with quinine and keeping himself awake with black coffee, killed himself slowly and methodically; for he gave the village and his wife twenty-three out of the twenty-four hours of his day and night. Not that he had any false pride in his endurance. On the contrary, he clamoured for help to Exeter and to London. From London no help came, for the whole country, you will remember, was swept by influenza that year, and the cities and the towns had louder voices than one weak hamlet smothered in the circle of Devon hills. But Exeter promised reinforcements, and until help came the doctor and the sexton carried on as best they could, while the death-mists filled the village and wrapped round the cottages as with shrouds. The doctor and the sexton found themselves tiptoeing through the streets, afraid to disturb the white silence of sickness and mist.

'Do you notice that the birds have stopped singing?' said the sexton.

'I wonder,' said the doctor,' that the buds don't drop off the trees and the beasts don't fall down in the fields. I tell you, the valley is poisoned.'

To which the sexton retorted that the plague had its moods. It was after men this year, not birds of the air or beasts of the field.

And indeed, two months from that wet, mild Christmas, the diminished village vestry had been forced to buy the field adjoining the churchyard, and the village was as empty as if a war had swept it. Fourteen years later it could send but three men to the aid of gallant little Belgium. And for all these deaths the doctor blamed himself more bitterly than he blamed the plague and told himself that if he lost his son or his wife it would be a just punishment for putting his private loves before the needs of his fellow-men.

The child came vigorously into the world in spite of the father's fears. But the doctor's wife resented its healthy wail. She thought herself dying, and in the selfish delirium of fever cried out that the child must die with her. She must have something to fill her arms when she lay in the grave. But it was a disgrace if the child died unchristened. What were they to do? It was so wrong of the rector to die before the child was christened.

To please her the doctor crossed the child's brow with water. But she only turned wearily on her pillow, asking for the god-parents: and when he told her, his voice shaking, that they themselves could stand godfather and godmother to their own child, she screamed at him weakly that there must be a second godfather. Had he no proper pride? Why didn't her brother come from Birmingham? It was only just across the road. Of course the child must have a godfather. He was to go out and get one—get one!

So crying she fell back into sleep. But for her husband and physician there was no sleep, since at any moment the night bell might jangle. He sat upright on the cane chair, snatching what rest he could that did not involve loss of consciousness; but sleep, true sleep, he knew for his enemy. He fought sleep as Jacob fought the angel at Peniel. He felt the thumbs of sleep upon his eyelids, and resisted that pressure till the thumbs shifted and laid themselves leadenly on the burning centre of pain at the back of his neck. When he rose to turn down the spindling lamp the attack of sleep shifted again. Now it wooed him in a woman's voice from the straw matting on the floor. He yearned for the floor. The floor was strewn with roses and pillows, and sweet scents came up from it. To lie down at full length upon the matting would be ultimate bliss.

But the acrid smell of the lamp was his salvation. It gathered to itself the smells of sickness and reminded him that he was a doctor. He reeled towards it and did at last manage to turn the little wheel which controlled the wick. It was a tremendous effort, but his will and his finger and thumb accomplished it, and as the flamelet dimmed he had a shadowy vision of God's finger and thumb idly twisting the rings of Saturn, dimming the planet's light. Triumphant he jerked his head round towards his wife and as he did so she opened her eyes.

'Has he come?'

'Who, my dearest?'

'The boy's godfather?'

The doctor's exhausted brain responded to the last demand he was to make upon it that night.

'They're sending over a man from Exeter to help us. He's coming to-morrow.'

'I want him now.'

'Go to sleep, my darling!'

Godfather Death

But the sick woman struggled up from her pillows. He slipped an arm under her shoulder.

'What is it, dear?'

'He's come!' she gasped. 'Let him in!'

He laid her down and turned to listen.

'There's no one.'

'I heard a footstep. Go down and see.'

He was long past thought. He was an automaton, directed by any will. 'Go down and see!' rang in his ears like the first commandment on Sinai. He went out and down the creaking staircase, seeing his way by the moonlight that filtered in through the landing window. Was his wife right? His ears were so ringing with the drugs he had taken that he could not tell. Then he saw that the night bell was still swaying, noiseless and lively on the wall.

At that he pulled back the bolt and flung open the door. For a moment he saw nothing but the mist, flowing, solid as a river, down the village street. Then from the mist emerged a figure.

'May I come in?' said the figure.

'Come in!' said the doctor.

He stood back to allow the stranger to pass, but whether it was the mist or a man who entered the doctor was never afterwards able to say, though his little son, growing out of babyhood to the age of inquisition, flogged him with questions on Sunday afternoons.

'How tall was he, Father? Taller than you?'

'Much taller.'

CLEMENCE DANE

'Tall as a tree?'

'Huge.'

'Was he kind?'

'Comforting.'

'Did Mother like him?'

No answer.

'Was she glad to see him?'

No answer.

'She must have been if she went away with him.'

The widower shivered and roused himself. The boy must be amused. It was a lonely house for a little boy.

'Shall I tell you about Robinson Crusoe?' he asked, pulling the child on to his knee.

'No! Tell me more about my godfather. He's a doctor too, isn't he?'

'Yes.'

'The greatest doctor in the world?'

'Yes.'

'Have you ever seen him since?'

'Often.'

'When shall I see him?'

'Soon, I think,' said the little doctor, coughing.

And putting the child off his knee he went across to his untidy desk and wrote a long letter to his brother-in-law in Birmingham. The small boy, an hour later, playing his favourite game with a looking-glass, deciphered snatches of sentences on the blotting-paper.

Godfather Death

'Settle him at a good school . . . solicitors will pay the fees . . . question of weeks now . . .'

The word 'school' excited the small boy. Still more exciting was the visit with his father to Exeter. There was a trunk and an outfit. There was to be pocket-money. There was a farewell at the railway station and dozens of strange boys. His father, crumpled up with coughing, waved to him as the train began to move. And then the small boy, hanging out of the window, saw behind his father a tall figure, and called out loudly in instant recognition of an old tale—

'It's my godfather! Look, Father! Just behind you! Make him come here! I want to say how-do-you-do.'

But the train moved too quickly for him to hear his father's answer. Nor, indeed, did he listen, for all his attention was on the vague figure which, as the train drew out, laid a friendly hand upon his father's shoulder.

'That was my godfather,' he told the carriage.

'Where?' said the other new boy.

'Just beside my father. Look, my father's taking his arm.'

'I don't see anyone,' said the other new boy, jostling him for a last look at Exeter station.

'You are a cuckoo!'

'Well, what's he like?'

The little boy's answer described a demi-god. For the unknown godfather continued to obsess his imagination. His father was a funny little man, bald and bowed, with a nervous stammer. The boys would be bound to laugh at him.

CLEMENCE DANE

Now if his godfather would only come to see him how different it would be.

'My godfather's a regular giant. He could pick up one of you in each hand and use you as dumb-bells,' boasted the small boy.

'What's his name?'

'Clement, same as mine. I'm his godson.'

'When is he coming to see you?'

'Any day now,' said Clement.

But it was the uncle from Birmingham who came a month later to tell him that his father had died, and that he must be a good boy and work his hardest. There was money to get him through school and Cambridge, but after that Clement must depend upon himself, though his uncle would help him, of course, as much as he could. He would try him in the business at any rate.

'But I'm going to be a doctor, like my father and my godfather.'

'I'm your godfather,' said his uncle.

'Was it you who came that night?'

'What night?'

'The night Mother went away.'

'I don't know what you're talking about,' said his uncle crossly.

'Then you're not my godfather,' said Clement.

'My nephew's a little backward. You know what it is— an only child, and my poor brother-in-law was an eccentric,' explained the uncle from Birmingham to the house-master,

Godfather Death

and when he got home— 'Boy's a half-wit!' said the uncle to his wife, who then and there gave up the idea of asking Clement to stay with them in the holidays.

But Clement did not feel himself injured by their neglect. He liked spending his holidays alone in the emptied house. The house-master and his wife gave him the run of house and garden, and for the rest knew enough to leave him alone. He throve, and instead of his nurse's country tales he had books, books, books. Inheriting his father's painful energy he worked like a beaver, and when he was not working, dreamed the ambitious dreams of a lonely boy. He was to pass all his examinations. He was to discover the cure for cancer. He was to be the greatest doctor in the world. His godfather would help him in this. One day his godfather would come to see him and they would discuss together the art of healing.

But he no longer mentioned his godfather to the other boys. He was old enough to know that his father's tales, told to amuse a child, were best kept to himself. He believed in his godfather, but he was no longer sure that other people would believe. As he moved up through the school and his teens, however, he himself thought less often of his godfather. The figure faded into a dream and was all but forgotten. Yet not quite forgotten; for he refused to be confirmed, and gave the outraged school chaplain the glibbest reasons for his refusal. But the real reason was the knowledge that all good godfathers turned up at the confirmation service, took their godsons out to dinner, and gave them a present.

CLEMENCE DANE

But suppose his godfather did not appear? No godfather, and no present? Then the whole secret fantasy would be betrayed, nullified. He would have nothing left to think about at nights. No. He would not risk it. He continued to pose as doubting Thomas, and would not be confirmed.

As there was no one who cared to coerce him he had his way. He had his way, too, over his later education, for he put two years on to his age and so scrambled into the last years of the war. But he never reached the front, for he slipped under the wheels of a gun-carriage one wet morning, and the whole contraption rolled over him. Thereafter came hospital, screams of pain, morphia. Looking up to thank the doctor who thus brought him ease, he saw once again the face which his father had so often described, which he himself had seen so long ago in Exeter station. The rest of that wild night he passed in familiar talk with his godfather Death. For his godfather had introduced himself by name.

'I am the sure physician,' said his godfather; 'the clement physician, and my other name is Death. I have no children,' said his godfather, 'but you are my godson, and that is a link between us. While you live I have a stake in the world.'

'That amuses you?' asked the boy, looking up into the hollow eyes of his dream.

'It's a new experience,' confided the godfather. 'I have so few adventures. People die with such sameness. It pleased me that your father asked me in and shook my hand. Nobody has ever done that to me before.'

Godfather Death

'My father was an eccentric,' said Clement, and as he spoke the face of Death changed, and he was quite sure for a moment that his uncle from Birmingham was standing by his bedside. 'Are you my uncle or my godfather?' he demanded fretfully.

'Your uncle is dying in Birmingham,' said Death. 'I am going back to him in a moment. I shall stand at the head of his bed and I shall breathe on him with my cold breath, and that will be the end of him. He will leave you half his fortune. Then you will be free to study in the great universities. You will travel from city to city, and you will sit at the feet of the great physicians until you become greater than all of them. When next you see me you will be the greatest physician in the world. Meanwhile you are going to get well, for I am standing at the foot of the bed, not at the head.'

'But—the war?' said Clement.

'I have harvested that field. Two months gleaning and the war will be over, and you will begin to work. Then you will become as famous as my godson ought to be.'

'I'm not clever enough,' said the boy fretfully. 'I can work and I can do with very little sleep, and I have never wasted time on liking people. All that counts in my favour, I know. But I'm not clever.'

Death smiled. 'I have given you a present. That's better than cleverness.'

'What present? I know a boy whose godfather gave him an Austin Seven. What are you giving me?'

The figure of Death shifted and wavered and became the shadow of the nurse moving about the room. 'My secret,' said the shadow.

'What secret? '

'Hush!' said the nurse.

'Think!' said Death.

But the boy fell asleep before he could think, and in the morning woke much better, but still thinking of nothing and remembering nothing. Not till the news came of his uncle's death in Birmingham, carefully and kindly broken to him by the pretty nurse, did he remember that dreamy talk with his godfather. So it was true! It was no dream. But what was the secret? 'Think, Clement, think!'

But for months, for years, the secret continued to elude him. It was not until his examinations had been brilliantly passed, not until his apprenticeships were over, that enlightenment came. He had seen many deaths. They were the concern of the hospitals. But when he bought his practice, when he attended his first private case, then he knew fully the weight of his responsibilities, then his eyes were opened and he saw. For his own experience and the far greater experience of the night nurse told him that the patient could scarcely live. But, looking up from the flushed, unconscious face, he saw, suddenly and without surprise, the figure of his godfather standing at the foot of the bed. And Death smiled at him and nodded encouragement. Then he knew the secret: then he knew that Death at the foot of the bed would be a kind godfather, dropping in to greet his young protegé

Godfather Death

Life. But Death at the head of the bed would always be the King of Terrors.

'She will live,' said Clement to the distracted husband of the patient. 'I've told the nurse what to do. Ring me, of course, at the faintest alarm. I will come in again in the morning. But she will live. Go to bed and rest. She will live.'

She lived to tell her friends, and Clement's practice prospered. And because he never held out false hopes he acquired, besides a reputation for infallibility, a name for honesty. Who shall decide when doctors disagree? The answer was to call in Clement. With extraordinary rapidity he became an international figure. His fortune was immense, and, being his father's son, it may be said that he earned it. He liked money, but even more he liked hard work.

Yet he was unhappy; for his lonely infallibility oppressed him. He still knew that he was not clever, and would have given all his fame for the skill that saved lives. Indeed, as the years went by, he learned to dread his godfather's welcoming smile even more than his scowl: and he thought sometimes that Death, who knew everything, knew of this growing distaste. His godfather had never spoken to him since he was famous, and his welcome, or so Clement fancied, had long since grown less cordial. Was it possible that he, Clement, had been too successful? It was a familiar situation, of course. Father and son—uncle and nephew—these partnerships are hell for all concerned. 'Why doesn't the old man retire?' demands youth. 'My boy, when I was your age——' retorts eld. Clement, physician and father confessor, had heard each side of the question often enough and had given good soothing advice. Now it occurred to him that it was his question too, and that his own godfather might be regretting their partnership. It was true that for years now the luck had been with Clement. Eight times out of ten, nowadays, his godfather would be standing at the foot of the bed, and his smile had grown jealous and cold as Clement pronounced judgment. Indeed, one terrible night, his godfather had left his station at the foot of the bed, and with one malicious glance at Clement, had stalked to its head, and the patient, with a loud cry, had turned on the pillow and died.

'Cheat!' muttered Clement, and he hated his godfather, melting before his eyes into the shadow of the curtains and stirring them with his cold passing. Nevertheless, it was not till Clement married that the estrangement was complete.

Clement had been summoned to the bedside of the richest man in the new world. He flew to him over three thousand miles of sea and another three thousand of land, arriving exhausted, disinterested, driven as usual by his inhuman will to work. He did not know that life, for once in league with his godfather, was setting a trap for him. But as he stepped out of the plane and looked at the anxious group awaiting him, he was lost. For the daughter of the rich man had herself come to meet him, and Clement, who never looked at women, discovered in the one fateful glance, that beauty has grey eyes and short fair hair. Beauty paints her finger-nails and her lips, and is still beauty, aged twenty-two.

Godfather Death

She drove him herself through orange groves set in dazzling sand, and from some dreary class-room reading the word 'Hesperides' floated into his mind—'the garden of the Hesperides.'

'The singing and the gold,' said Clement aloud, dreamily: and she flashed a kind look at him, knowing his thought.

It was the beginning of a swift intimacy. For she was feverish with anxiety and the fear of grief, and talked to him with confessional sincerity. That she should love her father so honestly was a reproach to him; for he had grieved but little for his own father. He saw that her soul was as lovely as her body and adored her the more, and found himself madly promising that he would save her father, and adorning his mad promise with boasts of all the other lives he had saved.

And so they came at last to the blue and golden shores of the Pacific and to her home. Without stopping to rest or change his coat, he went to the sick man's room, a conqueror. Anxious colleagues awaited him. These he could over-awe, humour, conciliate, control. He heard his own voice, glib and authoritative:

'All in good time, gentlemen! First let me see the patient.'

Oh, they were easy to control. But he had another colleague who would be less easy to control, and he wondered what they would say if they heard his thoughts instead of his words.

'All in good time, gentlemen! First let me consult my colleague. Where does he stand? Is he at the foot or the head of the bed?'

Then at last he entered and, as he feared, as he knew already, his godfather was standing at the head of the bed, one bony hand grasping the bed-post. The face of Death was the face of an enemy, and as he bent over the sick man he felt the cold breath of Death upon his own neck. In despair he made the necessary examination, in despair straightened himself, his lips framing a 'no,' and turned to tell his colleagues that which they already knew.

'No! No hope! No chance at all!'

But as he was about to speak he saw, behind them, in the doorway, the face of the girl, radiant with hope and promise. He could have disappointed her hope, but he could not deny himself her promise. He had for so many years been accustomed to take everything he wanted. Having courage, he made up his mind.

'The patient,' he said deliberately, 'is lying in the wrong position. He must not face the light. Put pillows at the foot of the bed. Lift him out and let him lie the other way round.'

His colleagues protested at that. The patient was at the last gasp. It was folly. It was fatal. It was quackery. Their distinguished colleague was overtired from his journey. He did not know what he was saying. But Clement, ignoring such murmurs, slipped his arms under the sick man's body. The frail carcase was no weight to his great strength. He lifted it, bedclothes and all, and laid it gently down again so that the head lay where the feet had been. And as he did so the laboured breathing grew easier and the sick man opened his eyes.

'He will live,' said Clement softly to everyone in the room. 'He will live many years.' Then he quailed, for Death in the shadows stared upon him with a livid countenance. His eyes were on that countenance as he dealt politely with doctors and nurses, and his mind, working independently of his tongue, proffered desperate excuses. A man must love. A man must marry. Godfather Death, in his own interests, must overlook this slip.

'What's that? Do you think you can over-reach me because you are my godson?'

'But how will you reap your harvest, Godfather, in the years to come, if a man may not beget children for you? Forgive me this once!'

'You had better not try it again.'

'Never, Godfather, never! Never again.'

Then he felt a touch upon his arm, and turning, saw the girl for whom he had thus embroiled himself, standing beside him, weeping with thankfulness and joy. Then he turned to his godfather, saying:

'It was for her. Now that you see her even you must understand and forgive me.'

The girl looked up at him.

'Why are your lips moving?'

He took her hands. 'I will tell you one day—one day soon—when your father is well.'

CLEMENCE DANE

And then, as she looked at him consciously, for it was one of those mutual first-sight romances, he muttered within himself piteously:

'Forgive me, Godfather, this once!'

But he spoke to the empty air. Threatening Death had made himself scarce. Life was in the sick-room, and Love. He took it that he was forgiven—this once.

But he was not prepared to bring the matter to proof. He knew well enough that he had given his last verdict, though he did not instantly announce his withdrawal to the world. Instead he devoted himself to his new adventure of love: and presently he married beauty with the grey eyes and short fair hair. Then it was natural that he should, for a time, give up his professional work. He had not had a holiday for ten years. He deserved a year's honeymoon. But he assured everyone that he would come back into harness at the end of the year.

But at the end of the year he still found a dozen good reasons for not coming back into harness. And in his heart he knew that he would never come back. Why should he risk his happiness?

For he was as happy as a king, as happy as a schoolboy, and in his wife's eyes he was both. She was enchanted by the folly of her famous king, by the kingliness of her schoolboy. And he, whose early teacher had been Death himself, found it exquisite to learn from the companion he loved, how to be young. He discovered that he had never had youth: and she was deliciously full of pity for the motherless, dry-eyed, hard little boy of thirty years ago, as lonely in his deserted village as the lame child in Hamelin. Soon she was asking him to take her down to his Devon village. She wanted to see the churchyard where the nameless Spaniard was buried in the year of the Armada. She wanted to see the stone in the wall with the fossil in it. She wanted to see the green village pond and the dance of will o' the wisp. She wanted to pick foxgloves from the gorgeous hedges and hunt wild raspberries in the clearing on the hill-top. She wanted, in fact, to recapture the years of Clement's life which she did not possess, could not share. She wanted to clothe herself in his past, to quote familiarly his memories. And so it was she, finally, who persuaded him to buy the rambling, derelict farm-house in which his father had lived. They enlarged it, annexed the neighbouring orchards, and enclosed it with gardens. They made it their toy and their summer palace.

And though they had the five continents to explore, though she had her penthouse in New York and her Californian estate, though he had his great town house and the villa at Como, still it was to their Devonshire toy that they returned again and again. And each time the visits grew longer, and each time they left more reluctantly in search of the amusement they really did not need, for they were their own perfect entertainment. They grew lazy-minded in the soft warm air: the green wall of hills was a barrier that they did not wish to surmount, a screen and shelter from a world which bored them.

It was at the end of their third summer that Clement, watching the manœuvres of the swallows overhead, said wistfully to his wife:

'Time to be off.'

'Why?' she answered reluctantly. 'I'd like to have a winter here. I order Michaelmas daisies and I never see them bloom. Let's stay on.'

'Won't you find it very dull? '

'We ought to pamper the village at Christmas-time, as they do in Dickens. There should be hampers and a tree.'

'It's damp here in the winter.'

'I don't care. I was brought up in the desert. I love the green wet look of everything. Rain's a green colour, do you know? Let's stay!'

'As long as you don't mind. I love it here, of course.'

'I know you do. And I love what you love.'

So it was settled, and they stayed on, rejoicing over their log fires within doors, over the smell of burning leaves drifting in through ever-open windows, over the fantastic procession of the clouds from hill-top to hill-top, over the gleams of sunshine and the smell of the fine relentless rain that soaked the woods, slid across the meadows, drained the lanes and rolled on down the ditches to the village pond. As autumn passed mistily into winter they concerned themselves with parish matters. There was a new stove in the church, and the organ was mended. Puddings bobbed in every saucepan that Christmas, and the tree in the village school-room was hung with presents which were not bought at Woolworth's.

Godfather Death

They enjoyed their benevolence in the picturesque village that was visited by so few gaieties. It was not till the Christmas decorations had been taken down that the village, nevertheless, had its winter visitors—white mists, winter rains, unseasonable warmth, colds, coughs, weaknesses, the plague!

'For that's what they call it here,' Clement said to his wife.' It's only influenza, of course. In the old days it swept the villages. A good thing in some ways. Overpopulation is the curse of England. All the same, my dear, you'd better get away.'

'Shall you?'

'I'll follow you.'

'If you stay, I stay. You say yourself you've got it in hand.'

And indeed Clement's promptness had done much. There had been a generous cheque and supplies ordered from Exeter and London, an importation of nurses and an exportation of the sick. Nevertheless the toll was heavy, as day after day the death-mists filled the narrow lanes and shrouded the cottage gardens.

'How silent it is,' said his wife to Clement, staring through her bedroom window across the sheeted valley to the emerging hills. 'Do you notice that the birds have stopped singing?'

'I tell you the valley's poisoned,' said Clement anxiously. 'I wish to God you'd go up to town.'

'I'm not going to desert the village. I've never had a village of my own before.'

'As if I couldn't look after them.'

'And who's to look after you? Besides, I want him to be Devon born. You mustn't thwart me. And look how well I am.'

And looking at her he had to own that she was blooming. Approaching motherhood suited her. She carried her burden with an air of triumph. Wouldn't it be foolish to thwart her, when all was going so well?

So he contented himself by extracting a promise from her to keep within the house and grounds, surrounded her with cares and advices, and a barrage of disinfectants. Nevertheless he watched her anxiously, and several times tried to assert his authority; but each time he was defeated by her obstinate gaiety, her defiant health. And in spite of his fears her prophecies were fulfilled. All went well, and a few weeks later the desired son was safely born.

They assured him, at least, that all went well. For he himself was struck down, on the morning of his wife's confinement, with a mild but maddening attack of that very plague against which he had so vigorously legislated: and for the next fortnight he lay fretting and helpless in a distant part of the house. But all went well, eh? 'Has everything gone well?'

'Now you mustn't worry yourself, Sir Clement. We would tell you, of course. The child is going on splendidly. You mustn't excite yourself so, Sir Clement. All's well.'

Thus sweetly they mouthed at him, and would not let him get up. But when at last, by sheer will-power, he wrenched himself out of bed and got himself into his clothes and out of the room, then he discovered, of course, that which he had known already. Didn't he always know better than any

Godfather Death

of them? They'd been lying to him. All was not well. In weakness she had been an easy prey to the all-conquering plague, as he had feared, as he had known. Had he ever been wrong in his diagnosis of any patient? And this was his wife. Would his instinct fail him about his own wife?

Waving them all aside he got himself shakily along the corridor and into his wife's room. On his way to her he paused at the door of the nursery, but he did not go in, though his ear noted with satisfaction his son's healthy wail. But he growled out as he passed:

'Take the child into a room further off! And keep the door shut, can't you? His mother will fret if she hears him cry.'

But the mother was beyond fretting. Indeed, as he came into the room and looked down upon the mother of his son, his first emotion was a desperate revolt against the unfairness of destiny. His wife had done as she promised. She had kept herself strong and well and brought his child safely into the world. Why should she be cheated of her triumph? Why should she be struck down and robbed of her right to his homage? Then his revolt turned to bitter self-reproach. Why had he let her stay in this infected air? He knew why! In his selfishness he had hated to be without her. He had let himself be persuaded by her. He had weakly delegated his authority, and here was his reward.

He called her softly by name and her eyelids flickered; but she did not open them. Weakly he dropped into a chair at the foot of the bed and his own eyes closed. Then he felt a glass at his lips. The nurse, with her damnable efficiency, was playing the ministering angel. He opened his eyes to wave her aside, and across her pink large hand saw the head of the bed and the bed-post with a bundle of bones clasped upon it—ten living bones, white, clenching and unclenching, intertwined. His slow gaze travelled upwards from those twisting bones, lost themselves in an infinite darkness, travelled upwards and met Death's eyes.

He stared for minutes—hours—eternities—into those threatening eyes, and throughout that uncounted period of time his tongue was occupied with the appalling labour of creation—the creation of shaped sounds, words, sentences. He thought to himself that his wife's birth pangs could not have been greater than these pangs of his will. His will triumphed. His tongue obeyed. A lucid sentence spoke itself.

'Lift her up and let her lie with her head at the foot of the bed.'

There was a confusion of protest about him, pink hands waving, a shrill voice. All this he flung aside. He had his arms round his wife's small, dear body. He was staggering through space with an orris-scented weight in his arms. He was collapsing upon that weight, sheltering it with his dissolving body. He was close to a white face. White lids were lifted. There was light in the beloved blue eyes beneath the lids.

Then he was no longer touching her body: then he was swaying: then he was erect: then he was facing his godfather.

'She will live,' said Clement arrogantly, without fear. 'She will live.'

Godfather Death

'You've cheated me twice,' said Death, and laid a hand upon his arm. But Clement was not troubled by the pressure, only by the complaint; for he no longer had any grudge against his godfather. His godfather had been kind to him. He didn't want to cheat anyone who'd been kind to him.

'You needn't take hold of me,' said Clement slowly. 'I'm quite ready to come.' And he followed his godfather obediently out of the room, down the stairs, along the passage [91 with the oak panelling that he and his wife had found together somewhere, centuries ago, through the door which was bolted and had its knocker and its letter-box, but no substance whatever, and so out into the village street which was filled with mist.

'Do you notice that the birds have stopped singing?' said Clement to his godfather, as they drifted on through the whiteness: and when the church tower loomed out at them—'Don't we stop in the churchyard?' said Clement.

But already they had passed the churchyard wall, and the stone with a fossil in it, and the village pond: and were following the track of the stream into the swamp itself.

He had forgotten that the swamp was so big. The mists receded as he looked about him, and the swamp was an endless plain. No sunshine poured down. There were no dragon-flies, no bumble-bees, no shouting children plunging after the candlesticks. But the candlestick flowers grew everywhere, just as they had grown in his childhood, thousands and thousands of candlesticks with yellow flames at the top, some large, some half size, some quite small. Then he saw that they were not flowers, as he had always thought, but true tall candles, burning in their sticks. And as he watched some of the flames were extinguished, and some burned more brightly, and others again dwindled and wavered, till he was dazzled by the perpetual leap and flicker of the myriad flames.

'Now, Godson, at last you know everything,' said his godfather's voice at his elbow. 'I promised that you should know everything. Those candles are men's lives. The tall ones belong to children, and those half-burnt candles are middle-aged folk, and the little ones belong to the old.' Death paused, and Clement could see out of the corner of his own eye how Death looked at him sideways and smiled a little. 'Though the candles of children and lusty young people are often very small,' said Death.

'Show me my son's candle,' said Clement, softly, to his godfather.

'It's fine and tall,' said Death: and he pointed to a lovely flame that leaped and flickered on a level with their eyes.

'And his mother's?' said Clement.

'Fine and tall,' said Death again.

'Show me the flame of my own life,' said Clement hoarsely.

'Why, there it is!' said his godfather: and he threatened with his foot a flattened candle-end that lay in the grey grass at their feet. It was no more than a little pool of wax with a black, crooked, over-long wick in it, and the wick had dropped sideways back into the wax, smoking and blinking.

Godfather Death

'That?'

Death laughed.

'Not so fine, eh? Not so tall?' he chuckled.

The breath of his laughter swept across the plain like a wind, and all the flames flickered, and one or two went out.

But Clement was staring at his flame of life, flickering wildly at his feet. In the heart of the flame he saw, minute but very bright, his wife's face, and he remembered that his wife loved him. Behind her he saw the walls of his home, and behind those walls the green ramparts of his birthplace. Beyond them again he saw the chequered world with its cities and he remembered that its cities had honoured him.

Then he clutched Death's robes, crying:

'I'm your godson, Death! Remember how much you have given me—love and wealth and fame. Give me then one more gift. Give me the life to enjoy them. Light a new candle for me, Godfather, and let me go home.'

'You don't understand,' said his godfather. 'A candle must go out before a candle can be lighted.'

He spoke in his customary voice, the voice that was a rubbing of grasshopper thighs, a stirring of winds in withered gardens, a rattling of dried beans in their frost-bitten pods. Nevertheless, his godson fancied that there was a yielding in it, and all the scheming, ingenious elements of his mind, all that made him what he was and prevented him from being greater than he was, prompted his next words.

'Put my candle-end upon a new tall candle, then it will go on burning when the old one comes to an end. Do it for me,

Godfather!' ordered Clement. 'Don't you see how easy it is? There—take that tall new candle!'

'If you choose,' said his godfather: and, stooping, he lifted the dribble of wax between the bones of his finger and thumb.

Breathless with hope Clement watched his godfather, and as the two flames approached he felt his weakness leaving him and new strength pouring into his veins. And he called out in his desperate relief:

'This is my true present, Godfather! You give me my present at last.'

'Are you grateful?' said Death. 'It's your son's flame.'

'My son's?' began Clement. But whether he would have protested at such a borrowing he never knew; for Death, with a malicious look, laid the candle-end so clumsily upon the new tall candle that it could not keep its place. Its last meltings guttered down the smooth new side, and in those gutterings its wick slanted and choked, and its feeble flame was extinguished. And as the flame died Clement fell also, and lay still upon the grey grass.

But the tall candlestick which was the life of his son burned on steadily in the face of Godfather Death.

Godfather Death

The Fisherman and His Wife

E. M. DELAFIELD

Once upon a time there lived a young author, who was also a fisherman, with his wife, in a very tiny little cottage on the edge of a Devonshire cliff, and every day the young author went out fishing for the purpose—naturally—of catching fish. In this he was no more often successful than are the majority of anglers, and his wife—an unreasonable and overbearing young modern if ever there was one—made herself exceedingly disagreeable about it quite often.

One day the husband—whose name was Alured—went out as usual, and after a good deal of patient waiting about—also as usual—he felt something pulling at the end of the line. And when he drew it up, he found a huge flounder on the hook.

Alured was pleased at this, but less pleased when the flounder suddenly began to speak, although not very distinctly, because of the hook.

'Fisherman!' said the flounder, and added—unnecessarily enough—'listen to me.'

Alured very kindly took the hook away, but he did not put the fish back into the water, wishing to hear what it had to say, and being also well aware that flounders would not emerge from the ocean every day of the week just for the sake of conversing with obscure young writers.

'I am not a real fish,' said the flounder earnestly. 'I am an enchanted prince. I shall be of no use to you if you land me and take me to your home. I shall not even taste good. Put me back again into the water and let me swim away.'

Alured, a man of few words himself, listened attentively to the eloquent speech of his captive, and replied, kindly but shortly, that there was no need to have said so much about it. The idea of cooking and then eating a talking fish was entirely repugnant to him, and he had no greater desire than to put it straight back again into the sea from whence he had all unwittingly taken it.

'I am indeed obliged to you,' said the flounder civilly, and it gave a kind of bow.

Alured bowed back again, and then enquired if the flounder wished to say anything more. On being assured that the flounder had finished speaking, Alured then returned it to the clear water.

The flounder sank to the bottom, and Alured got up and went home, feeling that any other haul he might make would merely come as an anti-climax.

'Did you catch anything to-day?' asked his wife, Barbara—and she asked it in a tone which clearly implied that she expected a negative reply.

'No,' said Alured negligently. 'That is to say, I did catch a flounder, but as he said he was an enchanted prince, I let him go again.'

'*Must* you be funny?' asked his wife wearily, having quite evidently not believed a word of it.

Alured explained that he was not, at any rate intentionally, being funny, and that this curious occurrence had really taken place. It took a long while, and more talk than he cared for, to convince his wife, and when at last this had been achieved, Alured almost at once wished it undone again.

For the first thing Barbara said was:

'Did you ask him for anything?'

'No,' said Alured. 'What should I ask him for?'

'Good heavens!' cried Barbara, 'we want all sorts of things. Money, of course, and a bigger house—and then we should have a better social standing—and a car, and a wireless——'

Alured, who wanted none of these things for himself, replied very coldly that the fish had said nothing to raise any such extravagant hopes, and that there was no reason to suppose he could or would give them anything at all.

'You might at least have asked,' said Barbara sulkily. 'Still, it isn't too late. Pop along back to the beach, and see if you can see anything of him.'

'I can't possibly ask him for cars and houses and social standings,' protested Alured, making the great mistake of arguing, instead of flatly refusing at once. 'Besides, how do you suppose he's going to get them from the bottom of the sea?'

'If he's really an enchanted prince, he can do it easily. Besides, you needn't ask for everything. Just say we'd like a little sea-side villa, instead of this horrible tumbledown cottage.'

And she hustled him out of the place.

Alured, far from happy in his errand, returned to the shore, and recited a rather vicious little poem that he had made up as he went along, in order to relieve his annoyance:

> 'O man, O man—if man you be—
> Or flounder, flounder in the sea,
> Such a tiresome wife I've got
> For she wants what I do not.'

He could not help hoping that the flounder, by this time, was half-way across the Atlantic, and would pay no attention.

The flounder, however, on the contrary, shot up to the surface and said quite amiably:

'Well, what does she want?'

'Well,' returned Alured apologetically, 'you know when I caught you this morning? My wife feels that I ought to have asked you for something. She thinks I might have wished, and that you might have granted the wish.'

The Fisherman and His Wife

'She does, does she,' replied the flounder not unpleasantly. 'Wish away, then.'

'My wife would like to have a sea-side villa instead of our present cottage,' said Alured, intentionally disassociating himself from these ambitions, which he thought foolish.

'Go home,' said the flounder. 'She has it already.'

And it disappeared into the water.

Alured went home without hurrying himself, and was not particularly pleased when he saw that, where the cottage had once been, Barbara was now installed in a little brick villa, with a slate roof, and two bow-windows, and a sign hanging in one of them: 'Apartments to Let.' Barbara, however, was delighted, and showed him the aspidistras, and the dining-room suite of fumed oak, and a number of pictures of young people in Empire clothes feeding swans, or saying goodbye, or riding on horses, and any amount of linoleum both upstairs and down.

'Isn't it all marvellous?' said Barbara. Luckily, she did not seem to expect any reply.

In a little while Alured became used to the villa, and by the time he had painted 'Mount Blenheim' on the gate, he almost liked it.

Unfortunately, Barbara chose that moment to become thoroughly tired of it.

'It's absurd,' she said firmly. 'It won't do at all. Pop along to your flounder and tell him we must have a decent labour-saving bungalow with a garage.'

Alured disliked the idea of this second popping even more than the first, but, as will already have been perceived, he was one of those unfortunately-constituted people who will do almost anything for the sake of a quiet life.

So, with the utmost reluctance, he again sought the flounder—and it seemed to him anything but a good omen that the sea, when he got there, should be of a strange purple colour, and not clear at all. He stood and looked at it distastefully, and muttered his piece of poetry as before:

'O man, O man—if man you be—
Or flounder, flounder in the sea,
Such a tiresome wife I've got
For she wants what I do not.'

'Well,' said the voice of the flounder, 'what does she want?'

'Oh,' said Alured, 'she wants to live in a labour-saving bungalow, with a garage.'

It sounded a poor sort of wish, but the flounder merely said: 'You can go home. She is already standing in front of the door.'

And so she was, and it was a spectacle that Alured viewed without any enthusiasm whatever. He disliked the bungalow at sight, and—for that matter—Barbara also.

She, however, was enthusiastic.

'Isn't it *heaven*!' she shrieked excitedly, and she ran about, and showed him the rustless steel furniture, and the electrical appliances, and the flat roof on which she said they would sun-bathe.

Alured thought it all frightful, except the bath-room, which had a green-tiled pool sunk into the floor, and even that reminded him of the sea, and his interviews with the flounder.

He did not feel in the least certain that Barbara would for long remain content with the labour-saving bungalow—nor did she. Their social standing having, as she had expected, improved with the size of their house, it seemed desirable to Barbara that they should entertain on quite a large scale.

'A country-house would be much better than this,' she said. 'Then we could have house-parties, and entertain the neighbourhood, and invite distinguished people to stay.'

"'I can call spirits from the vasty deep'" witheringly observed Alured, meaning to imply by this quotation that it would be one thing for Barbara to invite distinguished people to stay, and quite another for them to accept.

The quotation, unfortunately, struck Barbara quite differently.

'Off you go, then,' she returned briskly. 'Tell the flounder that we must have a fine country-house. One of the stately homes of England.'

'The flounder will never do it. Besides, I can't go on asking for things like that.'

'Why not?' said Barbara callously. And she added, to show that she, too, could quote: "'Youth will be served.'"

Alured crawled, rather than walked, to the sea and was dismayed, rather than surprised, to find that it had turned a very odd, dark wine-colour, and that the waves were lashing about ominously.

E. M. DELAFIELD

Being, like all of us, very much the slave of habit, Alured recited his poem once more, although he by no means viewed it as being one of his masterpieces.

It served to bring the flounder to the surface.

'What does she want?' the fish rather curtly enquired.

'A stately home of England,' Alured answered, feeling much ashamed.

'Go home, she has it already,' the flounder replied, and it disappeared again before Alured could frame suitable thanks and apologies.

He told himself that he had a very good mind not to go home at all, but this was not really true, because natural curiosity was as strong in him as in everybody else, and he wanted to see what the flounder had accomplished this time.

He was not left long in doubt.

The flounder, very economically, had retained the labour-saving bungalow—but it had become the mere lodge of Alured's and Barbara's new home.

It now stood just behind a superb pair of ornamental gates, flanked by stone pillars with gigantic stone pineapples on the top. Park walls stretched away into the distance, over-shadowed by tall trees.

The avenue, bordered with magnificent beeches on either side, was a great deal longer than Alured thought in the least necessary, as he walked and walked and walked, hoping eventually to catch sight of the house.

After crossing two ornamental stone bridges, and seeing a herd of deer, and a small marble pavilion that well deserved its name of Folly—at any rate in the opinion of Alured—he at last saw the mansion. It stood in the midst of a *parterre*, with a flight of stone steps leading to a terrace, and such a quantity of brilliant flowers were to be seen that Alured's heart sank within him, thinking of the gardeners.

But worse than gardeners awaited him. At the large double-doors of the mansion stood two powdered footmen, in knee-breeches, silk stockings, and yellow-and-red liveries.

Alured, at the sight of them, nearly turned straight back down the avenue of beeches once more—but the thought of its great length deterred him. Also the footmen, who were evidently very well trained, did not embarrass him by taking any notice of him. A very quiet elderly man dressed in black came out from amongst a cluster of marble pillars and said gently:

'Her ladyship is in the yellow boudoir, my lord. Tea has just been served there.'

Alured thought, *The hell it has*, but aloud he merely said 'Thank you—er—' and followed the butler down a long, softly-lighted hall, panelled in cedar-wood and with a few Persian rugs lying about the parquet flooring, and down two shallow steps, and through an orangery filled with flowering plants and shrubs, and up some more steps, and into an octagonal sitting-room, hung with yellow brocade, where Barbara sat amidst yellow upholstery, with an old gold tea-service on a little table in front of her.

She had the strength of mind to say quite calmly 'Tea, dear?' just as she used to say it in the kitchen of the original cottage.

E. M. DELAFIELD

Alured took the tea, because he felt badly in need of it, and he also took some of the pâté-de-fois-gras sandwiches off one of the gold plates, and insensibly these did something towards calming him. Nevertheless, he spoke shortly and sharply to Barbara, and said that he hoped she was satisfied *now*.

All that Barbara replied was:

'I think you'll like the library, and the picture-gallery, and the cellar.'

'The whole thing is preposterous,' said Alured sternly. 'You ought never to have asked for anything of the kind.'

'The library is lined with books, up to the ceiling. Your poems are there.'

'That is of no importance,' returned Alured proudly. But actually the flounder rose highly in his estimation on the spot.

'As for the cellar, it's completely stocked with vintage port and things,' said Barbara—and Alured could not help hoping that she had not spoken in this casual and feminine way to the butler. He was quite likely enough to despise them for the upstarts that they were without any such additional *faux pas*.

'It really is rather magnificent,' Barbara said. 'There's a muniment-room, and a priest's hiding-hole, and a haunted room. And a staff of nineteen indoor servants, and as many outdoor ones.'

'Shall you be able to manage them?' sceptically enquired Alured, who well remembered the great and many difficulties complained of by Barbara in her dealings with a single charwoman.

The Fisherman and His Wife

'There is a very experienced housekeeper downstairs, to whom I shall delegate a certain amount of responsibility,' replied Barbara.

She had an answer to everything, reflected Alured resentfully.

The country-house was very fine indeed, and on the whole Alured liked it better than any of the other places in which he had been compelled, by his wife's ambition, to live. His chief difficulties lay in intercourse with the butler, of whom he was terrified, and in the continual struggle to reconcile his way of life with his principles, which were highly democratic.

After a time, both these trials became less. He gradually grew accustomed to the butler, and his principles underwent, as do so many principles, certain modifications, that enabled him to take advantage of his circumstances without despising himself for so doing.

Just as he had reached this agreeable stage, Barbara sprang upon him a fresh mine.

She called him one morning to the terrace.

'Just look at this marvellous view,' she cried. 'Wouldn't it be fun to be king over the whole country?'

'Not to me it wouldn't, dear,' said Alured in a rather superior tone. 'You forget that I don't believe in a monarchy.'

'No more you do,' said Barbara. 'Well, that simplifies things, in a way. I will be king.'

Alured tried to believe that he had failed to understand her meaning.

'You mean,' he suggested carefully, 'that you would like to be Queen, were such a thing possible. Which of course it isn't.'

'I said King, not Queen. And you can go to your fish and tell him so.'

'Barbara,' said Alured, commanding himself with some difficulty, 'this has gone far enough. Too far, some people might say. It is entirely out of the question that I should go near the flounder again, especially for such a ridiculous purpose. Let me hear no more of your being King.'

But he heard a very great deal more, and the end of it was that, almost without knowing how he had got there, Alured once more found himself at the edge of the sea. This time the water was dark-grey, turgid and tumultuous, and smelling rather disagreeably into the bargain.

Alured groaned aloud, but repeated, from sheer force of habit, his poem:

'O man, O man—if man you be—
Or flounder, flounder in the sea,
Such a tiresome wife I've got
For she wants what I do not.'

It might not be great poetry, reflected the unhappy author, but at least it was true, particularly the third line.

Once more it brought the flounder to the surface, and Alured could not but perceive a marked absence of suavity in its abrupt enquiry:

'What does she want this time?'

'Oh dear!' said Alured weakly, and could get no further.

'Speak up,' said the flounder sharply.

'She wants to be King,' faltered Alured, wishing that the beach would open and swallow him. It did no such thing, and instead, the flounder told him to go home, his wife was King already.

Sustained only by a faint hope that perhaps Barbara had been transported to Windsor Castle, Alured took his way home.

He saw at once that the country-house had undergone a transformation suitable to the new dignity of its owner. It was even larger than before, a flag flew from the top of a huge tower, and sentries stood at the gates.

Indoors, there were more footmen, more red velvet, and a greater number of rooms.

And there was a throne-room.

In the throne-room, as might have been expected, stood a throne, and on the throne was Barbara, wearing robes of state, a gold crown studded with diamonds, rubies and sapphires, and holding a gold sceptre in her hand.

It did not add to Alured's calm to notice, as he immediately did, that there was not even a little throne for him, next to Barbara's.

'I hope you're satisfied,' he remarked bitterly.

Barbara's reply struck death to his soul.

'We shall see,' she calmly returned.

Alured emitted a short, unpleasant laugh, and was at once informed by Barbara that, if he were not very careful, he would find himself under arrest for lèse-majesté.

It will be readily believed that the new state of affairs was not conducive to a happy domestic life.

Barbara was busy nearly all day with ministerial conferences, processions, and other state functions. She took very little notice of her husband, beyond once offering him the post of Poet Laureate.

Alured without hesitation refused it.

Later on, he came to feel that this gesture had been far too reminiscent of that which is known as cutting off one's nose to spite one's face—but self-respect would not allow him to do anything about it.

Time hung heavy on his hands. He felt no desire to write poetry, knowing only too well that poetry does not come forth from palaces, but from places like pitheads, or cottages on cliffs, or bed-sitting-rooms in Bloomsbury.

As for his other occupation, fishing, Alured never wished to hear the word mentioned again. Who knew what might not result from any further catch of his?

He read the *Life of the Prince Consort*, and reflected that Albert the Good had at least taken up his position of his own free will, which was more than could be said for himself. And he felt a morbid certainty that, in the event of his death, Barbara would be content to perpetuate his memory in some quite small and insignificant way, not nearly as grand and expensive as either the Albert Hall or the Albert Memorial—let alone both of them.

Alured, in fact, was rapidly sinking into a permanent state of melancholy introspection, when he was summoned one day to the Royal presence.

'Our trusty and well-beloved servant, Alured, We are about to entrust to you a special mission,' said Barbara, with an air of graciousness that, together with her method of speech, seemed to Alured wholly intolerable.

'What?' he asked, as inelegantly as possible.

'It is Our wish to become Emperor, instead of King,' Barbara said. 'Go to the flounder, and instruct him accordingly.'

Alured said 'What' again, but this time it was a frenzied ejaculation, full of horror, astonishment, and disapproval. It left Barbara quite unmoved.

'Go,' she repeated, and pointed with her sceptre to the door.

Alured went.

Democrat or no democrat, he found it next door to impossible to defy a monarch.

Only too soon, he found himself on the familiar shore, repeating the familiar lines, before an ocean which was neither more nor less than inky, with flying scuds of spray, towering waves, and a worse and more pronounced smell than before.

The flounder appeared in the midst of all this disturbance, and asked in a loud, angry voice:

'What does she want now?'

E. M. DELAFIELD

'Oh!' said Alured frantically. 'It's absurd. It's simply out of the question. She doesn't know what she's talking about. I can't possibly ask you such a thing.'

'Then why come at all?'

Since Alured could not think of any answer that he cared to make to this question, he received it in silence.

'Come, come,' the flounder said more gently; 'you had better speak out like a man. What is it?'

'My wife has got it into her head that she would like to be Emperor,' said the unhappy Alured, feeling more and more how outrageous was such a suggestion.

'I realise only too well,' he added, 'that you are probably as unwilling as unable to accede to any such monstrous request. I will go back and tell Barbara that the whole thing is out of the question.'

'No, no, don't be so impetuous,' the flounder wearily replied. 'When you go home, you will find that she is Emperor already.'

'No, no! It's too much,' cried Alured.

'You saved my life, after all,' the flounder pointed out— although not very enthusiastically.

It then dived into the foam and was lost to view.

Alured turned homewards, feeling unspeakably depressed.

His only consolation was that Barbara had now reached the summit of human greatness, and there could be nothing further left for her to demand.

From King to Emperor was no such great step as all that. Even Barbara could not sit upon more than one throne, nor wear more than one crown, at a time.

The Fisherman and His Wife

She held more conferences than ever, and received a number of foreign potentates, ambassadors, and emissaries, and was obliged to conduct her conversations with all of them through interpreters, as she knew no word of any language except English.

She also became rather overworked, and inclined to be irritable as a result. Exactly the same thing had happened in the old cottage and bungalow days, when the oil-stove had given trouble, or the weekly books had gone wrong.

Alured had not had very much sympathy even then with tantrums other than his own, but now—when Barbara had such grand and splendid responsibilities to account for her fractiousness—he felt less able to endure it than ever.

He suggested to her that she might like to entrust him with some difficult and delicate diplomatic mission, of the kind that could not be given to any ordinary representative, the true reason being that he was anxious to get right away, both from the Castle and its Imperial owner.

Barbara's reply was an outburst of fretful and exhausted weeping.

'The fact is,' she sobbed, 'you none of you think of *me*, destroying myself with hard work. I haven't got time to turn round, simply, and it's one thing after another, and I don't get any thanks for it, from anybody, and I wish I was dead.'

The unworthy thought flashed for a moment through Alured's mind that this, on the whole, was the most sensible wish that his wife had as yet expressed. He did not, however, go so far as to take her at her word and rush off with her latest aspiration to the flounder. Instead, he told her curtly, but not unkindly, to pull herself together and added, after the manner of husbands, that perhaps what she needed was to go upstairs and lie down for a bit.

'What I need,' said Barbara, 'is a change. I'm simply worn out.'

'Well, take a change. There's Balmoral, I suppose,' said Alured, who did not care for Balmoral himself.

'I mean a change from being Emperor,' Barbara explained, with more tears.

'Would you like me to take it on for you, temporarily? To be perfectly candid,' said Alured, 'I've always thought it was more of a man's job than a woman's.'

'I don't agree with you,' Barbara replied. 'No, that wouldn't do at all. But I think that, instead of being Emperor, I had better become Pope. The position is, if anything, still higher, and the life is a much more restful one. So be off with you to the flounder, and tell him to make me Pope.'

Alured kept his temper with extreme difficulty.

'To begin with,' he said, 'there is only one Pope. Even the flounder can't suddenly appoint a second one. And to go on with, I refuse to ask him for anything more. Quite definitely.'

'But you can't refuse,' his wife pointed out. 'You forget that I'm still Emperor. This is an Imperial command.'

'My Good Heavens, Barbara—' Alured began, just as he might have addressed her in the old days on the subject of the bath-water, or the unsatisfactory cooking of the bacon for breakfast.

The Fisherman and His Wife

But in the old days Barbara had not been in a position to summon a platoon of guards, which she now immediately did, and bade them remove Alured in disgrace from the Royal presence.

For the next week he was kept in a kind of honourable captivity, without chains, but also without books, amusement, or any of the more interesting varieties of food. He was then conducted formally by his guards into the presence of Barbara. Dismissing the guards, she again repeated to Alured her determination to become Pope.

'I've quite made up my mind,' she assured him, 'so you may just as well go sooner as later. You'll have to, in the end.'

There was only too much truth in the assertion, as Alured felt. In an indescribable state of rage and apprehension, he took his way yet again to the seashore.

As he went, he wondered bitterly what unpleasant manifestations of Nature would meet his gaze. An earthquake would not have surprised him in the least.

There was no earthquake, but the waves were colossal, and dark fiery red, and the smell that had been noticeable before had now become a most fearful stench.

Alured decided at once that it was out of the question for him to face the flounder in these circumstances. Unfortunately, it seemed equally out of the question for him to go back to the castle, with his mission still unfulfilled.

He hovered about in a most miserable state of indecision, but presently the force of association became too strong for

him, and he began to mutter the lines of poetry that he had
so often spoken on the same spot:

'O man, O man—if man you be—
Or flounder, flounder in the sea,
Such a tiresome wife I've got
For she wants what I do not.'

And lo and behold! the flounder reared itself up out of the
raging waters and glared at Alured in silence.

'I don't know what to say,' the poet stammered, 'I can't
apologise sufficiently. You've done such a tremendous
amount for us already. It's outrageous presumption to suggest anything else . . . I assure you, no one can realise it better
than I do.'

'Go on,' said the flounder sourly, as Alured paused in utter
confusion—and its tone implied that there was at least one
other person to whom Alured's presumption was fully as evident as it was to himself. 'What does she want now?'

Alured, obliged to bellow so as to be heard above the roar
of the elements, shouted at the top of his voice:

'She wants to be Pope.'

'Go home!' shouted back the flounder. 'She is Pope
already.'

And it plunged furiously away.

Alured returned to that which had now become a Vatican.
It was a strange state of affairs.

Barbara seemed to have assimilated to herself all the out-
ward pomp and splendour of the Papacy, with but little of its

The Fisherman and His Wife

accompanying wisdom. So, at least, it appeared to Alured. The white robes, the triple diadem, and the throne were all there: but where were the concomitant prayings and fastings? Nowhere, so far as Alured could see.

Barbara held a great many audiences, and received quantities of pilgrims, and evidently liked seeing them go down upon their knees in front of her, and respectfully kiss her extended hand.

In other words, she seemed to become daily more and more arrogant.

Alured had less place than ever in the scheme of things. He spent most of his time talking to various unoccupied officials, whose only function was to swing censers and carry lighted candles in the processions.

The Papal Court was not nearly as comfortable as the original country-house had been, and the books in the great libraries had been taken away, and a number of dull theological tomes, many of them written in Latin, had been put there instead. As for the picture-gallery, it was still there, but all the pictures now represented holy and distinguished persons undergoing a variety of unpleasant experiences, such as being broken on the wheel, pierced with arrows, or roasted alive. It gave Alured no pleasure whatever to gaze upon them.

But Alured and pleasure had long been strangers.

Occasionally he looked back to the distant time when they had lived in the little cottage on the cliff and when Barbara, though self-willed and tiresome, had been far indeed from the degree of megalomania to which she had now attained. Alured often asked himself how he had ever come to give way to her in the first place, and he realised that, having once done so, it had become increasingly difficult to stop.

'"Facilis descensus"'—he murmured to himself,—for there was a good deal of Latin in the surrounding atmosphere, one way and another, and it was becoming natural to him to think in this classic way. Sometimes he wondered whether any further ambition could or would occur to Barbara, but to what more she could aspire, unless it were to the complete control of the sun, moon and stars themselves, he could not imagine.

It was, in a way, almost a relief to him when the sword of Damocles descended at last.

'Alured,' said the Papal Barbara, with pontifical dignity, 'I desire that you will go to your fish. Tell him that I am tired of being Pope. I wish to become instead the head of the B.B.C.'

Alured very nearly said, Is that all? for this seemed to him a retrogade, rather than a forward, step. But in another moment he realised that, retrograde or forward, he had no wish to ask anything more of the flounder.

This time, he decided to try reasonable persuasion.

'That is all very well,' he inaccurately observed, 'but have you considered what a great deal of trouble we have already given to this much-enduring flounder? On the occasion of my last approach, I found him far from amiably disposed— and no wonder. In any case, I think it extremely doubtful whether the flounder is in any position to do as you suggest. These appointments . . .'

The Fisherman and His Wife

'When I require your assistance, Alured, in assessing the wisdom or otherwise of my determinations, I will apply for it. In the meanwhile,' said his wife, 'you will oblige me by obeying my injunctions instantly, and conveying my instructions to your fish.'

Alured retired—walking backwards—from the Papal presence.

'I had better go to the flounder,' he thought, with the calm of complete despair. 'No doubt he will be furious—and quite right too—and perhaps he will cause the sea to rise up and drown me. That will be an end of the whole ridiculous situation, and I shall not regret it in the least.'

And he became lost in a typical author's day-dream of himself, as a second Shelley, lying drowned and beautiful on the shore. But the shore, when he reached it, was pervaded by so frightful a smell that he relinquished the vision at once, and looked anxiously out to sea.

The horizon was pitch-black, and something that Alured much feared to be a small—but still quite sufficiently large—tidal wave was rolling up, and the sky was sulphur-coloured, and the wind was howling and shrieking all round him.

In all these circumstances Alured did not expect the flounder to wear any appearance of benignity, but even so he was scarcely prepared for the concentrated fury with which the fish suddenly shot to the topmost crest of the tidal wave and addressed him:

'What in the name of fortune have you come to suggest *this* time?'

E. M. DELAFIELD

Like many possessors of the creative gift, Alured was apt to find himself totally devoid of ideas at those moments in which he most required them.

Nothing whatever occurred to his mind as being a suitable rejoinder to the flounder's enquiry, and he could think of nothing better than an almost automatic repetition of his original trope:

'O man, O man—if man you be—
Or flounder, flounder in the sea,
Such a tiresome wife I've got
For she wants what I do not.'

The rejoinder of the flounder to this was as terrifying as it was unexpected. It gave a loud, cynical laugh.

'Stop!' cried Alured. 'I will say nothing more, I have said far too much already. It is entirely scandalous that there should have ever been any further question of your granting my wife any more wishes.'

'Make no speeches,' said the flounder very angrily indeed, 'but tell me at once what it is that she wants.'

At the same moment the crest of the tidal wave, which had all this time remained as it were poised, in the most singular manner, toppled so perilously that Alured was driven into immediate speech through sheer terror.

'She wants to be head of the B.B.C.,' he cried loudly.

Whether or not the flounder replied with the words 'Go home' Alured could never afterwards be sure. For just as he

The Fisherman and His Wife

was expecting to hear them, the tidal wave, with force and fury, broke over him.

Stunned, drenched and blinded, he was conscious of absolutely nothing whilst this cataclysm was actually in progress, save of the fleeting realisation, seized upon by his writer's instinct, that the simile of a cork at the mercy of the waves was, if hackneyed, at least entirely accurate in reference to the helplessness of man.

Eventually he found that he was lying, bruised and battered, far up on the mainland, where the wave had evidently tossed him.

Alured sat up and gazed round him.

A familiar, and not unwelcome, sight met his eyes.

The tiny cottage in which he and Barbara had lived in pre-flounder days still stood on the edge of the cliff.

Smoke rose from one of its two chimneys.

Alured rose stiffly and painfully and made his way towards the cottage. Something between a hope and a suspicion was already at work within him, and he was not altogether surprised by the sight of his wife, outside the door. She was wearing neither imperial crown nor Papal diadem, still less had she the appearance of a person in control of such an organisation as the B.B.C. She was, on the contrary, wearing a very old blue gingham frock, and a pair of worn rubber shoes.

When she saw Alured she said:

'Well! I suppose this is the end of it all. Here we are back again, in the old hovel. Did the flounder lose patience?'

'Yes,' said Alured, 'he did. I always told you what would happen.'

'It must have been your fault,' said Barbara.

In a very few moments they were in the midst of one of their old quarrels. Actually, this exercise now had some of the charm of novelty, since it had been impossible for them to dispute on anything like equal terms during the regal, imperial, or pontifical phases.

It was rather a long while before they settled down again as before.

Barbara, in moments of forgetfulness, was apt to behave as though she still occupied one or other of the exalted positions that she had once adorned, and the awakening from these temporary illusions was never agreeable.

Alured, on the other hand, wasted a certain amount of time and energy in regretting those opportunities of which he felt himself to have made so little use.

For, he thought in his secret heart, if only I had had any sense, I should have wished for myself, and not for Barbara. Now, if *I* had been emperor, Pope, or head of the B.B.C., what a good job I should have made of all or any of it!

His convictions on the point grew, in fact, to such dimensions, that he eventually took up fishing again.

The flounder, however, with great wisdom, failed ever again to reveal itself.

The Fisherman and His Wife

Little Snow-White

LORD DUNSANY

With reverent apologies
to the memory of Grimm.

It will of course be remembered that Lord and Lady Clink, after the second marriage of the former, did a good deal of entertaining at their house in Grosvenor Square. Ostensibly the innumerable parties were to amuse Blanche, the daughter of Lord Clink by his first marriage; but, as she was often in bed before they started, there were those who attributed the lavish entertainment to a certain frivolity in Lady Clink, or a merely perverse intention to flout those taxes that are so much a feature of our country. Of these entertainments it is scarcely necessary to remind the reader, culminating as they did in the festivities on the occasion of the coming out of Blanche Clink, an event scarcely likely to be forgotten, either on account of the magnificence of

Lady Clink's hospitality or because of the unusual circumstance that Blanche came out at the age of seven. But I am a little ahead of my story, which really begins to have a certain significance when Lady Clink purchased a gramophone, some years before Blanche came out. Gramophones had been improving every year, and the improvement most noticeable to the vast majority of us was a gradual reduction of price, until the best gramophone that money could buy in, say, 1920 could be bought in 1930 for the price of one of the cheapest ten years earlier. And that is all that is really of interest to most of us. But if instead of watching a good gramophone come down to the price of a quite common machine, one had watched the other end of the market, one would have seen some very wonderful gramophones indeed. One of these Lady Clink purchased. It is unlikely that anyone in the Clink household saw anything out of the way in this gramophone: all they ever heard of it was Lady Clink muttering apparently to herself:

'Oh gramo, gramo, gramophone,
Which of us is the fairest one ?'

and they paid little attention to the words, wrongly supposing them to be poetry. Then Lady Clink would turn on the gramophone, and it would say, or rather intone:

'Thou art the fairest, Lady Clink.'

And that was all.

Little Snow-White

All the housemaids heard it at one time or another, so that when this monotonous noise varied, about the time of Blanche's coming out, they said: 'She's got a new record.'

And what they heard this time, following her lady-ship's usual muttering, was:

'Thou wert the fairest, Lady Clink,
But Blanche is fairer now, I think.'

And there was ample reason for Gladys' comment to one of the other housemaids: 'Doesn't seem to take to her new record.'

A few days after that Lady Clink sent for one of her chauffeurs. She was in the library alone when the chauffeur was shown in.

'Shut the door, Clutch,' she said. And then she said: 'Clutch, I want you to take Miss Blanche for a short run.'

'Yes, my lady ?' said Clutch.

'And don't bring her back,' she continued.

'Not back, my lady?' said the chauffeur. He had had odd jobs to do before, but he wanted to be sure.

'No,' said Lady Clink. 'You know; an accident.'

Clutch stood there silent.

'Do you want your wages raised?' she said. It was a taunt, not a question. His wages were so absurdly high already that any request to raise them would be fantastic.

'It would be a bit difficult, my lady,' said Clutch. 'The job, I mean.'

'Nonsense,' said Lady Clink. 'Do you know how many people are killed on the roads in a week? What's one more dead body in London?'

'There'd be an inquest . . . ,' he was beginning.

'Driver exonerated from all blame,' snapped Lady Clink with finality.

'Very well, my lady,' said Clutch.

'Ask her to step out for a moment while . . .'

'Leave it to me, my lady,' he said.

'And, by the way,' said Lady Clink, 'bring me her heart and her tongue.'

So that was settled, and Blanche was sent out in the Daimler to do a little shopping.

It was to Oxford Street that they went, and there, when Blanche got out to enter a shop, Clutch, giving some hasty excuse, drew up the car on the opposite side of the road. Soon she was out with her purchase and crossing Oxford Street, and at the same moment Clutch fixing her sternly with his eye drove the heavy Daimler towards her. But the moment that Blanche perceived his fatal intention she cried out: 'Ah, dear chauffeur, give me my life and I will run away into the traffic, and never come home again.'

This speech softened the chauffeur's heart, and her beauty so touched him that he had pity on her and said: 'Well, run away, poor child.'

But he thought to himself, 'The motors will soon run over you.' Still he felt as if a stone had been taken from his heart

Little Snow-White

because her death was not by his hand. Just at that moment a young pedestrian came stepping carelessly off the pavement, and as soon as he clapped eyes on it the chauffeur ran it down, and picking up the tongue and the heart from the mess carried them back to Lady Clink for a token of his deed. But now poor Blanche was left all alone, and was bewildered by the sight of so many lamp-posts, and knew not which way to turn. Presently she set off running and ran over pavement and road, and motors sprang up as she passed them, but they did her no harm. So she went northwards, on and on through the night.

That night Lady Clink spoke late with her cook, whom she usually only saw after breakfast.

'Gizzard,' she said, 'his lordship will be dining out to-morrow, and I should like a nice light meal in my sitting-room.'

'Yes, my lady,' the cook answered, and was about to come in with a suggestion of several dishes, when Lady Clink cut her short. 'Just a tongue and heart of an eland,' said Lady Clink, 'that Clutch has brought back from the butcher's. And Miss Blanche will be staying away for some days.'

She had got the idea of an eland from the cross-words, and, as they always called it an African deer, she had only the vaguest idea what the animal was. Her cook, whose information came from the same sources, received the relics, wrapped in a bit of newspaper, without any further question, except for the professional question, 'How will you have it done, my lady?'

'Au gratin,' said Lady Clink, and the interview ended.

Now, by the time that that dinner was served, Blanche had arrived at one of a row of houses in a small mining town, and entered to rest. There she saw a table all ready spread, with seven plates on it and a rasher of bacon on each, and beside each plate a bottle that she recognised as containing Guinness, some of which she drank, as she had heard that it would be good for her; and then she ate some of the bacon. She took a little of the bacon from each plate, so as not to take away the whole share of any one. Along the wall there were seven beds. Presently she lay down on one of the beds, after trying several to see which suited her best, and being tired she very soon fell asleep. And after a while the seven miners came in, who had been working overtime, and who lived in this room. And the first thing they saw was that someone had been eating their rashers, and the next thing they saw was that someone had been at their Guinness; and all of a sudden one of the more observant saw Blanche asleep in a bed. At this all seven shouted for surprise, although not loudly enough to wake her. And there they let her lie, the miner whose bed she had taken sleeping for one hour of the night with each of his mates in turn. In the morning when Blanche awoke she was frightened to see the miners. But they were friendly and asked her name, and why she had entered their room; and then she told them her story, how her stepmother would have had her killed, but the chauffeur had spared her life, and how she had wandered northwards until she came to their house.

Little Snow-White

When her tale was finished, the miners said: 'Will you see after our household: be our cook, make the beds, wash, sew, and knit for us, and keep everything in neat order? If so, we will keep you here, and you shall want for nothing.'

And Blanche answered: 'Yes, with all my heart and will.' And so she remained with them, and kept their house in order. In the mornings the miners went into the mine and searched for coal, and in the evenings they came home and found their meals ready for them. During the day the maiden was left alone, and therefore the good miners warned her and said: 'Be careful of your stepmother, who will soon know of your being here: therefore let nobody enter the cottage.'

And so the days passed; and then one day Lady Clink went again to her gramophone, which, as I think I said, was the best that money can buy and told the absolute truth, and she turned it on after triumphantly asking:

'Oh gramo, gramo, gramophone,
Which of us is the fairest one?

And the gramophone answered:

'Thou wert the fairest, Lady Clink,
But Blanche is fairer now, I think.
Beside the coal-mine darkly black
She lives with miners—hills at back.'

And then she knew that the chauffeur had deceived her and that Blanche was still alive.

Those who have never been social climbers may not understand how important it is to be indisputably the best-looking person in as much of the world as one knows anything of: to Lady Clink this was vital. To begin with, the considerable sum of money she had spent on the gramophone seemed absolutely wasted, and for every kind of reason she felt her position to be practically impossible. In this mood she set out to find Blanche.

And before many days had passed she came to the mining area under the hills, disguised as a pedlar. And there she cried out the pedlar's cry: 'Fi goo say. Boo goo say.' Which means 'Fine goods for sale. Beautiful goods for sale.' And Blanche peeped out of a window.

'Good day, my good woman,' said Blanche. 'What have you to sell?'

'Fine goods for sale. Beautiful goods for sale,' replied Lady Clink and showed some stays of all colours.

'I may let this honest woman in,' thought Blanche; and she unbolted the door and bargained for a pair of stays. Then when they were bought Blanche looked at the bright things and said: 'What does one do with them?' For she had never seen a pair of stays before.

And Lady Clink said: 'One laces them up like this.' And she fastened up Blanche in the stays.

Now it is unjust to make even a villain out worse than she is, and so I should like the reader to understand that Lady Clink probably laced the stays no tighter than she was accustomed to lace her own in the days when all but the most abandoned wore stays, and when even those neglected them only in Africa. But Blanche, who was unaccustomed to stays, dropped down apparently dead.

And so the miners found her when they returned from searching for coal. They raised her up, and when they saw she was laced too tight, they cut the stays in pieces, and presently she began to breathe again, and by little and little she revived. When the miners now heard what had taken place, they said: 'The old pedlar woman was no other than your wicked stepmother. Take more care of yourself, and let no one enter when we are not with you.'

Meanwhile Lady Clink had reached home and turned on her gramophone, repeating her usual words, to which it replied as before:

'Thou wert the fairest, Lady Clink,
But Blanche is fairer now, I think.
Beside the coal-mine darkly black
She lives with miners—hills at back.'

Which terrified Lady Clink, for she knew that it was one of those gramophones which can speak the truth. So she determined this time to destroy Blanche for certain, and she disguised herself as an old widow and set out once more for the hills of the mining country. There she knocked at the door of the seven miners and called out, 'Good wares to sell,' till Blanche peeped out, but only to tell her that she dare not let her in. But the disguised Lady Clink said: 'Still, you may look.' And she held up all the instruments of a shampoo, with a permanent wave to follow. The sight of these things pleased the maiden so much that she allowed herself to be persuaded and opened the door, and the old woman said: 'Now let me do your hair properly.'

So she washed Blanche's hair and shampooed it; and then she said: 'Would you like it dried by our special process?'

So Blanche said 'Yes,' as ladies frequently do upon such occasions without knowing much of the process. And Lady Clink turned on a gas upon Blanche's hair that dried the hair very quickly, but which at the same time stopped the girl's breathing, as can easily happen with this method of drying the hair, and she fell to the floor and lay still.

Fortunately evening soon came, and the seven miners returned, and as soon as they saw Blanche lying like dead on the ground they suspected old Lady Clink, and soon discovering the smell of gas in the air they opened the window and so revived Blanche, and she related all that had happened; and they warned her again against old Lady Clink, saying: 'Don't you go letting in nobody.'

Meanwhile Lady Clink had returned to Grosvenor Square, and went to her gramophone this time with the feeling that she stood at last alone at the very top of that ladder that she spent her life climbing. 'Oh gramo, gramo, gramophone,' she repeated, 'which of us is the fairest one ?'

'She's at that new record again,' said one of the housemaids. 'Doesn't seem to enjoy it much,' said Gladys; for the

Little Snow-White

gramophone gave the same answer as ever. Naturally she swore that Blanche should die, even if it cost her own life. So she went to the room in which she had, locked up, a box of apples from an orchard that had been sprayed with an arsenic solution, which was used to destroy insects. The apples were ripe, and good to look at, and rain and wind had long ago removed all traces of the solution from the sides of the apples; but sufficient of it remained, as Lady Clink knew, for her purpose, in the hollows where the apples joined on to the stalks. So she disguised herself again, and went back to the mining town, and knocked at the door and Blanche stretched out her head. But she only said: 'I dare not let anyone enter; the seven miners have forbidden me.'

'That's a bit 'ard,' said Lady Clink in disguise. 'I shan't be able to sell my apples. But ye can 'ave one for nothing.'

'No,' said Blanche, 'I daren't take it.'

So Lady Clink began eating the apple herself, both sides of it; and when little remained but the middle Blanche reached out a hand from the window, for it looked a very good apple and it almost seemed as if soon there would be none left. And almost the first bit she ate was the bit at the end, where the apple joins on to the stalk and the arsenic lay in the hollow. And then she fell down dead. 'Ah,' said Lady Clink, 'the whole Miners' Union can't wake you now.' And she went back to Grosvenor Square and turned on the gramophone.

'She's at her old record again,' said Gladys. For this time the gramophone replied to Lady Clink's question:

LORD DUNSANY

'Thou art the fairest, Lady Clink.'

And she left the room looking so happy that they all said afterwards: 'Can't see myself bucked up by a dud record like that. But there's no accounting for tastes.'

But when the miners came back and found Blanche, and saw that they could do nothing for her, they were very unhappy. And after a while the first miner said to the second: 'What will we do about it, mate?' And the second miner said: 'I don't know, I'm sure.' And the third miner said: 'There'll be an inquest and all that.' And the fourth miner said: 'And the police.' And the fifth miner said: 'And us appearing in Court.' And the sixth miner said: 'And I don't know what all.' And the seventh miner being a man of few words said nothing, but just looked at Blanche.

And in the end they decided to keep her where she was and to say nothing about it. So one of them who had a friend in the Glaziers' Union got six pieces of plate glass of the right lengths, and made a glass coffin and put her in, for she looked too fresh to be buried, as is always the case with arsenic. And they wrote in golden letters upon the glass that she was the daughter of Lord Clink, and they put the coffin at the end of the room and locked the door when they went to work, and no one knew anything about it, which they decided was much the best.

Now an effort to outdo Selfridge's had recently been made by Mr. Mooch, and his son Harold Mooch had occasion to travel in that part of the country looking for a few suitable coal-mines to buy, and he happened to come to the house of the seven miners to ask them for lodging for the night. This they gladly accorded him, and being a particularly observant young man, he soon noticed the glass coffin that stood at the end of the room, with the golden letters telling that Blanche was the daughter of Lord Clink. And when he saw it he said to the miners: 'We will buy it from you at a good price, and will pay all costs of packing and cartage ourselves.' But the miners would not sell their little maid. So Harold said: 'Then give her to me, for I cannot live without her.' And when the miners saw that he was so much in earnest, at last they gave him the coffin, and he ordered his chauffeur and valet to put it into his motor. And in the morning he went away with it, from the house of the seven miners.

[133

Now Harold Mooch's chauffeur was by nature a careful driver, but as he was seldom allowed to do less than fifty he was only at his best on a good main road. On the road on which he was driving now, cut up by heavy lorries, there were frequent ruts and hollows, which, when one is doing fifty, give rise to considerable bumps. And one of these bumps shook the bit of apple out of Blanche's mouth, the bit where it joins the stalk, where the arsenic solution had gathered. And the effect of this, as anyone who understands poisons will tell you, was to bring Blanche alive again. She sat up and opened the lid and asked Harold Mooch what was happening. Full of joy Harold answered: 'You are safe with me,' and began to tell her what had happened to her, and how he would like to marry her, and asked her to accompany him to the shop that his father was building along the whole of one side of Piccadilly. And Blanche consented, and I don't think I exaggerate when I say that their marriage was the smartest one of the whole of that London season. Abler pens than mine have described the bridesmaids' dresses, and in every single case the entire description has been printed on the front page; while were I to tell you the actual measurement of the head-lines you would scarcely believe my figures.

To so smart an event as this it was barely possible that Lady Clink should not have been invited; and invited she was. The invitation card, in keeping with the smartness of the event, was in exquisite taste, unless for one minor detail, which Lady Clink, delighted by the magnificence of the card, entirely overlooked, and that was that, in the case of so important a young man as Harold, it had not been thought necessary to put the name of the bride; so that she only knew she was going to the smartest wedding of the year, without actually knowing whom young Mooch was going to marry. What is, however, far more important, when one is so much in the public eye as was Lady Clink, she dressed for the occasion with especial magnificence. On a basis of chiffon rouge, at once seductive and alarming, she wore a truly exquisite jenesaisquoi, that had been specially sent by Pucille from Paris by air. Then she had flounces of tulle, caught up by delicate elephant-green furbelows, topped with a perfect ensemble of pale chinoiseries that had once belonged to Marie Antoinette, the whole toned down with svelte by Julie Limited and trimmed with boar's-tooth blue, in such a way as to lend a refined distinction. In this exquisite kit, and hung with the blackest pearls, she drew herself up before her gramophone and turned it on after her usual question:

'Oh, gramo, gramo, gramophone,
Which of us is the fairest one?'

And it replied:

'Thou wert the fairest, Lady Clink,
Young Mooch's bride's more fair, I think.'

Picture her standing there in her finery, all torn by petty emotions, the pettiest of which was perhaps her angry resolution never to give her gramophone another new needle, and another of which was not to go to the wedding, against which pulled, equally petty, the miserable feeling of curiosity to see this bride of young Mooch, and her reluctance to be left out of any smart function; and these last two emotions won, and she went to the wedding.

But when she saw it was Blanche that had got young Mooch, her fury was indescribable. She remained rooted to the spot, neither kneeling nor sitting down on the proper occasions, and no one was able to make her behave any better. And that, as things fell out, was the last social function that Lady Clink ever attended, for the story of her behaviour was reported next day in such quarters that the Lord Chamberlain cancelled her presentation at Court, striking out her name in red ink with his own hand and carrying away the

LORD DUNSANY

page upon which her name was written, with a pair of silver tongs. And so Lady Clink was never heard of again; but Harold and Blanche lived happily ever after, and she was frequently to be seen in the rooms of the big Piccadilly store, where she took a lively interest in Conditions and studied the ramifications of Up-to-date Service.

Little Snow-White

Aladdin

Or, the
Undertaker and
the Demon

ANNA GORDON KEOWN

Once upon a time there lived an undertaker, a brisk, rosy little man who possessed, but did not rejoice in, the singular name of Aladdin.

Such a name is bound to prove an embarrassment, and in the dour Scottish township to which he had come in pursuance of his profession, Mr. Aladdin many a time had cause to sit down and wish himself a MacGregor.

But all the wishing in the world will not, to be sure, vouchsafe to a southerner a northern name, and the undertaker, of a temperament naturally sanguine and industrious, was not the man to be beaten by sour looks. Opposition did but spur him on to renewed effort, and although he might not be able, by dint of sheer professional enthusiasm, to persuade his fellow-townsmen to die, yet, by throwing them a meaning smile as he passed upon his way, by cracking his whip with a peculiar flourish, by a thousand and one subtle devices known only to the members of the Melancholy Brotherhood, he did encourage them to suppose that, should a really agreeable funeral at any time become necessary, here was the man to conduct it; a supposition which he most certainly justified.

For thirty years then, and with unfailing cheerfulness, he buried the Lamented Hostile and the Deceased Suspicious, and at the end of that time, having won for himself laurels no less substantial than those subscribed by reluctant clients in the past, he retired.

Now in a former reincarnation, as you will doubtless recollect, Aladdin lived in a palace, possessed riches and concubines, married a lovely princess, and all by the simple expedient of polishing a lamp. About our modern Mr. Aladdin there was no nonsense of the kind.

The house to which he had retired, a house set demurely between kirk and police-station, boasted a polished door-knocker, a housekeeper with a squint, and a glimpse of the loch lying winking below the hill. Nobody in his senses could have mistaken No. 2 Stone Street for a palace.

Then again, Mr. Aladdin was a bachelor. No princess, lovely or otherwise, had ever crossed his path, and as for concubines, creatures notably out of place in a household situated beneath the very nose of the kirk, Mr. Aladdin frankly preferred cucumbers, expending, indeed, a great deal of time and money upon these interesting vegetables with a view to increasing his prestige at the local show.

All things considered, the analogy between the modern and the ancient Aladdin was of the slightest, and more particularly as the modern Aladdin possessed not a single lamp: indeed, had it not been for his fatal itch to *polish*, an itch handed down to him by a progenitor of whom he had never even heard, the autumn of his life might have passed in respectable obscurity, and the astonishing history which we are about to relate would, in all probability, never have been written.

But the itch, little as its owner suspected it, was there, and upon a certain drowsy day in mid-July, when the sunshine outside his windows was humming with bees, and his housekeeper, Mrs. Proudie, had just set before him his after-lunch coffee, Mr. Aladdin looked up, struck between the eyes, as it were, by a sudden unaccountable resolution.

'I must certainly polish up my Gaelic,' said he.

It was now that the fun began.

Replacing his coffee cup in its saucer, he proceeded, with the utmost recklessness, to recite certain Gaelic incantations learned of bearded beldames down by the shores of the loch, incantations whose melodious cadences he rolled round his tongue with a scholarly zest, and of whose sinister meaning he had no more idea than the man in the moon . . .

Now the formula of a charm acts very much as does the formula of a safe: given the correct number-sequence, the

ANNA GORDON KEOWN

safe will open; given the correct charm-sequence, magic will be made manifest. To the uninitiated (and who, after all, so uninitiated as our undertaker?) the possibility of arriving at such a sequence was one in twenty thousand. Yet this is precisely what happened.

Conscious of a notable chill in the room in which he sat, he beheld, confronting him from his own hearthrug, a full-grown, hairy demon. The demon was stark naked.

Mr. Aladdin was deeply embarrassed.

For several seconds he stared at the intruder in painful silence; at length, remembering his manners with an effort, he broke that silence with a feeble 'How d'you do?'

Folding his arms across a chest hairy as a ram's, fixing his brilliant eyes upon Mr. Aladdin's face, the demon grinned impudently.

'As to that,' he said, 'it's a little early to make any definite statement. We must simply hope for the best.'

With these words he seated himself in the undertaker's armchair by the fire, picked up the *Church Times*, and fell to reading it with such perfect unconcern that, had it not been for his horns and his tail, he might easily have been mistaken for a Christian gentleman newly strayed from the Turkish bath. Many a Christian gentleman has read the *Church Times* with less lively interest, but on the other hand, there were the horns and tail as large as life, and upon these the undertaker gazed with pardonable horror and excitement.

Was that Mrs. Proudie's step in the passage, Mrs. Proudie come to remove the tablecloth? He devoutly hoped not. The thought of being discovered by a pious woman in conversation with a naked man alarmed him beyond measure. In sheer desperation he blurted out, 'My good Sir . . . My good Sir . . . It's simply not possible for you to remain here. To be candid, I expect distinguished visitors this afternoon . . . the minister himself, and three sidesmen with him, coming to discuss parochial matters. Do but consider my reputation as a churchman! At the risk of appearing inhospitable I really must beg you to leave . . .'

[141

For the second time the demon grinned.

'Nonsense,' said he, 'nonsense. Am I not your devoted slave? Are you not my well-beloved master? When you journey forth, I journey forth. When you stay within-doors, I stay within-doors. Pray let us have no more words about it.'

And he went back, with obvious zest, to his *Church Times*.

Mr. Aladdin stared aghast. Here was a pretty kettle of fish. Here was a nice dilemma for a man with social aspirations, a man who has buried three mayors and kept his horses (dyeing the latter black as jet in every particular except their teeth and their grateful, astonished eyes).

'But,' he began. And even as he spoke, he recognised the futility of argument. About the manner and pronouncements of the demon there was a finality which admitted of no dispute.

'Quite evidently it's a deal easier to call 'em into existence than to make 'em disappear,' thought the unfortunate under-

ANNA GORDON KEOWN

taker, and now, the parlour clock striking two, he realised that he must call up all his powers of resource if the situation were not to prove too much for him. Addressing his unwelcome visitor with what politeness he could muster, he said briskly:

'Very well then. So be it. In that case, the first thing to do is to find you some clothes. Behind the times as Drumlochrie may in many respects be, it's no place for a naked man. We're somewhat different in figure, still, I daresay I can rig you up.'

His glance resting upon Mr. Aladdin's tubby body and wrinkled trousers, the demon ran experimental hands down his own lean flanks.

'To wear the garments of so elevated a being,' he began, 'were to experience the most profound delight. On the other hand, I should much prefer . . .'

But the undertaker was in no mood for objections.

'Follow me,' he commanded.

Now the stairs in No. 2 Stone Street were narrow and difficult at the best of times, and Mr. Aladdin had scarcely reached the first landing when, hearing sounds of distress behind him, he looked over his shoulder to see the demon climbing up on all-fours.

Man of the world as he chose to consider himself, the sight unnerved Mr. Aladdin.

'That won't do,' he protested sharply, 'that won't do at all. Go down again.'

For a moment the demon stood there defying him.

Aladdin

'What won't do?' he muttered, a sullen expression distorting his normally pleasant countenance.

Quite suddenly he turned and climbed down again.

'You will find me exceedingly willing to learn,' said he with unexpected meekness.

'Good,' said his master, 'then watch me. Grasp the rail in your right hand, so. Now place your right foot on the stair and raise yourself. Now your left. See how I do it.'

Mr. Aladdin's stout little figure waddled upstairs, the demon in his wake. Arrived at the top, he turned to beam.

'Excellent. Quite excellent. Already you do it nearly as well as I myself. You promise, I see, to be an apt pupil.'

But the demon looked depressed.

'Alas!' said he, 'you flatter me. My belly does not waggle from side to side as yours does. I do not puff and pant. I implore you to be patient with me.'

These words, innocent in themselves maybe, struck a sad chill in the heart of our undertaker. Once a considerable athlete, he was naturally sensitive upon the subject of his increasing girth, and he now shot the demon an angry glance from under his bushy brows.

'No need to pant when you are standing still,' said he crossly. 'You are not a dog.'

'Certainly not,' said the demon, 'far from it. I take myself to be a male human being. Am I right?'

Mr Aladdin led the way to his bedroom. 'Perfectly right,' said he, smiling in spite of himself, 'perfectly right. But a male human being is simply known as a man.'

ANNA GORDON KEOWN

'But a male human being,' repeated the demon, 'is simply known as a man.'

'That's it,' said Mr. Aladdin, and he began to consider, as he pulled odd garments from his wardrobe, how best he should tackle the problem of the horns and the tail. Here was a difficulty demanding the deepest thought; it was not, however, insuperable. At the end of five minutes, a five minutes occupied by the demon in making faces at himself in the mirror, in brushing his tail with a clothes-brush, and in hanging ecstatically out of the window, Mr. Aladdin's mind was made up.

'You shall wear this,' he said, producing from a chest of drawers his magnificent undertaker's suit of rusty black, 'you shall wear this. In the lining of the coat I will cut a hole with my penknife, and (are you paying attention to what I am saying?) into this hole you shall tuck your tail. With the help of heaven,' added he piously, 'together with good management, nobody will suspect its existence. Kindly leave my clothes-brush alone and come away from that window.'

'Certainly,' said the demon, 'certainly I will.'

'Very well then. Get into the suit without delay.'

The demon was obedience itself. Relinquishing the beautiful clothes-brush, he struggled into a suit which ended high above his ankles and far above his wrists. With his tail tucked in and his neck adorned with a stiff collar and tie, he stood regarding himself blissfully in the glass.

'I look very nice indeed,' said he, smiling childishly. But the smile died quickly. There was no need for him to tap those tell-tale horns of his with skinny forefinger; already his master had guessed the cause of his anxiety.

'Just so,' said Mr. Aladdin,' just so,'

He was sitting on the side of his bed swinging his legs; to tell truth, he was beginning to enjoy himself immensely. When he spoke again it was with an air of authority.

'You shall wear my top hat,' he decided, 'both indoors and out of doors you shall wear it. Never for a single instant must you be seen without it. You understand?'

The demon appeared to understand perfectly.

'And now,' continued Mr. Aladdin, 'there is another little matter,' and he unlocked a small brown box and produced a splendid watch-chain.

'This,' said he kindly, 'you shall wear upon holidays and high days. It will lend cachet and tone to the whole rig-out. A little old-fashioned, perhaps, but still quite in the mode, and if I ever find you fiddling with it or treating it carelessly, back it shall go into its box under lock and key. Is that clear?'

The demon was radiant. He said it was perfectly clear.

'Good,' said Mr. Aladdin.

It was an arresting figure which followed him down to his front parlour a few moments later; the minister and his three sidesmen, seeing the towering, top-hatted stranger over by the fireplace, stood stock still in astonishment. The minister in particular couldn't take his eyes off him; never in his life had he imagined the existence of anything so magnificently sombre. With a politeness very different from his usual suave condescension, he begged to be introduced.

ANNA GORDON KEOWN

Mr. Aladdin gulped. Many a time in the past he had cajoled clients into extravagances far beyond those dictated by prudent affection; faced with a situation like the present, that practised eloquence was to stand him in good stead.

'Why certainly,' said he, 'with all the pleasure in life.' And he now announced, upon the spur of a moment particularly inspired, 'Allow me to present to you my brother. My brother, you must know, is a bishop, a missionary bishop. He comes to me on a short visit . . . a holiday made necessary by his health . . . from islands west of Europe . . . islands so very far away that really and truly they can scarcely be considered to be anywhere on the civilised map. Civilised, did I say? Snakes. Wild boars. Every kind of monster, both by land and sea. Only one boat wins through to home waters in ten years . . . gobbled by sharks . . . riddled by whales . . . terrible . . . unthinkably terrible.'

Receiving this surprising information full in the face, Mr. Aladdin's audience blinked defencelessly; encouraged by this sight he continued, in an undertone intended solely for the newcomers; 'Cannibals . . . child-eaters . . . converted mumbo-jumbo worshippers . . . my brother over-conscientious . . . health ruined . . . climate a swamp . . . you notice he is obliged to keep his hat on in the house . . . you naturally wonder why . . .'; and now, concluding his oration with a low hiss which caused the minister to start violently, he added the awful word 'ASTHMA.'

It was the longest speech he had ever made in his life. And by far the most effectual.

'If I'd thought all night I could have hit upon no better fib,' thought he to himself complacently, and indeed it was not difficult to read upon the faces of his visitors the dawning of a respect which no mere thirty years of undeviating truthfulness could have evoked. A retired undertaker is one thing. A retired undertaker boasting a bishop brother with asthma is another.

So courteously did the minister question the distinguished stranger as to the habits, appearance and beliefs of his far-off flock, so entertainingly did the stranger reply, that parochial business for the time being was completely waived, and upon the striking of four o'clock on the parlour mantel Mr. Aladdin, keeping his wits with difficulty and pretending not to notice Mrs. Proudie's expression of awe, ordered a tray of tea and a plate of buns.

Never before had the minister broken bread in his house, and it was with considerable pride that Mr. Aladdin did the honours of his plush-covered table. As for the demon, he was carrying off the situation unbelievably well. A little uncertain as to the management of his tail, he had excused himself from leaving the fire on the plea of a treacherous climate.

'In the country where I live,' said he, 'business is invariably carried on lying down, owing to the overpowering heat. No man would think of moving without his private pillow, and if you were to come into the market when the moobungs (that is to say, fruits) are being sold, you would scarcely hear the crying of the blaterhoodoos (that is to say, merchants) for the harmonious snoring of the general public.'

ANNA GORDON KEOWN

To this story, and to many another like it, the company listened with grave attention, only the minister daring to interrupt with an occasional cough or a polite 'Weel weel!' and upon the company taking its leave Mr. Aladdin congratulated the demon in no uncertain manner. He also ordered the spare bedroom to be swept and made ready, an order which, when she learnt that they were to house a live bishop, Mrs. Proudie was only too ready to execute. From this day onwards life assumed a different aspect for our hero.

Never, up to the present, had he been able to cut a social dash in any broad sense of the word; apart from the privilege of subscribing to the minister's funds and of taking round the plate on Sundays, his amusements had been almost entirely restricted to cucumbers. Never, never had he been invited out to parties, a form of dissipation for which he secretly longed, and at those minor church socials to which he was occasionally bidden, the good citizens of Drumlochrie acknowledged him with a mournful inclination of the head, as though they saw in him a perpetual funeral rather than a warmhearted little man hungry for friendship. All this was now altered.

News of a missionary bishop unable to dispense with his hat spread like wild-fire in a town avid for gossip. The minister's wife relayed it to the sewing guild, the sewing guild to the Girls' Friendly, the friendly girls to their sweethearts, and in two days' time Mr. Aladdin and his demon awoke to discover themselves the most sought-after men in the town. Polite notes showered a letter-box hitherto innocent of correspondence other than bills, carriages were frequently to be seen before the modest hall-door; wherever they went, the undertaker and his brother, there were sure to be greetings and handclasps, invitations to high tea, and affectionate inquiries concerning the bishop's asthma.

All this was pleasant to a degree, and Mr. Aladdin enjoyed it; had it not been for his anxiety on the score of the demon's behaviour his happiness would have known no bounds. In this respect he need have feared nothing. At high teas, at meetings, at receptions arranged in his honour, the bishop comported himself with a patronising affability which won all hearts. The presence of that commanding figure and shining hat were sufficient in themselves to procure the success of any gathering, and Mr. Aladdin, moving in the wake of so brilliant a personage, had to pinch himself in order to remember that here in fact was no bishop, but rather a fraud, a creature with horns and tail, a monster.

Invitations to 'speak' poured in upon his distinguished brother; with all such invitations Mr. Aladdin took a considered line from the start.

'Pray do not press him,' he begged. 'It hurts him to say "No," but there it is . . . doctors unanimous . . . throat trouble . . .'

Against this edict the demon rebelled as openly as he dared.

'I *want* to speak,' he protested, 'I want to show off my lovely suit and my watch-chain. Where's the point in being smart if nobody sees me?'

ANNA GORDON KEOWN

But his master remained firm.

'You shall *not* speak. It would be highly indecent and extremely unsafe. As for nobody seeing you, will your vanity never be satisfied? Four nights this week,' said he, proudly expanding his chest, 'four nights this week we have supped in houses other than our own, and to-night, as you will remember, we attend the annual concert of the Lads' Forward Movement. There you may enjoy publicity without risk, and if I hear another word about this "speaking," off comes the watch-chain for good and all. I mean it.'

'Yours to command,' said the demon,' mine to obey,' but he now added slyly, as though talking to himself, 'Dear me! How terribly awkward it would be for my adored master if my top hat were to blow off when I walk with him in the windy high street.'

Despite this threat, the harmony of the home was but little troubled by active insubordination. If occasionally the demon grew sullen, murmuring that he would assuredly display his tail in public, take off his hat to the ladies, or otherwise disgrace his master, one look from Mr. Aladdin was sufficient to recall him to a condition of abject obedience.

To tell truth, our demon had a past, and that a very unfortunate past; in previous incarnations he had been guilty of more than one unforgivable blunder, and these blunders had considerably shaken his nerve. There was, for instance, that occasion upon which, commanded to produce a princess, he had procured a camel, leading it blandly in by the nose to the feet of an amorous and infuriated master. Even now, breakfasting thousands of years later with Mr. Aladdin in his sunny parlour, this painful episode recurred to vex, causing the demon to shiver so violently that his new master, always kind-hearted and considerate, rang the bell and ordered more coal to be put on the fire. Our demon, in short, was the victim of an inferiority complex which not the wearing of a gold watch-chain could completely cure. Even in his present existence he sometimes made mistakes.

It so happened that at the concert of the Lads' Forward Movement, a concert for which Mr. Aladdin and his brother were accorded seats of honour, the pianist was a rollicking young woman by the name of Ogilvy. Now the demon, trained by long practice in finding lovely women for exacting taskmasters, had a roving eye. No sooner had Miss Ogilvy struck her first resounding chord than, consulting his programme with a deal of shortsighted fidgeting, he gave a loud snort. This snort, in the rows immediately before and behind, was charitably ascribed to asthma. Actually it was nothing of the kind.

It would have been an exaggeration, perhaps, to describe Miss Ogilvy as a lovely woman, but in a community not over-blessed with beauty she certainly appeared a fine upstanding creature. The enthusiasm with which she banged her piano argued youthful energy, and she possessed, moreover, a cast of countenance distinctly oriental in mould, her grandfather having been a philandering sailor. The applause following upon the first song had scarcely died, when the bishop, leaning towards his brother and speaking in a voice which must have penetrated to the furthest ends of the hall, was heard to remark:

'Should you like me to buy Miss Ogilvy for you? She is young and plump, and I daresay I could get her at a reasonable price.'

These words, emanating from a highly respectable prelate, caused, as may be imagined, a good deal of nudging and staring, and it was not until the general coffee-drinking half an hour later that his brother, looking somewhat flushed, was able to explain the extraordinary occurrence.

'In his lordship's diocese,' said he, smiling unhappily, 'the parishioners are mainly cannibals, and it is their uncomfortable custom to admit to the church choir only those who are young and plump. These choir members they buy in, paying them for their services. My dear brother was so much impressed by Miss Ogilvy's performance this evening that he suggested her acquisition for the kirk harmonium. Not . . .' he added hastily, seeing the eye of the official harmonium player fixed gloomily upon him, 'not, of course, that we could possibly better our present musician, Mr. MacReady. That goes without saying.'

Once arrived home, the undertaker delivered a lecture suitable to the gravity of the occasion and the enormity of the offence.

'But I thought I was *pleasing* you,' whimpered the demon, almost in tears. 'It's very poor fun for you having that cantankerous Proudie woman about, and you can't deny she squints dreadfully. Miss Ogilvy is a charming young lady, her piano would fit nicely between the sideboard and the tallboy, and here she could bang away to her heart's content. Think of the long winter evenings! After Miss Ogilvy had finished banging, she would draw the curtains and set the kettle on the fire. I shouldn't be at all surprised if she made you a nice cup of tea, and you know perfectly well that's more than the Proudie has ever done.'

'Miss Ogilvy,' replied Mr. Aladdin, shocked, 'comes of a most respectable family. Her father is the leading dentist in Drumlochrie.'

'That,' said the demon, 'is all to the good. He will pull out your teeth for the sheer pleasure of it. What you need is Romance with a big R, and now, when it's offered to you, what do you do? You refuse it.'

'Romance?' said the undertaker. 'Fiddlesticks!'

But inside himself he wasn't so sure. For a long time now he had secretly admired the delightful Miss Ogilvy; strange indeed that his demon should have noticed the one young lady in Drumlochrie who, when he met her out shopping, had power to put him in a bashful flutter. The more Mr. Aladdin pondered the demon's words, the more sensible did they appear; deep down in his heart he began to cherish an ambition of which, in former days, he would never have dreamed.

'To-morrow evening,' said he briskly, anxious that the demon should not guess how deep an impression his words had made, 'to-morrow evening I go to the monthly "social." For you I have refused, fearing there might be prayers. If,

ANNA GORDON KEOWN

however, you will promise to behave yourself, coming in carefully on the "Amens," I daresay I might stretch a point and take you with me.'

Hearing these joyful words, the demon's depression vanished.

'And may I sport my watch-chain?'

'Certainly, my dear fellow,' replied Mr. Aladdin, whose mind was at the other side of the town with Miss Ogilvy; 'most certainly you may.'

So the matter was settled, and next evening the pair of them, Mr. Aladdin in his best grey suit and the demon splendid in black, betook themselves to the social. Gone were the days when Mr. Aladdin, pushing the door timidly open, crept into a back bench. With the towering figure of the bishop beside him his entry, as he realised with satisfaction, was in the nature of a social event.

'Bear in mind my instructions,' he whispered, as, opening the door with a proud authority, he motioned the bishop to precede him. Already the fun was at its height.

Urns were hissing, jaws were munching, and the minister was in the act of reading out the week's notices. Through silent rows of masticating parishioners Mr. Aladdin piloted his demon; cornering him discreetly between himself and an urn, he turned politely to the lady on his left. With this lady, under cover of the minister's announcements, he engaged in one of those particularly stimulating conversations for which Scottish socials are famous.

'A fine night, Mrs. Pim.'

'It's no bad.'

'How is your husband to-night?'

'He's bad.' Here Mrs. Pim helped herself to a fourth bannock. 'Awfu' bad,' she added, between mouthfuls.

'Is he indeed, Madam? I'm sorry to hear it,' said Mr. Aladdin, his professional interest aroused.

Mrs. Pim washed down the bannock with strong tea.

'Eh weel! He'll be worrse before he's better, I'm thinkin'. There's no knowin' which of us'll be the next to go.'

'True enough,' agreed Mr. Aladdin, taking a thoughtful glance round the assembly and forgetting, for one delightful moment, that he was retired from business. 'True enough!'

Refreshed by this interchange of thought, he now caught for the first time, and to his unqualified horror, the drift of the minister's remarks.

'And I've nae doot he'll do us the grate honour of speakin' a few worrds. Comin' frae a far-off heathenish country he'll hae much to tell us for our guid, and I'm sure he'll noe refuse us just this once. . . .'

Before Mr. Aladdin well knew what was happening, the bishop was on his feet, and there now followed such a harangue as never, surely, since the world began, enlivened a kirk social.

Opening his oration with many an expression of seemly piety, the demon gradually and unobtrusively changed his tactics; before three minutes were gone he was inciting his simple audience to every crime on the calendar, but in such subtle phraseology that not the minister himself, poor

ANNA GORDON KEOWN

trusting soul, had the slightest suspicion of its infernal drift. Only Mr. Aladdin, gazing desperately around him upon the spell-bound company, grasped in some measure the trend of the discourse, but even he, sworn admirer as he was of inspired eloquence, was carried away upon the tide of general enthusiasm.

When the bishop sat down, you might have heard the proverbial pin drop. Imperfectly as they had understood his lordship's arguments, the good folk of Drumlochrie yet recognised a fine speaker when they heard one, and the clapping and floor-thumping which burst forth upon every side made the demon flush with modest pleasure.

'Without being unduly puffed up,' he whispered to his master, 'I think I may claim to have surpassed myself.'

If he had expected praise from this quarter he was doomed to disappointment. Mr. Aladdin looked at him darkly and said nothing.

'I say I think I may claim to have surpassed myself,' reiterated the demon more loudly, and he was just about to remove his hat and mop his brow when a sharp kick on the shins recalled him to a proper sense of his responsibilities. This incident, as may be imagined, greatly perturbed Mr. Aladdin.

The fact of the matter was this: despite its many charms and advantages, the situation threatened to become dangerous. For one thing, there was the Proudie. The manner of that joyless female was daily growing increasingly joyless; in his more fearful moments Mr. Aladdin believed that she suspected the truth, and in this belief, had he but known it, he was not far out.

To serve early morning tea to a bishop who sleeps, not in his bed like a Christian, but stark naked upon the floor, was almost more than Mrs. Proudie could put up with. Upon two occasions she thought she saw (naturally, so modest a woman did not remain to stare, but setting the tea just within the door, averted her horrified gaze as soon as might be) something in the nature of a tail ... impossible, of course, but unless those sharp eyes of hers deceived her. . . . Bishop indeed! Mrs. Proudie bided her time, said nothing and looked a world of smothered emotion.

Secondly, there was Mr. Aladdin's courtship of Miss Ogilvy. Since the demon had obligingly voiced his private inclinations in this direction, he hadn't allowed the grass to grow under his feet. Unknown to the demon, he had obtained the consent of the young lady, together with the approval of her parents, and it now began to strike him, as it strikes many a man contemplating matrimony, that where two are company, three are none. Yet how to shake off the demon?

Halfway to Miss Ogilvy's house of an evening, a blush rose stuck jauntily in his buttonhole, and in his heart the dreams of a happy lover, Mr. Aladdin's attention would be arrested by the sound of panting in his wake; turning sharply round, he would find the missionary bishop grinning at his elbow. This was too much! Conscious of the extreme ingratitude of his own conduct, he began to cast about for a means of getting rid of his benefactor.

ANNA GORDON KEOWN

'By Gaelic I called him into being,' said he to himself, as he sat stiffly beside Miss Ogilvy beneath the pink satin lampshade in her father's parlour. 'By Gaelic, perchance, I may persuade him to vanish.'

In his bath, in his bed, in the company of his beloved cucumber frames, the undertaker took to muttering all such incantations as he could conveniently call to mind. Alas! The perfect charm-sequence does not wait upon men twice in a lifetime; as far as results were concerned he might have been repeating nursery rhymes. The demon flourished, Mrs. Proudie glowered, Miss Ogilvy languished, and the situation became hourly more unsatisfactory. It was not until many weary days had passed that he bethought himself of an expedient. It occurred to him at breakfast.

Speaking with an abruptness which made the demon scald himself with the coffee, he remarked:

'Next Sunday I am off on a nice little jaunt to Wales . . . to bury my nephew. I fear I shall require my suit.'

The demon stared.

'Yes, and my top hat too,' continued Mr. Aladdin, steeling his heart against the demon's expression of piteous dismay. 'It has occurred to me,' he continued, gathering courage as he proceeded, 'that a holiday wouldn't do *you* any harm, you look as though you could do with a little fresh air. Now whereas lots of people here in Drumlochrie possess watchchains, nobody at THE TOWERS has ever seen one, and should you by any chance decide to go to THE TOWERS, you would be certain of being enormously admired.'

At the words 'enormously admired' the demon cheered visibly.

'Where are these towers you speak of,' he inquired cautiously, 'and are you quite sure nobody there would have a watch-chain?'

'THE TOWERS,' said Mr. Aladdin, trying to speak calmly, 'is a nudist camp, and as for the watch-chain, I'm prepared to swear there won't be another in the whole place. THE TOWERS,' continued he, quoting by memory from a brochure carefully hidden away in his desk, 'THE TOWERS is the spiritual home of right-thinking and nice-minded peoples. It is surrounded by health-giving woods and sylvan orchards, it lies open to the four winds of heaven, and it is situated high above sea level. In a civilisation given over to noise and false modesty . . . modesty . . .'

Here Mr. Aladdin's memory unfortunately failed him. He put on his spectacles and continued more simply, 'It will cure your asthma for certain.'

'I haven't got asthma,' the demon pointed out.

'For heaven's sake don't start arguing,' implored his master. 'Now here's another very important point. If you choose to go about without clothes at THE TOWERS, nobody will care a pin. You've complained a lot lately, you know you have, about the scratchiness of my under vests.'

'So I have,' agreed the demon doubtfully, 'and they *are* scratchy, but . . .'

'Needless to say,' continued Mr. Aladdin suavely, 'the four winds of heaven (upon which this nudist camp appears to have a unique claim of some sort) would blow upon no visitor so distinguished as yourself. Not only would you dazzle the right-minded and nice-thinking peoples with my gold watch-chain, but upon second thoughts I should be prepared to lend you my umbrella.'

'Your best umbrella?' asked the demon quickly.

Mr. Aladdin hesitated. The sacrifice involved was a severe one, and he had intended, quite frankly, to part with his second-best; thinking the matter over quickly he decided to be ruled by circumstances. A new umbrella, after all, may be purchased any day of the week, whereas in the whole wide world there was but one Miss Ogilvy.

'My new umbrella,' said he, 'the one with the ivory handle.'

The demon was radiant. As always, his radiance soon gave way to depressing doubts.

'My horns?' he asked anxiously.

'They'll love 'em,' said Mr. Aladdin largely.

'And my tail?'

'Perfect, my dear fellow, absolutely perfect for a place of the kind. Nature's their watchword at a nudist camp.'

'Is a tail nature?' asked the demon, still rather anxious.

'Surely, surely,' replied Mr. Aladdin vaguely. Now that he had Miss Ogilvy to think about, his mind often wandered.

'I can't travel naked to THE TOWERS,' objected the demon, whose sense of propriety had come on astonishingly in the last six months.

Mr. Aladdin had thought of this.

'You shall travel south in my suit and top hat,' said he generously. 'Arrived at THE TOWERS, you will strip and post them back to me.' And he rang the bell for a Mrs. Proudie piously eavesdropping.

'His lordship,' said he, 'is going away this afternoon on a round of important visits. You will kindly pack for him in my beautiful new suitcase with the shiny straps. The motorcar will be at the door shortly after lunch.' His plans once matured, Mr. Aladdin sat back to congratulate himself upon his own tireless ingenuity. The bishop was beside himself with joy and excitement, Mrs. Proudie had twice smiled her thin-lipped smile, and it really did seem that everything, including the bishop, was going off splendidly.

But our human triumphs have a habit of turning dull in the mind which conceives them, and when, after a hastily partaken lunch, they stood awaiting the car on the front steps, Mr. Aladdin's heart sank. Ogilvy or no Ogilvy, he was going to miss his companion.

Beneath the weight of coming separation the bishop bore up manfully. He was dividing his last moments with his master between kissing his hand to Mrs. Proudie through the railings, playing with the straps of the suitcase, and craning his neck for the expected car.

'Will it *never* come?' cried he, indecently agog to be off. Mr. Aladdin was hurt.

'Send me a line from time to time,' said he. 'I shall be anxious to hear how you get along at THE TOWERS.'

ANNA GORDON KEOWN

The bishop did not reply. He had stopped his light-hearted play and was standing, legs far apart, deep in gloomy thought.

'It's going to be extremely difficult to wear it when one is naked,' he grumbled.

'Wear what?' asked Mr. Aladdin.

At that moment the car arrived. Without so much as a handshake or a word of farewell, the bishop prepared to depart. Chattering of future conquests like a happy child, armed with his master's ivory-handled umbrella, he skipped nimbly out of sight, banging the door after him. It was not until the taxi had started away down Stone Street that he appeared at the window.

'I've got it,' he shouted gleefully, showing to the full extent of his gums that surprising grin which Mr. Aladdin was never to see again; 'I've got it . . . I shall tie it round my stomach with a stout piece of string.'

Sindbad the Sailor
His Eighth and Last Voyage

ERIC LINKLATER

It is related that there was once, in the antiquity of time and the procession of days, a porter in the city of Baghdad, called Sindbad, who by the inscrutable purpose of Allah was raised from poverty to a pleasant estate and the enjoyment of plenty. He attracted the attention of a wealthy merchant whose name was the same as his own. This merchant, who had made many voyages and encountered a multitude of curious adventures, was called Sindbad the Sailor, and his chief pleasure was the entertainment of selected friends. Having assembled such a company and regaled them with strange meats and unusual wines, he would call for silence and relate to them the story of one or other of his seven voyages. Sindbad the Porter, being a willing listener and resourceful in the discovery of expressions of surprise and admiration, speedily became the favourite guest, and Sindbad the Sailor presently appointed him to be his major-domo. Then for a long time they lived together in perfect joy and friendship.

But when Sindbad the Porter had heard the seven stories of the seven voyages repeated seventy times, a weariness fell upon his spirit, and he said to himself, 'I think it is easier to become inured to hardship itself than to the narration of tales of hardship.' Thereupon, having made into a parcel such of his belongings as he thought would be useful to him, he left the house of Sindbad the Sailor and joined a party of merchants who were setting out on a far journey in the hope of selling their goods at a profit commensurate with the distance they would travel. But before they had gone very far they turned aside to examine a ruined tower where gold was said to be buried. This tower was the abode of an evil Jinni who was so enraged by the merchants that he attacked them, and having slain some made prisoners of the rest. Among the latter was Sindbad the Porter. In the passage of time the captive merchants, all but Sindbad, fell sick and died, and after many years the Jinni himself grew old. His vigilance having relaxed, Sindbad the Porter at last succeeded in making his escape. Travelling slowly, because of his great age, he came again to Baghdad and entered the city by the gate of the caravans.

He soon observed that great changes had taken place in the manners of the people. Women, not all of them veiled, moved freely in the streets, and the grave demeanour of the merchants had been equally impaired by an excessive devotion to commerce and their immoderate pursuit of pleasure. Such music as he heard was nothing like the songs that Ishak of Mosul and Abu Nowas had been wont to sing, for it was vulgar in tone, undisciplined in its rhythm, and the words were not likely to commend themselves to persons of taste and discrimination. Yet notwithstanding these and many other signs of decadence, the city was wealthier than it had been and the people were clearly accustomed to all kinds of luxury.

[165

Making his way to the house of Sindbad the Sailor, Sindbad the Porter was overjoyed to learn that his former benefactor was still alive, and having requested a slave to go before and announce his name, he followed as quickly as his shrivelled legs would bear him. The two old men embraced with tears and exclamations of joy, and in the pleasures of reunion the many years of their separation were soon forgotten.

As in former times the great hall was arranged and ready for feasting, but now there were no guests to share the delicacies displayed upon gold and silver plate, but only a few servants, old themselves and stooping beneath the burden of their years. With praiseworthy discretion Sindbad the Porter made no allusion to this state of affairs, but having washed his hands sat down and ate his fill. When the meal was over he related, with commendable brevity, all that had happened to him during his imprisonment in the Jinni's tower, and then, observing an expectant look in the eyes of Sindbad the Sailor, enquired if he had recently undertaken any journey by land or sea that could compare in interest with those of his early manhood. Sindbad the Sailor replied that he had but lately returned from a voyage so remarkable in every way that all the stories he had previously told were nothing compared with the astonishing adventures he was now prepared to relate. Thereupon Sindbad the Porter disposed himself with all the comfort he could, and Sindbad the Sailor began the story of his eighth and last voyage.

You must know, my friend—yet none but Allah knows all—that for many years after you set out upon your disastrous journey, I continued to live in Baghdad, enjoying to the full the great riches I had gained. I took unfailing delight in providing lavish entertainment for my friends, and I gave bounteously to the poor, the widow, and the orphan. So great was my enjoyment of this kind of life that I felt no desire to incur the dangers and uncertainty of foreign travel, and had it not been for the earnest entreaty of the Syndic of the merchants I would never have gone to sea again.

I must tell you, however, that there was a fly in the ointment of my beatitude. It grew increasingly clear that the people of Baghdad were becoming so addicted to worldly pleasures that their wits were now entirely spent in devising new fashions of amusement, and though I seldom went out into the streets and the bazaar I readily perceived the decadence of the time, the decay of morals, the decline of learning, and the desuetude of skilful playing upon stringed instruments. Consider my disgust, however, when I heard that many people, discontented with the felicities of dry land, were seeking idle happiness at sea. I was filled with anger to find that the hardships and peril of seafaring, from which I had won all my wealth, should now be thought an occasion for mirth, and my indignation knew no bounds when I was told that in the port of Bassora a trading vessel was being refurnished with great luxury for no better purpose than cruising in search of pleasure. It was in order to confer with me about this foolish project that the Syndic of the merchants came one evening to my house, and such was the power of his eloquence that before he went I had agreed to undertake yet another voyage.

The Syndic did not hide his contempt for people who would pay large sums of money in order to experience the tedium and dangers of the sea, but he was careful to explain that the company of merchants who had chartered the vessel had every hope of making a good profit on the venture. He then declared that he was anxious to obtain the services of someone well acquainted with remote and interesting parts of the earth, who would act as commentator, guide, and director to the passengers.

I answered that in all Baghdad there was no one whose knowledge of curious islands and the monsters who inhabit them could equal my own, and I related for his instruction the story of my voyage to the Island of the Rocs, and some part of my adventures in the Mountain of the Dead.

'It is well known that your experience is unique,' he intervened, 'and that is why I have come to ask you to accept the

ERIC LINKLATER

office of mentor, or cruise director, upon this new voyage. For your services we shall pay you the sum of ten thousand dinars.'

After some further conversation, in which I made it clear that my life in Baghdad was so pleasant that I had no desire to exchange it ever again for the insecurity and toil of seafaring, it was agreed that my fee should be twenty thousand dinars, and that I should enjoy in addition the sole right of trading and bartering for curios, ornaments, and other trifles of the kind that travellers are accustomed to purchase in foreign parts. These negotiations having been concluded, I embarked on a river vessel bound for Bassora, and spent some days examining the ship that was being refitted there.

I found that she had been equipped with every imaginable luxury. A great hall, such as you will see only in the houses of the wealthiest merchants, had been constructed in the hold of the ship, and in the fore part a hammam had been built. Every one of the passengers had a room of his own, fully furnished with a mat, a mattress, a ewer, and a basin, and such quantities of meat, fruit, and delicacies of all kinds were being carried aboard as would glorify the kitchens of the Caliph himself. There was, in short, comfort enough to satisfy a Sybarite, and I marvelled afresh at the wit of man that will both invent a new desire and devise its gratification.

When the time grew near for the ship to set sail, the passengers arrived in Bassora and came aboard. They were eighty in number, and of all shapes and ages. Ya Allah! there were women less comely than the hinder parts of a cow, stricken with age and wizened by the years. There were men whom rich living had swollen to the size of an elephant, and others in whom excess had dried up all their sap, making mummies of them before their time. Yet good and evil lie in the same Hand, and all this ugliness came side by side with a great deal of beauty. Among the passengers were several girls very disturbing to the senses, and my attention was specially taken by a virgin with remarkable hips, and by another more lovely than the moon upon her fourteenth night. There were also some very handsome young men. There was in particular a youth called Hassan, upon whose cheek the rose had written its beauty and whose waist was pliant as bamboo. The darkness of his eyes was more dangerous than a scorpion's venom, and the movement of his walking, if seen from behind, was like the undulation of sandhills. The faces of the old women darkened with desire when they observed him, and the young women trembled and grew pale.

The Emir Muhamad Al-Hashami, the Caliph's lieutenant in Bassora, together with the chief magistrates and a huge crowd of idlers from all the seventy streets of Bassora, came to bid us farewell, and there was a great hubbub on the quay when we cast off the mooring-ropes. But the clamour on board was nearly as great, for all the women babbled together, and the men likewise, and among the crew there were musicians who played upon a variety of instruments, so that the captain had great difficulty in making his orders heard. By the mercy of Allah we at last came to open sea, and on the second day I summoned the passengers into the great hall

ERIC LINKLATER

of the ship, and delivered to them a discourse upon foreign travel. I dealt with the natural features of the islands we were to visit, and I related such part of my own adventures as I thought likely to improve their understanding of the manners and customs of the natives, and to help them in identifying cannibals, ogres, and marine monsters. But even thus early in the voyage the passengers showed no great willingness to learn or to listen, but rather chose idly to talk among themselves. It is well known that Allah hates him who yawns: how then shall He excuse those who, without hiding their shame, fell fast asleep while I was describing the fearful rhinoceros, whose horn is ten cubits long, with which it will pierce and kill the largest elephants; but the fat of the elephant, running down into the eyes of the rhinoceros, blinds it and makes it fall, whereupon a roc, swooping down from its nest in the mountains, will often carry off both animals to feed its young?

There was a woman among the passengers, a widow called Dalila, whom I came to fear more than the roc itself. She had once, no doubt, been handsome enough, but that time was long past. Yet a fire made with cow-dung will keep its heat though it shows no flame, and the heat of youth was still so strong in her that she spent her whole time in pursuing some man or other, now the captain, now that rose of youth, Hassan, and now myself. Nor, in the small confines of a ship, could one escape her loud voice, her ogling smiles, and her provocative gestures. So presently I thought of a scheme by which we might rid ourselves of her, and one day, chancing to notice a kind of mound or hummock in the sea, I cried 'An island! an island!', and bade the captain steer towards it.

The passengers all ran to that side of the ship from which the island could be clearly seen, and I rubbed my hands to think that my plan would shortly be successful. For you must realise that this was no island, but a giant whale, basking on the surface of the sea, and perhaps that same whale on whose back I had so rashly gone ashore on the first of my voyages. But as we came nearer the passengers began to laugh and to utter scornful remarks, and when I repeated, 'Here is a desert island: who would like to go and explore it?'—knowing that Dalila was always the first to claim her share in any pleasure—there was a general cry, 'O Sindbad, now you are talking through your turban! That is no island, but a whale, and what you would have us think are rocks and trees upon it, are no more than barnacles and a little green weed.' As Allah lives, the people of to-day will believe nothing, for they have neither faith nor manners, and so my plan for getting rid of the widow Dalila was ruined, and all the passengers made mock of me.

But I remembered for what purpose I had accompanied them, and I controlled my anger. Presently I summoned them again into the great hall and told them we were now approaching an island that was one of the most dangerous places on earth, for it was solely inhabited by apes and ogres. I said that we would sail close by the shores of this island, but that on no account would we cast anchor, for then a multitude of apes would overrun the ship and make us their prisoners, and that would be the end of us.

Now on the following day we came within sight of the island and steered towards it. When we were no more than the third part of a parasang away, the captain uttered a loud cry, beat himself on the face, tore out the greater part of his beard, and rent his garments. 'What is the matter?' we asked him. 'O passengers of pleasure,' he answered, 'the wind has changed and we shall not be able to weather that point. Now we are lost indeed, for we must either shipwreck or anchor in this little bay, and when we cast anchor the apes will have us in their power.'

Despair seized me on hearing this, and retiring to my cabin I fell swooning on my mattress, where I remained for some hours. When I recovered my senses I mounted with great caution to the deck, and there, as I had expected, hundreds of those abominable monkeys were congregated, so that I gave up all hope of ever returning to Baghdad. To my surprise, however, I soon perceived that the monkeys were peacefully inclined, and were indeed earnestly engaged in trading with the passengers. They had brought for sale flasks of distilled wine, baskets of fruit, curios of native workmanship, and drawings of a facetious and obscene character, for which the passengers paid as much as five or six dirhams. Seeing this my anger knew no bounds, for the right of trading and bartering had been assigned to me, and by this traffic I was being defrauded of my just profit on the voyage. So calling together the captain and the sailors I bade them drive the monkeys out of the ship, and when that was done we set sail again, for the wind had come into a more favourable quarter.

But the passengers were ill pleased, especially those who had not yet bought any of the obscene pictures, and told me I had no business to banish the apes, who, they said, were truly not apes, but a very hairy sort of negroes.

'O people of foolish and insatiable desire,' I answered, 'you have just been saved from a great danger, and I advise you to be very careful not to abuse again the patience of Destiny in so insensate a manner.'

Sailing a little farther we came to that part of the island where the ogres lived, and no sooner had we rounded a certain headland than we saw several of them standing upon the beach. Again I warned the passengers of the danger they would incur by going too near, but once more I was overruled, and the solicitations of Budur, the virgin with remarkable hips, and of Zaynab, on whose face the full moon shone—Ya Allah! did she not shine upon it?—persuaded the captain to approach the shore. Great was my terror when I recognised the abominable and distinctive features of the people whose captive I had once been, and who had, as I recalled with horror, eaten so many of the comrades with whom I sailed upon my third voyage. But Budur and the lovely Zaynab, together with the other passengers, made exclamations of pleasure and amusement when they beheld the extreme ugliness of the ogres, and when the latter, swimming out to us, had surrounded the ship, they threw down copper coins into the water for which the ogres dived, and having retrieved them stowed them away in their capacious mouths. Then, treading water, they appealed for more coins, uttering a strange cry like '*Gilly-gilly-gilly-gilly!*' Nor were they satisfied till swimming had exhausted them and their mouths were full.

We were now but two days' sailing from the most perilous part of our voyage, and with the utmost gravity I warned the passengers of the appalling consequences that would ensue if they did not behave with caution and propriety when we landed on the Island of the Rocs. I told them that the distinctive features of the island were the huge white eggs of the rocs. These eggs, as large as a palace, commonly lay in smooth grassy places, and must on no account be damaged. They should even refrain from writing their names upon the eggs, a practice they were prone to indulge in when visiting tombs and other monuments. I waited with no little trepidation for the conclusion of this adventure.

To my surprise, however, no rocs' eggs were apparent when we came within sight of the island. We lay close to a large promontory that was green with well-tended grass, though here and there in the grass were sandy pits, and some parts of the grass were closer cropped than others. These parts were decorated with little flags. And when we examined the place more attentively, we perceived, lying on the grass, a large number of small objects, white and round, like the eggs of some little bird. Seeing these the passengers grew very excited and shouted, 'The golf, the golf!'

Now this shouting astonished me, for I knew of no bird called the golf, and since its eggs were so small the bird itself could not be large. I therefore saw no reason to be excited about it, and as none of the marvels we had previously seen had aroused any great interest among the passengers, I could not conceive the nature of this little bird whose eggs had suddenly filled them with enthusiasm. Nor was I pleased when, mocking me, they told me it was no bird but a game, and they were now going ashore to play with the eggs. This they did, beating them with clubs they had brought in readiness for such a chance, and indeed the eggs were hard to break. Yet some of the passengers, after many strokes, succeeded in splitting and cracking them. Allah alone knows what other games are now played in Baghdad—for I do not often leave my house nowadays, and have not for many years—but few, I think, can be more foolish than this one of breaking unbreakable eggs.

Yet so fond of it were most of the passengers that they insisted on staying in the island for many days, and every day they played at it from morning till night. On one of these days I was walking far inland, finding solace in the contemplation of beauty, and admiring the handiwork of Allah, who will plant His flowers in great abundance by the most desolate of streams. Musing upon His benevolence I was interrupted by a loud and familiar voice, and looking up I beheld the widow Dalila. She told me that she had never learnt to play with the golf's eggs, and leering at me in a most unpleasant manner she said there was a better game, that two could play at, in all whose subtleties and devices she had been expert for many years. Hearing this, the earth darkened be-

ERIC LINKLATER

fore me and my soul was filled with despair, for that game is worse than hell if one cannot choose one's opponent freely. My hands shook and my forehead was bedewed with sweat as I strove to talk of other matters and to take her mind from this horrible game. But she would not leave me, and all day she followed me, holding me fast by the arm and practising a multitude of tricks that were meant to awake desire, but which, indeed, only increased my hatred of her. The next day and on the following day I suffered this same torture, until I remembered my dreadful experience when the Old Man of the Sea perched himself on my shoulders and made me his slave. But he was not more horrible to my senses than the insatiable Dalila.

In this extremity I remembered the device by which I got rid of the Old Man. For I had filled a gourd with fruit juice, and let it ferment, and drinking this he became drunk, and I threw him off and killed him. On the third day of my torment with Dalila I took with me a flask of strong wine and gave it to her. This she drank, but it had no effect on her other than encouragement to redouble her demands and to sing some improper verses. My unhappiness was now complete, and I thought with great bitterness of the folly that had induced me to leave Baghdad on a voyage so unnecessary and fraught with hazard.

I was rescued from the depths of my misery by the providential arrival of the youth called Hassan. You must know that we were reclining in a dell some distance from the fields where the others were playing their game with the golfs' eggs, and by Hassan's appearance it was clear that some disaster had occurred. Sweat stood on his brow of alabaster like dew on white roses, and his breathing was so laboured that his breast rose and fell in delicious agitation. He said that while they were playing their game the sky had suddenly grown dark and a great flock of crows, descending on the fields, had carried off all the eggs. Whereupon the players, scattering in pursuit of the birds, had taken to the woods and were even now searching for their nests. It was obvious to me that these birds were not crows, but golfs, which, returning from some other island whither they had gone to feed, pounced upon their eggs to rescue them. But I said nothing of this, for I saw that Hassan was in distress, and I had also thought of another scheme to get rid of Dalila.

She had now lost all interest in me—praise Him who established fickleness in women to conserve strength in men—and was ogling Hassan in a truly revolting way. Hastily I suggested that I should go and look for the golfs in this direction, while they sought in another. Dalila immediately exclaimed that this was an excellent plan, and though Hassan protested indignantly she led him off into the darkest part of the wood.

I made my way back to the ship, and by nightfall everybody had returned, exhausted by their search, except Hassan and Dalila. Persuading them that I knew of another island near-by, where the fields were larger and more numerously favoured by golfs, I prevailed upon them to set sail at dawn without waiting longer for that terrible woman and the unfortunate youth.

ERIC LINKLATER

Such was the passengers' immoderate desire to continue their game that they were quite willing to do this, and after having lived with Hassan and Dalila for several weeks, no one was sorry to abandon them. Dalila had offended all by her disgusting manners, and Hassan, despite his beauty, was no longer popular: for he had caused dissension among the old men, the younger men were jealous of him, and the young women had

discovered that beauty is not always accompanied by those virtues most truly desirable in a man.

Although my unhappiness had been sensibly relieved by the disappearance of Dalila, I was by no means satisfied with the situation in which I found myself, for I could take no pleasure in the society of these worthless and foolish people, and my discomfiture was aggravated when I discovered that several of them were writing an account of the voyage with which they meant to entertain their friends when they should return to the City of Peace. My own account of the islands we had visited was already well known in Baghdad, and these new descriptions were not only quite unnecessary, but being at variance in several particulars with what I had told, were likely to cause confusion in the minds of the people, and might even persuade those envious of my wealth and good fortune to doubt my veracity. I also learnt that the crew of the ship had by now no more liking for our passengers than I myself had. For the sailors said they could scarcely attend to their work by reason of the foolish questions they must always be answering, and at night they were impeded in their handling of the sails because on every coil of rope there were nesting, like turtle doves, young men and women. And among the crew there were certain virtuous eunuchs who looked after the passengers' rooms, and they were greatly incensed by having been so often put to shame in the early hours of the morning, when, entering familiar rooms, they frequently intruded, all unwittingly, upon comparative strangers and scenes of intimate felicity.

In this rebellious mood we reached a land familiar to me by reason of the awful fate that, but for the mercy of Allah, had once overtaken me there. I had lived there for some considerable time, happily married and held in high honour by the king. But on the death of my wife—glory be to the Living who dies not!—I myself was confronted with death, for according to the law of this people, whenever a man or woman dies, the wife or husband is buried alive with the dead body. There is in the middle part of the country a hollow mountain pierced by a stone well, and the custom was to bury the bodies, the living and the dead, in the cave of this mountain, lowering them into the well by ropes. I had endured unspeakable horrors in the noisome darkness of this place, and only succeeded in escaping from it when I was on the point of going mad with fear and loneliness. The prospect of revisiting these scenes filled me with foreboding, but it was my duty to introduce the passengers to places of historical interest, and the peculiar peril of my sojourn there naturally endowed it with unusual claims to their attention.

When we landed I discovered, to my sorrow, that the king who had befriended me was now dead, and the country was ruled by his son. The young king was greatly interested to hear of my previous domicile in his country, and his admiration for me was sensibly increased when I described to him my escape from the charnel house in the mountain. He told me they had now given up their traditional custom of burial, thinking it too barbarous for this present age, but the mountain, he said, was still in almost daily use. I asked him how this could be, and he explained that the fame of their custom had gone abroad, and many visitors, curious to see this unique sepulchre, came to his country for no other purpose and were shown through the cave on payment of a small fee.

Now I must tell you that immediately before landing I had offered for sale among the passengers certain mementos of my previous visit: small jewels, that is, which I had removed from bodies in the cave. Having frequently displayed them to my friends in Baghdad, I thought now to dispose of them to people who would naturally be interested in them. But to my great disgust no one would purchase them, though the price I asked was ridiculously small, for some called me a robber and a pillager of the dead, and others denied that I had ever been in the cave at all. They interrupted, moreover, my description of the agonies I had suffered by rudely demanding how soon they were likely to reach another island frequented by golfs.

I was enraged beyond measure by these insults, and I found the prospect of journeying farther in company of people so devoid of piety and good manners more than I could bear. I was also perturbed by overhearing a conversation between the captain and certain members of the crew by which I was led to believe that they also had reached the limit of their endurance and were even now plotting to murder the passengers and continue the voyage as a trading venture.

Charged then with the double necessity of contriving means by which the passengers might escape this violent death—for they were in my care and I was responsible for them—and of securing my own release from further association with them, I cudgelled my brains for an acceptable plan. Two circumstances were helpful, the one being that the passengers proclaimed their eagerness to visit the charnel house and were willing to pay five dirhams apiece to enter it, and the other was the immoderate enthusiasm which the young king displayed for Budur, Zaynab, and two other young women. They were, it is true, exceptionally beautiful. Their skin was white as silver and soft as silk. Their waists were like branches of sweet myrtle, their mouths were anemones wet with dew, and their behinds like water-melons in their season. Each one was straight as the letter *alif*, and each had breasts like little gourds of ivory. They were, to be brief about it, perfection to the eye and extremely benevolent to the other senses, though to the understanding mind they betrayed faults too numerous to be counted. But youth is satisfied by what it can see or feel, and the young king thought he had never beheld girls more desirable than these four.

Taking him aside I opened my heart to him and proposed a plan. I said that the passengers, all but the four girls, were intolerable to a man of taste and that I desired to be rid of them. I then hinted that they might conveniently be detained in the hollow mountain.

The young king agreed that it was suitable for such a purpose. 'But,' he said, 'if I am to contrive this matter it is only right that I should be paid for my trouble.'

'Budur, Zaynab, and the other two girls,' I answered, 'need not go into the cave. I shall find some different entertainment for them, and as I am their guide and mentor, their cruise director, it is my privilege and responsibility to discover entertainment that will suit them.'

'O Sindbad,' he answered, 'I know the most delightful entertainment in the world.'

'Imprison the others in the charnel house,' I said, 'and the girls will become your property and you may entertain them as you please.'

Hearing this the young king immediately approved of my plan and gave orders accordingly. In the afternoon the passengers, all but the four girls, paid five dirhams apiece and were conducted by ladders into the charnel house. When they were all down a cover was placed on the well by which they had entered and great stones were piled on top of it. For some little time I listened to their cries of protestation and dismay, but their voices, often raised in expostulation, were by now so familiar to me, and indeed so distasteful, that their complaints and entreaties did not move me at all. There I left them, and that, so far as I know, was the end of them: it is written that every man carries his destiny about his neck. Then I delivered Budur, Zaynab, and the other two to the chief eunuch of the palace, and taking an affectionate farewell of the king I returned to my ship.

I took the captain and the crew into my confidence as to what I had done, and all agreed that my solution of the problem was admirable. Sailing early in the morning we made a good passage to the island of Serendib, where we sold the passengers' baggage at a very great profit. The people of Serendib had never seen anything to compare with the luxury of our late passengers' garments, or with the delicate design of their knick-knacks and ornaments, and they gladly paid an excessive price for them in pearls, camphor, and elephants' tusks. Greatly encouraged by this fortunate conclusion to our voyage we delayed no longer among the islands, but set a course for Bassora, and helped by favouring winds came there without mishap.

But before we arrived the captain and several of the crew came to me and said, 'O Sindbad, it seems to us that we may now be running into danger. For we sailed from Bassora with eighty passengers aboard, and we return with none. We cannot hope to avoid being questioned as to what has become of them, and if we tell the truth—Allah forbid such folly!—we shall all be thrown into gaol.'

I had given some thought to this matter, and I answered, 'There is no cause for alarm. It is well known that voyagers in distant seas must be prepared for many disasters, and many of the islands that we might have visited are perilous in the extreme. There is one, for example, that is infested by enormous black serpents, each a parasang in length, and their mouths are a hundred cubits wide. Had our passengers landed there they would certainly have been eaten by the serpents, and had it not been for my presence with you, as cruise director, you might well have been tempted to visit the island. It is, as it happens, a place of tempestuous winds, and if a storm had arisen while the passengers were ashore, and already in danger from the serpents, we should have been powerless to help them.'

'It is well to consider the possibility of such a mishap,' answered the captain.

'I myself have had adventures no less remarkable,' I said.

'That is widely known,' said the captain, 'and those who travel with you may well be thought to run the same risks.'

We returned to Baghdad, therefore, with easy minds, and when the Caliph's police officers, and the Syndic of the merchants, and the various relatives of the late passengers, expressed surprise at their disappearance, I satisfied their curiosity by describing the awful appearance of the serpents that had swallowed the pilgrims of pleasure, and the violent nature of the storm that had prevented us from landing and going to their assistance. There was naturally some talk and discussion about so unhappy an end to a voyage that was meant for pleasure, but no one thought of doubting my word, especially as it was fortified by the sworn statements of the captain and the crew, and the Caliph, after listening to my story with great interest, presented me with a robe of honour in recognition of my ingenuity and determined action in saving the ship when the sudden storm arose.

Sindbad the Sailor

Since then I have lived quietly in Baghdad, amusing myself with rare food and rich wine, with the conversation of selected friends, and the music of a lute-player who is skilled in all the twenty-one modes of playing. Nor have I forgotten to give bountiful thanks to Allah for His constant mercy and care in saving me from so many dangers.

Having listened with serious attention to this remarkable tale, Sindbad the Porter expressed his admiration of it in well-chosen words, and prepared to go. Sindbad the Sailor thereupon gave him a purse containing a hundred dinars, and invited him to dine in his company on the following night, 'For there is more in this story of my eighth voyage,' he said, 'than you can possibly comprehend in a single hearing. But you will understand it better and like it more when you have heard it a second, a third, or, if Allah wills, even a fourth and a fifth time.'

[185

[

Ali Baba
and the
Forty
Thieves

]

A. G. MACDONELL

Fergus O'Donnell Barber, who died some three years before this tale opens, was a strange mixture of idealist and small shopkeeper. During a lifetime of thrift and industry in the stationery line, with side-lines in sweets, cigarettes, newspapers, fruit-cordials, and cheapish ribbons, in the northerly town of Accrington, Mr. Barber never lost his grip upon the conviction that he was the descendant of the Celtic Kings of Ireland or, alternatively, of the Celtic Kings of Scotland.

It was the only fly in his regal ointment that he never could decide which of the two realms his ancestors had been called upon by God to rule. Sometimes he felt that the dreamy, poetical, fanciful mists of the Holy Island were rolling through his mind, and then he would be certain that he was the heir to all the Treasures of Tara, and would dreamily undercharge the urchins of Accrington for their paper twists of jujubes. At other times the wild surging blood of the hill-men would thunder through his veins, and he would grasp his yard-stick as if it was the cross-hilted sword of Kenneth Macalpine, and would deliver fiery orations to the Accrington Urban District Council of which he was a much-esteemed member.

Mr. Barber's mother had been an O'Donnell and her mother had been a Ferguson, but whether the O'Donnell had been a corruption of the Scottish variation of the name of the ancient House of Donald, or whether the Ferguson was a mistake for the Irish Fergus, were two questions that could never be satisfactorily determined.

So Mr. Barber alternated in his high beliefs between the two branches of the Gael. Now it happened that when his first son was born, the worthy shopkeeper was lapped in the mysteries of an Irish vision, and he insisted that the unfortunate child should be called Cuchullin Finmole Concobar Goll Casey. As only the last of these names was even remotely possible for everyday use in a world that is only too ready to enjoy a hearty laugh, the lad was called Casey, and later a nickname appeared from nowhere, as nicknames do, and he was usually addressed as Cassim.

It was in a very different mood that Mr. Barber welcomed the birth of his second son, and the hard-worked physician who attended Mrs. Barber was compelled to send three separate messages asking the triumphant father to refrain from chanting the reiving song of the Red Macraes at the top of his voice on the landing outside the bedroom. The second son, no less unfortunate than the first, was christened Muredach Conaill Aodh-na-Ardflaith Alastair. And he too, when the Inspiration of the Tartan Against All Else had worn off a little, and a cold world had to be faced, was called by the last of his sonorous string, and later he too got a nickname, Ally, short for Alastair.

This introductory note has been necessary for the better understanding of the subsequent history, for the characters of the two young men were without doubt much influenced by their strange heredity.

In the fullness of time Fergus O'Donnell Barber was gathered to his fathers, whether to the tinkle of a ghostly harp or the swift grace-notes of a pibroch, and he was borne to the last resting-place by the stout burghers of Accrington, each wearing strong boots and a massive gold watch-chain.

A few weeks later, a firm of solid and much-respected solicitors informed the two sons, now twenty-four and twenty-two respectively, that their father had left about nine thousand pounds in securities, stock, freehold, and goodwill, to be divided between them. The oleograph of Charles Stewart Parnell fondling an elk-hound was left to Casey, the album of picture post-cards of Edinburgh Castle, the Calton Jail, Princes Street, the bandstand at Portobello, Piershill Barracks, and Holyrood, to Alastair.

Cassim and Ally, with a loud and simultaneous whoop of joy, converted shop and jujubes and securities and goodwill into hard cash, divided it equally, and, shaking the dust of Accrington from their feet, bolted to London.

In London it was inevitable that Cassim should prosper. Inheriting all the tough business-instincts, the capacity for hard work, and the relentless realism of the Irish race, he invested his capital in the purchase of a partnership in the stockbroking firm of Messrs. Jogson and Batt, and married a widow whose advancing years, short temper, and unprepossessing appearance, was more than compensated by the excellent free-holds which she owned in the neighbourhood of Hampstead. Within a very few years, Mr. and Mrs. Casey were living in Avenue Road, Regent's Park.

Alastair, on the other hand, was a dreamy, unpractical Scotsman, and he soon found that he had no talents whatsoever for the maintenance of himself and the charming member of the Gaiety chorus who shared a divan with him in a studio in Flood Street, Chelsea. He was therefore compelled to become a novelist, and as he knew nothing about anything except life in Accrington, he naturally wrote novels about Mayfair. The Thames was in no danger of arson from either the books or their sales.

Casey, his veins full of an Irish puritanism, was somewhat shocked by Alastair's triple choice of partner, of companionate marriage, and of profession, but his disapproval was as nothing in comparison with Mrs. Casey's disapproval. She positively snorted whenever the sinful couple were mentioned, and was only reconciled to the singular remissness of the Almighty in not striking the whole of Flood Street with fire and brimstone, by His sensible notion of afflicting Alastair and his Carmelian with unrelieved and unrelievable poverty. Whereas virtue rightly flourished in Avenue Road.

The brothers seldom met, and it is likely that their lives would have drifted apart permanently, had it not been for the extraordinary chain of circumstances which followed the installation of the automatic telephone into the Sloane Exchange.

Alastair Barber, like all impecunious novelists, was on the telephone.

He could not afford the rent (or as we now say, rental) of the instrument, but like all impecunious novelists, he felt that if he were not on the telephone he might miss some golden opportunity of acquiring fame and, better still, fortune. And besides, Carmelian liked to ring up her girl friends every day between eleven and twelve, after breakfast. So Ally was a subscriber to the Post Office, and was attached by wires, but not by any feeling of affection, to the Sloane Exchange.

It will be remembered by keen students of the social phenomena of our times that the Sloane Exchange was one of the first to be modernised with those neat little dials and that maddening absence of anyone to swear at, and it will also be remembered that at first the system was very far from the perfection which it has since attained. Irritation in the Cadogans and the Cheynes and the Sloanes grew to annoyance, and annoyance grew to a mighty blasphemy, as the automatic system gained in strength and inaccuracy, and no one was more irritated, or blasphemed with a more intimate knowledge of Holy Writ, than Alastair Barber. For somewhere in the Sloane System there was some tiny technical fault, a short circuit perhaps, or a linking-up of one wire with another wire to which it ought not to have been linked up—one of those electrical mysteries which are beyond ordinary comprehension. Whatever it was, whenever Alastair dialled O for operator, he was invariably connected with the office of a financial house, presumably situated in the City of London. It was always the same office, for Ally came to recognise the voices of the various officials, the shrill cries of the stenographers, and even the tones, so musically attuned was his Scottish ear, of the different typewriters. After several days of fruitless blasphemy and equally fruitless complaints to those in authority, Alastair shrugged his shoulders and decided philosophically to be amused instead of angry. After all, he reflected, as he stroked Carmelian's red-gold hair, it was as if a God had transported him by magic carpet into a life that he knew nothing about. Indeed, it was as if he himself had been created a God, able to eavesdrop upon total strangers at an unparalleled distance. From being a nuisance, the short-circuit became a joy, and when inspiration for his new novel was tardy in appearance, Alastair often used to dial O and spend hours in a strange world of margins and mergers.

One day he dialled O and found that he had wafted himself down from the ether into the finance office, into the middle of an urgent conversation. A husky masculine

A. G. MACDONELL

voice was saying in an urgent whisper, 'Open Sesame. Ispahan Gold. Buy ten thousand, three and a half,' and a voice
somewhere else whispered back, 'O.K., chief. I'll ring you in
half-an-hour.'

Now, although the words Open Sesame meant nothing to Ally, being obviously some sort of code, any child
knew of the recent sensational fluctuations of the Ispahan
and North Persian Gold-mine Company. Clearly the first
voice had instructed the second voice to deal in these shares.
Half an hour later Ally heard the second voice report to the
first voice 'Shut Sesame,' and the first voice said 'Good boy.'
Next morning the newspapers announced that Ispahans had
opened at £2, 5s., had risen steeply in the afternoon to £3,
10s., and had then declined, under pressure of sudden and
heavy selling, to £3, 1s. 6d.

Ally was only a novelist, but even he could work out that
10,000 multiplied by £1, 5s. is £12,500. A nice little profit.

For the next two days Alastair Barber sat in his Chelsea
studio with his ear firmly affixed to the telephone receiver.
Even Carmelian's blandishments could not allure him from
the instrument, and Carmelian's blandishments were by no
means inconsiderable. But Ally was as flint. He had a vague
inkling in his mind that he was on to a good thing, which, if
properly worked, would bring him and Carmelian to a life of
perpetual bliss in Cannes, Rapallo, or St. Juan-les-Pins. How
right were those old Mahometans, reflected Ally as he shifted
the receiver from one hand to the other for the thirty-fourth
time since the Stock Exchange opened that morning, when

Ali Baba and the Forty Thieves

they decided that the Heavenly Paradise was nothing more, or less, than a perpetual afternoon with a Carmelian upon a Chelsea divan.

It was at about 2 P.M. on the third day of Alastair's vigil that he heard again the magic words, 'Open Sesame,' followed by the instructions, 'Shiraz emeralds a hundred and ten, sixteen thousand,' and then came the report two hours later, 'Shut Sesame.'

But during those two hours Alastair Barber had been busy. He had telephoned to his Bank and instructed the Manager to buy twenty £1 ordinary shares in the Shiraz Emerald Company, and to sell at 110. The Manager explained laboriously that (*a*) the purchase of 20 shares was an investment hardly worth making; (*b*) Shiraz Ordinaries stood at 14 and nobody in their senses would dream of buying them; (*c*) Shiraz Ordinaries would reach 110 at about the same time that the old cow jumped over the moon.

Alastair frigidly asked the Manager whether he would be kind enough to do what he was told, and the conversation came to an end. There is probably no class of professional man who can be so frigid with a Bank Manager as your novelist. The twenty shares were bought at 2.15 P.M. The news arrived in the City at 2.35 P.M. that an emerald vein of incredible richness had been struck in the Shiraz mines, and at 3.35 P.M. the shares had reached 115. About that time there was some rather heavy selling, and the market closed at 98½. But the Bank Manager, a gentleman with a sterling sense of duty, had realised Alastair's shares at 110, and the profit on his transaction, after deduction of commission and stamp duty, was somewhere in the neighbourhood of £90.

Ally and Carmelian dined at the Café Royal that night and drank a good deal of champagne.

Next day there was a flutter in Teheran Rubies which netted Alastair almost a thousand pounds, for he had planked his entire £90 (less the cost of the dinner at the Café Royal) upon the Rubies, and on the day after a magnificent affair in Bagdad Real Estate. Then came the hideous and abominable Saturday, upon which stockbrokers idle away their precious hours at Sunningdale or in the Hotel Metropole at Brighton. Alastair was peevish and fretful during that Saturday. But on Monday operations started again, and by the end of four weeks, Alastair had netted no less a sum than fifty-four thousand pounds.

Now, Alastair, being a man of letters, was also a man of sense. He knew, as so few other business-men know, when to stop. And when his profits had passed the fifty-thousand mark, he pulled out of the game. He married Carmelian, after a certain amount of hesitation, bought the lease of a large, gloomy, and impressive mansion in Queen's Gate, Kensington, and began to give dinner-parties. He also joined the Athenaeum Club. But some odd streak of prudence made him retain the Chelsea studio whence his riches had indirectly come, and made him also write an effusive letter to the local representative of the Postmaster-General, assuring him that the telephone in the studio was now functioning to perfection.

Ali Baba and the Forty Thieves

Cassim, an honest fellow at heart, was pleased at his brother's sudden affluence, which he ascribed to scenario-writing for the Gaumont-Persian Film Company. For, like all successful business-men, he suffered from the fixed delusion that scenario-writers were the most important, and the most highly-paid, people in the film-world. Mrs. Cassim, on the other hand, was doubly furious. For not only did Ally's rise to wealth undermine for ever her belief in the decency and fairminded-ness of the Almighty, but his visit with Carmelian to the registry-office at the back of Gorringe's deprived her of one of her most powerful subjects of invective. Mrs. Ally bought a cream-coloured motor-car. Mrs. Cassim squirmed. Mrs. Ally bought a set of furs. Mrs. Cassim wriggled with rage. Nor did she for one moment accept her good-natured husband's theory of the origin of the splendour. Dope, more likely, hinted Mrs. Cassim darkly. Or white-slavery. Or blackmail. Or all three. Week after week she goaded the good Cassim until at last he could stand it no longer. He took his hat and umbrella, went to Ally, and begged him as one brother to another to restore Mrs. Cassim's domestic felicity by divulging the sources of the new prosperity of the cadet branch of the Barber family.

Alastair, always ready to tell a good story, recounted, amid gusts of hearty laughter, the singular circumstance of the faulty telephone-circuit.

As the story progressed Cassim grew more and more thoughtful, and at the end, after a final guffaw from Ally, he sat in silence, staring absently at the unlit Corona-Corona cigar, which his host now purchased a cabinet at a time. At last he looked up and said, 'You might lend me that studio of yours, old boy, for a month or two. If you've quit the racket, you won't mind if I have a dart at it.'

'By all means, my dear Cassim,' replied his easy-going brother. 'But don't blame me if you get stung. By the way, have you any notion who these chaps are?'

'Of course,' answered the more experienced Casey. 'It can only be the Sesame Finance Syndicate, a group of the most daring speculators who have ever operated in the City. There are said to be about forty of them in it, and they work on an enormous scale.' Cassim lowered his voice. 'Between you and me, old chap, they're little better than robbers,' he whispered, and then he laughed. 'Still, I've no objection to picking up a bit of the swag, robbery or no robbery,' and he winked. Ally uncorked a bottle of Armagnac, and the two brothers raised the dark brown goblets in the air. 'Open Sesame,' they cried simultaneously and clinked their glasses.

'Gentlemen,' said the Chairman of the Sesame Finance Syndicate Limited, addressing an extraordinary general meeting of the shareholders (there were only forty shareholders in the Company, including the Chairman), 'this meeting has been convened to discuss the measures which we should take in view of a most serious crisis which has arisen in the affairs of the Syndicate. Briefly, there has been, for some months, a leakage of information. Gentlemen, I regret to have to say it, there is a traitor in our camp.'

Ali Baba and the Forty Thieves

'Do you suggest——' began one of the shareholders, a rosy Pickwickian man.

The Chairman held up his hand. 'I do not suggest anything against our shareholders. Their sense of honour is irreproachable. Besides, our profits have been so large that treachery is not worth while. No, gentlemen, the leakage must come from one of our employees.'

'What evidence have you got, sir, that there is a leakage?' enquired another shareholder, an elderly man who looked rather like a mediaeval saint.

[197

The Chairman picked up a sheaf of notes. 'The first indication I received,' he said, 'was on the occasion of our raid last month upon Caravan Tea. A block of 20,000 shares was bought seven minutes before we opened up. I thought at the time that it might be a coincidence. Then we attacked, if you remember, a few days later, Bagdad Merchandise. We began selling at noon exactly. Sixty thousand shares were offered at five minutes to twelve by someone else.'

'By whom?' shouted the thirty-nine shareholders angrily.

'Wait,' said the Chairman. 'When we wrecked the Widows' and Orphans' Trust, again someone was before us. And, clinching proof, gentlemen, three days ago we drove Desert Traction from 16 to 84. This same firm bought at 16 and sold at 82.'

Hoarse and inarticulate cries of rage resounded through the dignified boardroom.

'Now, gentlemen,' went on the Chairman, 'how did that firm of stockholders know that we were going to unload at 84? That is what I want to know.'

A. G. MACDONELL

There was a dead silence. 'As for the name of the firm,' he proceeded, 'that is also a puzzling matter. Messrs. Jogson and Batt are a very small, unobtrusive, hitherto unambitious, firm which has dealt mainly in Home Industrials. Suddenly it blossoms out as an adventurous raider. There are only two partners: Batt, who is eighty-eight years of age and stone deaf, and Casey Barber, son of a small north-country tobacconist.'

The Chairman of Sesame Syndicate was a born artist and he dearly loved a little drama, even in the hurly-burly of City life. He dropped his voice into a very casual tone, smothered a little yawn, and added, off-handedly, 'Two months ago Mrs. Casey Barber was modestly well-off. Yesterday she bought the Khoslov diamonds at Christie's for seventy-one thousand pounds.'

The Chairman got his dramatic effect all right. There was a simultaneous intaking of thirty-nine breaths which sounded as if the shareholders were hissing him. But the Chairman knew better. It was a spontaneous tribute to his artistry, and he smiled. 'Yes, it's Barber all right,' he said. 'But how he does it—that's another matter.'

'What are we going to do about it?' asked another shareholder, whose face was as full of wistful innocence as Little Lord Fauntleroy.

'I will tell you,' said the Chairman. 'Your Board of Directors has worked out a scheme for the annihilation of Mr. Barber, and in the meantime you may rest assured that no stone will be left unturned to discover the traitor. The scheme is as follows. We propose to carry out our ordinary routine for a raid next Tuesday. You will all be warned to have all your resources ready, in the usual way. Our whole machinery will be mobilised for a bear-attack on Overland Routes, selling down to 1 $^{3}/_{16}$. On the actual day, however, we will do nothing, and'— the Chairman's voice took on a steely rasp—'we will let Master Barber attack Overland Routes by himself.'

There was a ripple of applause. 'As to the source of the [199 leakage,' proceeded the Chairman, 'Mr. Barber is being shadowed night and day. Only this morning he was followed by one of our agents to a studio in a large block of studios in Chelsea. Our agent, a most astute man, marked the door of the studio with a cross in chalk, but unfortunately, when he returned after lunch with a colleague, he found his astuteness nullified by a tiresome urchin who had marked all the studios with a cross in chalk. However, gentlemen, it is only a matter of time. Meanwhile I am confident that we have got Mr. Barber hanged, drawn, and quartered. If there is no other business, I will declare the meeting adjourned.'

A fortnight later two visitors came to Ally's house in Queen's Gate on the same afternoon. The first was a stout, clean-shaven gentleman wearing a green suit, green shirt, green hat, green tie, and light-brown boots, and ornamented with a pair of horn spectacles and four chins. He announced himself to a surprised Alastair as Mr. H. Al Rashid, the London representative of Messrs. J. P. Morgan, and he bowed with an exquisite grace, in so far as his waist permitted exquisite grace, over the slender hand of Carmelian Barber. His errand was soon, considering that he was an American businessman, explained. Within three hours he had put all his cards on the table. Messrs. J. P. Morgan was, in common with many other old-established banking-houses, the Rothschilds, the Barings, the Hambros, the Sterns, Lazards, and the rest, out gunning for the Sesame Syndicate. The Syndicate was upsetting confidence; it was destroying credit; it was undermining stability. The international bankers were determined to put an end to its impudent series of robberies at the expense of the investing public. Mr. Rashid had very cleverly spotted the manœuvres of Casey Barber, had deduced that he was in the position to follow the Syndicate's game, had failed to get into touch with Casey, and had therefore come to Alastair for information. Alastair would have had no information to give him, had not the second visitor of the afternoon come rushing into the sitting-room where Alastair was closeted with Mr. Al Rashid. It was Mrs. Casey, covered with furs and diamonds, with the news, delivered hysterically, that Cassim had disappeared.

Mr. Rashid nodded his head sympathetically, and at the same time with an air of deep wisdom as a man might say, 'Dear lady, you have my sincere condolences, but I cannot honestly say that I am surprised.'

Alastair telephoned to the offices of Messrs. Jogson and Batt and found everything in the wildest state of confusion. The managing clerk, with tears in his voice, stammered out that Mr. Barber had sold Overland Routes to the tune of a quarter of a million sterling at an average of £2 a share, that

Ali Baba and the Forty Thieves

an immense bull force had entered the market and driven Overland Routes up to £4 ⁵/₁₆ and that the firm of Jogson and Batt, and Mr. Barber himself, were irretrievably ruined. Mr. Barber had not returned to the office since the catastrophe.

'Not at the office,' said Alastair, 'not gone home. There's only one place he can have gone to.' A quarter of an hour later, Alastair and Mr. Rashid entered the Flood Street studio and found the dead body of Cassim on the floor. A revolver bullet was in his brain and a revolver in his hand. Taking a sudden resolution, Alastair told the whole story from beginning to end to Morgan's representative.

Mr. Rashid listened intently and, at the end, said: 'See here, Mr. Barber, we've got to work together in this. We've got the cash resources and you've got this telephone mix-up. Let's pool them. And if we can smash the Sesame crowd, there's a hundred thousand pounds for you. Are you on?'

'Most certainly I am on,' replied Ally.

'Then the first thing,' said Mr. Rashid, 'is to get your brother's body out of here. We mustn't let the Syndicate associate him with this studio. They might get suspicious about the telephone. Ring for the caretaker of the block.'

Mr. Rashid tossed a rug over the body before he opened the door to the cheerful dame who answered the bell and waddled in.

Mr. Rashid, handing her a pound note, asked, 'Have you seen any queer-looking people about the studios lately?'

'Indeed I have, sir,' replied the caretaker. 'There was a man a week or two ago who followed Mr. Casey in and drew a

A. G. MACDONELL

big white cross on the door of this very studio, drat his impudence, the measly little stoat. "I'll know that door again if I see it," he thinks. "No you won't," I thinks, and I drawed white crosses on all the doors. The week after Mr. Casey comes in, and blimey if the little weasel isn't after him again, and this time it's a red cross. "I'll red-cross you," says I, and I drawed red crosses on all the doors. This afternoon it's a yellow cross, and I hadn't got no yellow chalk so I just rubbed it out.'

'Well done, Mrs. Jupp,' said Mr. Rashid handing her another pound.

At eleven o'clock that night Mr. Rashid and Alastair drove up to the studio in a large closed car with a brown, alert, dapper little man from the Persian Gulf, named Doctor Baba Mustapha, F.R.C.S. Dr. Mustapha was an extremely able young doctor and surgeon, who practised, very extensively, on lines which would have brought perspiration to the brows of the British Medical Council. His practice was mainly in Mayfair, but it extended as far east as the Whitechapel Road, and it was mostly conducted at night, and his fees were invariably paid in spot cash. No accounts rendered, and no cheques. With swift, dexterous fingers Dr. Mustapha stitched here and stitched there, covered the bullet-wound with pink wax, pushed and pulled and patted and arranged, and at last announced that he was finished. He then signed a certificate that the deceased had died of natural causes, pocketed the 150 pound notes which Mr. Rashid handed to him, bowed dapperly and departed with the body to a neighbouring undertaker with whom he had frequently collaborated in the past with the happiest results. Mr. Rashid and Alastair separated for the night. Mr. Rashid's parting words were: 'Keep your spirits up. Don't forget that Morgans are behind you. And if there is any trouble ring me up, or wire me. Morgiana, London, is our telegraphic address.'

'Gentlemen,' said the Chairman of Sesame Syndicate Ltd., at another extraordinary general meeting of the shareholders about a month later, 'as you know, your Directors took steps to eliminate the firm of Messrs. Jogson and Batt, who were seriously interfering with our plans. Those steps were almost entirely successful. The firm was hammered on the Stock Exchange; Mr. Jogson died of shock; Mr. Barber shot himself. So far, so good. But I used the phrase "almost entirely successful" advisedly, for I regret that we have been unable to trace the origin of the leakage. There is no doubt that the late Barber operated in some way, or worked with someone who was operating, from that block of studios in Chelsea. The doctor who attended him, a certain Oriental named Mustapha, has come forward in answer to an advertisement, and, for a substantial consideration, has informed us that he was summoned to that same block of studios, that he arranged the body so that no bullet-wound should appear, that he signed a certificate of death from natural causes, and that he subsequently removed the body and handed it over to an undertaker. All of which goes to prove the importance to our enemies of that studio. Furthermore, gentlemen, in removing the firm of Messrs. Jogson and Batt, we have not entirely destroyed our enemies. Operations are still being conducted, on a very much smaller scale than that of Mr. Casey Barber, but nevertheless sufficiently large to be irritating, and, gentlemen' —the Chairman's voice sank into a slow and impressive bass—'Mr. Casey Barber's brother, Mr. Alastair Barber, visits that studio every day.'

Again the Chairman secured the dramatic effect that he liked so much. The thirty-nine shareholders simultaneously said 'Ah!'

'Gentlemen,' said the Chairman, 'Mr. Alastair Barber must go the way of his brother.'

'Hear, hear,' cried the shareholders.

'We will lead him on gently,' said the Chairman, 'and then, just as we pounced upon Casey, so will we pounce upon Ally. This time the weapon of destruction will be Oil.'

Day after day Ally Barber sat in the Chelsea studio with the receiver at his ear, and day after day he passed on information to Morgiana, London, that colossal power of international finance. Several small coups were successfully brought off by Ally, investing on the advice of the Sesame Syndicate, and working through a broker recommended by Mr. Rashid. Then one morning came the message which Mr. Rashid was expecting. The voice had begun as usual with 'Open Sesame.' But instead of continuing with the usual curt instructions to buy or sell, had gone on, 'The biggest thing we've ever done, Sam; Colossal.' It was the first time on record that any refer-

Ali Baba and the Forty Thieves

ence had been made to the relative size of the proposed transaction. Then came the instructions: to buy Samarcand Oil, to buy every share in sight up to a hundred and fifteen shillings.

Ally instantly got on to Morgiana with the news. Al Rashid whistled. 'It's the big game at last,' he said. 'Come right along.'

All that day Ally bought Samarcand Oil. The market opened at 31, and it went on rising and rising under Ally's steady pressure, until it stood, when the Stock Exchange closed that afternoon, at 88½.

Next morning, before the House opened, Ally telephoned to Al Rashid in some alarm. He had already committed himself to the tune of nearly £300,000.

'That's O.K., big boy,' replied Al in the highest spirits. 'Morgiana is backing you. Stick to it.'

Samarcand Oil rose and rose and rose. It touched 100, wobbled back to 97, rose to 104, lurched to 108, and then, at 110, the great bear attack opened. Sesame Syndicate were in the field. The heavy guns thundered all along the line. The skirmishers ran in and out. The smaller fry bolted for shelter, and left the arena to the big men.

Samarcand Oil sagged to 95, and then fell like a plummet to 70. 'Barber is ruined,' the cry went round the markets with that strange swiftness with which news travels in the West. And then came the great counter-attack. Samarcands halted at 70; began even to creep up jerkily: 73, 74, 74 $^{3}/_{16}$.

The Syndicate flung in reserves, and drove the price down to 69. Recovery was swift, and at 80 the Syndicate launched another horde of reserves. It had no effect. Samarcands rose to 85. Men stared at each other with a wild surmise. Who had the nerve or the knowledge or the capital to resist the terrible Forty?

Seldom if ever has the Exchange known such a day. Business was suspended even in the Kaffir-market while the great struggle went on, and Kaffirs knocked about aimlessly, helpless in the unparalleled predicament of finding themselves without buyers.

Then the Syndicate, pale but resolute, mobilised their final reserves. They called up every asset and every ounce of credit, and went bravely into the turmoil. At the same moment the rumour, tearing along like a prairie fire, went blazing down Throgmorton Street. 'Morgiana is backing Barber,' A minute or two later Ally and Al Rashid appeared arm-in-arm, and laughing heartily, in the street outside the Stock Exchange, and Samarcand Oil rocketed to 126. The Sesame Syndicate was ruined.

Of the forty members of the Sesame Syndicate, only the Chairman of the Board retained his commonsense sufficiently not to throw his entire private fortune into the struggle, and he alone emerged unbankrupted. The other thirty-nine were entirely ruined, except for thirty-eight of them who had invested a certain amount of money in their wives' names. The thirty-ninth, being unmarried, had invested a certain amount of money in the name of a friend, Miss Lolita Sevillana, a dancer from Newcastle-upon-Tyne, but Miss

Sevillana wisely skipped out with the cash to Hollywood, and her unfortunate friend was left destitute.

But although the remainder of the raiders retained enough money to live on, nevertheless their power was utterly destroyed. Only the Chairman crept back into the City. He founded a new firm under the title of Codger, Hussein and Co., which was nothing more or less than a bucket-shop, and his profits were small and precarious.

As for Alastair Barber, he was now a man of such prodigious wealth that the University of Accrington, fully alive to the fact that the novels of so rich a man must be of exceptional merit, made him an Honorary LL.D., and in the following year he was awarded the Hawthornden Prize, and elected a Vice-President of the P.E.N. Club.

Puss in Boots

HELEN SIMPSON

Once upon a time there lived a miller who had three sons, and when he died he left all that he had to be divided between them. The eldest had the mill, which was on a particularly lovely stretch of river, not far from a cathedral town. He at once saw its possibilities; stopped the wheel, and buying a number of ladder-back chairs, together with a great many bright unfadable curtains, put up a sign on the high road:

YE OLDE MILL HOUSE
Luncheons and Teas.

And very soon was paying a fair sum in income-tax.

The second son inherited his father's old Ford lorry, and with this he managed to do a fairly good trade as a carrier.

The youngest son, whose name was Jack, had for his portion only the miller's black cat.

Jack was very well pleased with his share, and at once took the cat on his shoulder to the village cobbler's, where he ordered four little shoes of the finest leather to be made for it. It was his intention to go to London and seek his fortune there; he knew that the way might be long, and the hot asphalt roads trying to a cat's soft feet. He therefore paid for these shoes with the last of his money, and set out, quite penniless but happy, the cat sidling at his heels.

After travelling for many days he arrived in London. There he very soon found that the legend he read on the garages, Free Air, might have done duty under the City's coat of arms. He was moved on by a policeman whether he begged, or asked passers-by for work, or just stood; and at last was stirred with the toe of a boot from the steps of the National Gallery on which he had proposed to sleep. A neighbouring church crypt offered refuge for the night. There on a bench he disposed himself, first having begged a little milk from the vicar for his cat.

'It is a wretched meal for you, Pussy,' said he, 'who have so long been accustomed to the fresh mice of my father's mill. We are poor now; but we have at least this consolation, that we know ourselves to be honest.'

'And a silly consolation it is,' returned the cat. 'Move with the times! I know the secret of getting on in London; my ancestor five hundred generations back served with Whittington, and he handed down three useful precepts. The first is, Bluff; and the second and third are the same.'

'Are you inciting me to dishonest courses?' Jack asked. 'Honesty is the best policy anywhere, at any time.'

'Nonsense,' replied the cat, with insulting brevity. 'The first thing you do, my young friend, when we make our money, is to buy a copy of Florio's *Montaigne*, and read daily the chapter—I think it is numbered forty —which concerns our attitude to good or evil.'

'When we make our money!' echoed Jack, laughing. 'Why, Pussy, are you going to take a hand in my fortune?'

'That I am. For you must know that cats greatly enjoy the exercise of power, when they can depute it. They often feign indolence or unconcern in order not to be obliged to endure routine. You never heard tell yet of a cat turning a spit, but you must certainly have read of the cats of Cardinal Riche- lieu. These, lying upon the arm of his chair, gave him instruc- tions which he obeyed; and if you knew anything of history you would perceive that his policy shows all those qualities which we are apt to display in our private affairs; ferocity, patience, and frugality.'

'Am I then to take orders from you?'

'If you are wise, certainly. I might easily do better for myself; but I cannot abandon a boy who has respected my pride. When it was found that I was to be your only portion, your brothers expected you to kick me. Instead, you smiled and took me in your arms. Then with your last few shillings you paid for these boots, which have saved me many a blister on the long road to London.'

'I do love you indeed,' the young man responded. 'For that reason, and because I value your company, never speak to me again of making our living otherwise than honestly; for if you do we must part company.'

The cat eyed him; then, with a hoist of the leg like a shrug misplaced, set about its toilet for the night.

When Jack was asleep, deeply, for he was young and tired, the cat rose delicately and went out into the night air of London. Pigeons, fat and fuddled, leant against each other sentimentally all along the roof-ledge of the church. A steeplejack's ladder had been left leading to the tower, and up this, cautiously, and testing each rung with a paw after the cautious habit of cats, Jack's mentor proceeded. At the top he paused, selected a group, and sprang. The execution among sleepy birds was very great; six lay dead when the flapping escape of their companions allowed the bodies to be counted. The cat ate one, relishing its warm juices. The remaining five it strung together, and swinging them, approached a coffee stall, calling:

'Nice pigeons for pies!'

'Not me,' replied the coffee-seller with a wink at his customers, 'pigeons is too high-class for me. Cats is what we use in our veal-and-hams.'

The cat laughed politely, but repeated its offer, and named so moderate a price that after a little haggling for the fun of the thing, the coffee-seller purchased all five. The cat

HELEN SIMPSON

thanked him, and ran away, carrying two bright shillings in its mouth, towards the church, where Jack's sleep was still untroubled.

In the morning when they went out into the street the cat turned one eye to see that Jack was looking, and made a pounce on something in the gutter.

'A shilling!' cried Jack, delighted. 'Who can have dropped it?'

'Never mind about that,' answered the cat, 'it is treasure trove, and we will spend it on a breakfast.'

'No,' Jack answered firmly, 'treasure trove by law belongs to the Crown, and I shall hand the money to this constable, who is the Crown's nearest representative.'

This he did. The policeman looked at him, and then at the cat, which was tapping its forehead behind its master's back, and at last, slipping the shilling into his pocket, thanked Jack with some ceremony.

'You'll get a letter out of the Chancellor of the Exchequer for this, I shouldn't wonder,' said the policeman, 'and a piece in the papers.'

'That's all right,' said Jack, flushing with pleasure and moving on. His cat, following meekly, blessed the prudence which had allowed it to retain one of the shillings, and reckoned that a clearer understanding of Jack's character had been cheaply bought at the cost of the other.

Leaving Jack in Hyde Park, pleasantly occupied watching the Serpentine swimmers, the cat excused itself, and ran to Piccadilly, where in a most expensive flower shop it chose one single and exquisite rose. This it paid for with the shilling it had retained, begging the assistant to write on a card these words: 'My last shilling well spent in homage to a divine talent.' With this and the rose inside the box it walked back to the cool Park.

'And where have you been, Pussy?' Jack asked good-naturedly. 'Seeing the Queen? I wish I had twopence to buy a little fish for you.'

'Don't think of me,' said the cat, though it paid his kind thought the tribute of an arched back. 'I have a commission for you.'

'An honest one, I hope.'

'I have been asked to deliver this parcel, but I find it very inconvenient to carry, and have come to ask if you will oblige me by taking it to the Magnifique Hotel, which is not a great way from here. As you see, it is addressed to Briga Bortsch.'

This made Jack open his eyes, for even in the tranquil village near the mill there was a picture house where he had often seen and adored Briga. She had a soft yet frigid look like melting snow, and nobody could understand a word she said, which facts lent her mystery.

'You must give it into her own hands,' said the cat, 'those were my instructions. If she asks you any questions, don't speak, simply make the best attempt you can at a bow. You have not yet come to use words rightly, that is, lightly, and changing significance according to surface tension, as a bubble changes colour.'

'I can't tell a lie, if that's what you mean,' said Jack.

HELEN SIMPSON

'It is what I mean,' answered the cat, 'more's the pity.'

And it watched him with some misgiving as he set off. But his walk was good, his back slender and square, and so long as he kept his mouth shut the cat could not help having hopes of him.

Two hours later he returned, looking rueful and bewildered.

214]

'Well?' said the cat with impatience.

'I went to the Magnifique,' Jack began, 'and said that I had a message for Miss Bortsch. They answered that I was the four hundredth person who had told them that tale since eight this morning. I was about to give up the attempt, when they all turned away from me and began bowing, and who should step out of the lift but Briga Bortsch herself. She was very short, and looked common.'

'Ha!' said the cat. 'You associated with duchesses then, did you, at the mill? Common, indeed!'

'She had a face like a plate,' went on Jack, 'with a pattern painted on it. I was disappointed, for ever since I saw her in "Heart's Hell" I have thought of her as——'

'Yes, yes,' interrupted the cat, 'what next?'

'She saw me, and said something to the attendants, who very reluctantly let me come near. I held out the box without a word, and she took it, with a look that made me feel very uncomfortable indeed, as if she were undressing me with her eyes; a most un-English look. She opened the box and found the card with the flower; she read the card, and smiled. Then she beckoned me closer, and said, as near as I can remember:

"This is a very pretty message." I bowed. "Have you indeed not a single penny left in the world?" I turned out my pockets, which, as you know, were empty. She seemed pleased, and said: "Go up to my room and wait there for me. I should like to thank you privately." I obeyed her, and was taken in a lift up to a room more uncomfortable even than our rooms at the mill. It had metal chairs, and the furniture seemed all angles; the sofa, however, was very wide, and looked tolerably soft. After waiting an hour I heard a kind of bustle in the room next door, and five minutes later Miss Bortsch entered, wearing very little clothing, and that little transparent. I did not know where to look, and thought she must have mistaken the room; but she came up to me, rolling her eyes, and said something to the effect that she liked them shy. I bowed again, because I could not think of anything to say, and it saved me the embarrassment of looking at her. She took my hand and sat herself down on the very comfortable sofa, pulling me beside her, and began to conduct herself in such a way that there was no mistaking her intentions.'

'Very good,' said the cat, 'you have done very well so far. And did you gratify her on the sofa?'

'Can you ask?' Jack answered reproachfully. 'I hope I have enough self-respect not to lend myself to any such behaviour as that.'

'What!' said the cat incredulously, beginning to lash its tail. 'Are you saying that you refused?'

'Most certainly. What's more, I gave her my opinion of the sort of woman who tries to seduce a young man, relying on his politeness not to rebuff her. I told her that she ought never to allow herself to be seen, except on the screen; that her face was flat, her voice hoarse as a night-watchman's, and her morals those of—no offence, Pussy—a she-cat upon tiles. When I had done she flung herself on me, saying she had always craved a cave-man. I advised her to put on some clothes, especially a skirt, as her legs were bandy, and left.'

'John,' said the cat after a stupefied pause, 'I have been underestimating my difficulties. I knew that your head was thick, and your heart kind; but who could have supposed that you were that most disruptive of mortal beings, a prig? Nothing is more alien to the feline mind. Cats, a silly saying to the contrary, neither copy their neighbours nor condemn them; in other words, they are individuals. You, my unfortunate Jack, are a crowd in essence, seeing nothing clearly, neither your desires nor how to attain them. You must learn to lie; but it shall be under proper auspices, in the only way that a person of your temperament can achieve skill in this primitive art, which still is necessary for survival. You must stand for Parliament.'

'Do you imply, Pussy, that the elected representatives of democracy are liars?' asked Jack with some heat.

'I am saying,' answered the cat, restraining its feelings save for an occasional twitch of the tail, 'that it will do you no harm, as it did the prigs of three centuries ago no harm, to take a dose of Pride's Purge. Don't argue, but come.'

With that it led the young man to a house in which the National Corporation of British Millers was holding a meet-

Puss in Boots

ing, trying to think of some way to keep foreigners from grinding so much flour and selling it in England.

'Go in,' said the cat, 'and say what I tell you.' It gave him certain instructions, ending in a menacing tone: 'I do not suppose that even your conscience can find anything in that to object to.'

'Pussy,' the young man replied, 'as an animal, without moral responsibility, you take too much on yourself when you lecture me about right and wrong.'

'Lookers on see most of the game,' responded the cat. 'Do you wish to make your fortune? Then obey me.'

The young man accordingly mounted the steps of the house, and making his way unimpeded to a conference room where sat the thrones and dominations among millers he flung open the door and delivered this speech:

'Let us grow our own corn. Let England no longer live by pawnbroking, but by good grain out of her own earth. Dividends pass, but the bosom of Nature remains. More corn for England, and more grist to our mills!'

At this speech which, though the cat had devised it, represented Jack's own convictions very fairly, all members of the committee present sprang to their feet and acclaimed him as their spokesman and their candidate. He came out very much pleased with himself, and with money in his pocket, with which he at once proposed to buy some fish for the cat.

'You see, Pussy,' said he, 'that a man need not feign sentiments that are repugnant, whether of passion or otherwise, in order to get on in this world.'

HELEN SIMPSON

The cat, busy with fish, glanced at him once through slit eyes and smiled as it crunched a backbone, but did not speak, save to mutter to itself two sentences which had been handed down from a forefather, one Hodge, cat in his time to Doctor Samuel Johnson: 'Were not Dr. Dodd's sermons addressed to the passions? They were nothing, Sir, be they addressed to what they may.'

Next day Jack began to make himself known in his constituency. He drove about in a car, wearing the traditional miller's white hat, and made the acquaintance of a great many people who seemed to bear him no actual ill-will, though they asked one or two awkward questions about the dearer bread which his policy would necessarily involve. He told them the truth of this, as far as he knew it; that no nation could make on both swings and roundabouts, that it must pay for agriculture as a diabetic pays for insulin, not as a luxury but in order to keep alive. Astonished at being treated as reasonable beings, the electors rallied to him, and when polling day came Jack was returned by a considerable majority; a victory which he did not fail, in his conversations with the cat, to attribute to the impact of moral forces. The cat said nothing, but after staring at him for a long time suddenly licked itself furiously.

Jack, now John Millerson, M.P., went in triumph to Westminster, prepared to repeat there the tactics which had so delighted his patrons the millers. Half a dozen times during the first week he sprang up to utter his cry and propose his Bill, only to discover that he had not got his hat on; had not drawn a prize in the Parliamentary lottery which rules the bringing forward of Bills; or had not caught the eye of the Speaker, which appeared, whenever he rose, to be as conveniently blind as Nelson's.

After a course of this discipline, which Jack accepted as having been devised in past times by better men than he, and as lending dignity to what would otherwise have been a mere vulgar brawl, he began to forget himself as an individual, and to see himself as a part of the machine. He earned an occasional rating from his Whip, as a hound puppy may that goes off on the track of rabbits, by voting for motions put up by opposition members on the ground that they were sensible; and thus came slowly to perceive that enthusiasm would not do. He learned that lies and compromise enter into the composition of stable government as poisons do into remedies; that men and matters have their perspective, some to be judged best by standing near, others by withdrawing; and finally, that no society could hold together for long unless it agreed to regulate and limit the uses of truth.

By the time he had got all this into his head a general election was upon the country. He returned to his constituency with the manner and viewpoint acquired during a year in Parliament, and to his utter astonishment lost handsomely.

'Never mind,' said the cat, hearing the result, 'you have served an apprenticeship that will be of value to you all your life. You are now very well qualified to become a magnate of the press.'

'But I have no money,' said Jack.

'We can get that easily enough,' replied the cat, 'if you will attend to me. First of all, we must have a name for our journal, and this we will discover by means of a competition. We must invite people to send in suggestions, each accompanied by a postal order for 6d., and announce that a prize of ten thousand pounds will be given to the person whose idea for a name is finally adopted.'

'But we have not got ten thousand pounds,' interposed Jack.

'Leave that to me,' returned the cat.

It secured several hoardings on credit, and made the announcement. For three weeks, until the competition's closing date, Jack was kept busy putting elastic bands round postal orders, and at last, when the money came to be counted, it was found that they had received just ten thousand pounds.

'Wait a while,' said the cat, as Jack began to question. 'Give me one of those envelopes.'

And taking one at random it read the suggestion— which was, that the paper should be called *The Ego*— and announced that it would go at once and see the writer, a Mr. Bughouse, who appeared to live in some very poor locality. Jack made no further protest. The cat was his right hand, and he had political as well as religious precedent for refusing to his left hand all knowledge of that which his right was doing.

Arrived at Mr. Bughouse's door the cat observed that this lacked paint, gathered from the washing festooning the small garden that this householder possessed at least six children, and concluded that it would find him reasonable.

'I come to congratulate you as the winner of the Name competition,' said the cat, when the householder appeared, 'but I may say that our adoption of your suggestion has conditions attached. We cannot, for example, give you ten thousand pounds. The suggestion is not worth it, though it is the best of a bad bunch. We offer one hundred on condition—this is the crux of the matter—that you will sign a receipt for ten thousand.'

Mr. Bughouse began to protest; but the cat assured him that it was a question of one hundred or nothing, and declared that it could easily find another more amenable winner. At this moment the six children returned from school, and Bughouse, with a sigh, signed the receipt and received one hundred pounds cash down.

With this the cat returned to Jack; and though it did not recount the methods which had been employed, Jack knew by now enough of the ways of money to understand that all was not well.

'I am afraid,' said he, 'that you must in some way have deceived this poor man.'

'I have adopted a perfectly defensible financial practice,' replied the cat, 'for which I find example in certain dealings which have taken place recently in the bonds of a foreign country. This country announced that it could not pay interest on its own stock; upon which the bonds dropped to bed-rock, and at once this adroit government bought them in. Mr. Bughouse had only to hold on to his own idea and our promise; instead, he allowed himself to be stampeded.'

HELEN SIMPSON

'Well,' said Jack dubiously, 'but that was a foreign country. However, as you say, he has only himself to blame.'

The newspaper thus started with a capital of £9900, displayed a photograph of Mr. Bughouse's receipt on its front page in the first issue, and by devising a weekly competition on similar lines was able in a very short time to sell five million copies daily; despite which its advertising space, strangely enough, was not much sought after. Its policy continued to be directed by Jack along the lines of his speech to the millers, for though he had modified all public expressions of this opinion his heart was unchanged, and he really wished the mills of England to prosper. Since he had now a very great deal of money at command he was able to stand up for his policy in a practical manner, which had the approval of many patriots. He equipped a small private fleet of fast launches manned by young men dressed in crimson dungarees. These learned seamanship without costing the country a penny, and were reviewed from time to time by Admirals, who extolled the qualities of promptness and self-reliance which such a training must evoke. The manœuvres consisted of waylaying ships bringing flour from abroad, boarding them, and flooding the cargo with sea-water by means of special hoses. Experience thus was gained which might be of value in war-time, nobody (except the insurance companies) was a penny the worse, and the price of grain in England began gradually to rise.

After a time Jack Millerson, contented with the progress he had made but wishing it to have the sanction of tradition, sent up several members to put forward and support

his views in the House of Commons. This little block of fifteen men, sitting as Independents, at once took that position
which had been held in pre-war Parliaments by the Irish.
They were clever, they had lungs and impudence, and, as luck
would have it, the Government of the day was in the hollow
of their hands, since seven lost bye-elections had reduced
the Government's clear majority over both other parties to
thirteen. Unwilling to go to the country, the Prime Minister
had no choice but to fawn upon the Egoists, who, however,
turned out to be completely incorruptible, and referred him
to their Ljoeder, an Anglo-Saxon word having the same significance as Duce in Italian. The Prime Minister, who saw
no other chance of getting the Tinned Foods (Compulsory)
Bill through the House, determined to win Millerson, and
sent him an invitation to breakfast.

[223

'If you do as I tell you,' the cat exclaimed on being told the
news, 'there is a title in this for you.'

'I am not, I think, an ambitious man,' Jack responded.
'Anything I may have achieved has been for the sake of a
cause. As an individual a title would give me no pleasure;
as a recognition of what I have done for English milling it
would no doubt be welcomed by my followers.'

'Certainly,' said the cat, shaking its hind feet one after the
other in a cynical manner. 'You have no right to deny them
such an honour.'

'And you shall have a collar with a coronet on it, Pussy,'
cried Jack, 'and several new pairs of boots. I owe everything
to you, and I am not ashamed to let people know it.'

'There are moments,' responded the cat, not unmoved, 'when I wonder if it might not have been better to leave you as you were. At forty odd you are not grown up; you are credulous even to the extent of believing in yourself; and you are lovable. Such a man with power in his hands is more of a menace than Napoleon. But I shall never, now, get you back to your mill. Attend to what I say, therefore, and let us see how we can diddle the Prime Minister.'

Jack arrived at 10 Downing Street very early in the morning, and was led by his host to the breakfast table. No other person was present.

'Do you care for kedgeree?' asked the Prime Minister, lifting lids off hot dishes, 'or some of this bacon, or a couple of kidneys? I particularly want your opinion. They are all out of tins.'

'Thank you,' answered Jack, 'I prefer a little dry toast.'

'Made of home-ground flour, eh?' laughed the Prime Minister. 'Always faithful to principle, even in practice.'

And with no further reference to the object of their meeting, the Head of the Government proceeded to charm his guest. He spoke of sunsets on Welsh hills, of dawns down Scottish glens, of mid-days upon Yorkshire moors, and afternoons at Woking; he explored avenues; in short, went through all the motions and hoops of a politician out to wheedle his audience. Jack held his tongue, as the cat had told him, and looked at his plate. Suddenly, in the midst of a peroration on the beauties of phrasing to be observed in the draft of a new income-tax form, out slipped the question, very casually:

'And I suppose I may count on the Egoists in future?'

Jack did not answer, and the Prime Minister, after one enquiring glance, quitted the subject without in reality departing from it very far.

'I may say, my dear Millerson, that this is perhaps the moment to tell you of another matter. It is my intention to advise His Majesty that your services have been of a nature to command recognition. If, for example, you were offered a baronetcy, may I assume that you would accept?'

Jack looked at him, remembered the cat's injunction, and remained silent.

'Or if a baronetcy should seem to you insufficient, I believe that—your services have really been notable— even a viscountcy might not be out of the question. Of course in that case there would have to be an understanding. We need money, and we need support.'

Jack did not break his silence, but he drew out his chequebook and as though in a dream flipped the counterfoils past his thumb. The Prime Minister's starting eyes saw fairy sums recorded there, twenty thousand, fifty thousand paid out and noted in a scrawl.

'Fifty thousand and the support of the Egoists,' said he, confidently amplifying his previous statement. 'Considerable help to a Government which, I do not conceal from you, Millerson, finds itself at the present juncture in difficulties——'

Jack did not interrupt the Prime Minister. Faithful to the cat's precepts, he remained expressionless, flipping the counterfoils to and fro.

'An earldom!' cried the Prime Minister.

Jack did not budge.

'A marquisate, and by Jupiter that's my last offer. Take it or leave it,' shouted the Prime Minister in a voice of despair.

'I'll take it,' said Jack, and pulled out his fountain pen to write the cheque. The Prime Minister mopped his brow, bustled about, offered blotting-paper, and congratulated Jack on a decision that was as patriotic as it was personally advantageous. Jack, however, was not deceived. He had been warned by the cat that Prime Ministers were but mortal, their power over the Honours List not always as supreme as they pretended, and that cases had been known in which donors of money had waked on the fateful morning to find themselves *Gros Jean comme devant*. It had instructed him how to deal with this possibility; and thus, when the Prime Minister at last took the cheque from Jack's hands and surveyed it, his complacency was rudely disturbed.

'It is post-dated,' said he; 'that implies a spirit of mistrust which I am sorry to find in you, Millerson. And what is this extraordinary word?'

He pointed to the great sprawling signature, 'Carabas,' which trailed its way across the cheque's right-hand bottom corner.

'That,' responded Jack, 'is the title which I propose to take. You perceive that the cheque will not be honoured until the marquisate is legally mine. After the List is out, my Egoists shall be at your disposal. And now I have the honour to wish you, right honourable sir, a very good morning.'

Returning home, he reported to the cat the successful issue of their plan. In three weeks' time it would have the right to wear a coroneted collar, and boast itself the confidential cat of the Marquis of Carabas.

'All the same,' said he, 'though you have helped me very greatly, and though I should never have reached this eminence but for you, I cannot understand what impelled you to take all this trouble. You might have left me the moment we arrived in London, and have found at once a suitable place in some peer's household; in short, have become cat to a marquis in a hundredth part of the time, and with no trouble at all.'

'True,' said the cat, yawning, 'but you will remember —or more probably you will not—one instance given by the philosopher Diderot, who had made a study of our race. He observed that cats in the Champagne district never use a plate, and always drag their meat about the floor. The food is given them, but lacks savour unless they can pretend that it is stolen. One of my forbears was a cat from Rheims, and you will find that many men also have a touch of that quality.'

'Next,' said Jack, who had not been paying attention, 'I shall require your help to find me a bride.'

'Your title will do that for you,' answered the cat.

So saying, it folded its tail about its nose and composed itself to sleep.

HELEN SIMPSON

The Little
Mermaid

LADY ELEANOR SMITH

In Memory of Hans Christian Andersen: Whose genius lay
in an ordered simplicity of style, wedded to a supreme gift
for pathos and romance. His stories, fashioned
for the enjoyment of children, yet exercise over
mature people an even greater dominion.

It was the seventh day of July, which is the seventh month
of the year, and it was Mary's seventh birthday. There was
great excitement in the old French-Canadian farmhouse
where the Domvilles lived, for she was the youngest of seven
daughters and the seventh child of a seventh child. Everyone
knows that this has a mysterious significance. The coincidence of so many sevens invested the birthday with unusual
importance, and as Mary was the baby they all adored her,
although she was so unlike the other Domvilles that Nanny
called her a changeling. The first words she had learnt were

the names of her sisters: Ray, Josephine, Serena, Violet, Georgiana, and Blanche.

At the time of the birthday, Ray, the eldest, was twenty-three, Blanche was fourteen and Mary was seven years younger. The six elder sisters were as healthy as young animals, and had the dark exuberant beauty of gipsy girls. But Mary was different. She was a tiny creature with eyes too big for her heart-shaped face. It must have been the hot Canadian sun that had bleached her hair, for no one had ever heard of a fair-haired Domville.

All summer long she wore no shoes or stockings, and her body was as brown as an Indian's. The other girls were sunburned, but Mary was a little bronze statuette.

For many happy, careless years the Domville children had played boisterous games in the untidy garden on the shores of Lake St. Louis, but now that they were growing up they spent their time dashing about the countryside in disreputable Ford cars, or going to midnight picnics and barn dances dressed in cheap but pretty muslin frocks made for them by Nanny and Grandmother Domville. Even Blanche was now old enough to enjoy these sophisticated pleasures, so Mary was left to amuse herself. She was glad of this. She loved her sisters, but she was shy, and when everyone chattered and played practical jokes she would slip away to the cherry orchard where no one followed her. In the long grass spangled with daisies stood the marble figure of a boy. Grandfather Domville had brought it from Florence long ago. The marble boy was her most treasured possession; he always looked happy, and his eyes were not sightless like those of other statues. She told him all her secrets, and he smiled at her confidentially.

Sometimes she went down to the lake at dusk, and sat on the little pier that jutted out into the silent water. After the sun had set there was an hour of tender hesitation before night fell on the drowsy world and the stars came out one by one. Here she was often joined by Little Moose, an Indian who years ago had been her father's guide in the Laurentian Mountains. Her father and mother were dead now, but Little Moose had remained with the family, making himself indispensable in many ways. He received a small wage for helping in the garden, shining boots, and blacking fireplaces, but his real talents did not lie in this direction. There was nothing about the woods and rivers that Little Moose did not know. The animals and birds were his friends, and he knew the names of all the fish that darted through the waters of the lake.

Mary loved him, for he had taught her to paddle a canoe, to build a wigwam, and to swim and dive like a fish. On fine summer evenings he would light a fire on the beach, and roast potatoes or corn on the cob in the embers. Then he and Mary would squat together on the pier, munching in dreamy silence.

Sometimes for a treat he would take her to shoot the rapids near Windmill Point. This was a real adventure. Little Moose stood upright in the stern and guided the birch-bark canoe with agile movements. He swayed skilfully to and fro, and the canoe, obedient to every quiver of his body, slid between perilous rocks, lurched suddenly, righted itself, shot down foaming cataracts, and at last glided into deep and peaceful waters. Little Moose was no longer young, but the grace of the savage dies hard. His dark body, the cruel nobility of his features, achieved against the blue of noon a tragic beauty. As he surveyed the lakes and forests that were his birthright, the soul of a dying people brooded in his eyes.

Mary saw it and understood, although she was a child. She felt the Indian's loneliness, for, being as shy as a squirrel, she also was lonely. This was the bond between them.

In the winter the Domvilles moved to Montreal, where there were cinemas, theatres, and parties to amuse them, but Mary remained with her grandmother in the country. Mighty winds swept in from the Gulf of St. Lawrence, lashing the forest and felling trees in the orchard. Then the old farmhouse, frosted like a sugar-cake, was engulfed in mammoth snow-drifts, and glittering icicles hung from its crooked eaves. In the long winter months Mary and Little Moose skated across the frozen lake and tramped the white fields on snow-shoes. They knew the surrounding country for miles. They belonged to it.

But the winter was gone. It was July. The air quivered in the heat, and the flowers were so big and so extravagantly coloured that the garden looked like a jungle.

On the morning of the birthday everyone was up at dawn. Grandmother Domville and Cook were rather short-tempered, for the kitchen was like a furnace, and it was impossible to enter it without falling over cake tins, bowls of

LADY ELEANOR SMITH

jelly, and ice-cream freezers. Fifty guests had been invited, but there was food enough for an army. Ray and Josephine motored into Montreal with a list of necessities that had been overlooked. The younger girls hung coloured lanterns, and arranged rustic chairs and tables under the trees. The fireworks, with which they usually celebrated Dominion Day, had been saved for the birthday party. It was to be a grand affair.

At three o'clock in the afternoon Nanny pounced on Mary, who was happily making mud pies. She was soaped, scrubbed, and whisked into a stiff white muslin frock; her hair was brushed and tied back with a pale blue ribbon. The idea of the party terrified her, but as it was to be given in her honour she was determined to enjoy it. Released from Nanny's clutches, she ran to the orchard, where the marble boy was waiting amid the long grass and the flowers. She made a garland of daisies for his neck, and another for his head, then, standing on tiptoe, she kissed his marble cheek.

Little Moose found her there. He had brought her two chipmunks which had been trained to eat from his hand.

'Party begun,' he said.

The party was a thrilling nightmare. There were so many people, and they played such rowdy games, and everyone screamed all the time . . .

It was after tea, when little Jacques du Bonnet had been carried home after his fifth helping of ice-cream, that a new excitement occurred.

Blanche, who always knew everything first, climbed over the garden fence.

The Little Mermaid

'I've been over to the Wardens,' she panted, 'and what do you think? . . . the English cousin has actually arrived! Mrs. Warden is bringing him round here in a minute!'

Everyone began to chatter and shout again.

'He is terribly handsome, and he has just left Eton,' Georgiana proclaimed excitedly.

'Whoopee, whoopee!' shouted Blanche, 'won't it be thrilling to see what a real Eton boy looks like!'

Serena clapped her hand over her sister's mouth; Mrs. Warden and the English boy were already crossing the lawn.

Mary crept under the kindly branches of a syringa bush, hoping to escape notice. She stared at the ground, and listened to Mrs. Warden introducing her cousin. The young man's English voice was pleasant though unfamiliar.

They were approaching the syringa bush. She could see Mrs. Warden's little white shoes, and close to them a pair of big ones, coming nearer and nearer. Then Serena spoke the dreaded words:

'This is Mary, the baby. She is very shy.'

She was lifted to her feet, told to shake hands, and not to be a silly little goose. With a brave effort, she raised her head, and as she looked into the young man's face, her eyes dilated and she caught her breath. For it was not the face of a stranger. It was the face of the marble boy in the cherry orchard.

It was so hot that their light summer clothes seemed too heavy. The sun blazed down, although it was five o'clock in

the afternoon, and everyone welcomed Georgiana's suggestion that they should bathe from the yacht club pier. Soon
they were all splashing and ducking each other in the water.

Serena sat in the shadow of the bathing hut and talked
to David Darrell, the young Englishman, while Mary, in a
minute yellow bathing suit, crouched beside them.

'What fine swimmers those girls are,' said David, as Violet
and Georgiana plunged into the lake.

Serena nodded. 'Yes! The Domvilles always distinguish
themselves in the water! But you'll be surprised to hear that
this midget has them all beaten to a frazzle,' and she rolled
Mary over on her back as though she were a puppy.

'Really!' his voice was politely surprised. 'I wish she would
give us an exhibition!'

'I am afraid she won't. She's too shy.'

Mary exclaimed:

'Oh no, I am not. I would like to,' and she smiled at her
sister's astonishment.

'Get out of the way, everybody!' shrieked Blanche, who
had overheard the conversation, 'wonders will never cease!
Baby is going to perform in public!'

They were all delighted, amazed. They clapped and
cheered.

But for once Mary was not frightened. She had forgotten
their existence.

There were three diving-boards, but she climbed up to the
highest, and stood there in the sunshine with outstretched
arms.

The Little Mermaid

David Darrell grasped Serena's hand in real anxiety:

'Isn't she too small to dive from that height?'

'You wait,' said Serena; and at that moment the little bronze figure shot into the air, straight and swift. The blue waters opened at her touch, as if by magic, and she was gone.

For a long time she swam under water, searching the bed of the lake for treasure. She was at home in this shadowy world where the sun shone palely and fishes lurked in the gloom.

At last a bright shell caught her eye, and, seizing it, she floated upward to the surface. She found herself near the life-buoy, and clambering up, sat astride it like a water-baby on the back of a dolphin. Presently she slipped back into the lake, head first, brown legs flashing in the sun like a fish's tail. Rising again, she shook the spray from her long pale hair, and made for the shore.

He was entranced. He did not wait for her to climb on to the landing, but pulled her out of the water, threw her into the air, and caught her in his arms.

He told her:

'You are the cleverest baby in the world! You are a little mermaid!'

Then he put her down, and kissed her forehead.

She held out the pretty shell and looked into his eyes.

'This is for you,' she said gravely.

Supper was waiting for them when they returned to the old farmhouse; delicious cold confections invented by Grand-mother Domville and Cook, who was a genius. There were

LADY ELEANOR SMITH

lemonade and cider, ginger beer, and lager fresh from the ice. Then came the fireworks, and afterwards they lay under the stars breathing the sweet melancholy of the summer night.

David Darrell talked softly to beautiful Serena, and Mary sat at their feet. The garden slumbered in a deep enchantment.

Long after everyone had gone to bed, Mary crept downstairs. Like a little ghost she flitted to the cherry orchard, where the marble boy was waiting. She put her arms around his cold feet and gazed into his face.

As he looked down at her, his smile was infinitely sad.

It was the seventh day of July, and Mary was seventeen.

Nanny, who was now very old, sat in her big armchair putting the finishing touches to a white satin dress which Mary was to wear at her coming-out dance that evening.

'You must look your best,' she said: 'for to-night you will make your first appearance in the world.'

Mary knelt beside her on the faded nursery carpet. She had cut a picture out of a magazine, and was pasting it into a scrap-book. It was a photograph of the famous film star, David Darrell, and it bore the caption, 'David, the Prince of Lovers.'

She sighed, thinking of the years that lay between them.

She closed her eyes, but the beautiful face eluded her.

The coming-out dance was a greater ordeal than the party of ten years ago. The ball-room of the Ritz Hotel was brilliantly lighted, and innumerable young men, with red faces and perspiring hands, swarmed round Mary, who could think of nothing to say to them. She did not know that in her shimmering dress she looked like a moonbeam, and that other women envied her.

It was Serena who rescued her from the arms of a determined youth who had whirled her round the slippery floor until she felt giddy.

'The old woman from Gaspé is here,' she said; 'come and have your fortune told!'

They made their way to a little room leading off the hall.

The fortune-teller had shaded the lights, and had placed a stuffed owl on the back of her chair, for she was a great believer in 'atmosphere.' She showed her teeth in a hideous smile, and took Mary's outstretched hand. There was a silence, then she said:

'You are seventh child of seventh child. This mean you different from others. You have strange fate. You can get wish, but it bring only pain. Better give up wish, and be happy.'

Mary shook her head. The witch drew some withered herbs from her bosom. Tearing a feather from the owl's wing, she bound the two together with a thread, muttering strange words.

'Take,' she said, 'take, and you get wish, but you suffer much. I see death looking over your shoulder.'

'I am not afraid,' Mary answered, but she was trembling.

She stumbled into the hall, and collided with an ugly, thick-set man.

LADY ELEANOR SMITH

'Pardon me, beautiful,' he apologised, 'have some ice-cream. You look as if you had seen a ghost!'

He led her kindly to a sofa, and as they ate the ice-cream he talked about himself.

'My name is Phil Boardman. I'm American! Guess you can tell that from the accent! Ever been to Hollywood?'

'No,' said Mary sadly.

'Well,' he continued, 'it's a swell place. I have a beach-house at Malibu, and an Elizabethan manor at Beverley; fifteen bathrooms, and a major-domo!'

She asked shyly:

'What are you doing here?'

'Looking around for bathing beauties. I'm casting Paul Zenda's new picture. Lots of cuties where I come from, but they don't swim good enough.'

An idea took possession of Mary.

'I am a good swimmer!' she said.

He laughed. 'Have some more ice-cream?'

She said desperately: 'David Darrell thinks I swim like a mermaid!' It hurt her to pronounce that name.

Phil Boardman gaped. He talked no more of ice-cream. He looked at her seriously for the first time.

Paul Zenda and Phil Boardman sat at the edge of Hollywood's most beautiful swimming-pool.

The sun, blazing on the white house near by, dazzled their eyes, and they preferred to look at the water.

The Little Mermaid

'Swell dump you've got here,' said Boardman, as David Darrell joined them.

'Well, boys, let's get down to it,' said Zenda.

The bathing beauties made their appearance. They varied greatly in type, but little in opulence and vulgarity.

A red-haired Juno climbed the ladder and crashed into the pool. One by one the others followed, whirling through the air with incredible speed.

It was Mary's turn. She felt sick, but Phil Boardman gave her an encouraging wink. He had been very kind since her arrival. Perhaps her determination had touched him. She had sold a seed pearl necklace, her only valuable possession, in order to buy a cheap ticket to Hollywood.

At last the moment had come. Soon she was poised high above them, with the sun as a background. Far below she saw David Darrell; his eyes were fixed upon her.

She dived, and floated downward, like a bird with folded wings. The water received her lovingly, and her passing left the surface undisturbed.

'Looks like a slow-motion film,' exclaimed Paul Zenda, in amazement.

The red-haired Juno won the competition. She had the 'curves' that Mary lacked. She had 'S.A.'

'All the same, I would rather have the eerie one with the colourless hair,' insisted David, and he smiled as Mary approached him.

LADY ELEANOR SMITH

'I have dived for you before, Mr. Darrell,' she said; 'it was long ago, when I was only seven. You called me the little mermaid.'

Simeon, the negro boy from Alabama, shook the cocktails; Pack, the butler, placed them on a tray; Arnold, the footman, handed the tray to Mary, who carried it into the garden.

David Darrell was lying in his deck-chair near the swimming-pool.

'This rotten neuralgia is worse than ever,' he told her.

She knelt beside him, stroking his head with deft fingers.

'I have been speaking to Paul Zenda,' he continued; 'you are to have a part in his next picture. It is a promise!'

He patted her hand. 'You won't leave me, will you? You are the only bright spot in this confounded place! You are just like a nice little sister!'

'I won't leave you,' said Mary.

The days became weeks, and the weeks lengthened into months, but Mary's début in pictures was indefinitely postponed. She did not care. She was happy, for she knew that David needed her. She asked for nothing more. She had a little room of her own, and Mrs. Thomas, the housekeeper, was very kind. Her position in the household was not questioned, for David was considered to be 'eccentric,' and his whims were taken for granted. His 'little sister' stroked his head when it ached, and sang to him in a small, caressing voice. He was never tired of watching her dive, and he would follow her progress through the translucent blue of the pool

The Little Mermaid

as she swam under water, the long pale hair streaming behind her.

He said, laughing: 'If I put you in the sea, you would swim away to your own kingdom and never come back.'

'Would you be sad if I went away?' she asked.

'I couldn't get on without my little sister, now that I have found her.'

Mary smiled, and bent her head so that he did not see that there were tears in her eyes.

In February the Laurentian Mountains are wrapped in snow. The silent lakes are icebound, and wolves howl through the forests.

The first sequence of Paul Zenda's new picture was to be shot at Ste. Marie de Bon Secour, a tiny village not far from the St. Lawrence. Behind it towered pine-dark peaks which precipitated themselves into the mighty river, so broad at this point that it resembled the sea.

A number of log huts were provided for the Company, the largest of these being occupied by David, Paul Zenda, and Boardman. There was a good-sized living-room with comfortable chairs, and a vast fireplace, round which they crouched during the first four days when they were weatherbound and no work could be done.

At last the temperature rose, and sunshine streamed across the jewelled snow-fields.

Joe, the habitant guide, leaned out of the window, scanning the horizon.

LADY ELEANOR SMITH

'Soon we have blizzard,' he muttered.

'Not on a grand day like this,' David assured him.

But Joe was right. Day became night, black and terrible. The blizzard seized the cabin, rattling the windows, and pounding at the door like an infuriated giant. Clouds of snow whirled down the chimney and melted in the heat of the log fire.

Joe, sitting on his heels, mopped up the streams of water which threatened to flood the room. The kettle on the pot hook began to sing, and Mary made tea.

'Go and get David,' said Zenda, 'he's asleep.'

'If this don't wake the fellow he must be dead,' grinned Boardman, as he left them.

A moment later he clattered down the wooden stairs, and burst into the room. They guessed the truth from his face. David had gone. He was lost somewhere in the storm.

Mary stumbled to the door and flung it open. The blizzard, screaming like a madman, hurled her back into the room. It took possession of the house, overturning the chairs and the heavy dresser. In a moment the floor was snowed under. The three men, struggling frantically, closed and bolted the door, but Mary threw herself against it, beating with her fists. Boardman pinioned her arms, and, carrying her upstairs, locked her in her room.

At last the blackness gave place to a forlorn twilight, and the search party set out. They had forgotten Mary. Her window was blocked with ice, and could not be opened. She broke the panes with a wooden stool, and, wrapped in her blanket coat, climbed on to the roof and slid down into a snow-bank. Wading through it up to her neck, she reached the outhouse where the snow-shoes were kept.

A moment later she was trailing across the stark white fields. The newly fallen snow, 'unpacked,' yielded at each footfall, leaving a print inches deep, so that she could scarcely lift her snow-shoes. Often she slipped on icy crusts swept naked by the storm. The cold stung her face, freezing her breath, but she felt nothing—she was unconscious of her own weariness. It never occurred to her that she might fail. Instinct guided her across the trackless drifts, and so, at nightfall, she found him.

He was lying in a hollow left by a fallen pine. He had crept under the distorted roots and was sheltered from the wind by a blanket of snow. Kneeling beside him, she found that he was still breathing.

Suddenly a light shone out of the darkness. It meant that somewhere there must be a house, and with a stupendous effort she dragged him out of the hollow. The cold was getting the better of her now, numbing her feet and hands, creeping into her blood. But the distant light gave her courage and she struggled on, a few inches at a time. Her breath came in whining gasps, but the light beckoned, and she did not falter.

Hours seemed to pass; there was no house in sight. Her strength was ebbing, and she sank slowly to her knees, still holding him. Lassitude stole over her; she wondered vaguely if it were sleep or death.

LADY ELEANOR SMITH

The most magnificent 'camp' on the shores of the St. Lawrence belonged to Mr. Ashford Kent, the American millionaire. It was situated not far from Ste. Marie de Bon Secour, and from January until March Mr. Kent brought large parties there every week-end for the winter sports. There was nothing Mr. Kent liked better than entertaining his friends, and nothing that his friends liked better than being entertained, especially when they were offered an attraction such as David Darrell, the famous film star.

David basked contentedly in the sunshine of their admiration. His adventure in the snows had lent him a new glamour, and he graciously accepted his host's proposal that he and Mary should remain at the 'camp' for at least six weeks. He agreed that they both needed a long rest after their ordeal.

It was a pleasant life, for Mr. Kent allowed his guests to amuse themselves as they liked, and his daughter, Angela, was a perfect hostess. After dinner they played backgammon, or danced to the strains of the latest and most expensive radio on the market.

One evening an orchestral concert of 'Old favourites' was broadcasted from New York. David and Angela danced together in a shadowy corner of the living-room, and near them Mary, who was still very weak, lay on a sofa. As her eyes followed the dancers, she thought that it must be delightful to wear beautiful clothes and to look like pink and white ice-cream, cool, inviting.

'This is the "Waltz Dream,"' Angela said.

The Little Mermaid

'*You* are the dream,' whispered David. Her smile vanished and she closed her eyes. For a moment they both stood rigid, then she drew herself away, and told him, gently:

'Now you must dance with your little mermaid.'

'No, she's not well enough, and she doesn't like dancing anyhow.'

They were floating in each other's arms again.

She said: 'Thank God I found you out there in the snow that night, or we might never have met.'

He held her closely.

'You saved my life, and I shall never forget it.' Mary hardly recognised his voice. She was shivering, in spite of the blazing fire.

David had become Mr. Kent's permanent attraction. After making a film in Hollywood, he always returned to Ste. Marie de Bon Secour, and Mary went with him.

In summer the snow fled away to the North. The fields were a tapestry of flowers, and the great tidal river captured its blue from the sky.

The house was built on a cliff. Far below there was a ledge which jutted over the water. From it one could dive into a natural swimming-pool formed in the rock, which was emptied at low tide. Beside it rose a monolith of granite, resembling the figure of a man. It was known as Lone Indian.

In the hot weather Mr. Kent's guests spent most of the day swimming and sunbathing. To please David, Mary gave diving exhibitions, and whenever new people arrived, she was produced as a star turn.

Afterwards David would tease her affectionately:

'You're a little wonder, but you are getting too skinny.'

'Don't listen to his nonsense; we'll soon feed you up,' Angela would say with a friendly smile.

On a breathless night in July, David found Mary lying in the grass, near a bed of night-flowering tobacco.

He lifted her up, and putting his arm around her shoulders, he said:

'Can my little sister keep a secret?'

She looked at him in terror, but he could not see her face in the darkness.

He kissed her cheek, and his arms tightened around her.

She wrenched herself free, and ran away blindly—away from him—away from the house—away from them all.

Not far from the house there was a pine wood. As Mary reached it, the moon rose suddenly, casting her sickle over the dark world. A crackling of twigs broke the silence, and a man stepped out of the thicket.

It was Little Moose.

He had come to her many miles through the forests.

He took her in his arms, and, carrying her a little distance, seated her on a moss-covered tree trunk. Kneeling at her side, he took his hunting knife from its sheath and placed it in her hands.

'How did you know?' she asked.

The Little Mermaid

'Little Moose know many things,' said the Indian.

She pushed the long, clotted hair back from his eyes, and the knife fell among the pine needles. He ran his finger along the gleaming blade, and once more pressed the hilt into her hand. For a long time they remained there in the shadows.

They did not speak.

In the house, backgammon and dancing had begun. Presently Angela asked where Mary had gone.

'I don't know,' David said. 'She ran away into the woods. Leave the side door open for her. She loves roaming about at night.'

When Mary returned, the house was still. They had all gone to bed.

Cautiously she crept up the stairs, clasping the knife against her heart. Angela's door was ajar. She opened it, and approached the bed noiselessly. The moonlight was as bright as day, and she heard the faint sound of breathing.

She raised the knife with a hand that did not tremble.

But there was someone else in the room: a ghost, with staring eyes and a distorted mouth.

She took a step forward, and the phantom advanced to meet her. For a few moments she gazed, fascinated, at her own reflection in the mirror. Then the knife fell on to the carpet without a sound.

Soon she was standing on the rocky ledge overlooking the pool. There was stillness everywhere. A veil of mist floated up from the river. It twined around her body, encircling her head in a halo of silver. She was as unsubstantial as a wraith, and seemed to be part of this fairy world of shadow and moonlight.

For a long time she did not move, and she saw nothing.

Below her, the fugitive waters crept stealthily over the basin, leaving naked the fangs of rock at the bottom of the pool.

It was low tide.

Near by rose 'Lone Indian,' wearing the darkness like a shroud. So the figure of Death might stand, silent and watchful.

The little mermaid clasped her hands over her heart. Soon she would be flying through the night: soon she would feel the waters wrenching her shoulders as she sped, like a deep-sea fish, to the bottom of the pool. The icy water would hold her in a merciful embrace until she was numb, and there would be no more pain . . . no more pain.

With a sigh she lifted her arms above her head, and plunged into the darkness.

It was high tide.

The water, blue as forget-me-nots, gurgled into the pool. It lifted the little mermaid tenderly, smoothing her brow, caressing her long, pale hair.

She slept tranquilly upon its bosom, for nothing could disturb the peace that lapped her round.

The Little Mermaid

Little Red Riding-Hood

E. Œ. SOMERVILLE

Moira Cloca-dearg (and that means, in Irish, Mary of the Red Cloak, and the way you'd say it in English is 'Cloaka-dharrig') was a nice young girl of about seventeen years. She lived with her mother, a decent widow woman by the name of Margaret Sheehan, who had a small handy little farm that wasn't maybe more than a couple o' miles out from the town of Caherciveen in the County Kerry.

The neighbours put the name of Cloca-dearg on Moira for she having a tasty red coat, and a hood on it, that the Mother made for her to wear when she'd be riding after the hounds.

It might be thought a strange thing and against nature that a small farmer's daughter would have the way and the fancy to follow hounds. But sure these weren't grand English quality hounds at all. They were no more than only them big black dogs, Kerry Baygles they calls them, that the farmers' sons keeps to be hunting the foxes, that wouldn't leave a hen nor a goose in the country if they'd be let alone. And it was the way Moira seen pictures in the town of hunters in red coats, and after she getting the pony, the world wouldn't content her

without she'd get a red coat the same as she seen in the pictures.

But wait till I tell you how she got the pony that was as near and dear to her as the blood of her arm.

She had the fancy always to be going away by herself in lonely places. She would be by the way of going to school—that was a good two miles back in the town—and the Mother would give her a bit of soda-bread and one o' them hot-bottles with milk, for her lunch. But maybe in place of going to school at all, she would stray away in the hills, and queer stories she would bring back with her to the Mother.

One day it was a little old manneen that was no higher than her knee that met her, and requested her in Irish would she come with him to the Fort above on Slieve Liath, and see the neat pair of shoes he was making for one of the High Quality there, and he said he might make as good a pair for herself, once he had the length of her foot. She hadn't but ten years then, but as young as she was, she had sense. She thanked him kindly, but she told him she had all the shoes she wanted. Sure she knew well enough it was a Cluricaune he was, and if she put a foot into a shoe he made, if it was into the lake he went itself, she should follow him. She told the

Little Red Riding-Hood

Mother how she had met the Cluricaune, and that he had a neat red cap on him, and deeshy-daushy little leather apron, and a nice civil little old lad he was too, and good company. The Mother cautioned her she had no business keeping such company. But sure the world wouldn't stop her roaming that way. Every once in a while she'd come home and say to the Mother she seen this and that—a child, maybe, that she'd think was going astray, and she'd hear it crying, and would run after it different ways, and when it had her tired out, it'd soak away into the hill from her. Or she'd hear like laughing in the air, or horns blowing. There are plenty would friken at the like o' that, but sure that was all like nothing to Moira Cloca-dearg, for her being so used to it. And another day it might be the little manneen that she might see, from her, like, and he'd be gone again in the minute, but he might wave the red cap to her, like he was friendly to her.

There was a day when the Widow Sheehan had a couple o' hundred cabbage plants to set for her cows, and says she to Moira:

'Ye're so great with the fairies, it's a pity ye wouldn't ask them would they give me a hand to set the cabbages.'

Well, that I may never sin, if the next morning she didn't find the cabbage plants all set, but where were they growing only in the path down from the hill to the cottage! The poor woman had to give the day digging them out, and setting them where they should be in the potato-garden. And wasn't that like a lesson to Moira she should keep out from the like o' them? But divil a hair did she care.

E. Œ. SOMERVILLE

Moira was about thirteen years when her Mother sent her to go back in the hills to look for a milking-goat that had gone astray on her. The little girl was searching the hill, hither and over, till she was beat out entirely, and in the finish, when she could get no trace of the goat at all, she sat down to rest herself by one of them old forts that was back on the hill, Dun-na-shee it was called for being a place that the old people said was greatly resorted to by the fairies. Moira sat down on a big stone that was beside the ope in the wall of the fort. It was very early of a summer morning and the grass was grey with the dew. She heard a sound of music inside in the fort. Very light and sweet it was, and it came out to her through the ope in the wall. It went past her then where she was sitting. As the music went past her she saw the dew brushing away off the grass, like that people were passing, but not a sign of e'er a one could the little girl see.

Well, as tired as she was, she rose up and she followed the music. She told the Mother, after, she'd nearly have to dance it was that jolly. She hadn't gone above twenty perches when she came to a level place, with good grass and ferns, and a stream running through it, and a great growth of fox-gloves, that the people say is a great fairy plant—'Fairy Fingers' they calls it, but Lusmore is the name in Irish for it—growing thick by the stream, as gay as a garden. The stream was running out from under a big rock the size of a house, and beyond the stream, lying down under the rock in the grass, so cozy, what was there but me goat! And standing beside

Little Red Riding-Hood

her, taking a sup of water for itself, there was a pure white yearling pony! As white as the drivelling snow it was. You'd hardly see the like in a circus.

The music went winding on always. Round the far end of the big rock it went, but sure Moira Cloca-dearg forgot it entirely when she seen the pony.

'O my darling little pony-een!' says she, and she crossed the stream to the pony, and the creature stood, like as if it knew her, and looked at her as wise as a man. It was about the size of a good ass.

'O if I could carry you home with me!' says Moira, petting it.

'Ho, Ho, Ho!' says it, like it was agreeable to go with her.

She turned about then and roused up the old goat, and she said good-bye like to the pony—for how could she drive the two of them?—and she started to drive the goat down the hill. She was hardly past the level ground and going on down the glen, when she heard a sound behind her, and what was it but the white pony following after her!

When Moira saw the pony coming on this way, she was greatly delighted.

'Come along my little jewel,' she says, 'we'll live and die together!'

In the minute she heard a screech of laughter from back up the hill, and a horn blew a salute, like what a huntsman would blow when he seen the fox starting to run away. But Moira didn't mind at all.

E. Œ. SOMERVILLE

'Blow away!' says she, 'I have her now and I'll keep her!' says she, 'and Lusmore is the name I'll put on her, for finding her where she was, with the Fairy Fingers around her!'

But look, from that day out the fairies had a spite agin her.

That now was how she got the pony. Every step of the way home it followed her, and when the Mother seen it she was delighted altogether. 'For,' says she, 'in two years' time it'll be grown, and many a good basket o' turf it'll carry for us!'

Moira made her no answer, but says she to herself, 'It's me it'll be carrying, and not turf at all!'

The Widow Sheehan had a near neighbour by the name of John Wolfe. His farm was next to hers, and the name of it was Caherbrech, which means the Fort of the Wolves, and long ago they say there was wolves there in plenty. I believe there was one of them patriots one time by the name of Wolfe Tone, but John Wolfe had no call or claim to him; he was no patriot at all, but a quiet, respectable man, with no wish for fighting, and having a nice stall of cows, and a good share of money put away in the bank.

But the son he had was a wild lad. Cornelius was his name, and Curley Brech was the name the people had for him, and there was no mischief and tricks done in the country but what he was at the back of them. His near way to school was through the Widow Sheehan's ground, and it was hardly he'd pass her house without he'd do some mischeevious thing to her property or herself. He was older than Moira by three years, and he was the divil's own play-boy, and never tired with tormenting her and her Mother.

Little Red Riding-Hood

And as he got older it was only worse and more tormenting he grew. He was for ever running after Moira, and bringing by the way of presents for her Mother, pounds of butter,
or a leg of pork when his father'd have a pig killed; but if
he did, he'd hide them in some wrong place, like one time
when he had a comb of honey for her, and where did he
leave it only in her bed, and didn't the poor woman throw
herself down on it, and the curses she put out of her'd fill
a house, and her own child only to laugh at her! And there
wouldn't be a day hardly that he'd not be teazing Moira. He
was a great play-actor, and as full of tricks as a fairy. He'd be
waiting in an amberbush, maybe, to lep out at her, with an
old hat on him, the way he'd be a tramp, and then letting
on to console her, and trying to kiss her when she'd be crying with the fright—the raging scamp! And another day he
might steal his Mother's old clothes and dress himself like an
old woman, and come begging to the Widow for a sup o' tay
for God's sake. And when the creature'd have it made—for
mind ye she was charitable that way—nothing would content the old *calliach* that he let on to be. It'd be too wake,
or too strong, or he didn't want but the colour of milk and
she had it drowned with cream, or it was rotten with sugar,
and the like o' that. The Widow would get mad entirely,
and would bid him walk out of her house, and then the lad
would begin to strip the old clothes off of him and throw
them on the floor, and herself'd think it was a madwoman
he was, and would roar for the Polis, God help her, with the
Barracks two miles away!

[255

E. Œ. SOMERVILLE

Didn't he go one winter night with a pot of that red raddle that they mixes in whitewash, and he painted Lusmore, the white pony, with big patches of red, the same as a cow. When Moira went in the dark morning to feed her she thought it was a cow was in it.

'O Mother, Mother!' says she, giving the big mouth, 'The Fairies have me pony stole away, and a little rackling of a heifer left in place of her!'

It wasn't till the pony roared to her for her feed that she knew her. The Mother and Moira gave the day washing her, and in spite of them she was as red as a new-born child for a week after.

The Pony was up to three years when Curley Brech done this to her, and a fine stout puck of a pony she was too. Moira would ride her far and near in a grand saddle that had two crooked horns on it, the same as a Kerry cow. The Mother got it one time at an Oxtion.

'Here!' says the Oxtioneer, 'The man that brings this home'll get a kiss that'd wather a horse!'

'I want no kisses,' says the Widow Sheehan. 'I'll bid ye two pound for the saddle, and divil blow the ha'penny more I'll give!' And faith, she got it.

It was then Moira started to follow the hounds, and the Mother made her the tasty red riding-coat, and she put a hood on it, the way the girl'd cover her head if the weather'd be bad, and it was then the people put the name of Cloca-dearg on her.

Little Red Riding-Hood

Every Sunday and every Holy-day the boys would be out with the hounds. Eighteen dogs o' them there were of the black Baygles, and they'd mostly have a couple of bracket hounds—that's the way you'd say 'spotted' in English— white they'd be and black and brown spots on them, like them English hounds. They has the like o' them the way you'd see them away from you when the black dogs would hardly be seen at all, for the hills being so dark like. They were strewed out through the country. One lad'd have two, and maybe another three, and another might have but the one. Each hound would follow his own till they'd all be met together, and then they should be answerable to the horn. And who was the lad that had the horn only me bold Curley Brech! He was the leader for them, and an arch boy he was, that could run like a hound himself, and was as cute as a pet fox, let alone a mountainy one! All the lads followed after the dogs on their own legs, but if Moira got the chance when the Mother wouldn't know, she'd pounce up on the pony, and away with her after the hunt!

The way the huntsmen had, they'd drive the dogs before them till they'd find a fox, or maybe start a hare, and if it was a hare, that'd run back and forth round a valley, the boys would wait on a hill above and see the hunt, and run down and take the hare from the hounds if they cot her. But if it was a fox they had, it might be dark night before the lads'd see them again, and it'd be no better for Moira, and she on a mountainy pony that could run on the rocks like a bird. But sure the fox'd take the hounds away entirely, where horse nor man couldn't follow them.

As sure as Moira would be in the hunt it'd always be a fox they'd find, and back in the mountains he'd carry the dogs, and as sure as there's a harp on a ha'penny that'd be the fox they'd never ketch!

'And why not?' says you.

Because it'd be a fairy fox sure! It was the spite the fairies had agin Moira, for carrying away the white pony, that they'd keep a fox handy, and the dogs never be let ketch him, and them and Moira'd be put astray, and it might be dark night before she'd get home or the dogs either. Half dead they'd all be, and the pony the worst of all.

Well, there was a fine day came in Febbiverry, it was Valentine's day (and by the same token, that year it was the last day of Shraft) and Moira was eighteen years the same day. Her Mother says to her,

'Ketch the pony,' says she, 'and throw the saddle on her, and you'll go see your Grannema, and bring her the nice present that I have for her, and maybe yourself'd get a present from her, for this being your birthday. And,' says the Mother, says she, looking at Moira very sevare, 'Let you go straight there, and no idling and gosthering with any that'd be in your road, and if you meet that limb o' the divil, Curley Brech, mootching and purshawling,' says she, 'give him the go-by, cool and nice,' says she, 'Leave him go his way and you go yours.'

Little Red Riding-Hood

'Faith and I will too!' says Moira, '*I've* no wish for him, or the likes of him!' says she, as proud as the Queen of Spain.

The Mother then puts a nice pat o' fresh butter, and a nice comb o' honey, and a lovely soda-loaf, and a dozen fresh eggs in a basket, and Moira puts on her new red riding-coat, and away with her to ride across the hill to the Grandmother. (The grandmother was old Mrs. Dan Sheehan, that was Moira's grandmother by the father. She had a power o' money, and the Widow Sheehan, that was her daughter-in-law, was for ever sending Moira to see her, and paying her little compliments of eggs and butter, and the like o' that.)

Moira wasn't gone farther than John Wolfe's farm when who would she see before her only Curley Brech, and two hounds with him, and one of them was a big black baygle, by the name of Bugler, and the other was a little young bracket bitch, whose name was Comfort; and them was the two best hounds in the country.

Curley Brech ketches the pony by the head, and puts his arm over her neck. The pony wasn't but fourteen hands, and Curley was a tall straight boy.

'Where are ye goin'?' says he to Moira, grinning at her, and shaking her by the hand, and not letting it go. 'So smart ye look in your red ridin' coat, Darlin'!' says he.

'*I'm* not your darlin'!' says Moira, pulling the hand from him (but sure she couldn't keep from laughing at the impidence he had).

'For two pins I'd give ye a good box on the ear!' says she.

E. Œ. SOMERVILLE

'Ah, ye would not!' says Curley Brech, coaxing her, and looking at her the way you'd say he'd like to eat her. 'And listen,' says he, 'I'm waiting now for the hounds, and let you wait too and have a hunt.'

'And what'll I do with me present for Grannema?' says Moira.

'I'll run back with it to me Mother,' says Curley, 'and can't
ye get it from her when the hunt's over——'

Well now, that was where the mistake was for Moira. But to think of the hunt enticed her, and she was said by Curley Brech.

It was shortly then all the lads come along with the hounds, and me bold Curley outs with the horn, and off with them all up into the hill of Slieve Liath—that means the Grey Hill, but green and sunny it was that fine Valentine's Day, and sure a person's heart'd rise on a day like it, and the hounds playing around, and hunting through the rocks, and putting yowls out o' themselves if they seen as much as a rabbit or a weasel in the heather before them.

Curley Brech, with the horn, went on before the other lads, giving a shout now and again to hearten the hounds, and walking beside the pony, and looking at Moira, and saying to her to tell him when she seen a fox, 'for none of us,' says he, looking up at her so tender, 'has the sight to see a fox the way your blue eyes can!'

Moira wouldn't let on she heard him, but Curley seen the blush on her cheek, and he knew by her she was pleased.

Little Red Riding-Hood

They weren't gone deep into the hill at all when what'd Moira see close beside them, only the little Cluricaune, and he sitting on a flat rock and the tools of his trade beside him. He took the red cap off his head and he wove it to her. Moira returned him a salute.

'Who are ye saluting at all?' says Curley, looking around, but sure he hadn't *the Sighth*, the way Moira had. But old Bugler, that was the oldest of the hounds, saw the manneen, and the hair stood up on the poor dog's back, and he growled furious; and Comfort, the little bracket bitch, seen the manneen too, and she made a drive at him to bite him, but in the minute he was gone, and no trace of him on the rock!

'Ax no questions,' says Moira to Curley, teasing him, 'and ye'll be told no lies!' but she had it hardly said when she seen the manneen again, standing up on the rock, and waving his red cap up to the hill, saying 'Tally-Ho!' and giving little small screeches, that not a one heard only Moira, and old Bugler, and Comfort, the little bracket bitch. Moira looks up at the hill, and what was there but a big grey fox on a stretch of rock and he looking down at them as cool as a Christian!

'Look at him above! Look at him! Look at him!' screeches Moira, 'Tally Ho forrad!' says she, and she comminces to gallop at the hill, with Lusmore, the white pony, pulling mad, and old Bugler and Comfort out ahead of her!

Well, then was the ecstasies! Curley, and all the crowd of lads, shouting and legging it up the hill after Moira, and the hounds coming from all parts and sweeping through the

crowd! Believe me, the fox didn't wait long! What a fool he'd
be, with them black Baygles, like Black Death itself, yowling
after him! They gethered like bees on the rock he was on, and
then old Bugler threw up his head, and 'Yow! Yow! Yow!'
says he, 'Here's the way he went!' says he. And Comfort, the
little bracket bitch, give a squeal like ye'd say it was a pig and
it having the throat cut, and away on the line goes the two o'

them, and all the rest o' the dogs roaring after them!

By the mercy o' God there was a good cattle-track going
up the glen. Up it goes Moira, with the pony pulling like she
wanted to ketch the fox herself, and all the lads coming on
after her, and Curley Brech blowing his horn for fear would
any hounds be behind them (but faith, it wasn't long before
the breath failed him!). When they got to the top of the
glen, there was a level place that wasn't level entirely, for it
slanted up to another rise of hill. The hounds had it nearly
crossed when Moira got up to it. Boggy it was, but not too
deep; she faced the pony at it, and sure the pony went away
over it as easy and independent as a snipe, and Curley and
the boys following on always.

On the hill beyond the bog they could see the hounds,
but hardly. Them black hounds when they gets away in the
heather, melts like into it. You'd nearly say it was a shadow
only you saw, if it wasn't for Comfort, the bracket bitch, that
shewed where they were. White she was, and spotted, and a
yellow head on her, like her dam, that was an English hound
John Wolfe had one time. Great hounds to hunt they are,

and the cry they had was like a band o' music, and the sound went beating from one hill to another, most lovely.

As tired as the boys were, they couldn't stop running with that in their ears, and with the sight always of the white pony, galloping away before them up the next hill beyond, and as steep as it was, she facing up to it as hardy as a goat.

And as for Moira Cloca-dearg, she was in glory!

Not a thought in the world in her only to keep up with the hounds. Faith, she was as proud as that she wouldn't call the King her cousin! And no blame to her! Sure she had the boys all left behind, and the white pony under her ready to run to Cork! [263

Well, above that hill was another one, and it steeper again! I declare when a person'd be climbing mountains, the nearer he'd get to the top, the further off he'd find it! And that was the way for Moira. When she got above that hill, she seen before her a big stretch of wet watery bog, and a kind of an island in the middle of it, and a wide sort of a fence that divided the bog in two halves, and crossed out to the island, and follied on from it to the far side of the bog. And there were all the hounds, and they not running at all, but going this way and that, and the smell of the fox lost to them.

Faith the pony wasn't sorry at all to stand still, and Moira seen that out beyond the bog was hills, going away away, up into the sky, to further orders, as they say! Moira looks around for the boys, but deuce a one could she see.

E. Œ. SOMERVILLE

'O what'll I do now at all?' says she, and she mad with the hurry that was in her. 'It must be that blag-yard Fairy Fox we're hunting agin!' says she.

The hounds came up round her and stood there, and they waving their tails, and looking up at her, and blaming her for themselves losing the smell.

'Sure I can't help ye, my darlings,' says she to them, 'I d'no no more than yoursels what way is he gone at all!'

With that some o' them lies down and comminces to roll, and more comminces to scratch, and old Bugler comes up to the pony's shoulder, and sits down, and looks at Moira, with his long ears hanging down beside his nose, and his eyes drooping in his head, like his heart was broke. And Comfort, the little bracket bitch, strays away for herself, and goes wandering around, nosing every place, and getting no satisfaction. Moira was fit to cry; and not for herself alone, but for the dogs that were waiting on her, and she not able to do a thing for them.

And that now was the minute she heard the horn! Not Curley Brech's horn at all, but a little fairy horn, no louder than a blackbird's pipe, and it going on strong, blowing 'Gone away!' And then what did she see but two crowds of fairies, and they galloping along out of the little island, on the top of the fence across the bog! Some o' them was on little weeshy horses, and some only floating in the air, and all colours on them like butterflies! And then old Bugler rose up and begins to growl, and what was it but the manneen with the red cap beside her!

Little Red Riding-Hood

'Let you not go that way at all!' says he in Irish. Moira lepped in her saddle.

'And why not?' says she, jumping mad to start after the fairies; 'isn't that the way the fox went?' says she. 'Surely I will go!' says she.

'It's no good for ye!' says the manneen.

But there was no holding Moira. She ketches the pony by the head and away with her down to the fence that crossed the bog, and she screeching to the hounds:

'Forrad! Forrad! Forrad! Tally-Ho forrad!' Well! The hounds that were so idle and dull, come sweeping on after her like a flood of black water, and the young ones throwing their tongues, and not knowing the reason why at all—the creatures! Old Bugler and Comfort, the little bracket bitch, weren't running with the rest at all, but going one either side of the pony, and not a word out of them. When Moira comes down to where the fence started to cross the bog, all the pack mounts up on the fence before her, only Bugler and Comfort never stirs, and they stands still before Moira like they wanted to stop her going on the fence.

'What ails ye?' says Moira, scolding them; 'Get forrad there!' says she, ''Ware horse!' says she, very angry, riding at them.

They let her pass then, and up on the fence she goes after the hounds that was racing out along it with their heads down, and the cry that they rose then'd put the heart across in your body! Away they streams along the top o' the fence, the way

[265

the fairies went, and Moira and the white pony after them as clever as one o' them Frenchmen that can walk a rope!

But will ye believe me, half-way across the bog, when Moira got to the little island that was in it, she saw the hounds check, and then, one after the other, she seen them lep out of her sight!

Lusmore, the white pony, stops short.

266]

'What's the matter with ye?' says Moira, mad angry, hitting her a slap with the little *kippen* she had for a whip.

The pony walks on a few steps, and what was there before them but a gap between the island and where the fence continued on, twenty feet and more wide, of deep dark water! When Moira got to it, the most of the hounds was in it, swimming across, and the leaders climbing up on to the fence beyond, and follying on the way the fairies went.

Moira looks at the black water, and she knew then it was the divilment of the fairies that had led her that way, and if it wasn't for the pony being a match for their tricks, she might have galloped into it and never come out of it at all. (Sure bog-holes the like o' that goes down into the next world altogether!)

'It's as good for us to go home,' says she to Lusmore the white pony, and she like to cry, seeing the hounds going from her. She turns around and back with her along the crown o' the fence, and there was old Bugler, and Comfort, the little bracket bitch, sitting waiting for her.

Little Red Riding-Hood

'Shew me the way home, good hounds!' says she. Bugler looks up at her, and he growls.

And there was the Cluricaune sitting on a rise o' ground beside her, and he laughing at her!

'Bad luck to them fairies!' says Moira to him, 'putting me astray this way.'

'Why wouldn't ye be said by me?' says the manneen in Irish. 'Go home now,' he says, 'and do as your Mother bid ye.'

He commences to hammer at the little brogue he was making, and while Moira was looking at him, he soaked away into the hill.

It was only then that Moira thought of the basket she was to take to the Grandmother.

'O murder!' says she, 'Mamma'll kill me!'

It was well for her Bugler and Comfort was Curley Brech's, and it was for Caherbrech farm they made, and Moira after them, to fetch the basket. Five long Irish miles back in the hills she was; the rain had begun; she put the hood of the Cloca-dearg over her head, and followed on after the two hounds.

The day was closing in when she comes to Caherbrech. Mrs. Wolfe, that was Curley's mother, comes to the door, and Moira asks her for the basket.

'Sure Curley came back from hunting two hours ago,' says Mrs. Wolfe, 'and he said himself'd run over with the basket to your Grandmother. Come in, girl, out o' the rain, and have a cup o' tea, you're in the want of it, my dear,' says she.

'Thank you, Ma'am,' says Moira, 'I'd be thankful for it, but I must go see my Grandmother, and bring home the basket, or my Mother'll kill me.'

Mrs. Wolfe let Moira go then. Herself and the grandmother, that was old Mrs. Dan Sheehan, were for making a match with Moira and Curley, for the farms being convenient that way; they didn't say a word yet to the girl or the Mother, but Mrs. Wolfe knew well that the boy would be willing, and there was time enough, with them both being as young as they were. But sure women must always be matchmaking.

When Moira Cloca-dearg got to old Mrs. Dan's house, the half-door was shut.

'I wonder,' says she to herself, 'is she home at all?—But hardly she'd be out in the rain and it so late——'

She gets down off the pony and ties her to the gate of the garden, and knocks at the door of the house.

'The door's not locked at all,' says a wake kind of a voice inside, like a hen that'd have the croup. 'Come in, Asthore, come in why.'

Moira opens the door and goes in.

The kitchen was very dark, but she sees the Grandmother sitting back in a big old hurlo-thrumbo of a chair that she had, down by the fire. She had a big white cap on her, and a grey shawl over it, and an old quilt over her knees.

'Did ye get the eggs and the butter me Mother sent ye, Grannema?' says Moira.

Little Red Riding-Hood

'I did, I did, Asthore,' says the quare voice out o' the chair. 'Come here till I thank ye for them!'

Moira goes nearer, but she felt frightened like. She looks down into the chair. She sees nothing only the old woman's spectacles shining with the fire in them.

'Why have ye the specs on in the dark like this, Grannema?' says she.

'The way I can see you better, Asthore!' says the old woman. 'Come here to me, me eyes is dark, I can't see ye at all——'

[269

Moira goes closer. She looks under the big cap and the shawl, and she sees a big mouth, laughing, and it full of white teeth!

'O Grannema!' says she, 'When did ye get the grand new set o' teeth and the big red mouth?' says she, hardly knowing at all what was she saying for getting worse frightened every minute. ('It's a wicked fairy that's in it, and not Grannema at all!' says she to herself.)

'Those are me own teeth, child, sure I have them always!' says the wicked fairy. 'Come here to me and I'll show ye what I have the big mouth for!'

And with that, Curley the Wolf—for who was it but himself, the blagyard!—leps up out o' the old chair, with the cap and shawl and all falling from him, and he ketches the little girl and kisses her till ye'd think he'd ate the face off her!

'Let me go!' says Moira, trying to loose his arms that were round her. 'What have ye done with me Grandmother?'

E. Œ. SOMERVILLE

Curley Brech holds her tight.

'She's gone to settle with the Priest,' says he. 'There's time yet! This is the last day of Shraft, and I'll wait no longer,' says he; 'We'll be married to-night!' says he.

And so they were too, and if ye'll believe me, the little Cluricaune was before them, and they coming out of the Chapel, and he threw a little shoe after them that ye wouldn't get the like of in the whole world, no, nor in the globe of Ireland neither.

Little Red Riding-Hood

Cinderella

ROBERT SPEAIGHT

There dwells apart in a secluded valley somewhere in our
Western England a woman who has just entered upon her
middle age. The house where she has lived for the last fifteen
years is not remarkably different from many others in the
same village. The brick has weathered to a rich warmth of
red; the wistaria climbs above the porch profusely; the windows are hung with white muslin curtains; and the garden
is at all times gay with colour. The two narrow beds which
separate the front door from the gate are bright at different
seasons of the year with wall-flowers and roses, pinks and
nasturtiums, sunflowers and sweet-peas. But what I chiefly
remember from my single visit to the place is a rank of Madonna lilies.

It was this splendid array of bloom, sending a fragrance into the street, which emphasised the insulation of the cottage from the others in the near vicinity. It stamped it as a place apart. I seemed in that instant of my arrival to hear about it the vibration of a human story, but I found myself comparing it rather with the Norman Church, which stood a little way down the road, than with the buildings of its own kind. For there clung to it an air of dedication, and this impression was confirmed when the woman who owned it stepped out into the garden to meet me.

I have spoken of her as already in her middle age, but her face, which was quite unwrinkled, and her figure, whose lines were generous and full, retained still, or so it seemed to me, an active and yet a painful memory of youth. The history of some intense experience was written upon her brow, but to whatever she had known of pain or pleasure she was now reconciled, for there was a total absence in her expression of that conflict which wears down the resistance and withers the serenity of the soul. The steady glance of her grey eyes as she shook hands with me argued an interior content and an acceptance of all that she had suffered.

She took me into the house and pointed me to a deep armchair, whose covering of flowered chintz reflected the sunshine of her spirit. I observed an old Welsh dresser, a gate-legged table, a number of wheel-back chairs, and around the walls photographs of people she had known. I thought that I had never seen so many photographs together, nor had I noticed their number when I first entered the room. Boys

Cinderella

and girls, soldiers and sailors in uniform, judges and barristers in the pompous accoutrements of the law, here and there a priest in a cassock, two or three débutantes in their Court dresses, dozens of men and women of all ages, classes, and kinds, photographed in as many ways. I regarded these portraits so closely that the place seemed full of snapshots and enlargements, some fresh and others faded, but all eloquent, it seemed, of a purpose to which each contributed. They spread above the open brick fireplace and I thought that a day would come when they would cover the walls entirely. I was just observing a General's cocked hat several feet above me and trying to distinguish his features when the low, deep contralto voice of my hostess interrupted me.

'What are you staring at?' she asked.

'I'm staring at all your photographs,' I replied, 'and was wondering who all these people can be. Some of them look quite important.'

'They are all important,' she answered quickly, and I thought there was a rebuke in her tone.

'But who are they?' I persisted.

Then she said—a little shyly now—'They're just people that I have helped.'

Her words recalled to me the reason of my visit, and withdrew me from so curious a contemplation of the room. There was so little that was strange, although there was much that was remarkable, about this woman that I had forgotten her somewhat bizarre reputation. I could see that she lived apart from her neighbours, although from the greeting she gave to

ROBERT SPEAIGHT

some children in the street as she met me in the garden, I was sure that she did so from no misanthropic motive; and the rows of photographs confirmed the stories I had heard of the rich motor-cars and the well-dressed, distinguished people who were said to visit her continually. And then I remembered that other detail which had always puzzled me and which nothing so far had explained; that although her house was large enough to accommodate two or three people for the night, she invariably, and, it would appear, of set principle, slept and ate there alone.

I felt that she must be aware of my curiosity, because she broke in again upon my thoughts. 'Now perhaps you will tell me what I can do for you,' she said, rather with the air of a consulting specialist. I thereupon spoke with her upon a private matter for the space of about half an hour. I shall not re-tell it here for it does not concern my story. I was vexed upon some question of conduct and I had come to her in search of wisdom. Other people had frozen me with commonsense, but I had perceived the shallowness of their admonitions. They were reasonable and manifestly wrong. My own resolution needed to be quickened by a spark of divine folly, but I could not find among all the poets, the philosophers and the saints whom the Gods visit with their peculiar frenzy, the word that would redeem my weakness. I make no doubt that I did not look aright, or perhaps my vision was cloudy and my hearing dull. The woman indeed told me so herself. She maintained that her own solution of my problem, whose

Cinderella

justice I immediately welcomed, was derived from the stored wisdom of the world.

'The genius of man,' she told me, 'has always reached the same conclusion; and I know that it is right.'

I can still recall the certitude with which she spoke these words. The lift of her head and the warm accent of her voice are now with me as I write. They bespoke the conviction of her soul. They gave, too, the impulse of originality, the sign of experience to all that she had said. In that moment she seemed to have invented anew the maxims of the greatest minds.

I left her, well pleased with our conversation. I felt myself a renewed person. She accompanied me to the gate and I noticed that a row of hollyhocks ambitiously overtopped the wall. She must have followed the direction of my gaze, for she turned aside to attend to one of the tallest stems which was top-heavy and leaning away from its fellows. I watched her fingers deftly tie it in place with the others, and I thought I discerned in her movement an illustration of that principle of order which now lay, I knew, at the root of her dealings with men.

She shook hands with me before I went. Her grip was firm and friendly and the palm of her hand was cool. Her gaze, too, was candid, uncompromising, and serene. I was about to leave her when it occurred to me to ask her name.

'My friends call me Cinderella,' she replied, 'but I don't suppose that we shall ever meet again.'

ROBERT SPEAIGHT

I thought that I understood her meaning. The pattern of her life stood out before me in that phrase. I recalled the photographs in her room, and remembered in the light of my visit the stories of which she was the central and mysterious figure. I saw that she was friends with the whole world. I thought that I had only to go out into the highways and call aloud her name, for it to find an echo in every heart.

She was known as Socrates, as Shakespeare, as Christ are known. And she was loved as they. Yet although her name was mentioned daily on innumerable lips which called to her for sympathy and received from her the truth, she stood as unfathomably apart from this circle of suppliants as Christ stood from his disciples in the Garden of Agony, as Socrates stood from the Athenian youth in the Market Place, and as Shakespeare must have stood from the loud wits of the Mermaid Tavern, whose silence on the presence of genius in their midst is the most eloquent testimony we have to that man's pre-eminence among men.

It was when she said that we might never meet again that I realised the gulf between us. I then knew that her spirit, whose loneliness was the subject of general report, was not dependent upon any human solace. It was anchored to the eternity of God. Friendship, as I had known it with others, could never in this world be ours. Yet as I went away down the valley, with not even a look behind me to see if she were standing at the gate, I called upon her name with a tender familiarity, for I believed, and believed truly, that her influence was permanent in my soul.

Cinderella

I say that I did not look behind me; and there was a particular reason for my restraint. I may as well confess that I was intensely curious to learn the secret of Cinderella's life and to know the source of her wisdom. And I felt, as I went through the village, that if I turned my head in her direction this knowledge would for ever be closed to me. I felt I should incur her anger. I told myself that this fancy was absurd; of course the interior lives of such people were withdrawn from the eyes of men. Yet, as soon as I had rounded the bend of the road and was secure from that strong temptation, I was aware of having acted rightly in a critical moment; and all through that evening, as I dined alone and pondered the events of the day, my mood was one of real, though indefinable, expectation.

I went to bed early, and fell asleep as soon as my head had touched the pillow. I was very tired. During the night I had a dream. Its lucidity and completeness set it apart from the normal fantasias of sleep. It came to me with the shock of half-awaited revelation. It was Cinderella's secret. And then I could no longer doubt that the Gods, whom we disobey at our peril in such matters, had commanded me to inscribe her story.

In a large house which looks on to the same valley there once lived a man, his wife, and their three daughters. The man was noble, and like so many of his kind, he had been guilty of a great mistake. His wife was the first, the last, and the cardinal error he committed. She had the slim figure and the boyish look which in the early twenties can exercise so strange a fascination over men. She cut her hair; she wore trousers; her movements were sudden and nervous; her speech staccato. She lacked altogether the dignity, the repose, and the easy rhythm which lend a permanent beauty to her sex.

Such counterfeit attractions soon wane. They are not of the stuff to command the continual allegiance of man. Their appeal is to something superficial, restless, and almost perverse in his nature. They gratify his appetite for change. But his deeper capacities for fidelity and for worship it is not in their power to touch. And so it came about that Hester (for that was her name) began to lose her fascination for her husband. Where she had once been slim, she was now lean; where she had once been nervous, she was now neurotic. Yet for all this she had borne him three daughters, and that was why he refused to leave her.

The two elder daughters had inherited their mother's nature, which became more marked as they grew up. Their father viewed them, as he viewed his wife, with a sort of respectful disappointment. He could see the starching of their souls. But the youngest child was the offspring of his heart's desire. Even in the cradle she gave promise of a perfect womanhood; and as her hair grew more abundant and more magnificently dark, as her figure formed into wider contours and achieved a delicate and unconscious poise, as her voice deepened into the notes of the 'cello and her laughter into the sound of cascading streams, and as her spirit became ever more securely grounded in the traditions of honour and sanctity, he felt redeemed at last from the tragic error of his youth.

It is not difficult to imagine the life of this family: the father and his favourite daughter on the one hand; the mother and her two on the other. The father and Cinderella (for that was her charming name) would often go out together for the day and explore the high places of the hills, while the others remained at home, cultivating the art of criticism. In this they became quickly adept. There was no subject in heaven or earth upon which, as they grew older, they did not have a ready and a pronounced opinion. Their mother had schooled them carefully; and in all they did they were taught to eschew enthusiasm. They were remote from anything so energetic as attack, anything so serious as conviction. They recognised the importance of modernity and money, and while they would have said that all revolutions were vulgar and most religions were absurd, the title of Tory or Atheist would have equally displeased them. They believed in being up-to-date, only not too much so, and although they would have crossed the street to avoid a Liberal principle, as they invariably crossed it to avoid a cripple, they would probably have voted for the Liberal Party—if the Liberal Party had been alive.

It was not long before the two girls, Bridgit and Alathea, began to suspect in their younger sister a standard quite other from their own. It displayed itself in different ways—in a taste for Homer, Fairy-Tales, Church-going, country walks, and the novels of Sir Walter Scott. Her values were disagreeably romantic. On one occasion they discovered a poem she had written on a dead thrush. They laughed at it and then they burned it. Yet somehow they were afraid to boast of what they had done to Cinderella; her happy smile and untroubled mien filled them with a discomfort which left them dumb.

At last the day came, which comes to every lady of rank and fashion, when Bridgit and Alathea were due to be presented at the Court. They were then nineteen and eighteen years old, and Cinderella was a year younger. Bridgit's debut had been delayed for a year in order that she might be presented with her sister. No expense had been spared in coaxing their long, angular figures into the poor counterfeit of a curtsy, and once the fat little Jewish dancing master had turned to Cinderella in despair, as she happened to be passing through the room in the middle of a lesson.

'Here, you—you,' he had cried, 'I do not know who you are, but at least you look like a woman. Come and show these obstinate young ladies how to drop a curtsy.'

Now Bridgit and Alathea knew very well that Cinderella was an adept in this art; they had seen her practise it gracefully when the younger and the duller Princes had been invited to the houses of their friends. They were therefore very much surprised when she merely blushed at the dancing-master's request, and shuffled sideways out of the room with every mark of confusion. They could not understand why she had refrained from seizing this chance to humiliate them. They said to each other, what was perfectly true, that their sister was quite beyond them.

Cinderella

The first few weeks of the London season went gaily by, and the débutantes, newly arrived at their London houses, preened themselves day by day before their mirrors. The memories of the Chase, at which most of them were ardent, and of the Shoot, which most of them pretended to enjoy (although what they really liked was the foie-gras eaten at the wayside), were now forgotten as the day of their Presentation drew nearer. Through all the routine of the social round—in the crimson and gilt boxes at Covent Garden or moving elegantly among the orchids at Chelsea—they were relatively indifferent to every idea but this.

There was no house in London, however, to which Bridgit and Alathea could proceed. Their father was much too noble to be rich. And so during the exquisite length of May they sat in the garden reading *The Sketch* and *The Tatler* and observing how people in Society behaved themselves. They were wistful and curious by turn.

'What do you do to get into Society?' they asked their father one day.

'Nothing,' he replied brusquely. But they did not understand his meaning. Cinderella, who happened to be passing by at that moment—she had an irritating habit of always passing by when they were showing to their least advantage—looked over their shoulders at the illustrated journals, lying open on their laps. She too asked a question of her father.

'Why are these people's faces so wet?' she enquired bluntly. 'I suppose it comes from sitting in such stuffy rooms. Why don't they open the windows?'

ROBERT SPEAIGHT

'The rooms in which these people sit have no windows,' he replied; 'and if they had, the people would be too weak to open them.'

'But couldn't they tell a waiter to open them? That's what waiters are for.'

'No, dear. There are some things which even the rich must do for themselves.'

And she did not understand that he spoke of the windows of the soul.

At last on the Fourth of June, a day when the most eminent of our English schools is given over to very strange practices, Bridgit and Alathea proceeded with their mother to London. They could not stay with any of their acquaintances, for these, after the way of such people, were much too busy to bother about them; and they had no friends. So they had to stop at an exclusive hotel in Mayfair for the three days before the Presentation. Here on the third afternoon their father reluctantly joined them.

Cinderella, therefore, was left alone in the secluded valley. The servants had gone out for the day, and left her supper on the table. The place was extremely quiet. Her favourite wolf-hound slept on the sunburnt flagstones of the terrace, and only a few pigeons fluttered in and out of the dovecote. The heat was intense. It would seem to have compelled the land to a drowsy silence, and to have hushed the activity of men.

Cinderella remained in a deck-chair under the apple-tree. She slept a little in the afternoon. At half-past four she made herself some tea and brought it out on to the lawn. The flies buzzed around the fluted urn. Then, as the sunlight began to pale a little and the shadows lengthen visibly, she walked out of the small gate at the end of the garden on to the hill beyond.

She crossed two or three fields of barley and came out upon the heather, which tickled and scratched her bare legs. She picked her way instinctively to the top of the hill, for she knew every inch of the ground. She would often come here with her father in the evening; and sometimes before breakfast in the early morning. She would often come here by herself. She went forward briskly to the summit, which was crowned with a curious, low, flat stone.

Here she sat down and clasped her knees with her hands. The country, with its orchards, its rivers, its churches, its black and white villages, was plain to her for many miles. She could distinguish several places that she knew. But her view was cut short by the ridge of the Malvern Hills, which she re-membered her father telling her were rather like the hills of Umbria. It was many years since she had been beyond them, and they were still the horizon of her world. She was per-fectly content within her own valley. Sometimes, it is true, she had sat like this and wondered what exactly lay upon the other side, even fearing that she herself might one day be ex-iled thither. But she wondered without envy or unrest.

To-day she imagined the journey of her family to the great Court. The railway wound among the valleys and went clean through the hills on which her gaze reposed. After that you were in Middle England. Her family had gone a long way further than that. She fell to wondering what the Court was like, and how the King would be dressed. And she was just picturing to herself the ermine of his robe and the jewels in his crown, when she remembered that there was no Queen.

For Cinderella was living in an age comparatively golden, when the House of Stuart still sat upon the English throne. The ingenuity and the ineptitude which have always alternated in the policy of those Kings still dominated the realm. On the whole this was a good thing. Ever since the second and the more egregious George had been sent scuttling back to Hanover before the advancing armies of Charles the Third, when that perfect Prince had overcome the vacillation of his lieutenants at Derby, and proceeded with the help of a whole countryside to defeat the forces of the Crown at the Battle of Hounslow Heath; ever since the soul of Whiggery was buried beneath the ashes of Woburn Abbey, and the thud of Jacobite artillery had silenced for ever the harsh capitalism of the Shires, England had been powerful and feared abroad, peaceful and prosperous at home. Neither the cruelty of an uncontrolled industrialism nor the vulgarity of Imperial aggrandisement had sapped the soul of our people. Scarcely had Charles the Third (or Great, as he is commonly called) been crowned in Westminster Abbey according to the rites of the Catholic Church, than a measure of Home Rule was given to Ireland, he himself proceeding to Dublin, and there being crowned King of the United Irish Free State by the Cardinal Archbishop of Tuam. And soon after his return property was restored and consciences were free.

Charles had also commissioned the brothers Adam to build him a great palace, in whose elegance and symmetry the spirit of the period should be seen. This was finished in 1750. It now stood, the image of a lost urbanity, and although Cinderella had never seen it, she knew it well from photographs. 'What is Hounslow House like?' she had once asked her father. 'Gibbon in brick' was his terse and emphatic reply. It was to this great house that her family was now going, to meet a King who was without a Queen. It was just this that directed her thoughts into an unfamiliar channel. It was just this idea of a man without a woman that sent her heart thumping in her bosom and rippled the usual serenity of her mind. It was this, in fact, which awakened her to the intimate imagination of love. For the first time she looked beyond the Malvern Hills with a serious enquiry, for it occurred to her that a King might look with pleasure on a woman, and she wondered who that woman would be.

She turned to the West where the sun would presently sink upon the Welsh mountains. She felt she could hardly endure the splendour of its dissolution; there were times when there was almost too much beauty in the world. The silence and the mystery of the evening had left her with a new thought, and she decided to take it down into the valley.

She descended by a different path, and came out on to the road before the house. Coming up the drive she was astonished to see a large motor-car drawn up beside the front door. She noticed that it had no number-plate. It was some visitor, she supposed, paying a late call. And then she remem-

ROBERT SPEAIGHT

bered that the servants were out and that no one could gain access to the house. But in that case why was the car standing in the drive, apparently without an occupant? With a slight uneasiness she opened the front door with her latch-key. She passed into the hall and then into the drawing-room. There was no sign of anything unusual, and she was about to go through into the boudoir, when her breath left her and she clung to a chair for support.

She had caught sight, through the window, of a stranger standing on the terrace. It was a woman of elderly appearance, but her face was turned away and her body was bowed a little. She seemed to be intent on some immediate task, for she was apparently unaware of the opening of the door behind her, and she did not turn round as Cinderella came out into the garden. In a moment the reason for this became clear. Around her feet, and confused with the folds of her flowing dress, the four pigeons were collected and she was feeding them with fine grain. The wolf-hound knelt on the further side of her in an attitude of rare docility, and it seemed as if all the living creatures in the garden were obedient to the strange Lady. Cinderella was rooted where she stood. Presently the Lady brushed the last grain from her fingers, and with a gesture of dismissal to the pigeons she drew herself up to her full height. She was extremely tall, and her whole body had the habit of command. And then Cinderella noticed that her clothes were not cut in a modern fashion, but that equally she could not be described as in fancy-dress. Her hat was wide and wound with a voluminous grey veil, which recalled the first days of motoring. Her skirt swept the ground with an antique grace. You could not attach her to any period, but she rather seemed, as she stood erect in the last sunshine, to belong to the whole of time.

'I'm sorry you were out when I called. I hoped you would open the door to me.'

She spoke these words with her back still turned to Cinderella, but she swung round as soon as she had said them. Her face was the face which Cinderella had expected to see. It had the character of a wise maturity, but she felt that it would not alter with the years. Her hair, which was quite grey, was bound into two coils upon either side of her forehead, and her smile was ripe with charity. There was something fixed and therefore divine in her appearance; the autumnal grandeur of her face would never decline into the winter of old age.

'I came to take you for a drive,' she said sweetly, 'but you must hurry up, or you will be too late.'

It was on the tip of Cinderella's tongue to ask her who she was, and whence she came, and whither she would take her, but a glance told her that her visitant would not abide the question of mortality. She waited, instead, for her instructions.

'Cinderella,' the Lady continued, softly stroking her name, 'would you like to go beyond the Herefordshire Beacon into the Midland Plain?'

'Yes.'

'Cinderella, have you ever been in love?'

ROBERT SPEAIGHT

'No.'

'Cinderella, do you know what love means?'

'No.'

'Then listen, Cinderella—and weigh what answer you give me. Do you think that you could bear that knowledge?'

'Yes.'

'You are sure of that from the bottom of your heart?'

'Quite sure.'

'Very well, then, you must place yourself in my hands and promise to do as I tell you.'

'I promise.'

'Go upstairs, then, to your bedroom and you will find a new frock laid out upon your bed. When you have had your bath and put on your dress, ring for me and I will come.'

She went to her room and found all as the Lady had said. The dress was like the ones made for her sisters to wear at the Court, but it seemed to her more beautiful than theirs. It was made of white organdie and she liked to touch it with her hands.

She rang the bell and in a moment the Lady was with her, carrying a leather suitcase. Out of this she drew several flat boxes, and from these she took an amethyst brooch, which she pinned to her bosom, a diamond bracelet, which she hung on her wrist, and a fillet of emeralds, which she fixed on to her hair. She also put into her hands a bouquet of Madonna lilies.

Cinderella regarded herself in a mirror.

'I look very beautiful,' she said.

'Yes,' replied the Lady.

'I did not know I was so beautiful,' said Cinderella.

'That is the reason,' replied the Lady; 'but you know now: that is the reason also.'

There was a pause.

'Mayn't I wear any rings?' asked Cinderella.

'No,' replied the Lady. And they went downstairs.

Outside the house the car was standing, and a chauffeur in livery was holding open the door. He had not been there when Cinderella had returned home.

'Get into the back,' commanded the Lady, 'and listen to my last instructions. If you ask where you are going, if you ask any question about me, the car will immediately turn back. When you reach your destination you will remain there until midnight. On the first stroke of twelve, you will find the car waiting for you outside the entrance of the house to which you are going. It will not be there a moment after the clock has finished striking. Be careful.'

The engine of the car was started up, when a gesture from the Lady silenced it.

'I forgot to tell you,' she said, 'to take great care of your slippers. They were fashioned in silver thread by a very holy woman. I once asked her who they were for. Her answer was very curious. "For the feet that stumble and the heart that does not fail." See that you keep them on your feet, for you cannot enter this car without them.'

'What did the holy woman mean by that?' asked Cinderella.

ROBERT SPEAIGHT

'I cannot tell you,' said the Lady, motioning the driver to be off.

The car immediately began to move, and when Cinderella turned round to say good-bye she found that she had disappeared. Nor did this in the least astonish her; her mood was too acquiescent for surprise. She was never once tempted to ask a forbidden question; there was no need, she felt, since destiny had taken her by the hand.

Shortly before ten o'clock they entered the suburbs of London. They came at a great speed through Hyde Park, and Cinderella noticed that whenever they arrived at a crossroads the lights immediately changed to green. There was no obstacle in their way.

At last they reached the entrance of Hounslow House. It was clear that they were going to Court. Soldiers in big fur hats saluted as they passed. She inclined her head to them through the window. She thought that only queens were thus saluted and thus replied to the salute.

As they drove through the arch into the inner courtyard she heard the sound of music from above. It was the melody of a well-known valse. She wondered if her sisters were dancing it, and who were dancing it with them. A man in scarlet uniform with a powdered wig opened the door of her motorcar and stood at attention as she went in. She turned round to say a word to the driver, but the car and the driver had gone.

Cinderella was not afraid. She imagined she had dismissed them herself. She was taking part in the pageant of an earthly King but she would presently discover the meaning of a love that had no end on earth. For real love, she had read, was not subject to the doom of things. She walked with her head aloft into the Hall, and receiving as she went the lustre of the lighted chandeliers she advanced up the Great Staircase. The place was empty, though the noise of the Palace was high. She was next ushered into the Throne Room, where a brilliant throng was gathered. She had never been among so many people, but she noticed that although they pushed against each other they never got in her way. She walked slowly through them, dividing, it seemed, by her mere presence the white wave of excited youth.

When she had joined the first rank of débutantes she paused to look about her. At the end of the room the King was seated on a dais. She could see him quite clearly. His face was perfectly familiar, for it was the face of English history. It had at all times commanded the admiration or the obloquy of men. The hair was long for these modern times, as though he had reluctantly dispensed with the rich curls and the flowing coiffure of his forbears. The cheeks were hollow, the lips sensuous, the eyes uncertain, the expression weary. It was a face which asked for the loyalty of men and the love of women.

Cinderella could see that he was bored. The débutantes were not attractive. Around her were a number of flat girls, and she was thinking that she had never seen a flatter pair than the couple immediately in front of her, when she recognised them as her sisters. They made precarious curtsies, but it didn't matter very much, because the King was looking the other way.

ROBERT SPEAIGHT

When her own name was announced and she moved forward, he listlessly turned his head in her direction. She dropped a profound curtsy and smiled up into his face. He returned the smile. She rose to withdraw, but he beckoned her to come to him. She came and knelt on the steps of the Throne. He raised her on to a stool beside him.

'Send all these women away,' he said, turning to the Major-Domo. 'My family has never had a stomach for flat-chested women, and still they come—they come. Give me a little respite until eleven o'clock. I will try to continue then. And, Major-Domo,' he added, 'refuse admission to any woman with red finger-nails.'

The room emptied slowly. Cinderella looked up into his face.

'Why do you look at me like that?' he asked, when they had all gone.

'I love you,' she replied. 'A Lady came to me to-day and told me that I should discover the meaning of love. She sent me here in a fast car for you to teach me.'

'But why did she do that?'

'I asked her to.'

'How—asked her?'

'I just thought on the top of a hill this afternoon that it was a pity for a King to be without a Queen.'

'The whole of England has been thinking the same thought: but damn it, the women are so ugly. My ancestors had knowledge of the other sex. Mary, Charles, James—yes, even the gloomy James—Charles the Great—God! how

Cinderella

that name crops up like an eternal refrain in my family. Believe me, my dear, a dynasty is heavier than a crown.'

'You look very tired,' she said. 'Give me your crown; sit on the floor beside me.'

He did as she told him, and leaned his head against her knee. They did not speak for a few moments.

'A beautiful woman is a restful thing,' he murmured at last. 'My family has always depended upon women. —I like your dress.—I love you. Would you care to be my Queen?'

'Of course,' she answered; 'that is why I am here. The soldiers saluted me in the sentry-boxes.'

'They did, did they? If they'd done it to any other woman I'd have cashiered them.'

'They wouldn't have done it to any other woman. You know that.'

'So you're determined to be Queen, are you? All right, you'll be damned unhappy. What's your name?'

'Cinderella.'

'That's not a bad name. I hope you're not too religious. Religious women have been the curse of my family.'

'I believe in God.'

'There's no harm in that, so long as you keep it quiet. The Whigs used to call us a theatrical lot, and we certainly know how to make a good exit. Well, I'd better see some more of these tall Society girls. I'll see you later.'

She regarded him with a great pity: and then the pity in her look gave place to great hunger.

'You'll teach me,' she said; 'won't you?'

ROBERT SPEAIGHT

'Teach you—what?'

'The secret of love.'

'The secret of love! My poor child! Yes, I'll teach you that.'

'Where?'

'In the Oak Room—at half-past eleven.'

And then the doors were once more thrown open, the room filled, and Cinderella disappeared into the crowd.

She only wanted to be quiet, and she sought the silence of the long corridors. She forgot that the splendour of this palace would be hers, that the lackeys would obey her voice, that the women would curtsy around her. She did not dream of giving birth to Princes, of riding through the streets of London in a coach, of sitting on a throne, of wearing a crown. She only thought of an unhappy man. She only felt the burden of an illimitable love. She was oblivious of her own honours.

For a full half-hour she kept her vigil. She waited in lonely corners with her heart beating. At half-past eleven the King would teach her the mystery she yearned to know, and she prayed to God that she might be worthy of the revelation.

At twenty minutes past the hour, shortly after she had heard the striking of the quarter, she enquired of a servant the way to the Oak Gallery. It was in another part of the Palace and he told her how to find it. She went in silence down sombre passages lined with Chippendale and Sheraton furniture, all consonant with the architecture of the place, and past the embrasures of windows hung with brocaded curtains. She went with rapid footsteps, catching up the train of her dress, and the few people that she passed noticed that her eyes were shining.

She was just coming to a sharp turn in the corridor when she heard the sound of voices from the further side. She stopped dead. One voice she recognised; it was the King's. The other was the voice of a girl, evidently in great distress. Cinderella could not immediately distinguish what they said, but she was aware of a commotion in her breast which no argument could still. She quickly screened herself behind the curtain of the nearest window to discover what was going on.

The King now raised his voice:

'You were a fool to trust me. It is not in my nature to keep a promise to a woman.'

And a voice, light in timbre but tragic in its quiet appeal, replied to him.

'What about your martyred, sainted ancestor? He was a faithful man.'

'Poor, silly Charles,' said the King; 'he was a martyr and a saint and a magnificently self-conscious monarch, but I don't think that the rest of us would have described him as a man. Not in our sense of that word, at any rate.'

'And what is your sense of that word?' the girl broke in with indignation.

There was a pause in which Cinderella could imagine the shrug of the King's shoulders.

'The history books are full of our folly,' he replied at last. 'The quality of our manhood, like the quality of our kingship, will always be a matter for dispute. We have always been a boon to the historians.'

'My father is a yeoman farmer at Melton Mowbray. He says that his ancestors recovered their land when Charles the Great came to the throne. Your family was wise and generous then.'

'We have never been noted for generosity or wisdom, although we have sometimes been inspired by God. But we have understood the art of gesture.'

'I suppose you were inspired by God to invite me to come secretly to your Palace this evening,' she cried: 'I suppose that when I opened that gate for you as you were out hunting with the Quorn, and bandaged your head when your horse had thrown you, and took you back into my house and laid you on my bed and brought you hot things to drink,—not knowing who you were,—I suppose that you were inspired to make love to me when I came to see how you were in the middle of the night; I suppose that you were inspired to ask me to be your Queen.'

'It is rather difficult to live up to a legend,' he replied wearily, 'but I do my best. Surely it was obvious that I should ask you to be my wife, and surely it was obvious that I should break my promise. I thought you knew the rules of the game.'

'I think that Kings and their subjects play at different games,' she answered.

'You forget that in this, as in every age, I am the last of the Romantics. That is the secret of my success. I know that Romanticism returns.'

Cinderella

'I believe you live in a world of sentimental fiction.'

'That is the penalty for having inspired so much. Good-bye, Cinderella.'

'Cinderella?'

'Yes, it's such a pretty name and it's the name of such a pretty person. But you, too, are pretty in your own, your rural way. I should like you to take it as my parting present—I have no jewels handy. It will help you to remember me, perhaps.'

'I don't want to remember you. I only want to forget.'

'I can quite understand your feelings, but I am not easily forgot. There is no one who has lived so long in the memory of my subjects. And that reminds me—a soothsayer told me the other day that soon I should be a memory and no more, but a memory that would never die.'

He paused, and Cinderella could imagine with a dreadful distinctness the tear that he wiped away from his eye.

'Good-bye, and God bless you,' he continued in a lighter tone; 'go back to your farm and tell your father that I'm delighted he's a free proprietor. Not that we can take much credit for that—Charles Edward Stuart never had a taste for the Midlands.'

There was a moment's silence, and then Cinderella heard in front of her the swift passage of feet. Hurriedly she drew aside the curtain, and there passed her in that second a figure in white rushing down the dark corridor. It was lost at once in the gloom of the Palace, and there was nothing in the features of the girl which Cinderella could even roughly recall.

ROBERT SPEAIGHT

She would not have recognised her in the street. Her momentary vision was fixed upon one thing only—the agony in the girl's eyes. It was not for nothing that she had lived all her days in the country; she knew the look of a dumb animal in pain. Yet what she now saw was more tragic by far than this. There was less of query and bewilderment in that expression than an awful certainty of despair, a terrible conclusion of hope. It was an image of love's eternal crucifixion. It was love's mystery laid bare.

Cinderella did not wait an instant. She had achieved the object of her visit. She knew. She sprang from the embrasure of the window and fled for ever from the presence of the man whom she adored. His features were impaled upon her heart. She knew that she could never be happy upon the ruins of another's happiness, and that sin must be purged by sacrifice.

She had reached the head of the Grand Staircase when the clock struck twelve. She remembered the Lady's warning. She descended by two or three steps at a time. But so frenzied was her haste that it was not until she had almost reached the main entrance that she realised that she had lost a shoe.

Ten strokes had sounded, and she was paralysed with indecision. She saw the car awaiting her and the chauffeur holding open the door. She ran forward to jump inside, but the man leaped into his seat and the car had started off at a dangerous speed before she was at the bottom of the steps. She was alone at the portals of the Palace.

Cinderella

She turned back immediately, hoping that some miracle would attend the recovery of her shoe. She ran through the Hall, nearly at the point of tears, and was just beginning to climb the staircase, when she heard a voice loudly calling her by name. It was the King. She stopped in terror. The Palace reverberated with passionate, importunate cries. She was amazed that her name could sound so eloquent. And she listened with the tears streaming down her face to the breaking of a royal heart.

The voice came nearer. She dared not, would not meet him. The eyes that had transfixed her in the corridor intercepted the image of his embrace. She would make no more efforts to regain her shoe. She would fly.

Cinderella fled: out of the entrance, across the courtyard, past the astonished sentries, up Constitution Hill, along Knightsbridge, on into Kensington, Hammersmith, and Chiswick. She ran with her train dragging on the pavement, her stockings torn, her hair awry, her jewels lost, her heart broken. She remembered with a pang that there was no ring on her finger for her to lose; the foresight of the Lady had been remarkable. And no woman has ever fled from fire or pestilence or unwelcome suitor as Cinderella fled that night from the peril which is in the eyes of Kings.

It was here that I must have woken up. I can't remember exactly where the dream left off, but I think she had reached the beginning of the Great West Road. How she got back to her home I have never been able to discover: it is possible that she reached it by supernatural aid. But I did find out a few more details which complete the story.

As a result of the Court reception, Bridgit and Alathea became engaged to two middle-aged officers of the Coldstream Guards. They were immensely rich. The girls had one child apiece, which quite exhausted them. A year later their father died. This was a blow to Cinderella. But it was found that apart from the house and a yearly allowance to be paid to his wife, he had left her all his money. This was not a great deal, but it enabled her to buy a house, and it gave her a yearly income. And that was how she came to live in the small red-brick cottage in the valley.

Her mother remained in the old home until the notoriety for wisdom which Cinderella soon began to acquire among the local people embarrassed her beyond bearing. She heard that her daughter had composed three matrimonial disputes among the working-classes in a week, and when she discovered that one of these involved her own gardener, she decided to leave immediately. She sold the house for a good sum.

King Charles the Fifth raised a great hue and cry for Cinderella following her flight from the Palace. He found her slipper on the landing of the Grand Staircase, but although its photograph was reproduced in all the newspapers, its owner was never traced. Cinderella now understood perfectly how the 'foot could stumble and the heart could never fail.'

King Charles never married, but died of influenza two years later. A number of privileged onlookers were much moved by the piety of his last hours, and the Archbishop of Canterbury was in readiness in case he should want to join the Church of England; the Stuarts were always changing their religion. But he didn't, and was buried with great pomp. Afterwards the Crown lands were divided between a few very rich men, who got over a Balkan Prince—a member of the Greek Church—and made him King. This man couldn't understand a word of English, but he gave them all a barony, which was what they wanted. And then they divided the power of the country between them, some taking the newspapers, some the Parliament, some the Banks and others the land. The rest you know.

And all this time Cinderella was living alone in her cottage; yet she lived happily ever after, for she was the consolation of all her world.

'O, If I Could but Shiver!'

CHRISTINA STEAD

The day Lludd started work at Brice's, the rubber-stamp maker's, a dingy little hole down under the railway bridge, he ducked stuttering Andy, the senior apprentice, in the river. At night he related that he had seen Andy capering in a dunce's cap with his shirt-tails lifted, his way lighted by three dancing donkeys bearing lanterns, whispering in each other's ears and hee-hawing, followed by three geese and led forth by a suckling pig standing on its tail. Andy had a long face like a shoe, staring, beaded with fat sweat, and he wiped his brow constantly on his arms, so that its impression came off and his arms were presently covered with staring long faces. Andy stepped ever closer to the river, walked in, next trod in up to his knees and at last was drowned with only his old felt hat floating down the current, while the church bell gave out warning tones like the first grumblings of a storm. At this point in the story, Andy's father appeared with Andy pale as a junket, and Lludd, after staring for a second, burst into a lively laugh and shouted:

'Look at the senior apprentice! He knows his trade; he shivers like a half-set jelly, like a wet shirt on a clothesline, and I can't shiver at all. Oh, what a trade is that that men learn, that the innocent can't do at all and that old buffers do to perfection, shivering and palsying until the grave stills them forever. What a man I should be, what a rubber-stamp maker, if I could but shiver!'

That night the church bell jangled for a quarter of an hour in the middle of the night, and when the sexton went to investigate he was pitched head first down the stairs by a bogey and broke his leg; pigeons and fowls were loosed into bedrooms, goats and dogs strayed about the streets, the barnyards were stirred up, ghosts walked, bugles blew, lanterns flickered, door-bells rang with no one on the step, milk-bottles left on steps were filled with urine, letters were flung through letter-boxes threatening terrorism and extinction by the 'Horny Hand,' and other freaks and wonders took place which were blamed (and rightly) on Lludd and his juvenile band of townsboys. In the morning flocks of citizens passed by the public-house of Lludd's father threatening to boycott the house if Lludd did not leave town. Lludd very gladly agreed to. His father took him aside and said:

CHRISTINA STEAD

'Lludd, do you want to end up in prison? Have you made up your mind to a trade or a profession yet? I will do what I can for you, for no boy ever started off worse in life.'

'Father,' said Lludd after a moment's thought, 'do you know what it is? I can't do one thing, I can't shiver; that's what's at the root of all this. I'd like to learn to shiver, first of all.'

'Get out of my house, you jackanapes,' cried his father; 'don't let me see you again: you have no brains and no feelings.'

'Well, I'll go since you talk that way,' said Lludd. The old father watched him out the gate, called out 'Wait!' and Lludd waited. After a long time the father came out of the house with a bundle and a purse in his hand and said:

'Lludd, you're my son and you've been spoiled by a foolish mother: I blame her for your weakness, but perhaps there's something of me in your wildness, too: I ran wild myself once—but I know it leads to trouble. Still I can't let you go empty and naked into the world, at the next turn of the street to fall into God knows what company and monkey tricks, with your habits. Here's twenty-five florins I've saved, and here's a bundle with a shirt and a sandwich in it. But you get all this on one condition, that is that you swear me a solemn oath never to tell your name, or your birthplace, or your father's name and condition, to a living soul. You'll keep an oath you swear to your father whose face you'll never see again.'

'I never lie,' said Lludd, 'I'll promise.'

'O, If I Could but Shiver!'

In fact, only those who can shiver can lie.

'You can break your promise if you come back wealthy, honourable, famous or otherwise respected,' said the father, lingering a bit when the moment of parting came.

'I understand,' said Lludd, and turned away.

Lludd went cheerfully down the road, waving goodbye to dozens of people who had had fun with him. He went down the road and over the top of a rise and never thought to be seen in that town again. He cried out aloud:

'Now, I'm launched; a rover I am, a man I'll be; I'll make my way, I'll teach them a thing or two, I'll cut a figure in the world'; and he loped along the highway singing aloud to himself, 'O, if I could but shiver! O, if I could but shiver!'

At sunset a man came by and heard this song. 'Is that a folk-song, son?' he asked.

'A folk-song? No, it's no song. I've set out on foot to learn to shiver, because I can't. In fact, they've kicked me out of house and home simply because of that.'

'Impossible,' said the man; 'what, you've never shivered? I'll teach you to shiver in double-quick time.'

'Then, I'll give you ten shillings,' said the boy; 'there's no harm in your trying, but I warn you, no one has taught me yet.'

'Here is the spot,' said the man presently.

On a rise near the top of a hill near a thick, low copse, seven corpses hung on a great tree, the remains of seven murderers and robbers, so it was said, caught in a band when robbing a deserted castle.

CHRISTINA STEAD

'I will learn here?' said Lludd, uncertainly.

'I'll take my affydavy on it,' said the man.

'All right.'

The evening promised to be lowering and cold, the sun had gone down, swans and bitterns squawked over the sky and a wind had come up.

'Stay and see if I shiver,' said Lludd, 'perhaps I won't know when I do it.'

'You'll know,' grinned the man, 'after you've danced at the wedding of the Seven Ditch Crows with the rope-maker's daughters, for dance they will this night; but not I. You say you're out to learn; well, you'll learn this night from stiffs to fly and your skin will learn to creep. But for me, a bed in the inn and a steak: the steak is good if the inn is queer, and if the woman's garrulous, she keeps good beer. I'll come and collect the ten bob in the morning.'

'Good-night, sleep well,' said Lludd.

The man went off laughing to himself, and Lludd went up to the Seven Ditch Crows and sat under the dead men's feet for company, for he was most companionable. He lighted a fire, but at midnight the wind grew so cold that he did not know how to keep himself warm. The wind swung the bodies backwards and forwards and the ropes creaked, and Lludd said:

'They are rubbing against each other to get warm, but listen how they complain of the cold: here I am freezing by the fire; how much colder must they be up there!'

'O, If I Could but Shiver!'

Then he climbed the tree and cut them down one by one. He blew up the fire and placed the dead men round it. As they could not sit up by themselves, he propped them up with bits of brush. They sat there and never moved even when the fire caught their clothing.

'Take care, look out there, brother,' he kept crying, and he hopped about putting out the flames which caught their clothes and the brushwood, but when the flames burned the clothes right off one he got angry and shouted:

'Look after yourselves better, or I'll hang you all up again.'

The dead men remained silent while their few rags burned up—miserable sights they were, naked, dirty, scarred from their struggles, charred where they were burned, and the ropes trailing from their necks. But Lludd was tired; he had been walking all day; so he lost patience and hung them all up on the tree again, although they were very heavy.

Next morning the man came back and found Lludd ready to start.

'Now,' said he, 'you shivered, I bet.'

'How should I learn it with nothing but dead men around? Those fellows over there never opened their mouths and they were so stupid that they let their clothes burn—as for shivering, not likely! *They* don't know how.'

The man looked at Lludd nonplussed and went away saying:

'Never in my life have I met such a queer customer'; he was uneasy, he hastened his step and was soon out of sight.

CHRISTINA STEAD

Lludd walked a little way and perceived a small settlement beneath him, a country hotel, with a garden and one or two cottages about, and beyond, coming up through thick old trees, the smoke of a chimney.

'A nice place,' said Lludd, 'and if I didn't have to learn something in life, I'd stay here. But something's hidden from me; there's something wrong that I can't shiver.' And without thinking any more of the dead men he went on his way singing his tune, with the words, O, if I could but shiver!

A carter walking his horse along the road caught him up and asked:

'Hey, where are you from?'

'That is a secret.'

'A fine secret: who is your father?'

'No one must know.'

'Who wants to? What's your name?'

'I'm not allowed to tell.'

'It's not far you've come from; your shoes are clean.'

'I wiped them this morning on dead men's rags and all yesterday's dust is gone.'

'Where are you going to?'

'Wherever they teach men to shiver.'

'What's that?'

'I'm out on my travels to learn to shiver; then I'll make my fortune.'

'What do you see on my cart?' said the carter.

'J. Snooks, General Merchant,' said Lludd.

'O, If I Could but Shiver!'

'Well, J. Snooks, General Merchant, supplies everything to the neighbourhood,' said the carter, laughing, 'and even shivering I'll guarantee to supply. You'll shiver this night.'

Very soon they came into the dining-room of the inn, where the carter began calling:

'Mrs. Coppers, here's a customer for you; he's off on his travels and wants to learn to shiver.'

The landlord put his head round the door and exclaimed:

'Yes? Then there's work for him in this part of the country.'

Lludd stared at the landlord's face, which was excessively red and grown with very thick eyebrows, whiskers and beard, while his nose was too large. But with this grotesque and clumsy face went dark, quick-moving and observant eyes.

Near, in the middle of the small forest Lludd had seen, they said, was a great castle, perhaps the largest in the land, but deserted for fifty years past by the ducal family that owned it because it was haunted and could only be freed from ghosts, and its hidden treasure revealed, by a youth in his first bloom who would stay in the castle three nights in succession.

'Many have tried and none have dared stay even the second night,' said the landlady sadly. 'Seven men who tried lately were found hanged on a tree, on the hill beyond, in the morning. Don't try. What does it matter if you can't shiver? I don't see it can harm you; you're not so sensitive as other people.'

'You think so?' said Lludd, 'then that's it perhaps; and I must learn to shiver, at all costs.'

CHRISTINA STEAD

Then they told him the castle could not find a buyer; and the noble duke who owned it was obliged to live in a game-keeper's cottage with his three daughters, and try to marry them and keep a son in a cavalry regiment and two nephews in the navy on the miserable means left him. How he did it no one knew; but he had sold half his giant estate to a suburban development company for bungalows.

No one dared approach the castle, they told Lludd. Lights appeared at the windows at nights, fearful howls, hollow sounds of gongs and desolate cries were heard by those who went within a thousand yards of the walls at night. A cold wind blew continually from it, and the trees growing older and older, untrimmed, grown with moss and mistletoe, thick with rooks' nests, were fearsome even by day.

'There is one curious condition,' said the landlord: 'he who goes into the castle may take three lifeless objects with him.'

'Then,' said Lludd, looking carelessly out the window and seeing objects in the backyard, 'I'll take a fire, a wire and a piece of wax.'

That night, set in the great hall of the castle by the duke himself, whose eyes resembled the landlord's, Lludd picked all the locks he could with his penknife and his wire, melted the wax at his fire and took impressions of the other locks with the wax. On the second and third nights, despite some wretched bogeys and katzenjammer contraptions arranged in dark halls and doorways, and the effective use of tom-toms, bugles, sirens and other little wheezes, which the duke

'O, If I Could but Shiver!'

had fixed up to frighten off the scarey, Lludd discovered a very complete counterfeiting plant and a store of prohibited drugs in the castle. He now understood quite well how the duke kept, on his dwindling rents, three daughters to marry, a son in a cavalry regiment and two nephews in the navy. Then, because he was unable to shiver, Lludd was employed by the duke to distribute the counterfeit money round the country in the most handsome manner. Before a year was out he had a letter from his father telling him that he might tell his name since he had succeeded so well; but Lludd didn't care to. Lludd saw that the duke paid him off in good coin at the end of a year, when he thought the business in counterfeit coins had reached saturation point, and went his way, after having fallen in love with and seduced in turn the duke's three daughters and his middle-aged maiden sister. The duke, very properly enraged at his conduct, had Lludd arrested while discoursing with a dozen workmen in the ditch on the public highway adjoining his forests, because Lludd was heard to say (while exhibiting a bad coin to the workmen):

'See how rotten the king's head is! And you'll see that he's turned upside-down on that date . . .'

So Lludd was locked up for three years in a country gaol. He fretted and fumed, and his only thought was how to get out of gaol before the year was up. One day he went to the warder with his best manners and said:

'The men have nothing to do in the yard; why don't you let them dig little gardens round the cells?'

CHRISTINA STEAD

The warder, a kind man, agreed to that and gave the men small spades. Then Lludd began digging in his cell under the bed and made a tunnel. Each morning he covered up the hole, and before daylight put the excavated dirt outside the cells to make a garden. When he had made a hole so deep that a man could go into it and he needed a truck to take out the dirt, he collected match-boxes from all the men in gaol and made from the match-boxes a long train of little cars with which, patiently and laboriously all through the nights, they took the dirt out of the cell. Presently, after a couple of months, the tunnel went under the wall and came up into the bog which surrounded the gaol. And one night Lludd and a mate escaped and were never caught or recognised. For of course Lludd had not told his name. In this way Lludd was turned against the law.

Now, he was a long way from the place where he had concealed the money given him by the duke, but he began to journey towards it along the highways and byways. He lived miserably, poor amongst the poor, but nothing daunted him, simply because he could not shiver. He assisted at murders and druggings; he slept, without turning a hair, in a country inn with a trapdoor in the bar-room floor where drunken men were robbed and thrown head first, down into a deep well. In the stews, he slept one night with a Javanese girl of great beauty, whom he found dead the next morning from plague, puffed up, black and stinking. From her room he ran out naked into the streets, avoiding arrest by shouting 'I've got the plague, the bubonic plague.' He passed the night under a cart with a dead man and tried to warm him back to life by pressing his warm body against him, and he awoke in the morning with the dead man's jaw biting his cheek. He came once to a large town in the north and could find no hole to sleep in until he came to a decaying court hidden in a maze of rotten tenements, so bad and old that they seemed to tremble as you trod. He found them not deserted, but inhabited by more human creatures and more families than could fit into ten times as many mansions in the west-end. The one back window on the foul, green, rotting staircase, covered with rags, cobwebs and filthy emanations of households, was almost black with dirt. The pans had overflowed, and the mingled excreta and spittle of all the families in the house, most of whom were consumptive and otherwise ill, ran down the passage and the stairs, and in the centre of the court children played horses and made immature love round an open cesspool. In the basement a family of skeletons lived. The mother lay in a sort of slime in which rags could dimly be seen; she had just given birth to another skeleton with staring eyes. Little bags of bones which, worse luck, couldn't even be sold to the rag and bone man, clawed at him and begged in a gutter dialect. They were covered with sores and their hair was matted; they looked like animals, but they spoke Lludd's native tongue. Lludd looked at these creatures strangely, and he cried with true feeling:

CHRISTINA STEAD

'O, if I could but shiver,' for he realised that there was something wrong with him that he couldn't shiver at that. Thus he tried to tear out of his breast, in his boyish ignorance, the secret of immense success. He left this town, having had no luck in it, and struck out again along the high road, but when he came to the place where he had hidden his cash, he found the secret discovered and the money gone. Merrily he set out again, whistling and occasionally pondering on the strangeness of the world and its madness, beyond all that tales of ghosts and fairy-tales had taught him.

One day he saw a strange thing, like a large, tattered bird hanging to the telegraph wires. When he came closer he saw what it was, a man with burned clothing, blackened, contorted. Just then, some workmen came past and with hands wrapped in newspapers they got him down, the poor scarecrow. It was Peter Brownet, a down-and-out yokel who joined the army and who was accused of stealing the company cash-box because some money had been found on him. He committed suicide by climbing the telegraph wire and electrocuting himself. When Lludd looked at the death-dealing coins which still remained in the poor recruit's pocket, he saw that same bad shilling with the bad king's head which had caused his own imprisonment. But Lludd couldn't shiver although his middle was wrung with anguish. And he said:

'The open road, the free life, the tramp's life is too full of miseries; you see too much. I want to be cooped up, I want to wear blinkers, I'm going back to town,' and back he went.

In town Lludd met his brother Page, a theatrical manager. Theatrical people are very superstitious you know. The stage-manager somehow gets mixed into their religious beliefs—they think there's one aloft who's interested in their blowings and puffings and what they gross. Well, Page took Lludd to Madam Maritana, a wonderful parti-coloured ogress. Lludd walked up a littered lane between garbage tins next door to a theatre, where badly-mixed cats prowled, dogs sniffed trousers and old men poked in the rubbish. Up a wooden staircase black with age lived Madam Maritana behind a cretonne curtain. She wore two Paisley shawls and old Turkish slippers, had a moustache, gold-filled teeth and a port-wine breath.

'Do you wish to learn the secrets of the unknown,' enquired Madam Maritana after drawing the orange curtains; 'do you know what fate lies before you in the courses of the stars?'

'No,' said Lludd, 'I came to learn to shiver; I thought my brother Page explained.'

'To shiver,' exclaimed the lady, in a baritone voice, 'ho, ho, you are the young man who cannot shiver? You'll learn.'

'In this way?' asked Lludd a few moments later, when the lady, after gently massaging his hand and the back of his neck, approached her mouth to his own red and pouting lips. Maritana advanced the smallish foot in the Turkish slipper to Lludd's foot, murmured:

CHRISTINA STEAD

'Many learn this way.'

'Not me,' said Lludd.

The seer then rose, changed her dressing-gown in the corner, sprayed herself with Black Zebra perfume, brought into the room a large parrot and a crystal ball, and proclaimed:

'Lludd, prepare to see futurity!'

316]

She put the ball in front of him and begged him to keep his eyes fixed on it. She pressed a button, not unobserved of Lludd, and clouds assembled in the ball and began to fade away. The old one, leaning over his neck, grunted:

'Boy, what do you see now?'

'Nothing,' said Lludd.

'I see, I the seer.'

'You should.'

'I see that you will take a long journey, come into pots of money, marry a beautiful innocent girl who has known much misfortune.'

'Good, but when do I shiver?' said Lludd, who was single-minded.

'Now,' said the lady, 'your father's spirit stands before you, and with his index pointed at you says, "Son, I have a message for you; I can see you unseen and hear you unheard. Be here at Madam Maritana's place at three to-morrow afternoon and you will meet your fate and fortune."'

Well, Lludd fell into Madam Maritana's net too, but he made money out of it; he was no sucker like Page. He became the Fakir Prahna, the most celebrated society fakir of

'O, If I Could but Shiver!'

our day. He made lots of money. The women were all swarming at his feet; he performed for everyone of distinction, all the rich noddies, the old girls taking beauty treatment with their pekingeses, the timid Theosophical widows living on the alimony of husbands in India, the actors, the Monte Carlo hounds—the world of spirits, if you please, is just wild about them. His bank account swelled like a puff-ball, and Edna Freedom, the beautiful, wild and middle-aged wife of a leading rich Socialist minister, threw away home, reputation and husband to live with him.

Lludd had no bad habits and he got on. In this way he met his wife. She lived on an estate in the country with four brothers who were anxious to marry her off because she was almost forty and sentimental. She was severe in dress, cultivated in conversation, religious in practice and had a giant library. Madam Maritana saw how the land lay, introduced Lludd to her as secretary and librarian. The lady, named Esther, fell madly in love with Lludd and invented difficulties in the way of marriage to induce him to run away with her to Gretna Green. But Lludd waited, for her honour's sake, he said, for the marriage contract, which was not long in coming. The next year she had a child by him and he immediately became the perfect family man and she the perfect virago. The little brat had hardly learned to squawl like a human and not like a kitten before Lludd was festooned with the chains of domesticity. She was wifely too, the rich old bride; she put his slippers by the fire, had the finest dinners cooked for him, gave him a nightcap at ten at night, when he was used to sitting up larking, reading, dancing, listening to music till two o'clock in the morning. She even gave him an allowance for 'private pleasures,' went to the tailor's and chose his suits with him. She never left him alone for a moment, winter and summer, night in, night out. But there were no nights out, except when she went to the theatre and displayed the family diamonds. Then the young women used to look after Lludd regretfully and jeeringly as the smart young Alec who married the family diamonds and had been converted into a safe-deposit.

But pretty soon, Lludd met one who delivered him— in a way. He went down to an antique bookshop to get something rare and curious for Esther's birthday. Alone in the shop was a young, serious girl, in colouring all red, white and ebony, with hair beautifully curled up from her neck and that perfect, young, delicate, elegant beauty which looks divine with a long neck. She was retiring in manner because a maiden, and troubled by the sensation her beauty caused everywhere. She had a hesitating lower middle-class accent. What a beauty she was! Lludd dared not look at her straight but stole a thousand side-glances at her. After a few minutes' stiffness and silence, she moved gracefully about showing him the books he asked for. He found an erotic book which would please Esther, and as he stood looking through the illustrations she moved off and stood at some distance like an alabaster lamp in the dim of the shop. His heart was soft wax and moved round her image. He walked along the

'O, If I Could but Shiver!'

streets with wide and gleaming eyes thinking of the beauty, and he felt desire too, but that tender, painful desire which always overcomes one at the sight of a peculiarly beautiful and intricate design, as one of Cellini, or at the sight of a very fine stone Venus. The next day Lludd awoke from dreams of the girl with a burning love. He went back, bought Esther many books and made love to the girl. He told her all his ill-fortune, how he had been tricked into marrying Esther—a long and plausible history— how unhappy he was and the restrictions he suffered in. The letters he wrote her! He blushed himself when he re-read them, stealing them from a wooden box she kept them in.

[319

They ran away. He went with very little money, no clothes and a railway ticket, and she had a little bundle. He took a canoe moored in the river which ran through the estate and came into the great river and so to the city where she met him. At the landing-stage they set the boat adrift; nothing more than that.

After waiting two years, Esther divorced Lludd; but alas, by that time he had already taken and forgotten three or four girls. He particularly liked the bluff, artistic, ignorant art-school type of girl, a mixture of Burne-Jones and Marie Laurencin in face, odd greens and handwork in dress, who believes in Wiener Werkstätte work and art in a garret, on papa's meagre allowance; who is raving mad with love and spouts muzzy eloquence, deep-voiced from a deep bosom. He liked, too, the revolutionary girls who believed in them-selves and the flame of revolution and were equally mad with love and ambition. He vowed never to marry again—but he did. He married a girl with a china shop who had two thousand pounds of her own. She immediately gave him twins and they ate up the money (one thousand pounds as it proved) in no time at all. First of all, of course, they furnished a luxurious studio with Nepal furniture, Madras cloths and Chinese rugs, and after that they lived in the cheapest sort of hotel in one room with only their valises and the babies' crib. This second wife, Wanda, left Lludd in a year or two and went to live with her people, opening a second china shop. In the meantime, Esther sued Lludd for alimony, made false representations of his financial position and wanted him in gaol. He was now penniless, somewhat shopworn and couldn't recuperate his fortunes so easily; and he had an accident. In a fight with one of the art-school boys about one of the art-school girls he got his nose broken. It was reset at the public hospital by a harassed young doctor who was sandy and very plain, and it no longer had its fine outline.

Well, to make a long story short, just when Lludd was getting on foot nicely with a little business in ladies' gloves, financed by a madam who wanted to give up her house, and who would have married him, Esther had Lludd thrown into gaol for the alimony. There he stayed six months until Wanda, the second wife, got her people to pay it off. But by that time, of course, more was due and in six months Lludd was in gaol again. Lludd wrote to Esther from gaol a most pitiable letter, and Wanda went to see her showing her the

'O, If I Could but Shiver!'

twins and her belly in which was a third. But the four brothers threw them out bodily on the country road and Wanda came back sick, suffering, and full of reviling, to her parents.

Lludd came out of gaol and went to see Esther's brothers. The youngest, who had a little heart, took him aside to say:

'Esther doesn't want the money, she has more than she'll ever want: she wants to keep you away from the other wife— don't you know a jealous woman's a tigress?' and he advised Lludd to skip the country. So he started to leave all his troubles behind and begin in somebody's colonies. But Wanda got wind of it and had him arrested at the boat for wife desertion. For they had both heard of the amorous madam and were mad with jealousy. You have to beware of these great passions, they flow equally in all directions.

At last Lludd heard the charges were lifted and he was a free man. He walked out of gaol with greying hair at thirty and hid himself from them all, under yet another name, and with a moustache. He didn't answer telephones and moved from place to place. Soon again he had got someone to advance him the money for a refreshment shop business. He made a temporary husband for many a lonely girl. They were all grateful to him for his kindness and helped him when he was in trouble.

Then he got a delicate little note in the handwriting of Adora Lester, the beautiful girl from the antique bookshop. She told Lludd she had her job again and that her father would get him a job in the city if he got himself divorced and married her, since he had come to understand that all along

[321

Lludd had been the victim of misfortune. She mentioned a time, seven o'clock in the evening, when the shop closed and it was darkish. Lludd got himself presentable and went up with a little button-hole of carnations for her; but there, on the spot, was Esther, looking plump, well-dressed, and dark about the eyes. She had begun to make up, and as she got older resembled Madam Maritana more and more. By the hand she held a boy of seven or eight, Lludd's son, as he supposed, a sickly, dark, timid child, dressed in a lace collar and silk socks. When Lludd came up, he smiled and gave her the bouquet, and she said:

'I suppose you brought me a bouquet because you knew by thought-transference I would be here, you old mind-reader,' and with that she raised her arm, which she had held behind her back, and brought down across Lludd's face a great green-hide thong. Lludd let out a yell, but Esther laid it on, and presently people came running, although it was quiet there, near a museum, and heads popped out of windows. Men held her off, and presently, with his face and neck horribly marked, and the boy howling, Lludd made off. But Esther shook herself free and ran after him. Lludd was almost blinded and stumbled as he ran. He presently fell. In a moment she was there, pushing off the policeman, and saying:

'It's my lowdown runaway husband; I'll teach him to leave me for a pack of bitches.' She sang this out in her rich contralto which had something fearsome and inspiring in it.

'O, If I Could but Shiver!'

When Lludd attempted to get up, Esther let down a couple of stripes and yelled:

'Your madams won't like you now.'

They pulled her off, and she began to cry, saying:

'Lludd, if you'll come back, I'll forget everything; I worship you, I'll clean your boots.'

'I won't come back,' said Lludd, and fainted.

When he came to himself he was in a great, dark room, cool, sweet with the scent of flowers. He didn't recognise it at all. He felt a soft, kind hand on his and thought:

'It is Adora; at last she has brought me home.'

He felt around and switched on the bedside lamp. There, grinning horribly with love, like a man-eating ogre, with the green-hide bat across the chair, sat Esther.

'Lludd,' she said in her deep, coarse voice, and she opened her dressing-gown preparatory to coming into bed. She had got much older; she was wrinkled and wasted, but he saw the fires of passion still burned, from her intense and almost beautiful look and her welling eyes. She vaulted into bed, the savage, and at that, yes, at that, Lludd felt himself convulsed in a long network of cold sensations, as if a delicate knife gently lacerated and penetrated his skin and muscles; from head to foot shuttled the blades in all his limbs.

'Why are you shivering?' said Esther anxiously; 'why, you have learned to shiver!'

'Who is this coming?' said Lludd's mother a few days later, when a splendid automobile drew up before the public-

CHRISTINA STEAD

house. Looking out of the window they perceived a dark, fat, rich woman in furs and a delicate pale man with a silk hat.

'It is Lludd,' cried the father; 'he comes back riding in his own car: what a boy!'

'My brother was born under a lucky star; there he wallows in the Pearmain Million,' said Page at the theatre.

And Lludd, by shivering, shivering, day and night, made his money and keeps his place.

'O, If I Could but Shiver!'

The
Sleeping
Beauty

G. B. STERN

Part I

Once upon a time while the world was still young, a baby girl lay in a carved wooden cradle rocked by an ancient nurse, who, as she rocked, sang in a reedy quavering voice a soft lullaby:

'As I walked along
The Bois de Boulogne
With an independent air——'

The thousand wrinkles on her face twisted into a tender smile as she looked at the tiny rose-leaf face fast asleep on the pillow. Rose, that was the infant's sweet old-fashioned name.

Roy and Queenie, her parents, were passionately old-fashioned, and had been ever since they so unexpectedly got married and left London to dwell for ever at Briar Park.

'Reaction,' remarked their intimate friends. 'Reaction,' they repeated over and over again, with wise and owlish looks. For if they called it 'True Love,' it gave them a pain. And pain was so homely and hateful!

'Reaction. I give it a week.'

'I give it a month.'

'I give it three months.'

But they had been married now for four months and fourteen days, and neither of them thought, for one single instant, of separation or boredom. An exemplary and most devoted couple. Their friends were utterly disgusted:

'Positively, my dear, they've settled down in the country all among green grass and stuff like that. Mustard and cress. *Too* exclusive and unhealthy!'

Rose was the name of Roy's mother, and also, by a curious coincidence, of Queenie's mother; but Old Nurse never called the child anything but Beauty, from the moment of her birth.

To-day had been the Christening. Beauty had behaved beautifully; that is, according to the fatuous and doting crone who attended her; though Pollux, who as godfather had to hold the baby, would have testified differently.

There had been a little argument between Roy and Queenie over this matter of the Christening. They had agreed in wanting Pollux as a godfather: he was a darling, and the most generous person in the world. Pollux never said an ill-natured word about anybody; in fact 'Always-Ready-to-Pour-Oil-on-Troubled-Waters' was his nickname, though a little too long to be used in the give-and-take of daily life, even in those leisurely far-off golden days when our story happened.

But where the argument at the bedside began to be acrid, was on the question of the Feast afterwards. Queenie kept on insisting plaintively that she wanted a *quiet* Christening. Perhaps, who knows, she was a little influenced by the thought that in any case she herself would not be present, and that there was nothing more boring than to lie in bed and listen to chaps having a rowdy old time in the downstairs part of the house.

'My Brightest, you needn't even hear us; you're right away in a wing here, and I'll keep everything down in the old banqueting-hall. Not a sound will get through, even if we ramp and roar like hyenas. Not that we will,' he added quickly; 'I want a quiet Christening, too.'

Roy was not being strictly truthful. He was a reformed character, no doubt about it, not a shadow of doubt; reformed for life; positively Puritan; 'atta-lemonade' and all that. But there had been moments during the long four months and fourteen days spent tête-à-tête with Queenie at Briar Park, when he had wondered a little wistfully whether it would be always as dull as this; or whether in the rich fullness of middle age he might come to take a deeper interest in his own enclosed kingdom. For Briar Park was the old family seat. The antlered deer silhouetted permanently on the sky-line of his estate, the proud white peacocks strutting permanently up and down the balustrade of the terrace, the kine permanently knee-deep in the limpid stream (they never went in further than the knee), the carefully-preserved game that permanently sprang up and whirred away at the sound of his footfall through the home woods, the model farm, the slow-striking clock over the stables, his hounds surging round his feet like the waves of the Ionian Sea; would all these delights suffice in time to prevent him from feeling even one last lingering twitch of regret for those unregenerate pre-reformation nights about town?

All very well for Queenie; she had plenty to do making good resolutions and planning to bring up her infant by the impeccable precepts of the jolly old Fairchild family. He agreed, of course. Oh, he entirely agreed. Ankle-deep in buttercups his child should be brought up; waist-deep in rhododendrons. Porridge and cream for breakfast and Alphabet biscuits for supper. Not one lurid electric gleam, no sophisticated sinister sparkle of phosphorescence from the past life of Daddy and Mums, should ever shoot across that sunny daylight path . . .

But all the same, while she was still too young to be even atmospherically affected, he wanted a feast; he most stubbornly wanted a feast; good old Pollux and the rest of them; not many, just a dozen or so of his particular pals, and he didn't know what Queenie was making a fuss about!

'Pollux will expect it,' he urged, gently stroking his wife's soft bob of flaxen hair, 'and we might as well finish up the Pommery—it wouldn't last, of course, till she's fifteen' (all the children of Briar Park from time immemorial had come of age at fifteen), 'but I've a barrel of last year's vintage of Romanée-Conti laid down for her. They say it's going to be a dream.'

'*Roy!*'

'Oh, I shan't drink a drop myself. Nor of the fizz, either. But a Christening, you know, and the laws of hospitality! Pollux will expect it,' he repeated. 'Bit dreary for him just to come down and find only me and the stone ginger, and you in bed, and Beauty in her cradle. You know, my Brightest, I'm sure I've heard modern doctors say that cradles are unhealthy: something to do with the rocking, you know; puts funny ideas into a baby's subconscious.'

'I know, my Brightest, but Old Nurse took cradles for granted. She rootled round the dusty attics till she found one, and lugged it down.'

'Isn't she a bit dusty and unhygienic herself?' Roy pursued the subject; a safer one than the question of a Christening feast with the last of the Pommery. 'Oughtn't a brisk up-to-date children's nurse be under eighty-nine, or am I a faddist?'

Queenie sighed: 'She's ninety-one; and the world's bore. All very well for you, Roy; you don't have to listen. She talks nothing but proverbs; even when hell began, three nights ago, she talked right through that: "Once the Seven strew the sky, drop the latch, let none come nigh." "Once the Six are in the bin, bolt the door lest five come in." "Once the four fly through the trees, hold your thumbs and cross your knees." "Once——"'

'Good God!' interrupted Roy, aghast; 'do you think she's going to talk like that to our child? Why, it's immoral. Look here, my Brightest, shall I sack her or will you? It would Come Best from you,' he added, wishful always to spare her trouble.

'My Brightest, it's going to be terribly difficult for us to get a younger nurse, stuck right down here in the country, you know. Besides—this new generation of nurses . . . they're so damnably conventional! I mean . . . About us . . .'

Her flush of remorseful scarlet, the penitent quiver in her throat, all reminded her young husband that they had something to Live Down. Very seriously, he pressed a kiss on her forehead and walked with bowed head from the bedchamber.

So without further parley, Roy invited a few friends of his careless bachelor days (much more, as he said, to please Pollux than to please himself). And they sat down twelve guests at the banquet for Beauty's Christening.

The Pommery was consummate.

Nevertheless, the guests were nervous, except Pollux. Except Pollux, they were not at their usual ease with Roy. No other of their number had ever yet become a husband

and a father—Really, my dear, it was almost profane. Then after having had the grace to shut up about it for four-and-a-half-months and to go and bury himself, which after all, my dear, is what you expect, to come out like this into the open and give a Christening Feast! I mean, my dear, it's nearly obscene.

And then the legend of his severe conversion was causing acute discomfort. When they had discussed it in London, it had been screamingly funny; but face to face with the central figure of a morality play, actually hobnobbing with him, touching glasses—Let's not bluff about it, my dear, it's too devastating. My dear, I don't know why we *ever* came, do you? Just the most boundless devotion. My dear, do you think we shall have to *touch* the baby? That would be too ultra. I should simply swoon.

But the babe slept peacefully in her cradle up in the nursery, rocked by her ancient nurse, who sang in a reedy, quavering voice a soft lullaby:

'Maddermerzell from Ahmenteers,
Parlez-vous . . .'

And poor Queenie tossed and fretted in her big four-poster bed, stared ruefully at the great embroidered canopy, and damned the party at the banquet below, where she could not be present. And wondered if they missed her. And knew they did not. And thought: my baby is the pet and beauty of all the world—but swelp me, if I ever have another!

G. B. STERN

They had not got much further than the boar's head, when for the seventh time Roy stumbled to his feet, waved his glass aloft, and gave them: 'My daughter!' 'My daughter,' he repeated fiercely between two hiccoughs, 'the most beautiful, the most innocent, the most accomplished, the most chaste——' he wept a little. 'She takes after her father, she takes after her mother. She inherits their . . . their . . . their . . .'—he glared round suspiciously at his twelve guests. 'Well, why don't you say something?'

Roy's mood was powerfully intimidating. They hastily began to scramble for phrases that would soothe and propitiate him:

Of course, they said, Queenie's child would be beautiful and chaste; *of course*, they said, his child would have courage and good horsemanship; *of course*, they said, Queenie's child would have charm and a too marvellous figure; *of course*, they said, his child would have a brain for the higher mathematics ; *of course*, they said, Queenie's child would be seductive ; *of course*, they said, his child would have discrimination and breeding; *of course*, they said, Queenie's child would be bound to marry well; *of course*, they said, his child would have wit and subtlety——

'*Of course*,' Pollux said, 'Queenie's child——'

He was interrupted by a low, sneering cackle of laughter from the doorway:

And: 'Do pray go on,' remarked the thirteenth guest, the guest who had not been invited. 'I'm deeply interested; poignantly moved. You were saying that Queenie's child——?'

The Sleeping Beauty

Roy was the first to recover from the shock. Damon could be highly disagreeable, none knew that as well as he. In fact, since Damon had passed his seventy-ninth birthday, he had become a positive menace at parties; that was why Roy had deliberately not asked him for to-night. But still, as he was here, and not, most evidently, in a pleasant humour, for nobody likes to be excluded from Briar Park, Kingshire, better make the best of it and pretend the omittance had been accidental; the merest carelessness, in fact . . . You see, there had been a list, Damon, and then somehow they had made another list, Damon, and then they had copied out the first list, and the second list had got muddled so they had made a third list, and you know how it is, Damon, the second list had got put into the waste-paper basket, and they had had to make a fourth list from the first and third . . . And anyway, delighted to see you, Damon, and do sit down, and Jevons, bring another plate. No, I know we've only got twelve of the Sèvres, but break into the Crown Derby. No, no, no, I didn't say *break* the Crown Derby; break into it. Here's your very good health, Damon, you're looking grand! Isn't Damon looking grand? . . . Roy feverishly appealed to the company.

Damon advanced to the table, smiling evilly. A conspicuous figure, tall and emaciated, with stooping shoulders and hair dyed to such a hue of bright gold and brushed to such a burnish of smooth brilliance that it looked as though it were metal and would chink if you threw a coin at it. He always wore a long cape with fur about his neck and wrists, and a tall beaver hat. They say he had inherited both from his great-uncle, Lord George Hell.

'Please, please let no one break into the Crown Derby for me,' he murmured; 'just an old kitchen plate of the commonest pottery, cracked if you wish it. I only desire to be with my friends. Especially,' he added, his voice smoother than spun glass, 'especially at their periods of rejoicing. I heard a rumour that you were giving a party, Roy, and here I am.'

'I hope you haven't taken umbrage?' stammered Roy.

Damon pensively fingered his signet-ring . . . 'Perhaps ever so little umbrage. Yes. Perhaps.'

And indeed, he did seem a trifle nettled.

Silence lay leaden over the feast. Even Roy could not be merry nor hospitable while that sinister figure sat amongst them. He wished, now, that he had invited Damon, after all; then perhaps he might have refused, and this absolutely ghastly situation would never have arisen.

Would it be a good notion, Roy mused, to declare the feast at an end, even though it had advanced no further than the boar's head; and retiring behind the arras with his seneschal, give secret orders for Damon to be drowned in the barrel of supreme Romanée-Conti? Yes, but then what would his daughter's friends drink at her coming-of-age in fifteen years? Useless to hope that the addition of Damon would lend body to a wine that could be trusted by itself to be perfect in fifteen years. Well then——

'You were saying, all of you, you were saying, Pollux, that Queenie's child—? that Roy and Queenie's child—? Oh, I heard you: a compendium of all the milder virtues, the more shining integrities: loveliness, chastity, humility—— Well, if you ask *me*,' the thirteenth guest rapped out with sudden concentration of putrid poison in his tone, 'if you ask *me*, Queenie's child won't be long in her teens before she picks up the use of Queenie's pretty little needle; the same pretty little needle whose prick has sent so many of our débutantes to cold ruin and a colder death.'

[335

He spoke the prophecy with such gloating malevolence, that the other guests could only huddle together and whisper, with sidelong glances of helpless sympathy at the stricken father of the doomed child.

But Pollux had never been afraid of Damon.

'A fig for your black pessimism,' he remarked lightly. 'And cheer up, Roy. If your brat inherits Queenie's guts, even with this business in her blood, she'll fight it out of herself; and before she's out of her teens, I wager she'll be married and living happy ever after. Like Queenie. Whatever,' he added thoughtfully, beating down Damon with his own steady gaze, 'whatever a stylised ogre may care to say to the contrary.'

In the nursery far away upstairs, the babe woke up (Old Nurse had just nipped down to the kitchen for a stoup of posset) and wailed, pushing her little dimpled fist at some foe that threatened her from the empty air. Then, as though invisible comfort had descended, she sank to sleep again, her tiny rosebud mouth smiling at the future. . . .

G. B. STERN

Part II
Beauty's Fifteenth Birthday

Fifteen years fled by, while Roy and Queenie's little daughter grew daily in beauty and goodness and accomplishments; such was her charming disposition that Old Nurse boasted no one in Kingshire could hold a candle to it.

Like all converted rakes, Roy and Queenie had perhaps rather over-done the strict supervision of their adored only offspring. Morally speaking, they drew an invisible cordon round Briar Park, and only the most truly respectable, the most spotlessly unblemished, the most unassailably wholesome, the most ineffably dull, were allowed to pass their sentinel vigilance. They themselves, in the spirit of parental sacrifice, and frightened blue by Damon's prophecy (though to be sure Roy was too chivalrous to repeat it more than twice a year to Queenie), dwelt without grumbling in the same crystal vacuum, and brightly pretended to Beauty that this was the life and there was no other. Quite a lot of very nice county people called regularly and left cards; and Beauty was allowed to play with their sons and daughters. By reason of her sweet and unselfish temper she became a great favourite among them. Every now and then, certainly, Roy had gone up to town for a night or two to see his solicitor; and at these times Queenie was apt to retire into a little hermitage of her own and not be seen for a while. She slipped through a door behind the tapestry along the Long Gallery in the left wing, and mounted a winding stairway to a small octagonal room in the tower. . . .

The Sleeping Beauty

'Nurse,' piped little Beauty, when she was old enough to remark these disappearances, 'what's through that door and up there where Mummy goes?'

'Eh, my bairn, t'edn nowt but a wee sonsie lonely roomie. . . . And them that asks questions ere the brew be on the hob at Lammas, they du lose their tongues ere feathers strew at turn o' tide the homing peregrine. Do 'ee mark that, my butcha, my doushka machree, mein Herzensblut, and dinna fash ye no more.'

Even at an uncritical age, it occurred to Beauty now and then that Old Nurse's replies were not always to the point.

'But what does Mummy *do* up there?' she persisted, still curious.

Needlework, she was told. Just needlework.

It was difficult, in view of Beauty's strict bringing-up and the very severe standards of selection used on those who were allowed to become her companions, to decide exactly how her fifteenth birthday should be fitly celebrated. Celebration usually means a party, and a party usually means gaiety. Roy and Queenie could not but recognise that their little daughter's friends, the Amys, the Agathas, the Connies and the Lucys, if they were a little more than moron, were certainly a little less than merry. However, they were not going to break all their rules of decorum and propriety for young girls, simply for this one occasion. So they told Beauty that she might give a nice little feast for her birthday, and the invitation cards were printed in the following idiom:

[337

> I AM GIVING A LITTLE PARTY!
> DO COME!
> IT WILL BE SUCH FUN!
> *To*—Dora, Agatha and Bertram.
> *From*—Beauty.
> 5 to 9.   CRACKERS.

'A romp in the garden first,' explained Queenie to Roy; 'and then—we couldn't exactly give them tea, and we couldn't exactly give them dinner; but a sort of bobbery meal at six-thirty, don't you think, which isn't really either? with jelly and candied cherries and potted paste and lemonade?'

Roy shuddered; then pulled himself together and ejaculated solemnly:

'Very nice. Very nice indeed. They'll bring their governesses, I suppose. Dreadful women. Brrh!'

'*Roy!*'

'Excellent conscientious ladies, every one of them,' he amended in a hurry. 'And Beauty is a very fortunate little girl. A romp in the garden, and then a feast with jellies and things. Yes. Do we—er—romp and jelly with them?'

For the first time, their eyes met in deep and guilty understanding.

'Well, no, I thought not,' Queenie replied slowly. 'They're apt to get a little self-conscious, you know, if we look on and encourage them. I thought that as it was Beauty's coming-of-age, you and I might celebrate alone. A

carefully-chosen dinner, don't you think, in the small panelled room in the Left Wing? It's right away from everybody, and we shan't get mixed up in their innocent games.
And Roy, wasn't there something about—my memory was
not very clear at the time—but didn't you say, just after
Beauty was born, that you were lying down, no, laying
down, or *was* it lying down?—Burgundy, was it, or Bor-
deaux? I'm so ignorant!'

Roy understood now: 'The Romanée-Conti!' he shouted.
'Allelujah! If I hadn't completely forgotten! Queenie, you're
a marvel. What a vintage! We'll celebrate our little daughter's coming-of-age in a way to make her grateful to us all
her life.'

'Yes, dear,' murmured his dutiful wife.

Beauty was bored to death at the prospect of the party for
her fifteenth birthday. Ruefully she consulted the least awful
among her county friends, Henrietta Beatrice Victoria, as to
whether there were any legitimate way out of it?

'Imagine,' implored Beauty, 'imagine from five o'clock till
nine o'clock; five, six, seven, eight, nine; with Agatha and
Amy and Connie and Dora and Lucy and Bertram and Clar-
ence and Herbert and Patience and Anne, all prim and awful
in their accordion-pleated party-frocks and best suits. And
we shan't be able to get rid of them and get away by ourselves
to talk, as we usually do.'

Henrietta smiled her slow mocking smile:
'Don't forget there'll be crackers.'

G. B. STERN

She was a year older than Beauty; and her grandmother, a neighbouring dowager, was just beginning to notice that Henrietta was growing up a *little* on the wild side. She had not yet noticed it enough to confide her alarms in Queenie, who would immediately have placed the young girl on the undesirable list.

'I'll tell you what, Beauty. You know my brother Jack? No, you don't, he's never down here. I'll have a quiet talk with him from the village telephone-box, and make him run down, on your birthday, with some of his gang and as many cocktails as they can cram into thermoses. Oh, and I'll tell him to bring down some of the latest records, too, and we can dance. Your tunes are no good; they all date from the year One.'

'Oh, I don't know. I've got "Tommy-make-room-for-your-Uncle!"' And then Beauty flushed scarlet at the sound of Henrietta's scornful laugh. Her father had brought her down 'Tommy-make-room' last time he went to town, and she had thought it rather modern and dashing. To cover her mistake, she became enthusiastic over the notion of brother Jack, his gang, his cocktails and his new records, and begged Henrietta not to delay that important call from the village telephone.

But nothing ever works out as we imagine it beforehand. Or, as Old Nurse would less wordily have put it: 'Better the pot-ted pastes of peace eaten at the tables of harmony, than the vodka and Tokay of an inflamed spirit riding to destruction

The Sleeping Beauty

down the tipsy valleys of Sennacherib.' Or again, for Old
Nurse was rarely at a loss for a whole selection of proverbs
with which to drape every untoward incident: 'It be too late
to go vrothering after dung in a clean lane while the cows be
already passing.'

For Henrietta's brother Jack and his companions, who at
about seven o'clock turned themselves loose among Beauty's
quiet little birthday-party with something of the effect of
Comus and his rabble crew, were a great success with everybody except Beauty herself. Beauty was secretly disgusted. A
fastidious strain in her revolted at the sight of Amy and Connie and Dora and Lucy prancing about, clumsily uproarious,
under the stimulus of one and a half normal-sized cocktails.
Amy and Connie were not used to alcoholic drinks. In vain
their governesses went bleating after them, wringing their
hands and feebly expostulating. Comus and his rabble crew
dealt with this immediately by producing more cocktails and
forcing them with false flattery on the impressionable ladies.
The uproar grew, and there was nobody in authority to deal
with it.

Roy and Queenie, far away in the small panelled room
of the Banqueting Hall in the Left Wing, knew nothing of
what was going on. They were at their third bottle of vintage
Burgundy. Like rich hangings of muffled mulberry velvet,
it separated them from the frolicsome pinks and blues of
their good little daughter's coming-of-age party. Sleep was
marching towards them and would presently fold them in
his Burgundian arms. Sleep glorious and crimson-hearted as

G. B. STERN

the heart of the darkest rose in the garden. . . . Meanwhile they did not hear the shrill excited screams of laughter nor the wanton syncopated wails of the gramophone. Briar Park, for fifteen years a model home where gentleness and virginal mirth were in alliance with early bed-time and strictly tee-total diet, where the very sun seemed to shed its benison as though aware that here at least it would never set on the slightest scintilla of impropriety, Briar Park was now the scene of an indescribable orgy.

Neither Roy nor Queenie were aware that Beauty, their cherished little daughter, had disappeared and could not be found.

Suddenly their unhallowed peace was rudely disturbed. Suddenly Old Nurse burst into the room where they sat with their heads sinking deeper and deeper to pillow themselves at last on the two remaining plates which had not been broken of the famous Crown Derby.

'Waly, waly,' cried the faithful old retainer, unable even in this moment of crisis to make her meaning quite clear to the bereaved but unconscious parents: 'Du allmächtiger Gott. Haro! à mon aide! Que le bon Dieu ayez pitié de nous! Mene, mene, tekel upharsin! Ichabod, the glory is departed. Corpo di Bacco, ché fastidio! Shure the curse of Cromwell is on this unhappy house when 'tis meself is after seein' the Little Man in the rath. Eh, 'tis laāmentable! Curfew shall not ring to-night! Nem, nem, soha!' . . .

Beauty's mother continued to sleep with her head on the Crown Derby; but Beauty's father was just sufficiently awake

342]

The Sleeping Beauty

to grasp that something faintly unforeseen and maybe even lightly disagreeable had happened.

'Wharrisit?' he grunted thickly.

To make herself still clearer, Old Nurse threw her apron over her head, so that her further remarks came in muffled sobs and gasps: 'Curses come home to roost,' she wept, 'and what's bred in the bone will come out in the flesh. You canna make a silk purse out of a sow's ear. Like mother like daughter. The sins of the fathers will descend unto the children. Coming events cast their shadows before. Blood will tell. Blood be thicker than water. Blood will out. Blood——'

[343

Roy stumbled to his feet, hit her over the head with a full siphon of soda-water—he had been longing to do this for years—gave a satisfied grunt, flopped down in his chair again and fell asleep.

Part III
The Curse Fulfils Itself

The more she saw of her party, the more Beauty wanted to get away from it. This was not in the least what she meant by gaiety; nor, to her mind, was it an antidote for boredom. To her mind, it was just as boring as the party would have been had only Amy, Connie, Dora, Bertram, Herbert, Lucy, Agatha and the rest of her young neighbours of the county been present; had lemonade been the only drink, and crackers the only diversion. In fact, Beauty's reactions proved most curiously that she had been mysteriously dowered at birth with courage, chastity, a brain for the higher mathematics, good horsemanship, wit, subtlety, discrimination and breeding...

So at last, feeling a little sick, and especially resenting the unsober advances of Henrietta's brother Jack, she managed to escape from the party without anyone seeing her slip away. Wondering where she would be safest from pursuit till they had all taken their departure, she remembered how her mother had been wont at various times to seek solitude and spiritual refreshment through the narrow door behind the tapestry in the Long Gallery, and up the winding staircase into the wee sonsie roomie where, as Old Nurse said, she calmed her nerves with a little solitary needlework.

Beauty herself had been forbidden to seek this particular room; but to-day was an emergency, and surely Mummy wouldn't mind?

She drew aside the tapestry, opened the door hidden behind, and ran lightly up and up the spiral stairway that led into the tower. Sanctuary at last! And what a darling room, with a blue satin couch and cushions and everything! Beauty ran hither and thither with a child's curiosity examining the fittings and knick-knacks of Queenie's retreat. What pleased her best of all was a fascinating old-fashioned work-box, the kind that stood on legs, and was probably furnished within—Beauty had read about them in her book of fairy-tales—with little mother-o'-pearl reels and bodkins and pearl-handled scissors. Or perhaps they would be gold, she thought, clapping her hands.

But, alas, the casket was locked.

Beauty searched diligently until she found the key hidden in a secret drawer which sprang open as she ran her fingers over the surface of a small walnut writing-table of the Queen Anne period. (Why had Mummy never invited her up here to have a cosy tea-party, just the two of them, she and Beauty alone? How *odd* of Mummy!)

She fitted the key into the work-box and threw back the lid.

[345

What did it reveal?

A lovely rank of—were they pencils?—lying side by side on the velvet ridges; and below, on a series of smaller velvet ridges, a rank of little glass phials with long sharp tips, like little bottles in a doll's-house.

'Oh!' cried Beauty, ecstatic at so much symmetry and prettiness.

Then, as she gazed, a queer emotion possessed her; an emotion that was part desire, part memory . . . For she had seen this box before, open, and she had seen . . . Yes, it was coming back to her now: she had seen how the pencil and the doll's-house bottle were used together. This was not the first time, after all, that she had explored beyond the door behind the tapestry; not the first time that she had been in this wee sonsie roomie.

Memory struggled . . . Memory returned:

She must have been about three or four years old when, running along the corridor in search of Mummy, she had seen Queenie go through this door, and had slipped in after her, unperceived, and run up the stairs and stood for a moment at the door of the room left ajar; watching, rapt, puzzled . . .

A minute later, Queenie had seen her and had spoken to her sharply; bundled her downstairs; told her she must never follow her again; called Old Nurse and said: 'Take Miss Beauty at once to the strawberry-beds and let her eat all she wants!' Of course you forgot everything, eating ripe strawberries under the nets.

Now, very, very carefully, eyes big and shining, her lips parted a little with excitement, Queenie's little daughter did everything that she had seen Queenie do that time. She broke off the thin end of the bottle; and then, using the hypodermic syringe like a fountain pen, she filled it, withdrew it and even remembered to point it upwards, pressing the self-filler, so as to get any air out, before, trembling, she pricked herself with the needle.

Part IV
The Prince Arrives

The Leopard Moth was flying high when its engine konked. The pilot thought it an air-lock, glided down, tried to turn into the wind and failed. He was about fifty feet from the ground when he stalled. But he had had the presence of mind to tighten his belt, so that he was not flung forward into the cockpit when the plane crashed. Stunned and bruised, he

undid his belt, by a miracle, just before the machine burst
into flames. He had tried to turn off the petrol, but there had
been no time.

Surprised to be alive, Chalmers Prince found himself in a
queer formal pattern of hedges eight feet high, on the outskirts of Briar Park; the sun was flooding its evening benison
and farewell over the well-timbered garden, tennis court,
paddock, attractively matured fruit garden and orchard,
well-laid out lawn, rockery and shrubberies and ornamental
lake . . .

Luckily he was just taking a short flight for pleasure, and
had not been called out on a professional case; flying was his
hobby, though he sometimes used his Moth when somebody
was dying and likely to be dead at the other end of the county
before he could reach them by one of his several cars; for this
fortunate young doctor was rich as well as handsome, and as
good as he was valiant. *And* a bachelor.

He realised that he must fetch aid at once to cope with
the flames. He had not yet realised that he and his pet char-
ger had elected to fall into the precise centre of a large and
very efficient maze. Presently, however, it did occur to him;
but he was far too giddy and battered and bruised from the
accident to be able to keep a cool head and pick his way out
into the open from the numberless neat and mincing paths
which provided such an amusing puzzle for those who were
in no hurry.

G. B. STERN

Presently he began to shout, but nobody heard. The Leopard Moth was blazing away like mad. Surely somebody must see the flames and come rushing to give aid?

'I can't stand this any longer,' muttered Prince. He had to fight his way out; those high, smooth hedges were his bitter enemies, and he got a queer satisfaction out of forcing his way through the interlacing of tiny, obstinate twigs. By the

time he was free at last of the subtleties of the maze, free on strength and not by subtlety, he was terribly scratched and his clothes torn to rags. He paused for a moment to brush the back of his clenched fist across his forehead as though to brush away the memory of the terrible nightmare which had just befallen him . . .

And saw, a few hundred yards away, the towers and turrets of an enchanted castle, its grey stone drowsing in the wash of evening gold from the west. He ran towards it across the emerald-green sward softer than moss, in his ears the musical tinkle of rivulets clear as crystal. There was no other sound; even the birds were hushed in their branches; the dogs silent in their kennels; the doves mute in their cote; the horses dumb in their stables; the deer still under the immemorial elms; and all nature participated in the soundless magic which greeted Prince's arrival at what seemed like a palace veritably asleep.

The iron-studded oaken doors stood wide open. Too awed to shout, to clang the huge bell which hung on one side, Prince ran up the flight of steps and into the cool vaulted hall, hoping to find someone to whom he could re-

The Sleeping Beauty

late his mishap and who would give him the help he sorely needed. Still not a voice could be heard; no evidence of life. He opened a door, saying, who knows by what instinct: 'This should be the Banqueting Hall.' And indeed it was the Banqueting Hall, and Chalmers Prince stood amazed by the sight. Just inside lay the seneschal, breathing heavily, his eyes shut and his chain of office all awry. Around the room were about twenty young people flung about in careless, sprawling attitudes, some on the floor, some across the table, some on the steps that led to the dais, but all of them alike in this, that they were sunk in a death-like sleep.

'Drunk as lords,' reflected the young doctor. 'No help to be got here.'

He closed the door again and tried other doors; but silence bound the interior of the castle in a thrall that might have lasted a hundred years, so intense it was. If he could have heard a canary chirrup, it would have been a relief. He was getting frantic by now, rushing here and there, dashing up and down stairs, throwing open door after door. Presently, at the far end of the Left Wing, he came across another strange tableau in a small panelled room: a man and a woman, not young but still comely, fast asleep at a small round table which showed by the disposition of several empty bottles of Burgundy, that they had been feasting tête-à-tête. On the floor beside them, an old, old wrinkled, withered crone lay also unconscious, but not asleep.

If Prince had examined her more closely, he might have detected signs of a heavy blow on the head.

G. B. STERN

He dashed away again, rushing up and down, searching, never finding. Was there no life but his own, in all these vast halls and chambers and staircases? in these seven reception rooms, fourteen bedrooms, three dressing-rooms, five tiled labour-saving bathrooms, central heating, basins in bedrooms, large inglenook fireplace, convenient offices, oak floors and perfectly panelled interior?

He wandered on. At last, opening a narrow door from which the tapestry curtain had been pushed aside, he burst up the winding spiral stairs that led to the little room in the tower.

Lying in a pose of exquisite careless grace across a couch was a young girl, fast asleep. She was lovelier than any girl that Prince had ever yet beheld. Her long hair was strewn about the cushions, her soft lashes were dark little fans upon either petal cheek. Her lips, the hue and texture of poppies, were faintly parted. She breathed, that was all; and hers was not the stillness of childish slumber; say, rather, it was the stillness of one who lay under a malevolent spell.

'Drugged,' exclaimed our practical young doctor instantly, his experienced eye marking the symptoms; next, and not unnaturally, he spotted the work-table with its row of syringes, the broken phial and other casual evidence. Examination revealed that each phial only contained one-sixth of a grain of morphine sulphate.

Rapidly he ran over in his mind the antidotes. Caffein was best, but how could he make hot, strong coffee, here and

The Sleeping Beauty

now? Luckily, however, he had as usual in his pocket his case containing an injection of filocarpine nitres.

He felt her pulse and her heart; then gently, ever so gently, raised her head and bared her arm.

But before his remedy could have taken effect, he thought he saw signs that she was coming round. Her eyelids fluttered; she sighed . . .

The surge of passionate relief was too much for the most chivalrous Bayard. Her loveliness attacked his senses, undid his sanity. The little round room swam and trembled before him . . . his heart thudded and checked . . . the blood rushed through his veins with the roar of a cataract . . . She was so young . . .

Beauty opened her eyes, as Prince's kiss pressed ardently upon her mouth.

A cackling, unmelodious laugh from the doorway shattered the rapt moment.

Part V

They Lived Happy Ever After

'So of course I reported him and had him removed from the Medical Register,' explained Damon afterwards, in an overwhelming state of virtuous indignation, to an interested group of Roy and Queenie's old friends, at the Café

Sybarite. 'In all my ninety-four years I never came across a more flagrant case of violation of medical etiquette whilst in discharge of professional duties. Never. I just happened to hear—matter of fact, you told me, didn't you, Jack?—that there was a little coming-of-age romp going on down at Briar Park, and I thought: "Ah, me old chums and me little god-daughter"—Pollux was not present to contradict—"I'll run down and join them in time for a late tea." And then I saw the door left open up to the tower, and wondered whether Queenie... Well, anyhow, I thought, I'll toddle up and have a look. And would you believe it, there he was, kissing her; actually, the dastardly brute, the ravening barbarian, holding her in his arms and kissing her.'

We are pleased to be able to relate that the attitude of Damon's hearers was as correctly indignant as his own. Singly and in groups, they exclaimed that no retribution, no sentence, no banishment could be severe enough to punish a man who while-in-discharge-of-his-professional-duties could so far lose all moral sense as to kiss a young girl—not on the forehead, mind you, my dear, we're not narrow-minded and we have no objection to the forehead—but full on the lips, *before* she was quite conscious, and no one within call, and my dear, he didn't even ask her parents; such nice people, as we all know. Really, he might have been expected to recognise the difference between *one* class of girl and another. I don't wonder you were shocked, Damon, I'm shocked myself; too, too shocked, shocked to the core. In fact, I can't shake it off. I've conscientiously tried to, but I *positively* can't. Makes me shudder to think of it. What times we live in. Full on the lips, my dear; too dreadful, too jarring. She can never be the same again.

Fortunately, Chalmers Prince was wealthy as well as handsome, and as faithful as he was valiant. So he bought a new aeroplane, and in due course he and Beauty were married and set off on a long, joyful flight: [353

> 'Across the hills and far away
> Beyond their utmost purple rim
> And deep into the dying day . . .'

G. B. STERN

Big Claus and Little Claus

Or, Grimm's Not the Word

An attempt to put Hans Andersen On the Spot

R. J. YEATMAN AND W. C. SELLAR

Authors of *1066 and All That*

Old wine is often all the better for being re-bottled; perhaps old wives' tales are like that, too.

For instance, there is no doubt that old Uncle Andersen doesn't go down too well with the new generation—they say he isn't tough enough and complain of a total absence of pep, dope, yep, nope, etc., in his efforts to amuse.

But there's nothing wrong with his scenarios. Take this one about Big Claus and Little Claus that we drew out of the editor's hat. There's no denying that it's an absolutely Epoch-making, All-slaying, All-flaying, All-swindling production, featuring only two murders-which-didn't-come-off and three which certainly did (one an absolute cracker, done with a mallet), and a rattling old night-ride with a juicy old corpse, not to mention some beating-up, blackmail, black magic and a Married Woman's Shameful Intrigue with Sexton. (She jolly nearly sacrificed all for love.)

No, dear parents, these old stories need nothing more than a little re-direction and some new dialogue. In fact, whenever we find ourselves booked to tell some of your little nasties a bedtime story we just slip into the nearest Movie Palace to get the atmosphere, and when six o'clock comes the old tale goes something like this . . .

Once upon a time there were two chaps—all right, Teddy, two guys—called Big Claus and Little Claus.

And they were good guys, too, but they had one failing: they were both one-hundred-per-cent liars, like old Hans Andersen who invented this story and then swore it was all one-hundred-per-cent gospel.

To be fair to these Claus boys you got to admit that they were also undoubtedly a couple of born crooks and had the makings of Killers in a big way (No, Freda, they didn't have machine-guns—this is an old-time thriller, not an East-side family boast).

Apart from their names being the same there wasn't much to choose between these two ginks, anyway, except that Little was the smarter of the two, as you'll see later, and had only one horse, while Big had four horses and was just a dumb egg.

It was on account of this difference in the amount of horse-flesh they owned that one of these guys was called *Little Claus* and the other one *Big Claus.*

R. J. YEATMAN AND W. C. SELLAR

(No, Georgie, they weren't cowboys, they were Germans or something.)

Anyway, don't interrupt, because the killing begins right here.

You see, kiddies, it so happened that Big Claus used to loan his four horses to Little Claus (in exchange for something worth more), and every time he did that Little Claus used to go about shouting, 'Gee up, my five hosses!' (Aw, cutitout, Georgie, we just can't remember the German for that.)

Well, naturally this made Big Claus sore and he'd sing out 'Boy, only one-fifth of them hosses is yours.'

Little said that a bit of boloney was O.K. in an advertisement; but Big couldn't see it.

So what d'you kids reckon Big did?

No, Freda, he didn't bump Little off—at least, not yet. He did just what young Hughie, here, or Johnnie, dear, might have done—he up and hit Little Claus's *one* horse one grand sock with a croquet-racket. Flonk!

And did it die? And did the blood gush out and the brains and maybe the eyeballs? Don't ask, Teddy-boy; try it on your sister's dollie, or on your old Nannie, she hasn't long to live anyhow.

Let's get on.

Well, that settled the argument about Truth in Advertising, and there was nothing left for Little Claus to do but flay his one dead horse and then hit the trail for the next township to sell the raw hide.

(Yes, Georgie, he could have sold it right there in his own home town, but you must have a change of scene sometime in a feature story.)

Well, half-way to this next dump Little Claus starts to doss down for the night on top of a hay-stack when he notices with pleasure that he can pry down into the windows of the farm-house itself.

Inside he spies the farmer's wife making whoopee with the local Sexton—they were having champagne wine and kisses and chicken-à-la-King and doughnuts and everything.

Fact is, the farmer's wife was a Good Woman but she had one failing. Sextons. (Yes, Georgie, it was probably what they call a Sexton-Complex.)

Well, those two was all set for a hunky-dory soirée, and old-man Sexy had just finished telling her the latest dirt-track stories and the two of them was getting-down to a straight business conference about the best places for burying farmers who died unexpected, when who should they hear but the Old Man himself rolling home unexpected and also alive. Yes, Sir!

Well, the female's slick all right. She hides the *plat du jour* and *Cordon Rouge* in the oven, and old Sexy in ye olde oake cheste.

Fact is, this farmer was a good guy, but he had one failing; he just couldn't abide Sextons. No, Sir!

Of course, this was just jam to an all-round grafter like Little. Inside of three minutes he'd muscled-in on that family party and was giving them the works.

He played poor-man-lost; but you can take it from us, Teddy, he knew his way about. Well, the farmer's wife starts serving peanuts and gruel to the Old Man and the stranger within, but the Kid he'd thought up the cutest bluff ever. He just trampled on his sack with the hoss's hide in it, which he'd slid under the dining-room table, and then informed the company that the squeaks it made was a special high-power hoodoo he had control of, and that this hoodoo had condescended to load up the oven with swell eats and straight liquor for the benefit of self and partner.

Well, the stuff's there, sure enough, and so the farmer falls for the hoodoo, and the dame daren't squeal on the Kid, and bye-and-bye the old man gets so boozed-up he reckons he could face the devil himself.

'Nothing easier,' says Little, squeaking his raw-hide, 'my information is, Old Nick's around to-night in these parts disguised as a Sexton.'

That seemed likely enough to old-man farmer, who had always reckoned Sextons were the devil.

So the Kid says, 'Boss, if you look in that old oak chest you'll get an eye-full.'

It worked all right. That old hick was so taken in with the magic stuff he was right glad to buy the Kid's bag of squeaks for thirty bucks cash. What's more, he was so durned scared by what he'd seen in the old oak chest he threw that in too. Why, the old sucker even loaned Little a barrow to take it away in.

Big Claus and Little Claus

So Little lights out for home, and the first river he comes to he sings out 'Gosh, I'm that tired of toteing this old chest around, I guess I'll pitch it into the river.'

'Let me out of this,' hollers the Sexton.

'That'll cost you thoirty bucks,' says Little. And he got it. (You're right, Hughie, he'd got him cold.)

Now what does Little do? We'll tell you.

So soon as he gets home Little Claus says to Big Claus, 'Guess how much that hide fetched!'

'Ten dollars,' says Big. 'You're all wet,' says Little. 'It fetched sixty bucks,' and shows him his wad.

Big naturally deduces that raw-hides must have gone up in value overnight, so he reaches for his axe and steps out into the stable.

Whim! Wham! Whomp! Whump! He hits his own four horses over the head, and this time there was four times as much blood around, Freda, and maybe eight eyeballs arolling on the floor, and if this isn't a dandy tale!

Next thing, Big tries to sell those four hides for sixty bucks apiece. But folks just laughed at him, and pretty soon they reckoned he was crazy, so they naturally started beating him up with shoe-lasts and straps and any old thing, because that was how they used to treat anyone they thought was crazy in those days. (No, Georgie, they didn't sterilise him; they didn't know anything about science, anyway.)

Let's get on to the murders.

Big Claus naturally felt sore; so he planned to axe Little Claus while he was asleep, so as to get even with him. But

Little senses he was getting unpopular and put his Old Granny, who happened to have died that afternoon, into his bed; and when Big popped in that night and slugged her, Little lay quiet under the bed and thought what a good thing it was the old dame was dead anyway or she'd have been killed right then.

However, seeing the way Big was acting he guessed it was time he beat it. But by now he reckoned he was so smart he could sell anything for thirty bucks, even an old corpse. So he took the old dame along with him propped up in the back of the buggy, and you can just picture them, Teddy, driving along through the moonlit forest with the old mare nodding in front and the old dame dodding behind, clip-clop, flib-flob . . .

The next bit is funny.

About dawn they came to a road-house. Now, Little knew that the road-house proprietor was a good guy, but he had one failing—he couldn't abide deaf dames.

'Mornin', Boss,' says Little, 'would you oblige me by stepping out and serving my old Granma a can of rye: she's plumb deaf and she won't come inside; she says it isn't clean in here.'

At this the road-house man gets his dander up, but he draws the can of rye and steps out hollering, 'Hey, you old so-and-so, here's breakfast.' Granma don't answer; so he hollers again. Granma goes on acting like her soul was above rude road-house men, which it was by now, so the guy pitches the can of rye in her face and knocks her hipsy-tipsy out of the back of the buggy—kerflomp!

Big Claus and Little Claus

Little strolls out and hisses, 'Lookit, lady-killer, if that'd bin my buddy you just bumped off I'd skin you alive right now like I did Scarfaced Heimy down on the river-front in 'toirty-two. But seeing as how it's only my old Granma I'll take toidy bucks.'

Well, to cut a long story the road-house man paid up and thankful, and they buried the old lady under the porch, and as soon as he'd driven out of sight of the road-house Little Claus laughed all the way home and went and told Big Claus how someone got in in the night and slugged his gran' and how he'd cashed in for thirty bucks on the body, easyaseasy.

Of course Big was mad to think how he'd really done all the hard work on that job and had nothing to show for it, but he figures it's a soft racket and before you could say Jack Washington he was round at his own granma's shack a-socking her on the dome with his little mallet, Blunk, Blonk, Blosh!

But when he tried to get thirty bucks for the body all he got was very nearly lynched; because, you see, kiddies, the boys in town didn't understand he was only trying to get even with Little, really; they reckoned he was just trying to make money in a mean kind of way. (You're right, Georgie, no one ever got no sense out of a crowd of hick farmers.)

Consequence is, Big Claus had to beat it out of town, but on the way he was lucky and caught Little Claus when he wasn't looking and toppled him over into a big sack and roped it up and made for the river meaning to permanently drown Little Claus this time and so get even.

But Big Claus had one failing we forgot to mention. He was crazy about Church music. (Don't keep saying 'Sez you!' Teddy; this is all Mr. Hans Andersen's story and he always swore it was true to life.)

Let's get on, we've still got two more murders in hand.

Big Claus had nearly got to the river when he hears some elegant psalm-singing going on in an old Church near-by; so he puts down the sack and goes in to listen, figuring Little could never get himself out of that sack.

But Little had a hold of the right end of the stick this time. While Big was inside the Church an old bozo came by, driving a herd of steers. Little sings out 'O lordy, I'm so young to be on my way to heaven!' And this old bozo must have been absolutely nuts because he answers 'O lordy, I'm so old I don't seem ever going to get there,' and believe it or not, he let Little out of the sack and got right in himself because the kid lets on that if he did he'd soon be in heaven alright-alright.

So off goes Little with the herd of steers and bye-and-bye Big Claus comes out of Church and totes the sack with the old bozo in it down to the river and pitches it in—one-two-three—Splosh!

Half a mile on who should he meet but Little Claus, waiting for him with all that cattle.

'Say,' complains Big, 'what's the idea? Didn't I just drown you in the river? How many more times do I have to take you for a ride before you'll stay dead? And where'd you get them steers, anyway?'

Big Claus and Little Claus

'Boy,' says Little, 'you don't know nothing. Not till you've been drowned like I was by you.'

And then he spins him the craziest yarn about a beautiful country at the bottom of the river where he met a swell jane who gave him a present of a slap-up herd of de luxe farmstock. 'And Big, old man,' he finishes up, 'the last words she said to me were, "if you've got a buddy up there on land, tell him to come down and see me sometime."'

Well, the end of it was that this Big Claus actually allowed this Little Claus to rope him up in the sack and pitch him into the river, one-two-three Splosh, and so he was plumb-permanently drowned and Little was left alive with a herd of elegant cattle and ninety bucks in cash. But before you start razzing old man Andersen, Georgie, you've got to imagine how you'd feel if you *believed* you'd infallibly drowned young Teddy, here, and then he met you the next minute all alive with a herd of ritzy cattle to his credit. And you must all remember, kiddies, that in those old days people didn't know much about what folk feel like after they've been drowned. Which explains why Big fell for that story about the nice goings-on at the bottom of the river . . .

Anyway, the moral of this tale is that a high-grade grafter like you, little Georgie, will beat a dumb thug like you, pretty Freda, every time. Yes, Sir!

And now, children, good-night; we'll just put the lights out and then you can imagine you're Little Claus driving his buggy through the moonlit forest with that juicy old corpse behind . . .

R. J. YEATMAN AND W. C. SELLAR

Of course, it isn't so hot, really; for instance, it would obviously be more all-thrilling if the two chaps had been half-human-men-lobsters and called Big Claws and Little Claws (good names, huh?). In fact, if we could have worked it out on those lines, Mr. Metro-Goldwyn (or at least Mr. Meyer) might have actually made it into a real Feature Film with Boris Karloff doubling both the parts.

And again, no doubt it would have been more All-shuddering if Little Claus's Granma's eyeballs had rolled out, too, when he pasted her with the mallet—only the road-house man would have noticed she hadn't any eyes, wouldn't he?

Still, done this way, the story goes down fairly well, we find, with the next generation of dictators, and although the whole thing is rather difficult for people who were educated at Eton and Harrow, and Oxford and Cambridge, and so on, we still have hopes of fixing up a version of 'Little Goldilocks' that has machine-guns in it, for Freda, and of re-writing Sinbad the Sailor so as to provide a strong part for Mickey the Mouse and his girl-friend, for everybody in general . . .

Anyway, there's the Big Idea, ladies and gentlemen, and if you've children of your own and want to give them a New Deal we reckon it's up to you guys to do your own stuff . . .
Sez who?
SEZ WE!

Big Claus and Little Claus

Author Biographies

A. E. Coppard, 1878–1957

On the first of April, 1919, Alfred Edward Coppard declared his allegiance to the literary life: "I took a cottage in the country, lived sparely, and hawked my first collection of tales, *Adam and Eve and Pinch Me*, around the publishers." Born in Kent, Coppard was the eldest boy in a working-class family. His formal education ended at age nine, when he was apprenticed to a paraffin oil vendor. A voracious reader, he never forgot the privations of his childhood and was deeply ambivalent about working as a writer, suffering from what Frank O'Connor described as an "unearned income complex." Haunted by shame about his hardscrabble childhood yet also proud of his autodidactic energy, Coppard established himself in a world dominated by Oxbridge educated men and made a name for himself as a master of the short story.

Clemence Dane (Winifred Ashton), 1887–1965

Considered one of the most distinguished dramatists in interwar England, Clemence Dane is now best known for *A Bill of Divorcement*, which played on the London stage and was turned into a film starring Katharine Hepburn and John Barrymore. Born in Blackheath in southern England, she worked as a French tutor in Geneva, studied art at the Slade School in London and in Dresden, and taught school in Ireland. Her pseudonym, the name of a historic London church in the Strand, was adopted when she published her first novel, *Regiment of Women*, in 1917. The work depicted life at a girls' boarding school and launched a career in which Dane wrote plays, novels, detective stories, and also painted portraits (the National Portrait Gallery has two of her paintings).

E. M. Delafield (Edmée Elizabeth Monica de la Pasture Dashwood), 1890–1943

The daughter of a Count descended from the French nobility and of a prolific British novelist, Delafield was born in Sussex, England. A child of privilege, she entered a French religious order at age twenty-one in order to secure "work." "It was before the days when girls—at any rate girls in my particular walk of life—were allowed to take 'jobs,'" she later commented. When World War I broke out, she had already left the cloistered life and served as a nurse in a Voluntary Aid Detachment. Her first novel was published in 1917. One of the most prolific writers of fiction between the wars, she is best known for five books cast in the form of rambling diaries by the "Provincial Lady." Set in rural England, London, the United States, the Soviet Union, and wartime England, the five volumes combine satire and social critique with travelogue and political commentary. Delafield wrote about educational evils and hereditary weaknesses with the same energetic verve she brought to real-life stories about crime and justice.

Lord Dunsany (Edward John Moreton Drax Plunkett, 18th Baron of Dunsany), 1878–1957

Lord Dunsany was, by his own admission, first and foremost a soldier and sportsman, then a writer. Born in London, he spent his childhood in rural settings and was educated at Eton and at the Royal Military Academy at Sandhurst. After serving in the Boer wars, he succeeded his father as baron in 1899 and led the life of a country gentleman at Dunsany Castle, which had been in the family since 1190. A prolific writer, he began his literary career by publishing *The Gods of Pegana*, fantasy fiction set in an exotic Other World. Ursula Le Guin was to warn "unwary beginners" in fantasy fiction to avoid falling into the trap of the Dunsany style. Yet Guillermo Del Toro and Neil Gaiman have both acknowledged him as important influences in their work. Lord Dunsany branched out into plays, short stories, and novels later in his literary career and also wrote several autobiographical works.

Anna Gordon Keown, 1899–1957

Married to Philip Gosse, son of the poet and critic Edmund Gosse, Anna Gordon Keown was the author of a modestly successful drama entitled *The Cat Who Saw God* (1932). Her poem "Reported Missing," written during World War I, chronicles defiance at the news of a young soldier's death and remains today on the English literature syllabus in British schools.

Eric Linklater, 1899–1974

Born in Wales and educated at Aberdeen University, Eric Robert Russell Linklater grew up in the Orkney Islands. He studied medicine at Aberdeen, served as a private in the Black Watch Regiment on the Somme front, and worked as a journalist for the *Times of India*. Wounded at Voormezeele, he spent several months recuperating and returned to civilian life to continue his studies. At Aberdeen University, Linklater switched from medicine to English literature, receiving his M.A. in 1925. Alternating between a quiet life in his beloved home on the Orkney Islands and travels to Persia, India, China, Japan, and the United States, he wrote novels, travelogues, poetry, and fiction for children, winning the Carnegie Medal for *The Wind in the Moon* (1944).

A. G. Macdonell, 1895–1941

Born in Pune, India, Archibald Gordon MacDonell was educated at Winchester College in England and served in World War I as a lieutenant in the Royal Field Artillery of the 51st Highland Division. A victim of shellshock, he worked hard after the war to rebuild devastated areas of Poland and Russia and ran unsuccessfully for public office in the 1920s. Combining a passion for drama with a love of detective fiction, he was the author of many plays and murder mysteries. Today he is best known for his satirical novel, *England, Their England* (1933), in which a native of Scotland becomes a shrewd observer of British customs and a brilliant ethnographer who is "a stranger in a strange land."

W. C. Sellar, 1898–1951

Born at Golspie in Sutherland, Walter Carruthers Sellar served in World War I as Second Lieutenant in the King's Own Scottish Borderers. After the war he earned a degree in modern history at Oxford. With Robert Yeatman, he authored *1066 and All That*, a title inspired by Robert Graves's *Good-Bye to All That*. Although he hoped to devote himself to writing, financial constraints led him to spend most of his life teaching history at British schools.

Helen Simpson, 1897–1940

Born in Sydney, Australia, Helen Simpson traveled to England in 1914 to live with her mother. She studied French

at Oxford and joined the Women's Royal Naval Service, where she worked in the division of decoding. After the war, she returned to Oxford to study for a degree in music, but failed her examinations and turned to writing. The author of plays, translations, biographies, poems, detective novels, and cookbooks, Simpson is perhaps best known for her collaborations with Clemence Dane and for *Boomerang*, a novel
with multiple historical settings that ends in the trenches of World War I.

Lady Eleanor Smith, 1902–1945

The daughter of the Earl of Birkenhead, Eleanor Smith preferred her paternal ancestry (her great-grandmother was apparently a gypsy named Bathsheba) to her aristocratic title. She worked as a reporter and film reviewer, then became a publicist for circus companies. Her autobiographical reminiscences, published in 1940 under the title *Life's a Circus*, chronicled her picturesque adventures as a girl and as an adult. Several of her novels, among them *Tzigane* (1937) and *The Man in Grey* (1946) were made into movies.

E. Œ. Somerville, 1858–1949

Born in Corfu, Edith Anna Œnone Somerville was raised in County Cork, at a country house named Drishane. After her mother's death, she ran Drishane, importing cattle and hunting while also writing to support herself and her family. She attended Alexandra College in Dublin and studied art in Paris and London. In 1886, Somerville met a cousin named Violet Martin, and shortly thereafter the two writers formed a literary partnership, publishing fourteen books together, including *The Real Charlotte* and, most famously, *The Experiences of an Irish R.M.* After Martin's death in 1915, Somerville kept in touch with her writing partner through séances and kept her on as coauthor of her books.

Robert Speaight, 1904–1976

A British actor, director, and writer, Speaight earned fame when he played Becket in the first production of T. S. Eliot's *Murder in the Cathedral*. Speaight's many novels include *St. Thomas of Canterbury* (1938) and *The Lost Hero* (1934). He wrote a biography of Hilaire Belloc and one of Eric Gill, and published widely on authors ranging from Shakespeare and Teilhard de Chardin to George Bernanos and George Eliot.

Christina Stead, 1902–1983

Born in Sydney, Australia, Christina Stead spent most of her adult life abroad, first in Paris, then in England and the United States. The author of fifteen novels and several volumes of short stories, she also worked as a screenwriter in Hollywood. Peter Davies published her first novel, *Seven Poor Men of Sydney*, and helped to launch her career as a writer. Stead was an advocate of the "many-charactered novel," fiction that gave voice to a large cast of characters in a competitive metropolitan setting. Her best-known novel, *The Man Who Loved Children* (the title is ironic), was based on her own childhood and displayed the "intelligent ferocity" that was her goal in writing. The poet Randall Jarrell wrote an introduction for the first U.S. edition in 1965, praising the work for its capacity to "make you a part of one family's existence as no other book quite does."

G. B. Stern, 1890–1973

Born in England to second-generation Jewish emigrants, Gladys Bertha Stern (later Gladys Bronwyn Stern) attended the Academy of Dramatic Art in London after studying at German and Swiss girls' schools. A marriage in 1919 to the New Zealander Geoffrey Holdsworth ended in divorce, and Stern traveled to the United States to work as a screenwriter in Hollywood. Beginning with *Tents of Israel* and on through *The Young Matriarch*, she chronicled the fortunes of a modern Jewish family in London, St. Petersburg, and in European capitals. In addition to her many novels, she wrote a biography of Robert Louis Stevenson as well as two volumes on Jane Austen.

R. J. Yeatman, 1897–1968

Born in Oporto, Portugal, Robert Julian Yeatman served in World War I before receiving his B.A. from Oxford. There he met Walter Carruthers Sellar, with whom he would co-author *1066 and All That*, a parody of history books used in British schools. Yeatman worked as an advertising manager for Kodak and also wrote for *Punch*.